INVADER ZIM

VOLUME 9

™

Created by
JHONEN VASQUEZ

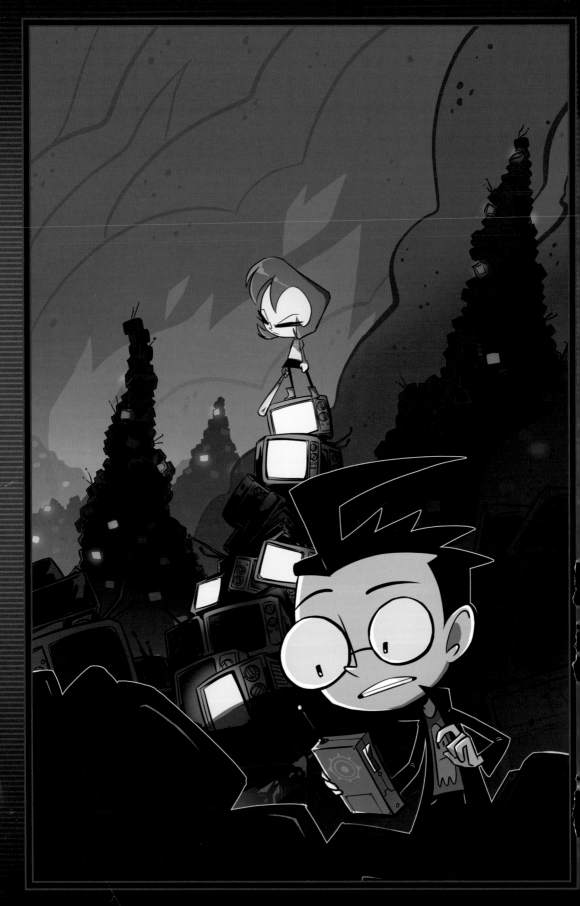

Illustration by MEGAN LAWTON

INVADER ZIM ™

VOLUME 9

Writer, Chapters 1, 2
SAM LOGAN

Writer, Chapter 3
STEVEN SHANAHAN

Writer, Chapter 4
ERIC TRUEHEART

Writer and Illustrator, Chapter 5
DREW RAUSCH

Illustrator, Chapters 1-4 and Letterer, Chapters 1-5
WARREN WUCINICH

Colorist, Chapters 1-5
FRED C. STRESING

Retail cover illustrated by
WARREN WUCINICH with **FRED C. STRESING**

Oni Press exclusive cover illustrated by
STEPHAN PARK

AN ONI PRESS PUBLICATION

Special thanks to **JOAN HILTY** and **LINDA LEE**

Designed by **KEITH WOOD**

Edited by **ROBIN HERRERA**

PUBLISHED BY ONI-LION FORGE PUBLISHING GROUP, LLC

JAMES LUCAS JONES, president & publisher · **SARAH GAYDOS**, editor in chief
CHARLIE CHU, e.v.p. of creative & business development · **BRAD ROOKS**, director of operations
AMBER O'NEILL, special projects manager · **HARRIS FISH**, events manager
MARGOT WOOD, director of marketing & sales · **JEREMY ATKINS**, director of brand communications
DEVIN FUNCHES, sales & marketing manager · **KATIE SAINZ**, marketing
TARA LEHMANN, marketing & publicity associate · **TROY LOOK**, director of design & production
KATE Z. STONE, senior graphic designer · **SONJA SYNAK**, graphic designer
HILARY THOMPSON, graphic designer · **SARAH ROCKWELL**, junior graphic designer
ANGIE KNOWLES, digital prepress lead · **VINCENT KUKUA**, digital prepress technician
SHAWNA GORE, senior editor · **ROBIN HERRERA**, senior editor · **AMANDA MEADOWS**, senior editor
JASMINE AMIRI, editor · **GRACE BORNHOFT**, editor · **ZACK SOTO**, editor
STEVE ELLIS, vice president of games · **BEN EISNER**, game developer
MICHELLE NGUYEN, executive assistant · **JUNG LEE**, logistics coordinator

JOE NOZEMACK, publisher emeritus

This volume collects issues #41-45 of the
Oni Press series *Invader Zim*.

Oni Press, Inc.
1319 SE Martin Luther King Jr. Blvd.
Suite 240
Portland, OR 97214
USA

onipress.com · lionforge.com
facebook.com/onipress · facebook.com/lionforge
twitter.com/onipress · twitter.com/lionforge
instagram.com/onipress · instagram.com/lionforge

First edition: April 2020

ISBN: 978-1-62010-692-1 • eISBN: 978-1-62010-704-1
Oni Press Exclusive ISBN: 978-1-62010-730-0

nickelodeon

INVADER ZIM, Volume Nine, April 2020. Published by Oni-Lion Forge Publishing Group, LLC,
1319 SE Martin Luther King Jr. Blvd., Suite 240, Portland, OR 97214. © 2020 Viacom
International Inc. All Rights Reserved. Nickelodeon, Nickelodeon Invader Zim and all related
titles, logos, and characters are trademarks of Viacom International Inc. Oni Press logo and
icon ™ & © 2020 Oni-Lion Forge Publishing Group, LLC. All rights reserved. Oni Press logo
and icon artwork created by Keith A. Wood. The events, institutions, and characters presented
in this book are fictional. Any resemblance to actual persons, living or dead, is purely
coincidental. No portion of this publication may be reproduced, by any means, without
the express written permission of the copyright holders.

Library of Congress Control Number: 2015950610

1 3 5 7 9 10 8 6 4 2

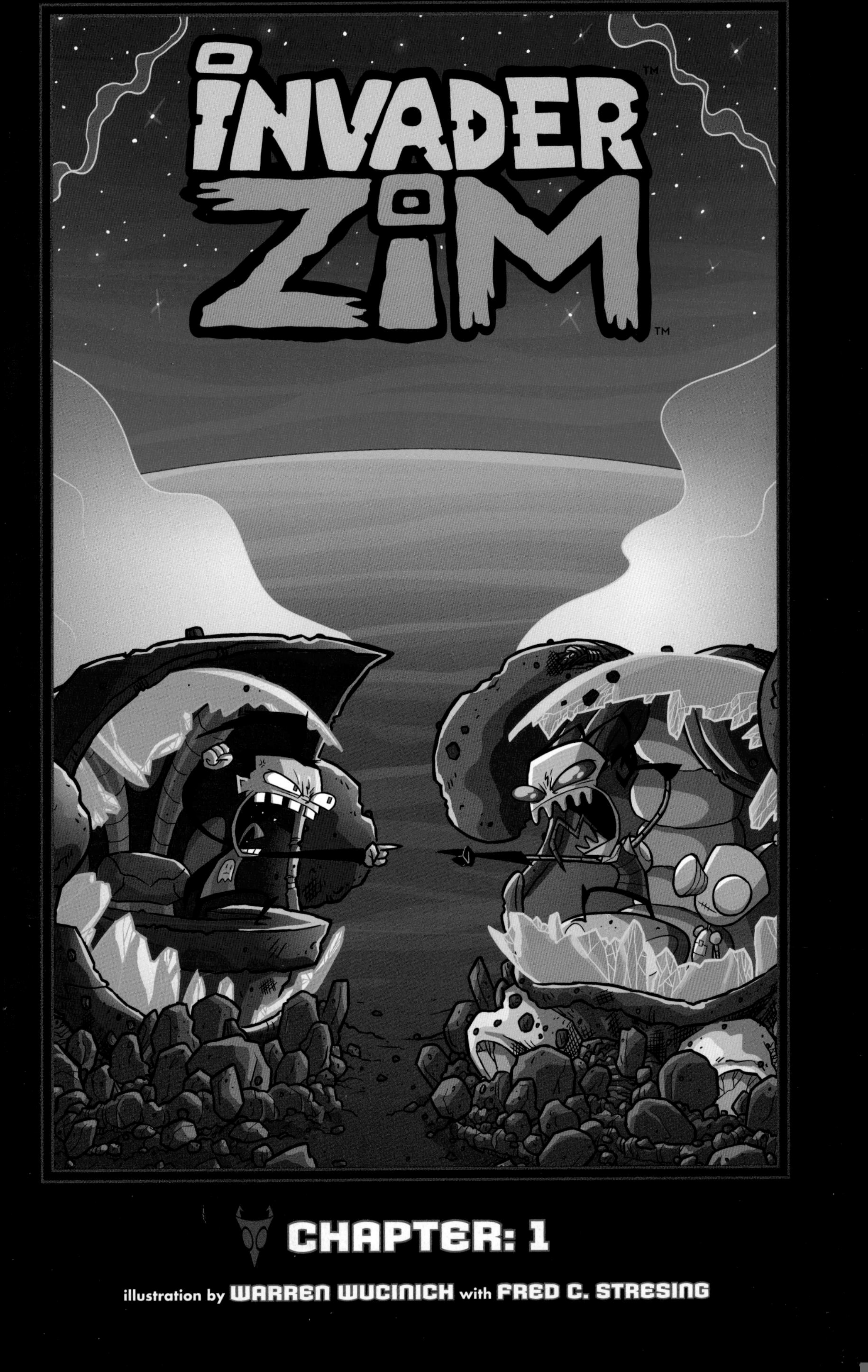
INVADER
ZIM™

CHAPTER: 1

illustration by **WARREN WUCINICH** with **FRED C. STRESING**

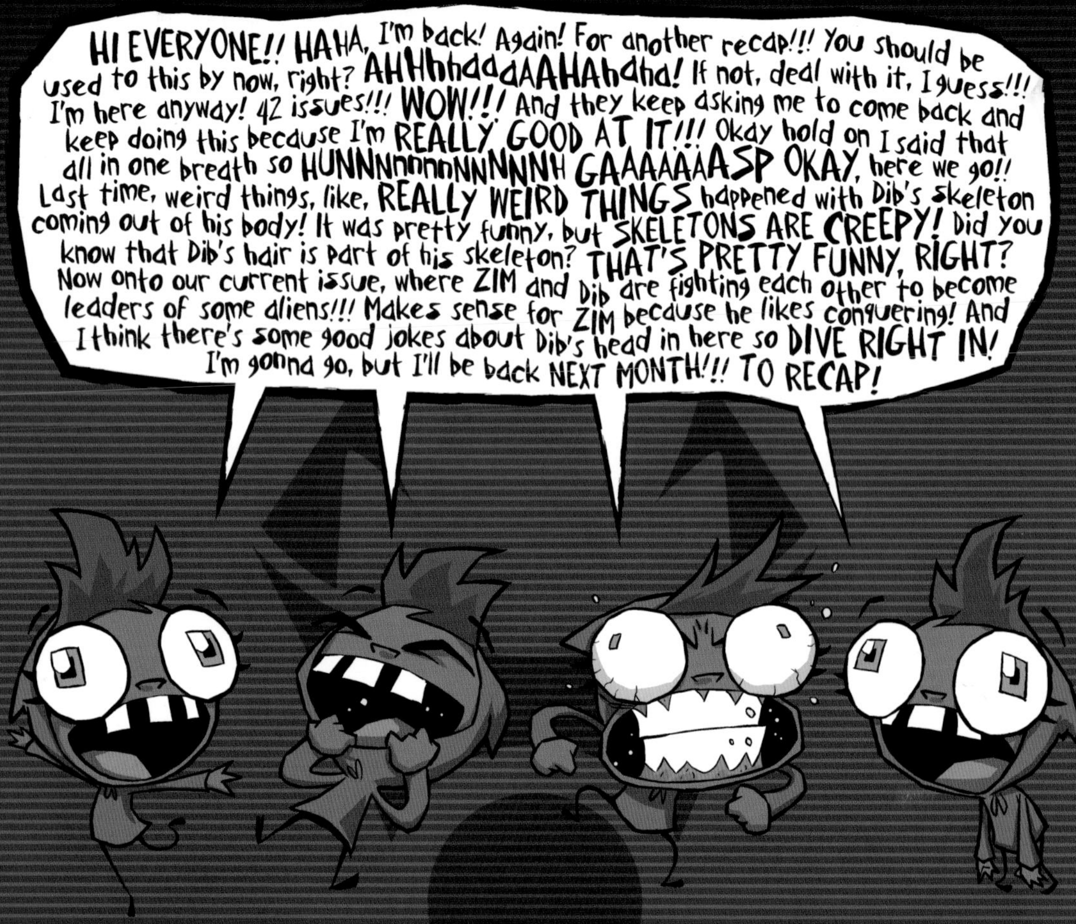
HI EVERYONE!! HAHA, I'm back! Again! For another recap!!! You should be used to this by now, right? AHHhhaaaAAHAhaha! If not, deal with it, I guess!!! I'm here anyway! 42 issues!!! WOW!!! And they keep asking me to come back and keep doing this because I'm REALLY GOOD AT IT!!! Okay hold on I said that all in one breath so HUNNNnnnnNNNNNH GAAAAAAASP OKAY, here we go!! Last time, weird things, like, REALLY WEIRD THINGS happened with Dib's skeleton coming out of his body! It was pretty funny, but SKELETONS ARE CREEPY! Did you know that Dib's hair is part of his skeleton? THAT'S PRETTY FUNNY, RIGHT? Now onto our current issue, where ZIM and Dib are fighting each other to become leaders of some aliens!!! Makes sense for ZIM because he likes conquering! And I think there's some good jokes about Dib's head in here so DIVE RIGHT IN! I'm gonna go, but I'll be back NEXT MONTH!!! TO RECAP!

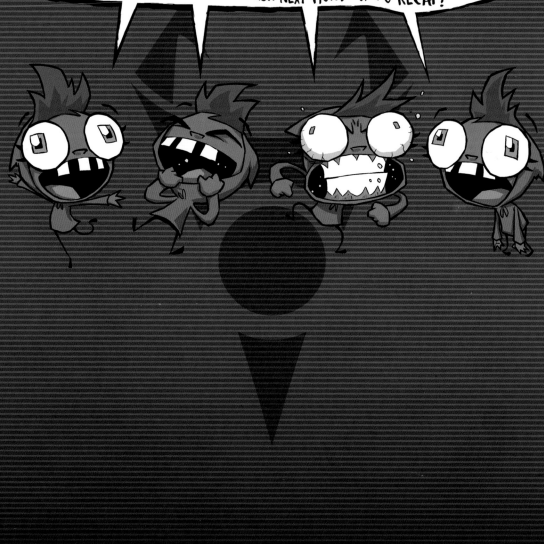

Recap Kid illustrated, colored, and lettered by

WARREN WUCINICH

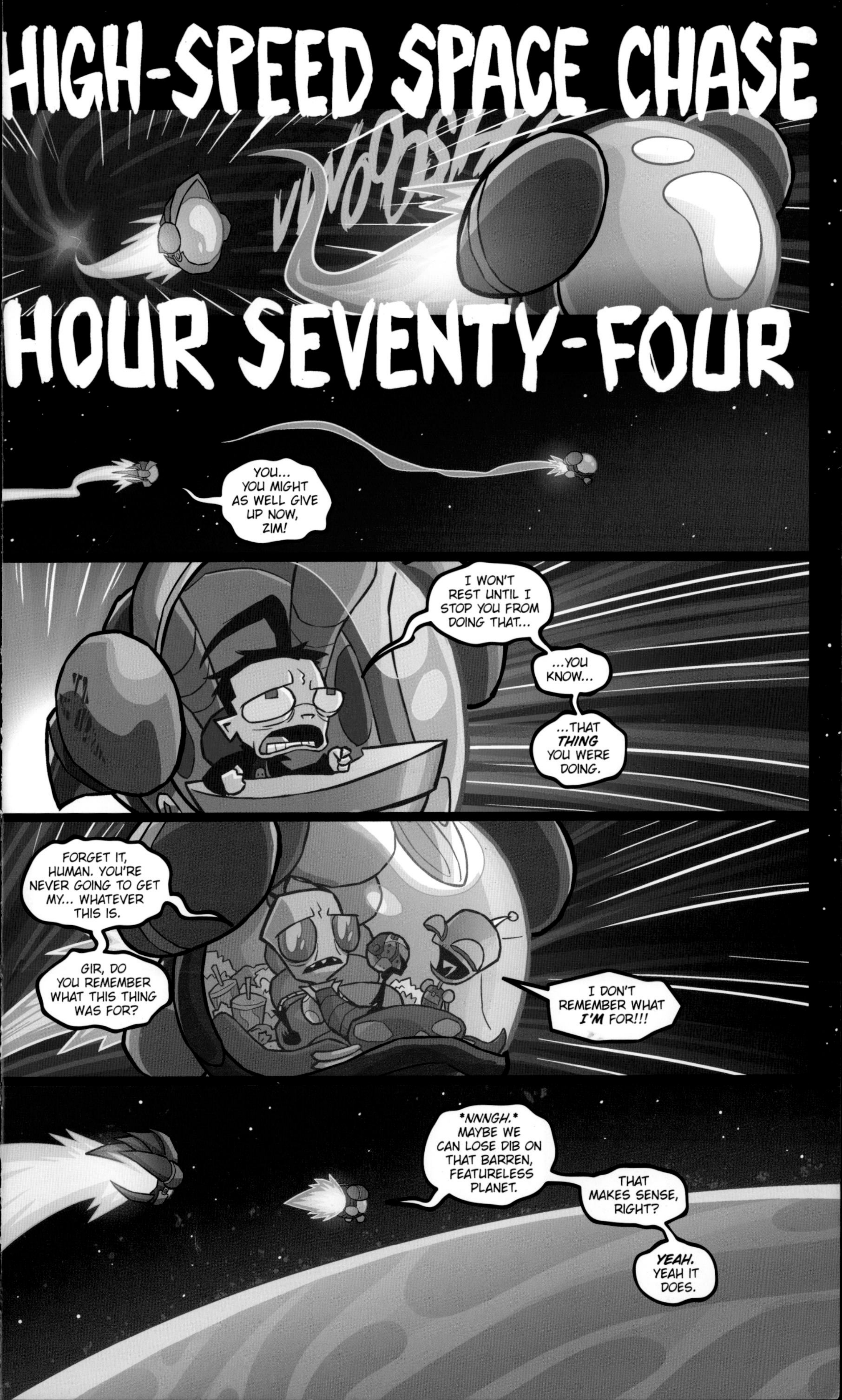
HIGH-SPEED SPACE CHASE
VVVOOOSH!
HOUR SEVENTY-FOUR
YOU... YOU MIGHT AS WELL GIVE UP NOW, ZIM!
I WON'T REST UNTIL I STOP YOU FROM DOING THAT...
...YOU KNOW...
...THAT *THING* YOU WERE DOING.
FORGET IT, HUMAN. YOU'RE NEVER GOING TO GET MY... WHATEVER THIS IS.
GIR, DO YOU REMEMBER WHAT THIS THING WAS FOR?
I DON'T REMEMBER WHAT *I'M* FOR!!!
NNNGH. MAYBE WE CAN LOSE DIB ON THAT BARREN, FEATURELESS PLANET.
THAT MAKES SENSE, RIGHT?
YEAH. YEAH IT DOES.

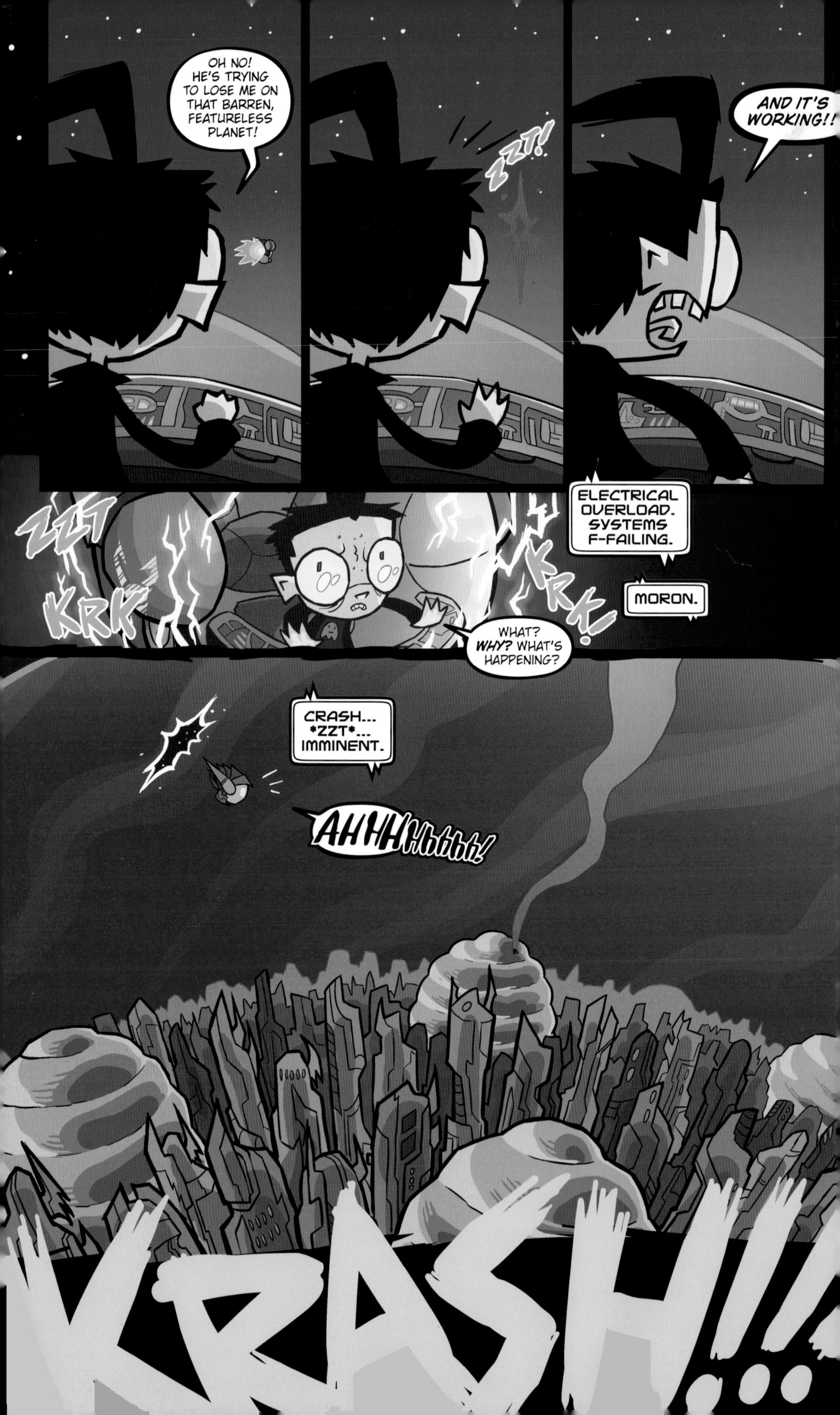
OH NO! HE'S TRYING TO LOSE ME ON THAT BARREN, FEATURELESS PLANET!
ZZT!
AND IT'S WORKING!!
ZZT
KRK
ELECTRICAL OVERLOAD. SYSTEMS F-FAILING.
KRK!
MORON.
WHAT? WHY? WHAT'S HAPPENING?
CRASH... *ZZT*... IMMINENT.
AHHHhhhh!
KRASH!!!

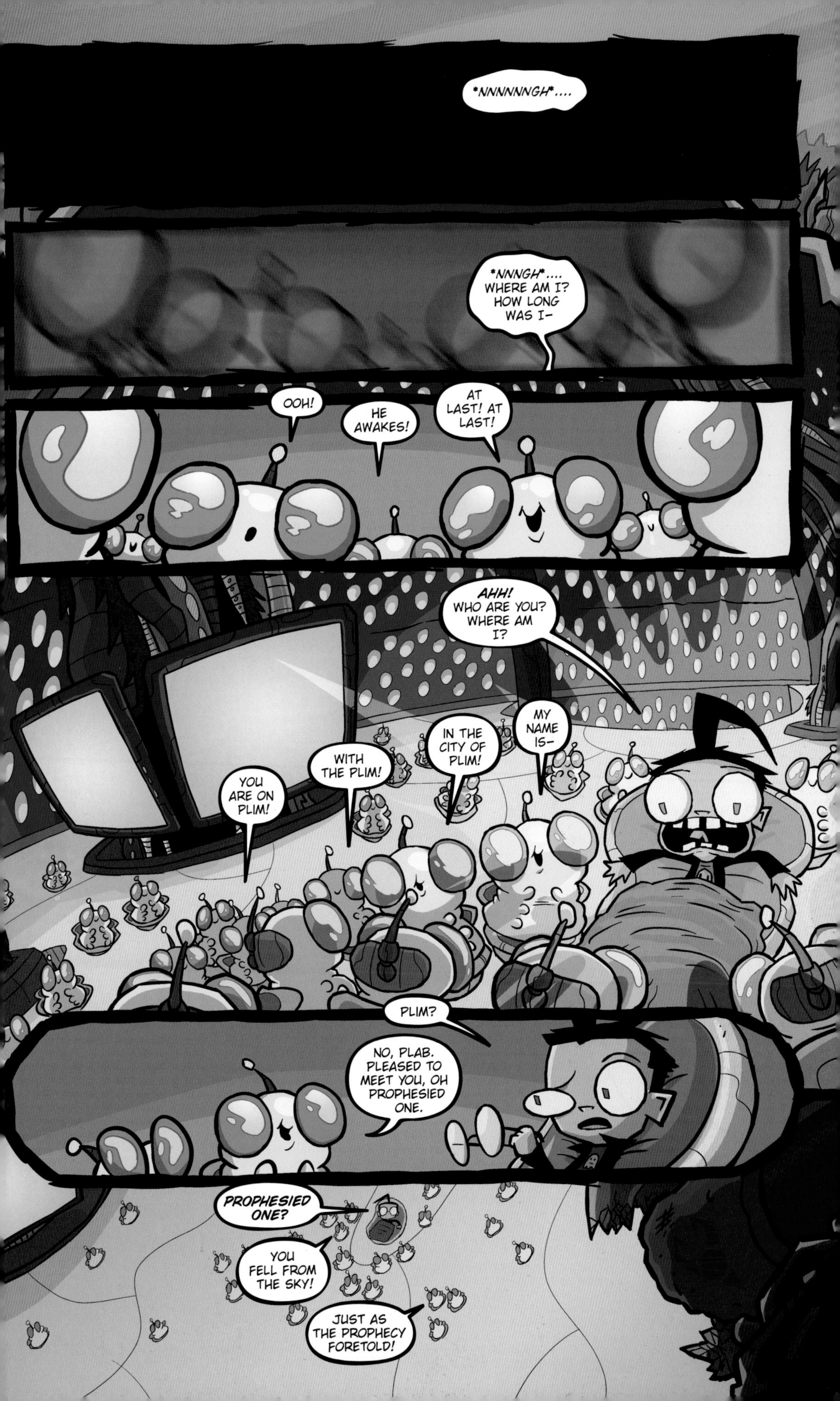
NNNNNNGH....
NNNGH.... WHERE AM I? HOW LONG WAS I-
OOH!
HE AWAKES!
AT LAST! AT LAST!
AHH! WHO ARE YOU? WHERE AM I?
MY NAME IS-
IN THE CITY OF PLIM!
WITH THE PLIM!
YOU ARE ON PLIM!
PLIM?
NO, PLAB. PLEASED TO MEET YOU, OH PROPHESIED ONE.
PROPHESIED ONE?
YOU FELL FROM THE SKY!
JUST AS THE PROPHECY FORETOLD!

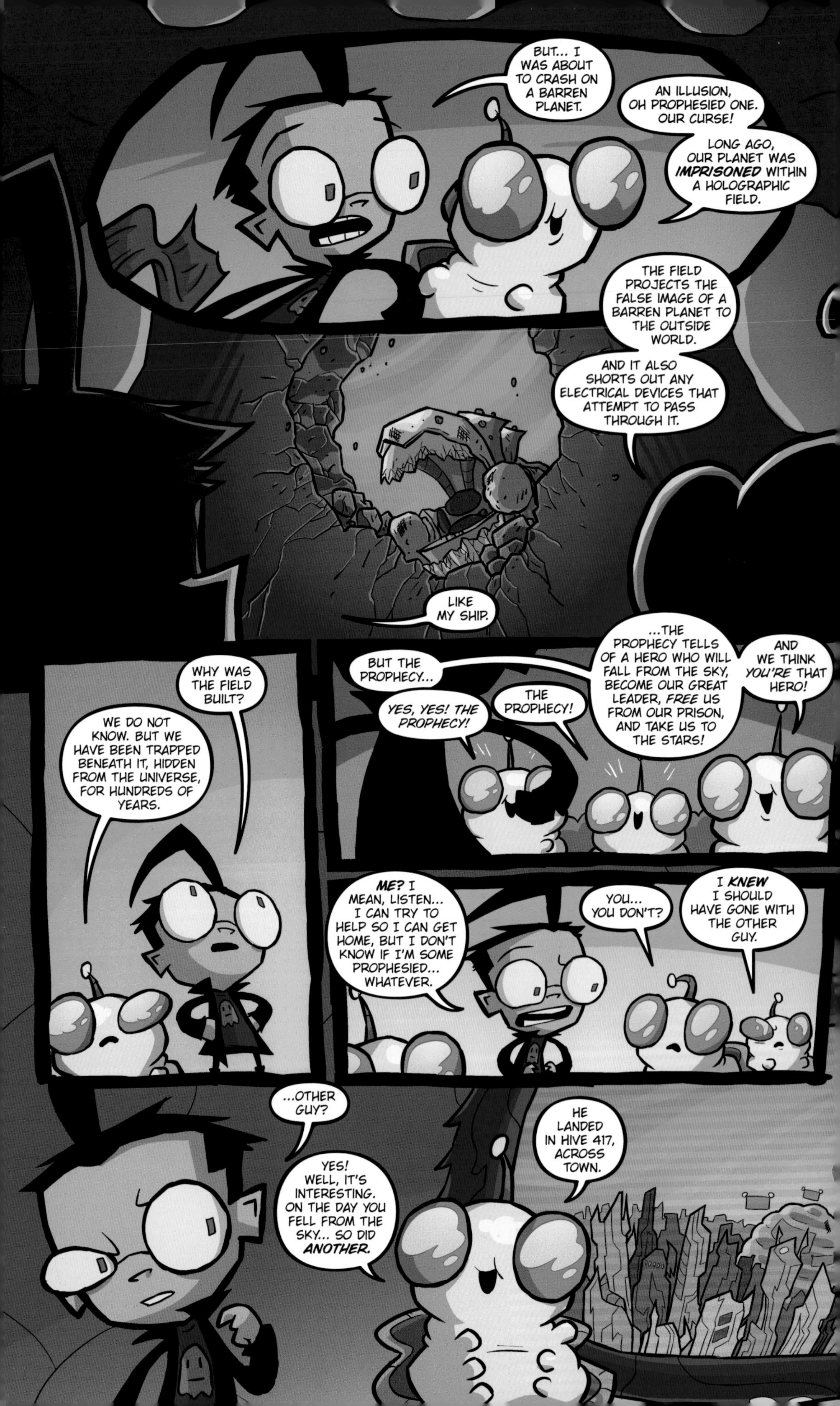

BUT... I WAS ABOUT TO CRASH ON A BARREN PLANET.
AN ILLUSION, OH PROPHESIED ONE. OUR CURSE!
LONG AGO, OUR PLANET WAS ***IMPRISONED*** WITHIN A HOLOGRAPHIC FIELD.
THE FIELD PROJECTS THE FALSE IMAGE OF A BARREN PLANET TO THE OUTSIDE WORLD.
AND IT ALSO SHORTS OUT ANY ELECTRICAL DEVICES THAT ATTEMPT TO PASS THROUGH IT.
LIKE MY SHIP.
WHY WAS THE FIELD BUILT?
WE DO NOT KNOW. BUT WE HAVE BEEN TRAPPED BENEATH IT, HIDDEN FROM THE UNIVERSE, FOR HUNDREDS OF YEARS.
BUT THE PROPHECY...
YES, YES! THE PROPHECY!
THE PROPHECY!
...THE PROPHECY TELLS OF A HERO WHO WILL FALL FROM THE SKY, BECOME OUR GREAT LEADER, *FREE* US FROM OUR PRISON, AND TAKE US TO THE STARS!
AND WE THINK *YOU'RE* THAT HERO!
ME? I MEAN, LISTEN... I CAN TRY TO HELP SO I CAN GET HOME, BUT I DON'T KNOW IF I'M SOME PROPHESIED... WHATEVER.
YOU... YOU DON'T?
I ***KNEW*** I SHOULD HAVE GONE WITH THE OTHER GUY.
...OTHER GUY?
YES! WELL, IT'S INTERESTING. ON THE DAY YOU FELL FROM THE SKY... SO DID ***ANOTHER.***
HE LANDED IN HIVE 417, ACROSS TOWN.

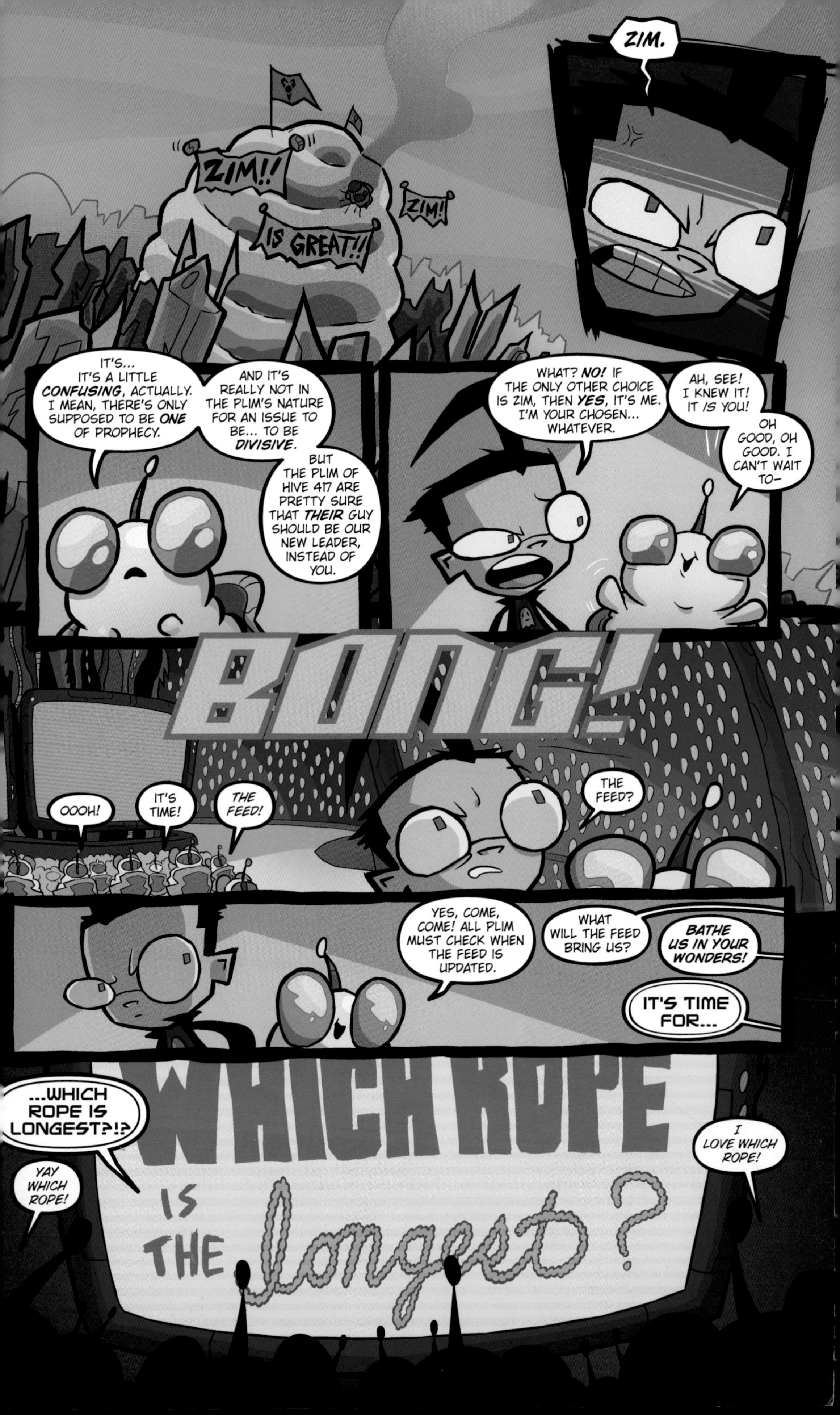
ZIM!!
ZIM!
IS GREAT!!
ZIM.
IT'S... IT'S A LITTLE CONFUSING, ACTUALLY. I MEAN, THERE'S ONLY SUPPOSED TO BE ONE OF PROPHECY.
AND IT'S REALLY NOT IN THE PLIM'S NATURE FOR AN ISSUE TO BE... TO BE DIVISIVE.
BUT THE PLIM OF HIVE 417 ARE PRETTY SURE THAT THEIR GUY SHOULD BE OUR NEW LEADER, INSTEAD OF YOU.
WHAT? NO! IF THE ONLY OTHER CHOICE IS ZIM, THEN YES, IT'S ME. I'M YOUR CHOSEN... WHATEVER.
AH, SEE! I KNEW IT! IT IS YOU!
OH GOOD, OH GOOD. I CAN'T WAIT TO-
BONG!
OOOH!
IT'S TIME!
THE FEED!
THE FEED?
YES, COME, COME! ALL PLIM MUST CHECK WHEN THE FEED IS UPDATED.
WHAT WILL THE FEED BRING US?
BATHE US IN YOUR WONDERS!
IT'S TIME FOR...
...WHICH ROPE IS LONGEST?!?
WHICH ROPE IS THE longest?
YAY WHICH ROPE!
I LOVE WHICH ROPE!

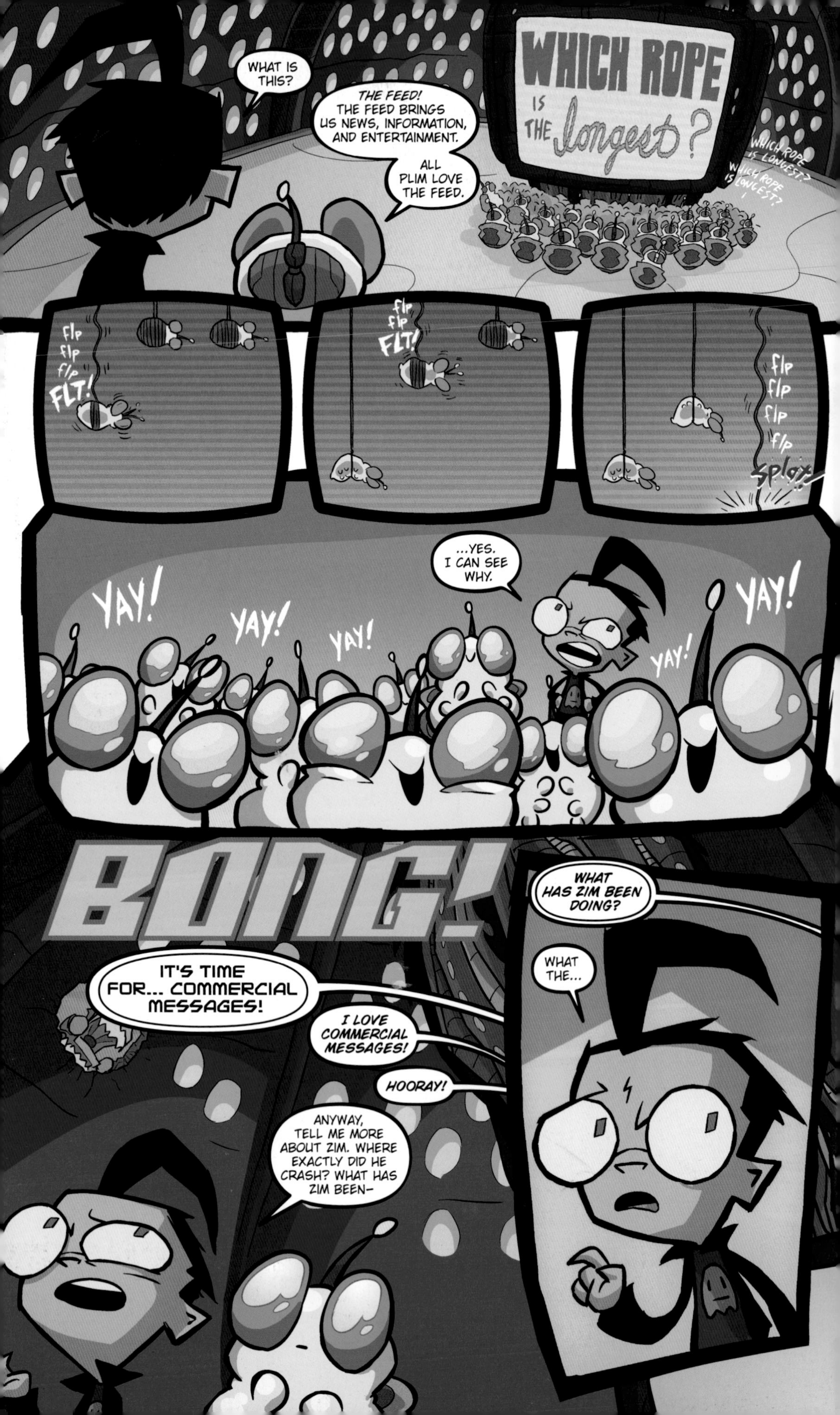

WHAT IS THIS?
THE FEED! THE FEED BRINGS US NEWS, INFORMATION, AND ENTERTAINMENT.
ALL PLIM LOVE THE FEED.
WHICH ROPE IS THE Longest?
WHICH ROPE IS LONGEST?
WHICH ROPE IS LONGEST?
FLP FLP FLP FLT!
FLP FLP FLT!
FLP FLP FLP FLP SPLAT!
...YES. I CAN SEE WHY.
YAY!
YAY!
YAY!
YAY!
YAY!
BONG!
IT'S TIME FOR... COMMERCIAL MESSAGES!
I LOVE COMMERCIAL MESSAGES!
HOORAY!
ANYWAY, TELL ME MORE ABOUT ZIM. WHERE EXACTLY DID HE CRASH? WHAT HAS ZIM BEEN–
WHAT HAS ZIM BEEN DOING?
WHAT THE...

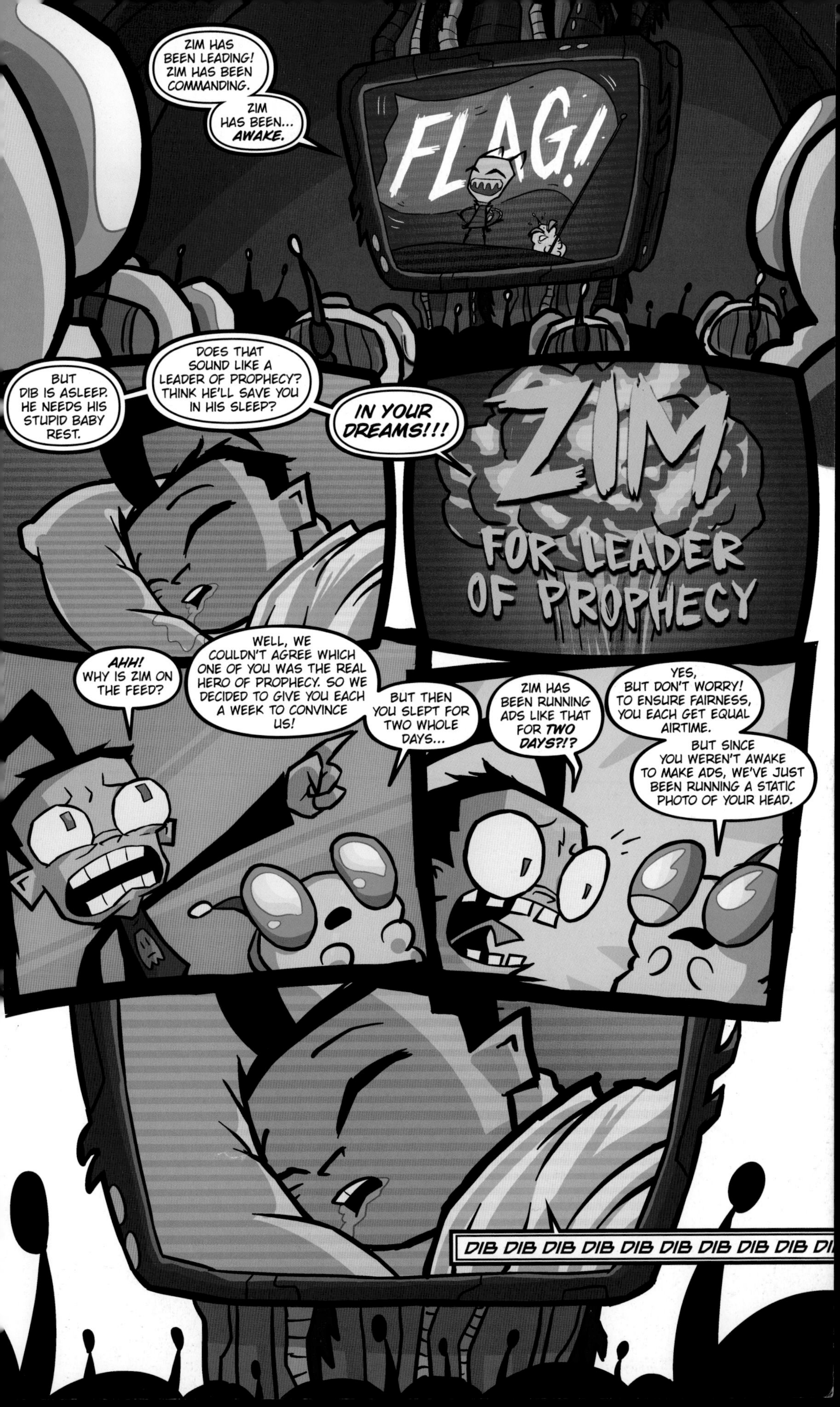

ZIM HAS BEEN LEADING! ZIM HAS BEEN COMMANDING.
ZIM HAS BEEN... AWAKE.
FLAG!
BUT DIB IS ASLEEP. HE NEEDS HIS STUPID BABY REST.
DOES THAT SOUND LIKE A LEADER OF PROPHECY? THINK HE'LL SAVE YOU IN HIS SLEEP?
IN YOUR DREAMS!!!
ZIM FOR LEADER OF PROPHECY
AHH! WHY IS ZIM ON THE FEED?
WELL, WE COULDN'T AGREE WHICH ONE OF YOU WAS THE REAL HERO OF PROPHECY. SO WE DECIDED TO GIVE YOU EACH A WEEK TO CONVINCE US!
BUT THEN YOU SLEPT FOR TWO WHOLE DAYS...
ZIM HAS BEEN RUNNING ADS LIKE THAT FOR TWO DAYS?!?
YES, BUT DON'T WORRY! TO ENSURE FAIRNESS, YOU EACH GET EQUAL AIRTIME.
BUT SINCE YOU WEREN'T AWAKE TO MAKE ADS, WE'VE JUST BEEN RUNNING A STATIC PHOTO OF YOUR HEAD.
DIB DIB DIB DIB DIB DIB DIB DIB DIB

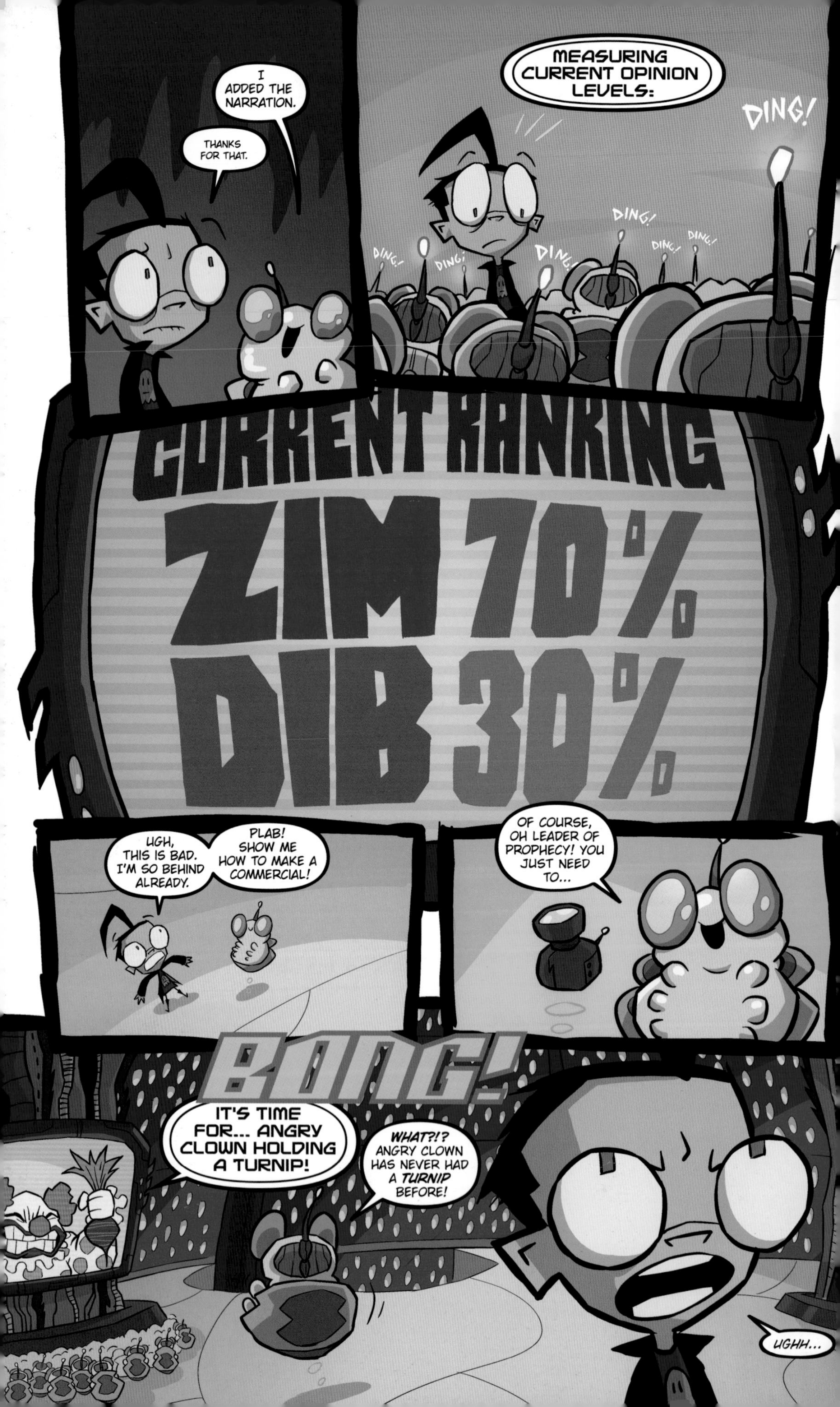
I ADDED THE NARRATION.
THANKS FOR THAT.
MEASURING CURRENT OPINION LEVELS:
DING!
DING!
DING!
DING!
DING!
DING!
DING!
DING!
CURRENT RANKING
ZIM 70%
DIB 30%
UGH, THIS IS BAD. I'M SO BEHIND ALREADY.
PLAB! SHOW ME HOW TO MAKE A COMMERCIAL!
OF COURSE, OH LEADER OF PROPHECY! YOU JUST NEED TO...
BONG!
IT'S TIME FOR... ANGRY CLOWN HOLDING A TURNIP!
WHAT?!? ANGRY CLOWN HAS NEVER HAD A TURNIP BEFORE!
UGHH...

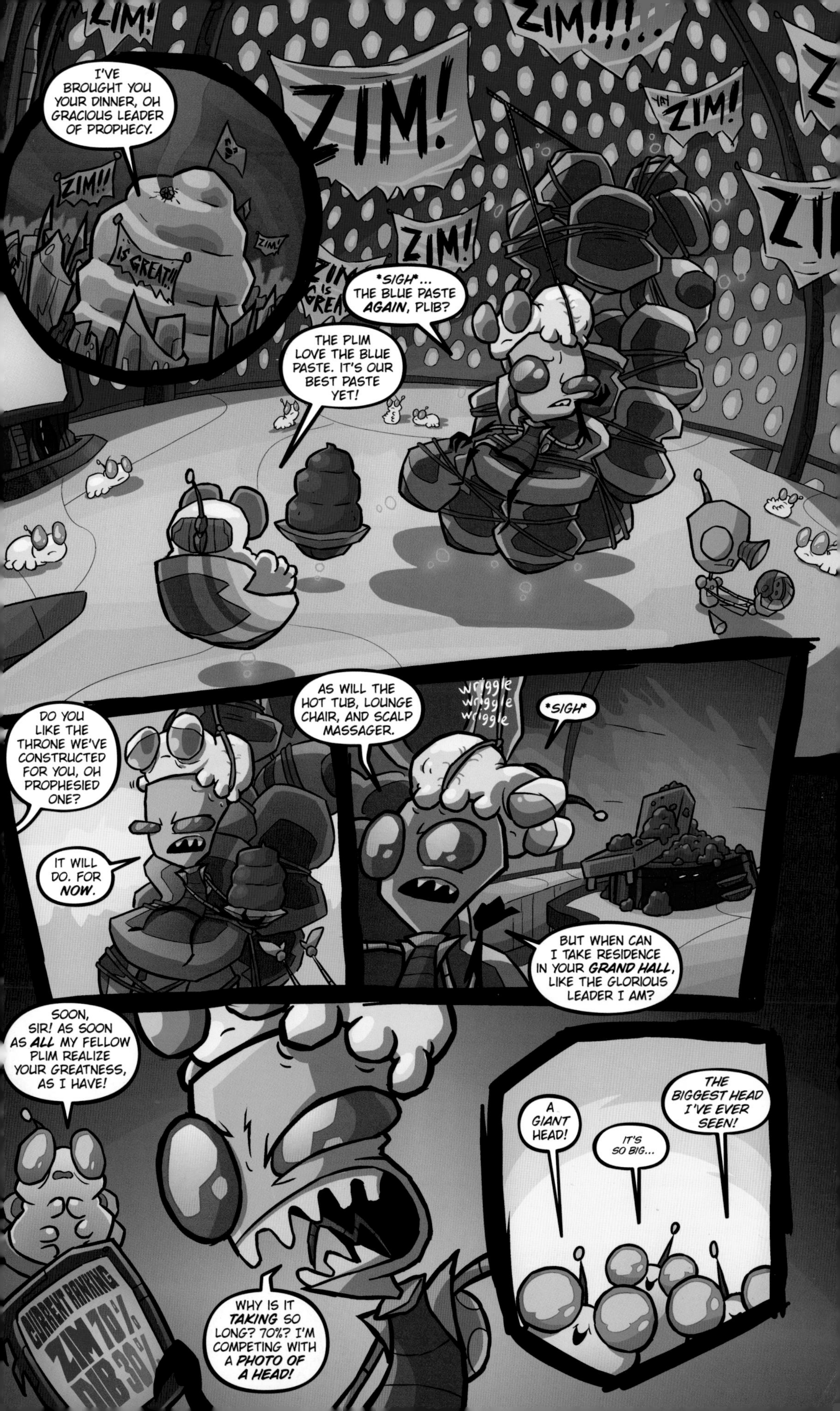

ZIM!
ZIM!!!...
I'VE BROUGHT YOU YOUR DINNER, OH GRACIOUS LEADER OF PROPHECY.
ZIM!!
IS GREAT!!!
ZIM!
ZIM!
YAY ZIM!
ZIM!
SIGH... THE BLUE PASTE AGAIN, PLIB?
THE PLIM LOVE THE BLUE PASTE. IT'S OUR BEST PASTE YET!
DO YOU LIKE THE THRONE WE'VE CONSTRUCTED FOR YOU, OH PROPHESIED ONE?
IT WILL DO. FOR NOW.
AS WILL THE HOT TUB, LOUNGE CHAIR, AND SCALP MASSAGER.
wriggle wriggle wriggle
SIGH
BUT WHEN CAN I TAKE RESIDENCE IN YOUR GRAND HALL, LIKE THE GLORIOUS LEADER I AM?
SOON, SIR! AS SOON AS ALL MY FELLOW PLIM REALIZE YOUR GREATNESS, AS I HAVE!
CURRENT RANKING ZIM 70% DIB 30%
WHY IS IT TAKING SO LONG? 70%? I'M COMPETING WITH A PHOTO OF A HEAD!
A GIANT HEAD!
IT'S SO BIG...
THE BIGGEST HEAD I'VE EVER SEEN!

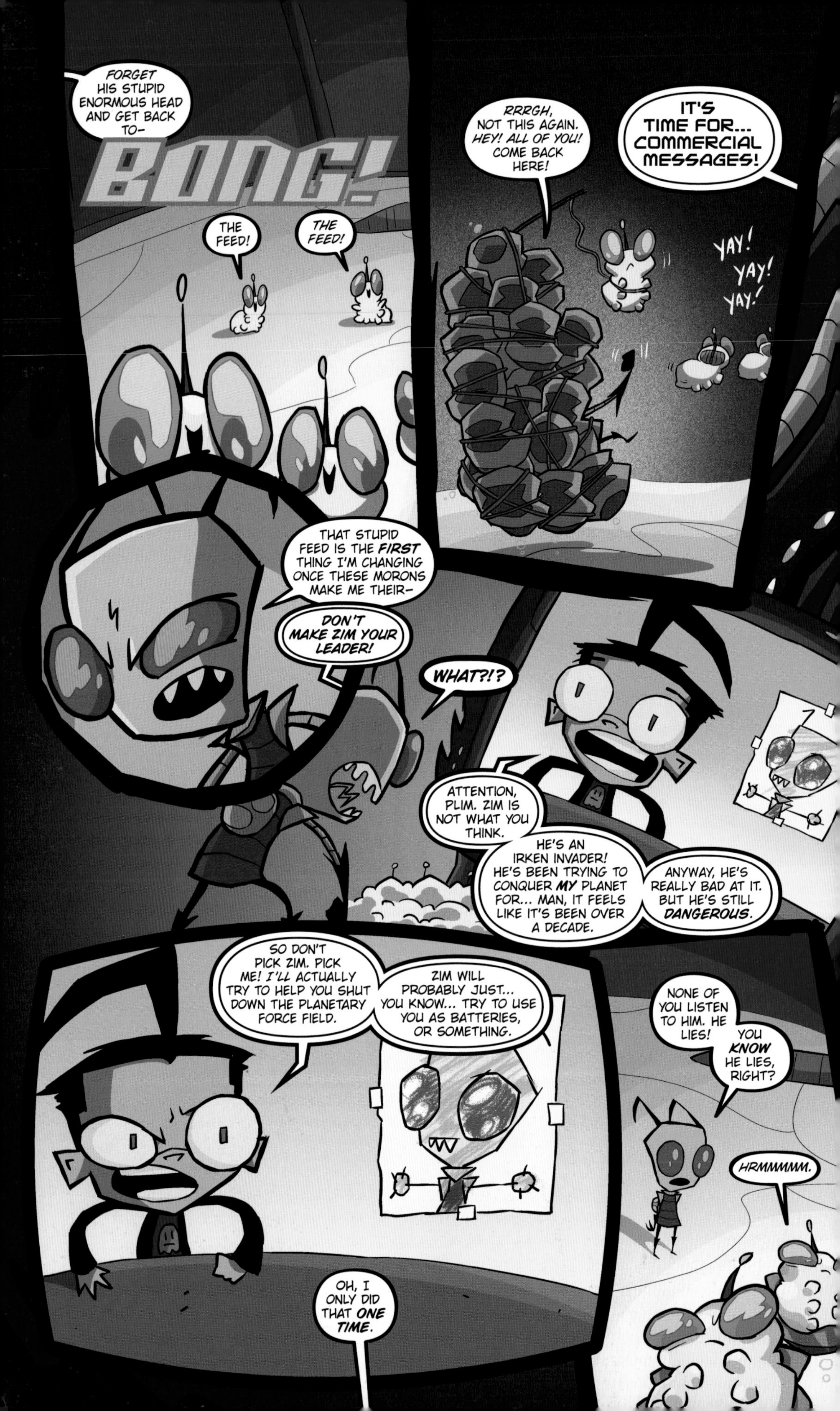
FORGET HIS STUPID ENORMOUS HEAD AND GET BACK TO-
BONG!
THE FEED!
THE FEED!
RRRGH, NOT THIS AGAIN. HEY! ALL OF YOU! COME BACK HERE!
IT'S TIME FOR... COMMERCIAL MESSAGES!
YAY! YAY! YAY!
THAT STUPID FEED IS THE FIRST THING I'M CHANGING ONCE THESE MORONS MAKE ME THEIR-
DON'T MAKE ZIM YOUR LEADER!
WHAT?!?
ATTENTION, PLIM. ZIM IS NOT WHAT YOU THINK.
HE'S AN IRKEN INVADER! HE'S BEEN TRYING TO CONQUER MY PLANET FOR... MAN, IT FEELS LIKE IT'S BEEN OVER A DECADE.
ANYWAY, HE'S REALLY BAD AT IT. BUT HE'S STILL DANGEROUS.
SO DON'T PICK ZIM. PICK ME! I'LL ACTUALLY TRY TO HELP YOU SHUT DOWN THE PLANETARY FORCE FIELD.
ZIM WILL PROBABLY JUST... YOU KNOW... TRY TO USE YOU AS BATTERIES, OR SOMETHING.
OH, I ONLY DID THAT ONE TIME.
NONE OF YOU LISTEN TO HIM. HE LIES!
YOU KNOW HE LIES, RIGHT?
HRMMMMM.

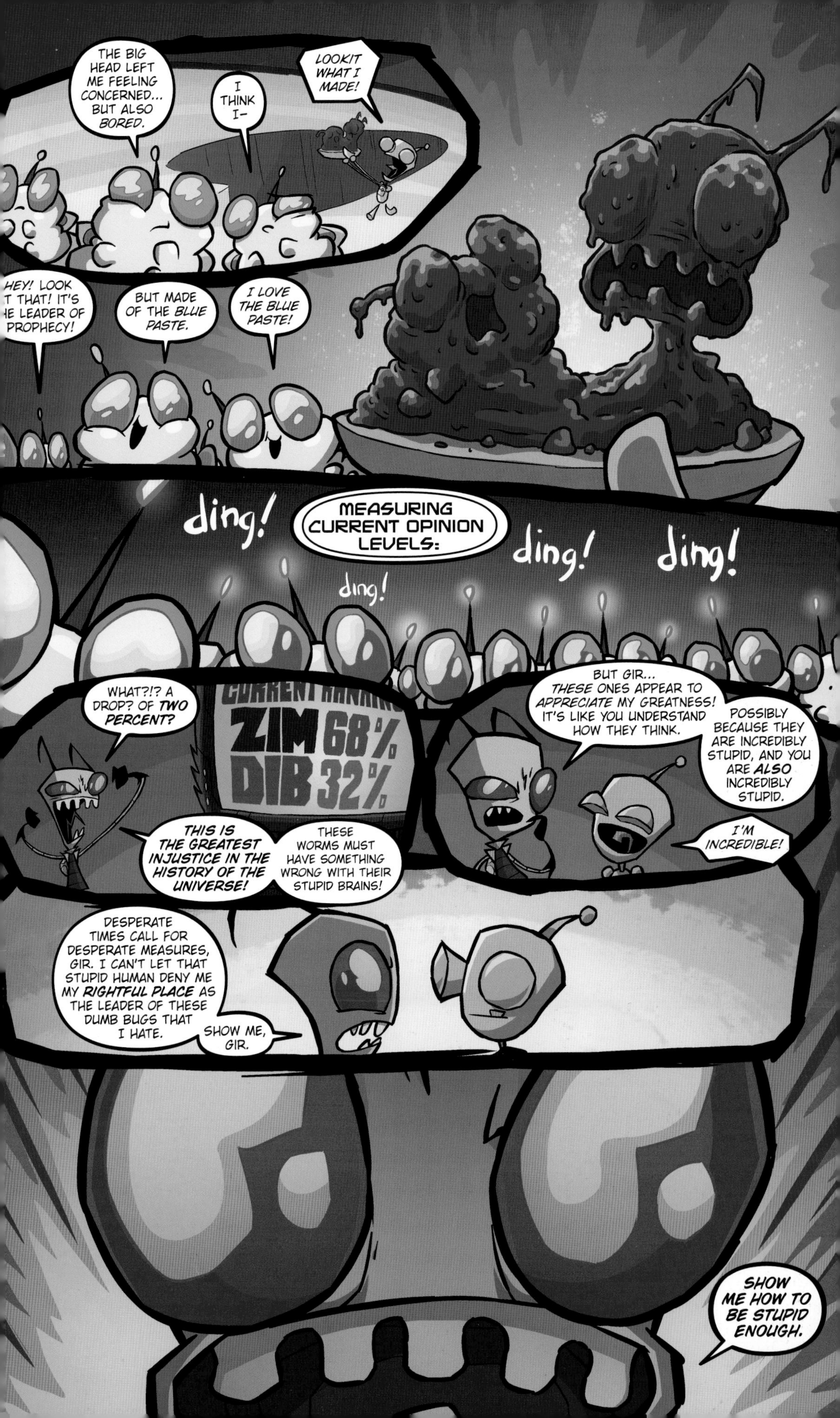
THE BIG HEAD LEFT ME FEELING CONCERNED... BUT ALSO *BORED*.
I THINK I–
LOOKIT WHAT I MADE!
HEY! LOOK AT THAT! IT'S THE LEADER OF PROPHECY!
BUT MADE OF THE *BLUE* PASTE.
I LOVE THE BLUE PASTE!
ding!
MEASURING CURRENT OPINION LEVELS:
ding!
ding!
ding!
WHAT?!? A DROP? OF **TWO PERCENT?**
CURRENT RANKING
ZIM 68%
DIB 32%
THIS IS THE GREATEST INJUSTICE IN THE HISTORY OF THE UNIVERSE!
THESE WORMS MUST HAVE SOMETHING WRONG WITH THEIR STUPID BRAINS!
BUT GIR... *THESE* ONES APPEAR TO *APPRECIATE MY GREATNESS!* IT'S LIKE YOU UNDERSTAND HOW THEY THINK.
POSSIBLY BECAUSE THEY ARE INCREDIBLY STUPID, AND YOU ARE **ALSO** INCREDIBLY STUPID.
I'M INCREDIBLE!
DESPERATE TIMES CALL FOR DESPERATE MEASURES, GIR. I CAN'T LET THAT STUPID HUMAN DENY ME MY ***RIGHTFUL PLACE*** AS THE LEADER OF THESE DUMB BUGS THAT I HATE.
SHOW ME, GIR.
SHOW ME HOW TO BE STUPID ENOUGH.

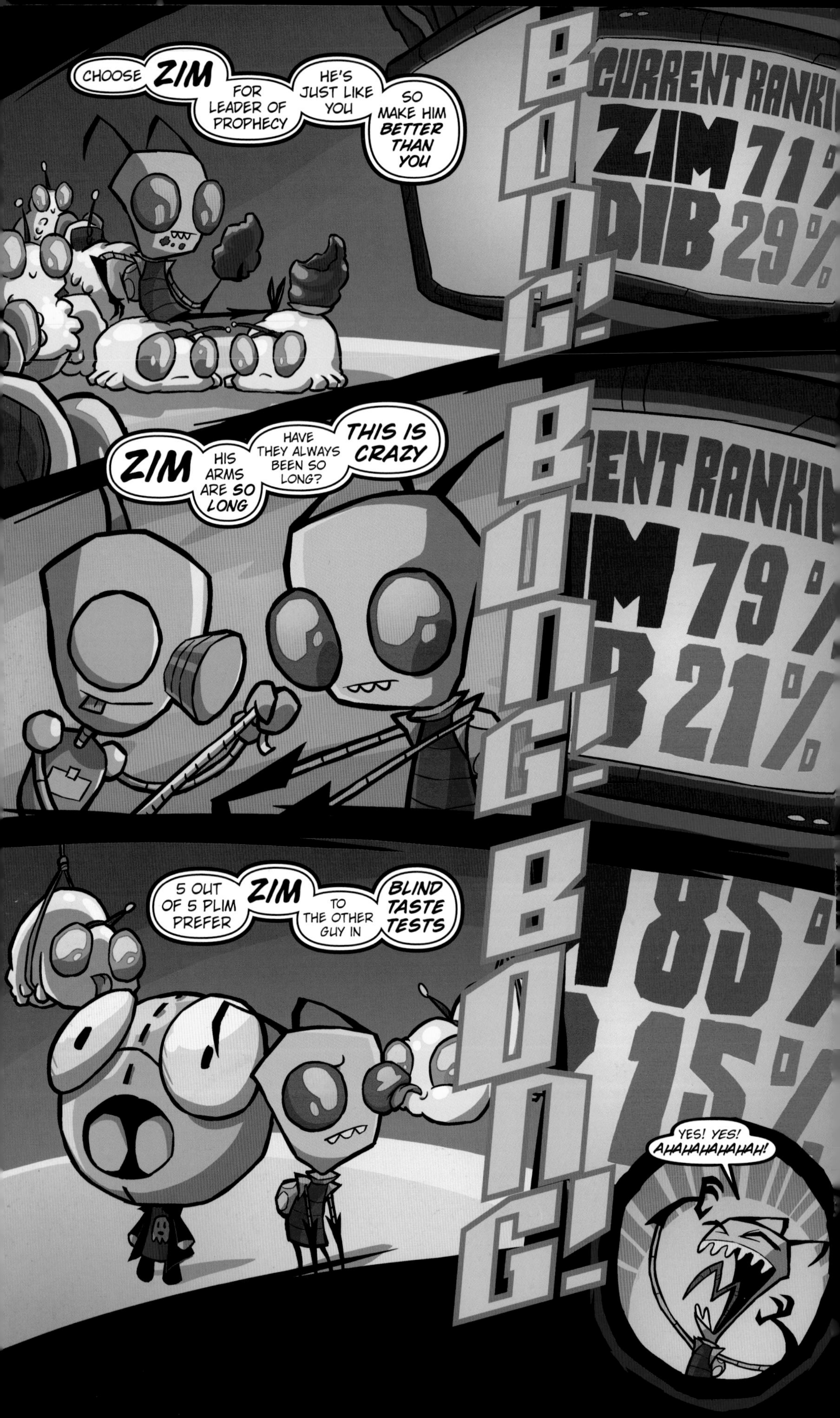
CHOOSE ZIM FOR LEADER OF PROPHECY
HE'S JUST LIKE YOU
SO MAKE HIM BETTER THAN YOU
BOONG!
CURRENT RANKI
ZIM 71%
DIB 29%
ZIM HIS ARMS ARE SO LONG
HAVE THEY ALWAYS BEEN SO LONG?
THIS IS CRAZY
BOONG!
ENT RANKI
M 79%
B 21%
5 OUT OF 5 PLIM PREFER ZIM TO THE OTHER GUY IN BLIND TASTE TESTS
BOONG!
85%
15%
YES! YES! AHAHAHAHAHAH!

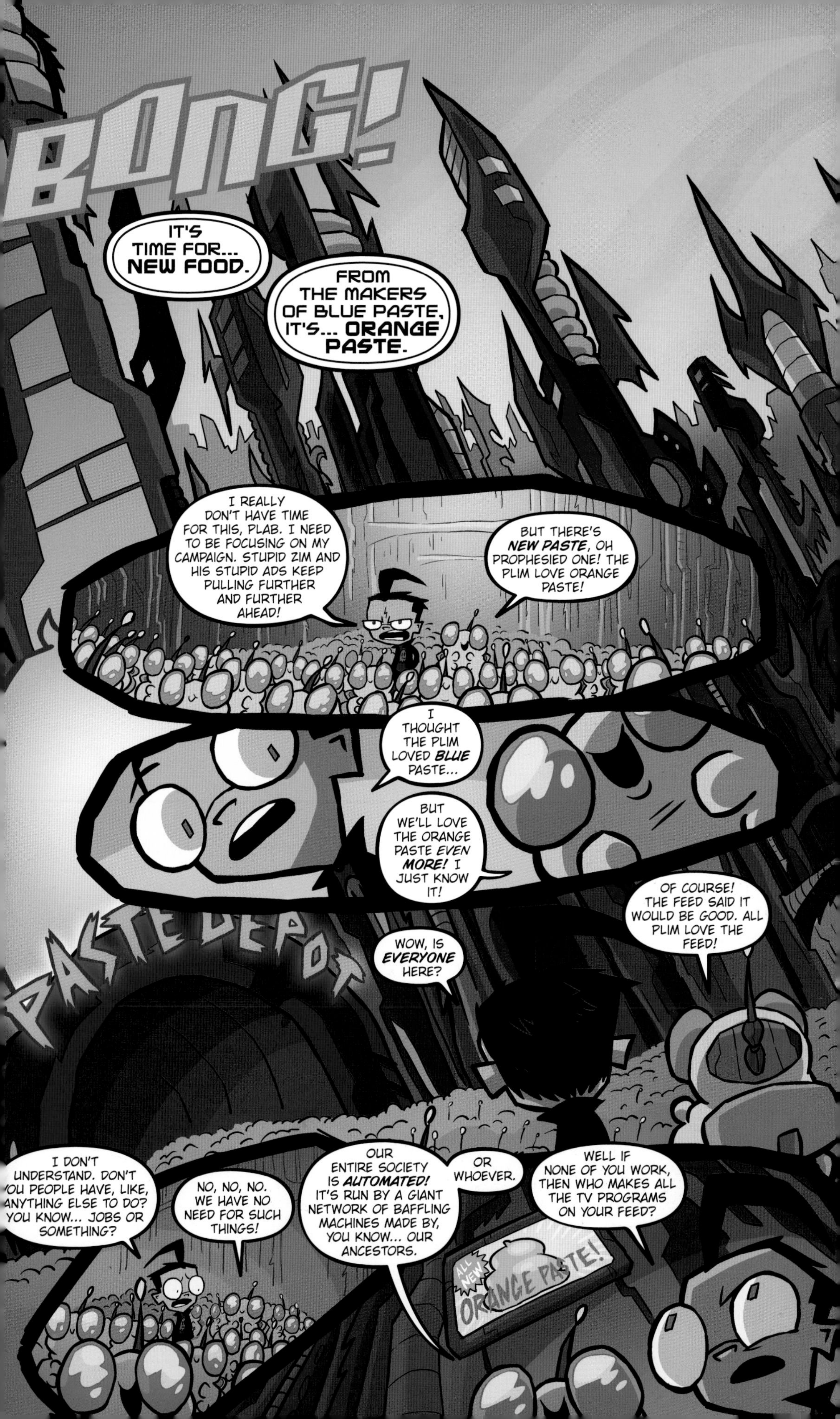
BONG!
IT'S TIME FOR... NEW FOOD.
FROM THE MAKERS OF BLUE PASTE, IT'S... ORANGE PASTE.
I REALLY DON'T HAVE TIME FOR THIS, PLAB. I NEED TO BE FOCUSING ON MY CAMPAIGN. STUPID ZIM AND HIS STUPID ADS KEEP PULLING FURTHER AND FURTHER AHEAD!
BUT THERE'S NEW PASTE, OH PROPHESIED ONE! THE PLIM LOVE ORANGE PASTE!
I THOUGHT THE PLIM LOVED BLUE PASTE...
BUT WE'LL LOVE THE ORANGE PASTE EVEN MORE! I JUST KNOW IT!
PASTE DEPOT
WOW, IS EVERYONE HERE?
OF COURSE! THE FEED SAID IT WOULD BE GOOD. ALL PLIM LOVE THE FEED!
I DON'T UNDERSTAND. DON'T YOU PEOPLE HAVE, LIKE, ANYTHING ELSE TO DO? YOU KNOW... JOBS OR SOMETHING?
NO, NO, NO. WE HAVE NO NEED FOR SUCH THINGS!
OUR ENTIRE SOCIETY IS AUTOMATED! IT'S RUN BY A GIANT NETWORK OF BAFFLING MACHINES MADE BY, YOU KNOW... OUR ANCESTORS.
OR WHOEVER.
WELL IF NONE OF YOU WORK, THEN WHO MAKES ALL THE TV PROGRAMS ON YOUR FEED?
ALL NEW ORANGE PASTE!

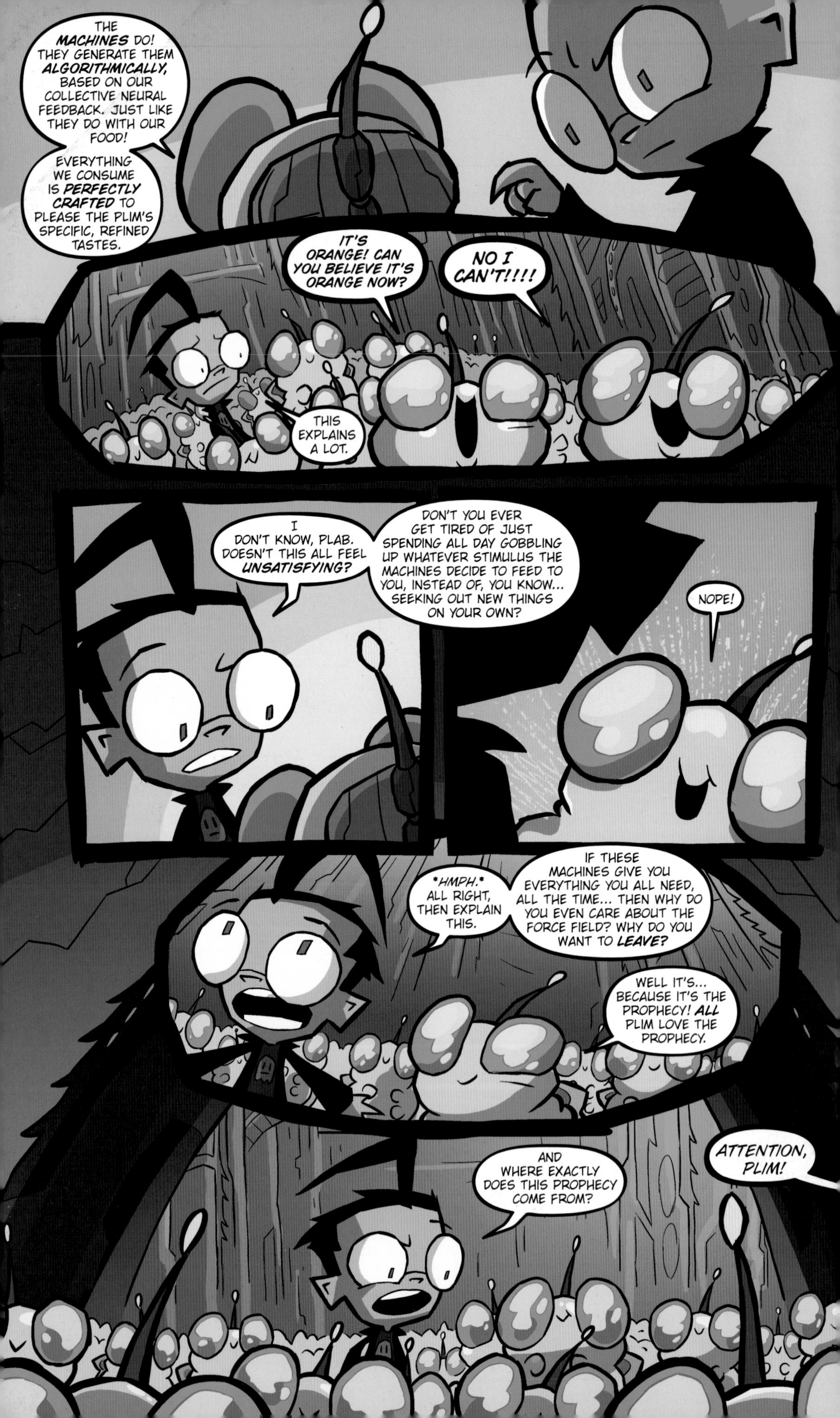
THE MACHINES DO! THEY GENERATE THEM ALGORITHMICALLY, BASED ON OUR COLLECTIVE NEURAL FEEDBACK. JUST LIKE THEY DO WITH OUR FOOD!
EVERYTHING WE CONSUME IS PERFECTLY CRAFTED TO PLEASE THE PLIM'S SPECIFIC, REFINED TASTES.
IT'S ORANGE! CAN YOU BELIEVE IT'S ORANGE NOW?
NO I CAN'T!!!!
THIS EXPLAINS A LOT.
I DON'T KNOW, PLAB. DOESN'T THIS ALL FEEL UNSATISFYING?
DON'T YOU EVER GET TIRED OF JUST SPENDING ALL DAY GOBBLING UP WHATEVER STIMULUS THE MACHINES DECIDE TO FEED TO YOU, INSTEAD OF, YOU KNOW... SEEKING OUT NEW THINGS ON YOUR OWN?
NOPE!
HMPH. ALL RIGHT, THEN EXPLAIN THIS.
IF THESE MACHINES GIVE YOU EVERYTHING YOU ALL NEED, ALL THE TIME... THEN WHY DO YOU EVEN CARE ABOUT THE FORCE FIELD? WHY DO YOU WANT TO LEAVE?
WELL IT'S... BECAUSE IT'S THE PROPHECY! ALL PLIM LOVE THE PROPHECY.
AND WHERE EXACTLY DOES THIS PROPHECY COME FROM?
ATTENTION, PLIM!

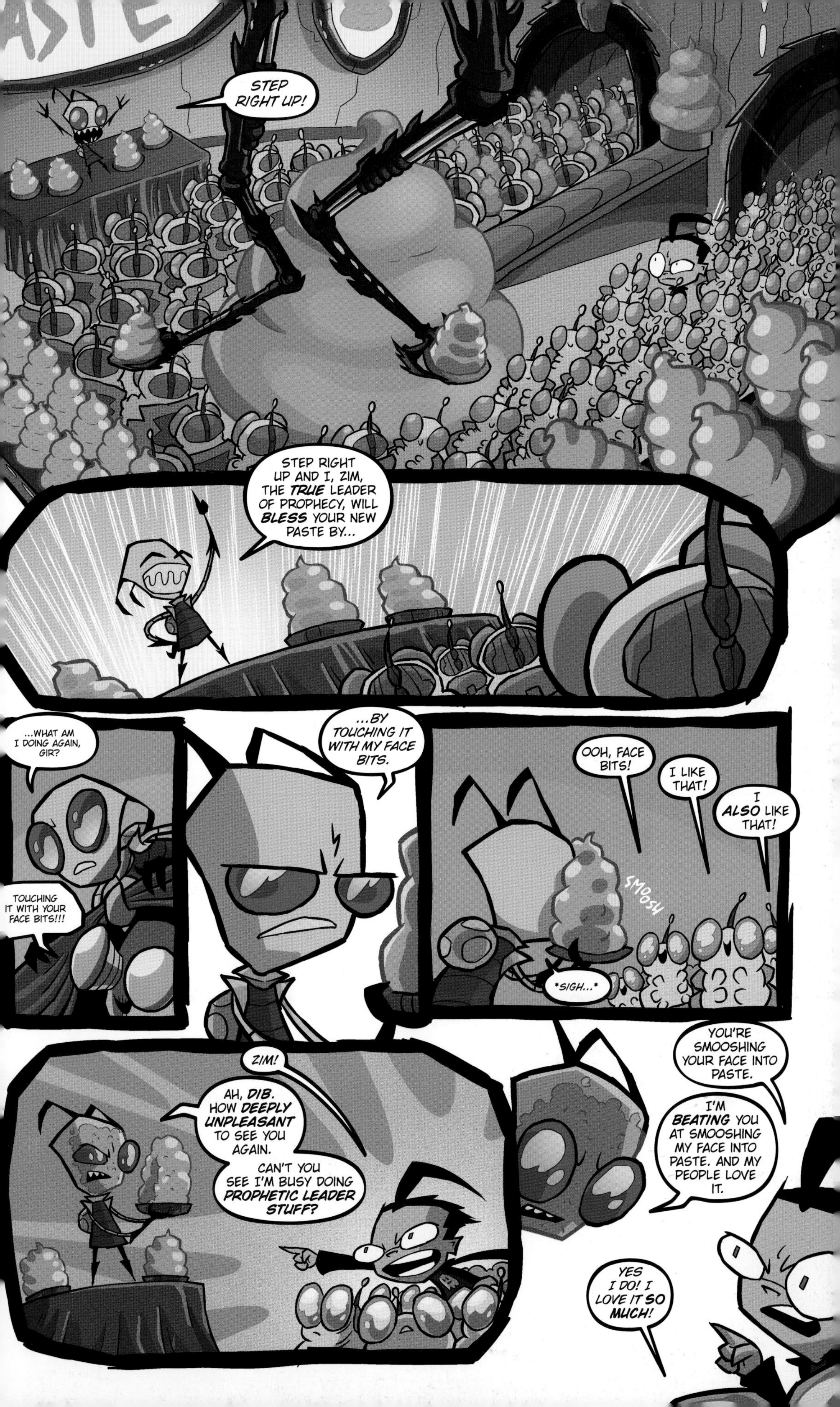

STEP RIGHT UP!
STEP RIGHT UP AND I, ZIM, THE TRUE LEADER OF PROPHECY, WILL BLESS YOUR NEW PASTE BY...
...WHAT AM I DOING AGAIN, GIR?
TOUCHING IT WITH YOUR FACE BITS!!!
...BY TOUCHING IT WITH MY FACE BITS.
OOH, FACE BITS!
I LIKE THAT!
I ALSO LIKE THAT!
SMOOSH
SIGH...
ZIM!
AH, DIB. HOW DEEPLY UNPLEASANT TO SEE YOU AGAIN.
CAN'T YOU SEE I'M BUSY DOING PROPHETIC LEADER STUFF?
YOU'RE SMOOSHING YOUR FACE INTO PASTE.
I'M BEATING YOU AT SMOOSHING MY FACE INTO PASTE. AND MY PEOPLE LOVE IT.
YES I DO! I LOVE IT SO MUCH!

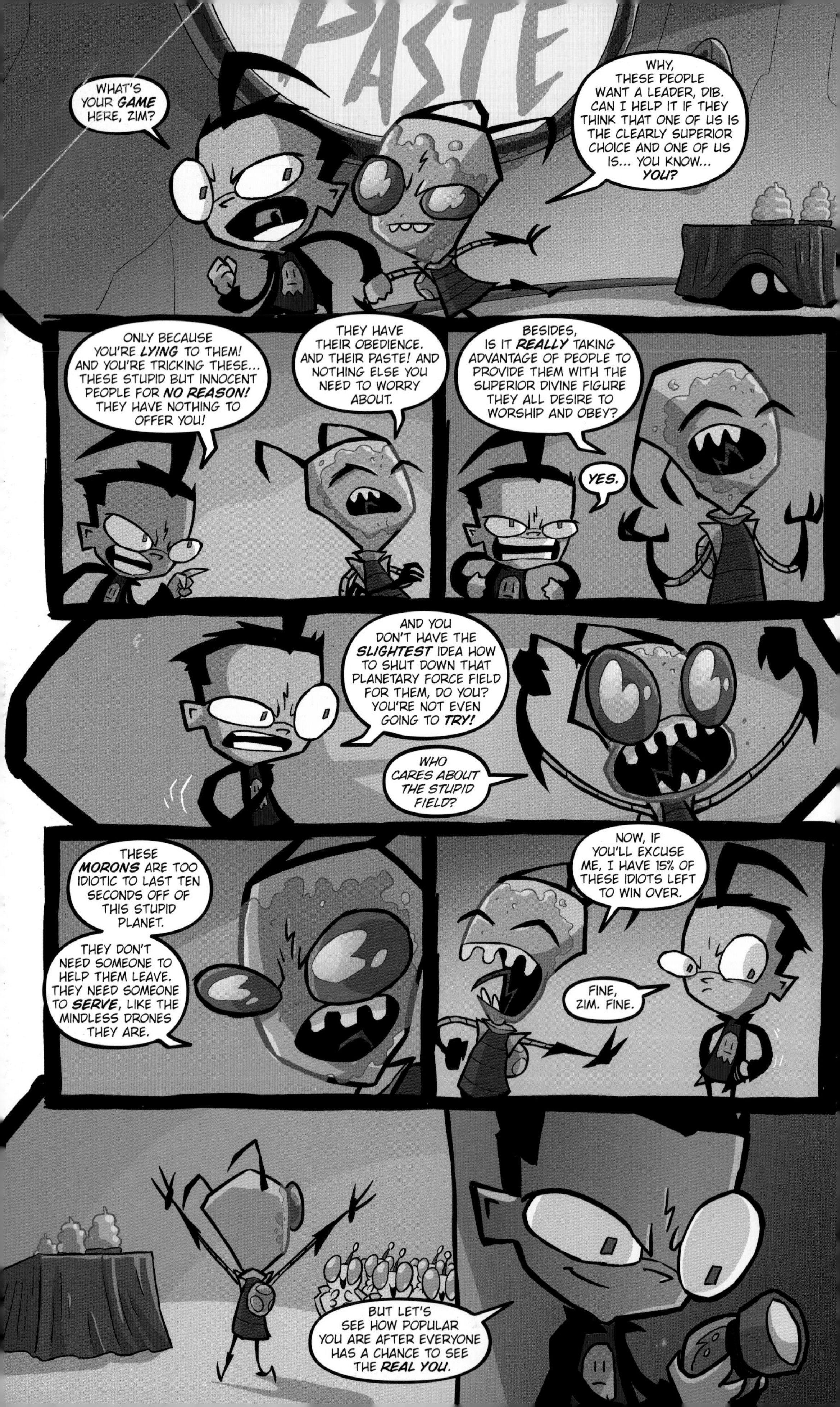

PASTE
WHAT'S YOUR **GAME** HERE, ZIM?
WHY, THESE PEOPLE WANT A LEADER, DIB. CAN I HELP IT IF THEY THINK THAT ONE OF US IS THE CLEARLY SUPERIOR CHOICE AND ONE OF US IS... YOU KNOW... ***YOU?***
ONLY BECAUSE YOU'RE ***LYING*** TO THEM! AND YOU'RE TRICKING THESE... THESE STUPID BUT INNOCENT PEOPLE FOR ***NO REASON!*** THEY HAVE NOTHING TO OFFER YOU!
THEY HAVE THEIR OBEDIENCE. AND THEIR PASTE! AND NOTHING ELSE YOU NEED TO WORRY ABOUT.
BESIDES, IS IT ***REALLY*** TAKING ADVANTAGE OF PEOPLE TO PROVIDE THEM WITH THE SUPERIOR DIVINE FIGURE THEY ALL DESIRE TO WORSHIP AND OBEY?
YES.
AND YOU DON'T HAVE THE ***SLIGHTEST*** IDEA HOW TO SHUT DOWN THAT PLANETARY FORCE FIELD FOR THEM, DO YOU? YOU'RE NOT EVEN GOING TO ***TRY!***
WHO CARES ABOUT THE STUPID FIELD?
THESE ***MORONS*** ARE TOO IDIOTIC TO LAST TEN SECONDS OFF OF THIS STUPID PLANET.
THEY DON'T NEED SOMEONE TO HELP THEM LEAVE. THEY NEED SOMEONE TO ***SERVE***, LIKE THE MINDLESS DRONES THEY ARE.
NOW, IF YOU'LL EXCUSE ME, I HAVE 15% OF THESE IDIOTS LEFT TO WIN OVER.
FINE, ZIM. FINE.
BUT LET'S SEE HOW POPULAR YOU ARE AFTER EVERYONE HAS A CHANCE TO SEE THE ***REAL YOU***.

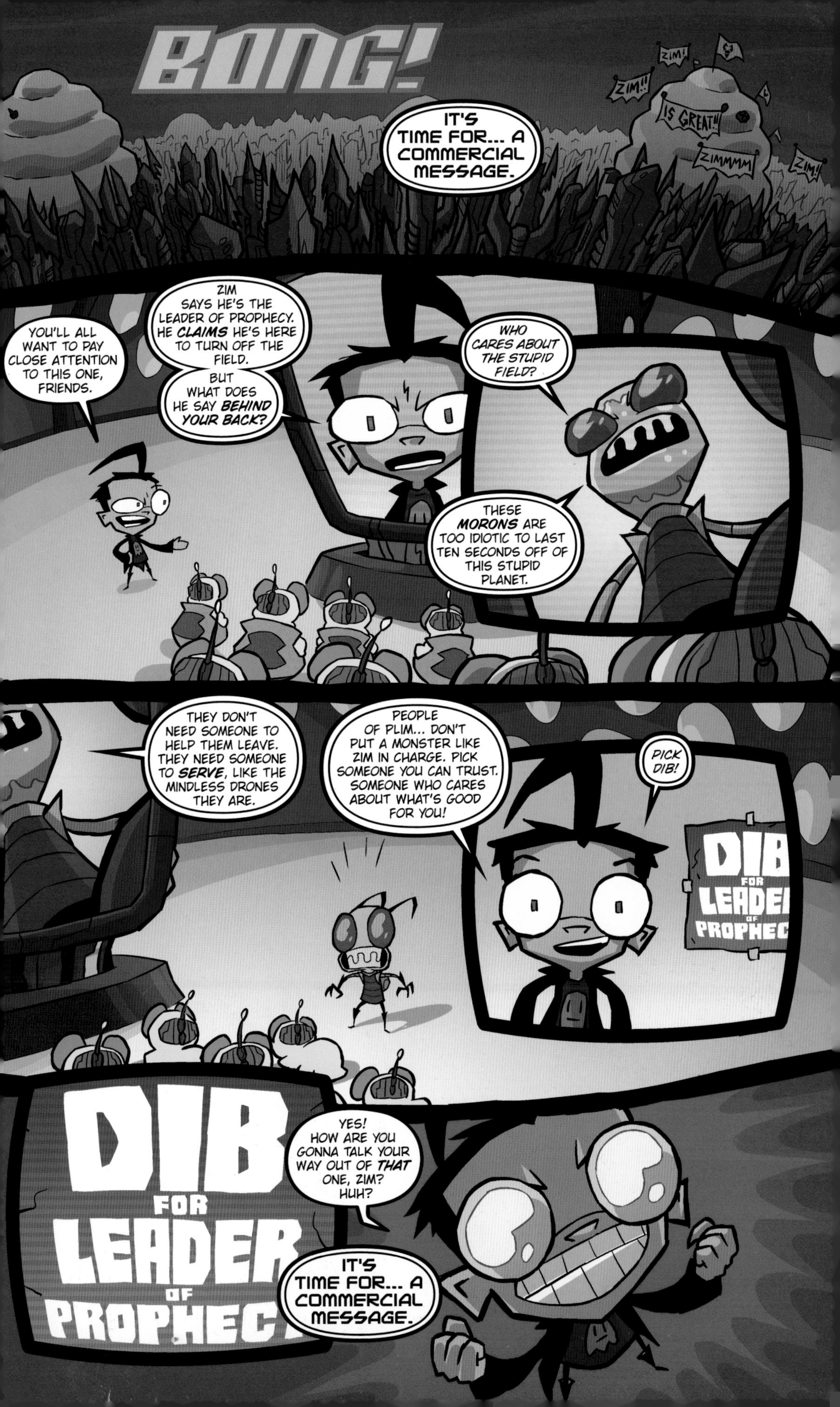

BONG!
ZIM!!
ZIM!
IS GREAT!!
ZIMMMM
ZIM!
IT'S TIME FOR... A COMMERCIAL MESSAGE.
YOU'LL ALL WANT TO PAY CLOSE ATTENTION TO THIS ONE, FRIENDS.
ZIM SAYS HE'S THE LEADER OF PROPHECY. HE CLAIMS HE'S HERE TO TURN OFF THE FIELD.
BUT WHAT DOES HE SAY BEHIND YOUR BACK?
WHO CARES ABOUT THE STUPID FIELD?
THESE MORONS ARE TOO IDIOTIC TO LAST TEN SECONDS OFF OF THIS STUPID PLANET.
THEY DON'T NEED SOMEONE TO HELP THEM LEAVE. THEY NEED SOMEONE TO SERVE, LIKE THE MINDLESS DRONES THEY ARE.
PEOPLE OF PLIM... DON'T PUT A MONSTER LIKE ZIM IN CHARGE. PICK SOMEONE YOU CAN TRUST. SOMEONE WHO CARES ABOUT WHAT'S GOOD FOR YOU!
PICK DIB!
DIB FOR LEADER OF PROPHEC
DIB FOR LEADER OF PROPHEC
YES! HOW ARE YOU GONNA TALK YOUR WAY OUT OF THAT ONE, ZIM? HUH?
IT'S TIME FOR... A COMMERCIAL MESSAGE.

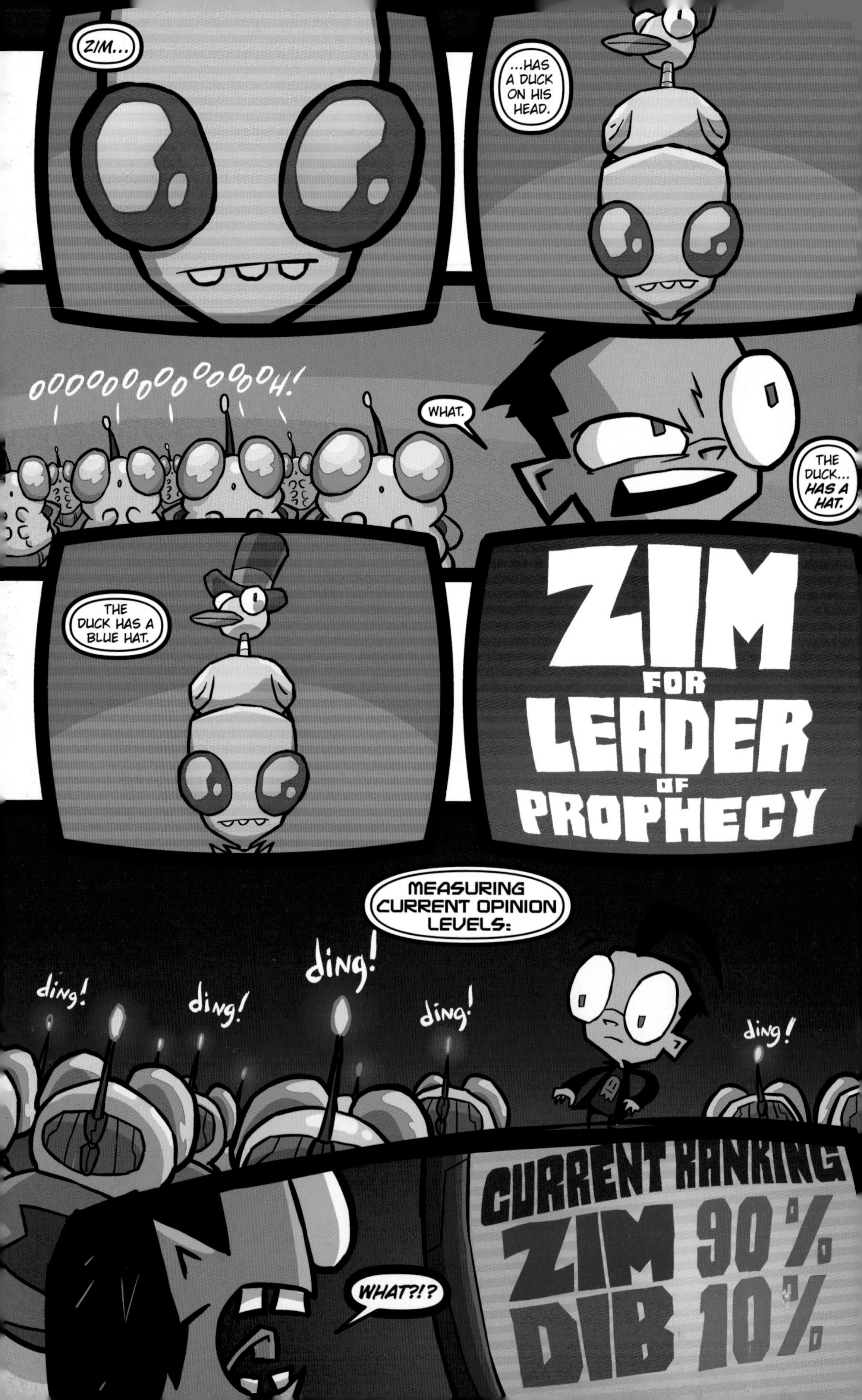
ZIM...
...HAS A DUCK ON HIS HEAD.
OOOOOOOOOOOOOOOH!
WHAT.
THE DUCK... HAS A HAT.
THE DUCK HAS A BLUE HAT.
ZIM FOR LEADER OF PROPHECY
MEASURING CURRENT OPINION LEVELS:
ding!
ding!
ding!
ding!
ding!
CURRENT RANKING
ZIM 90%
DIB 10%
WHAT?!?

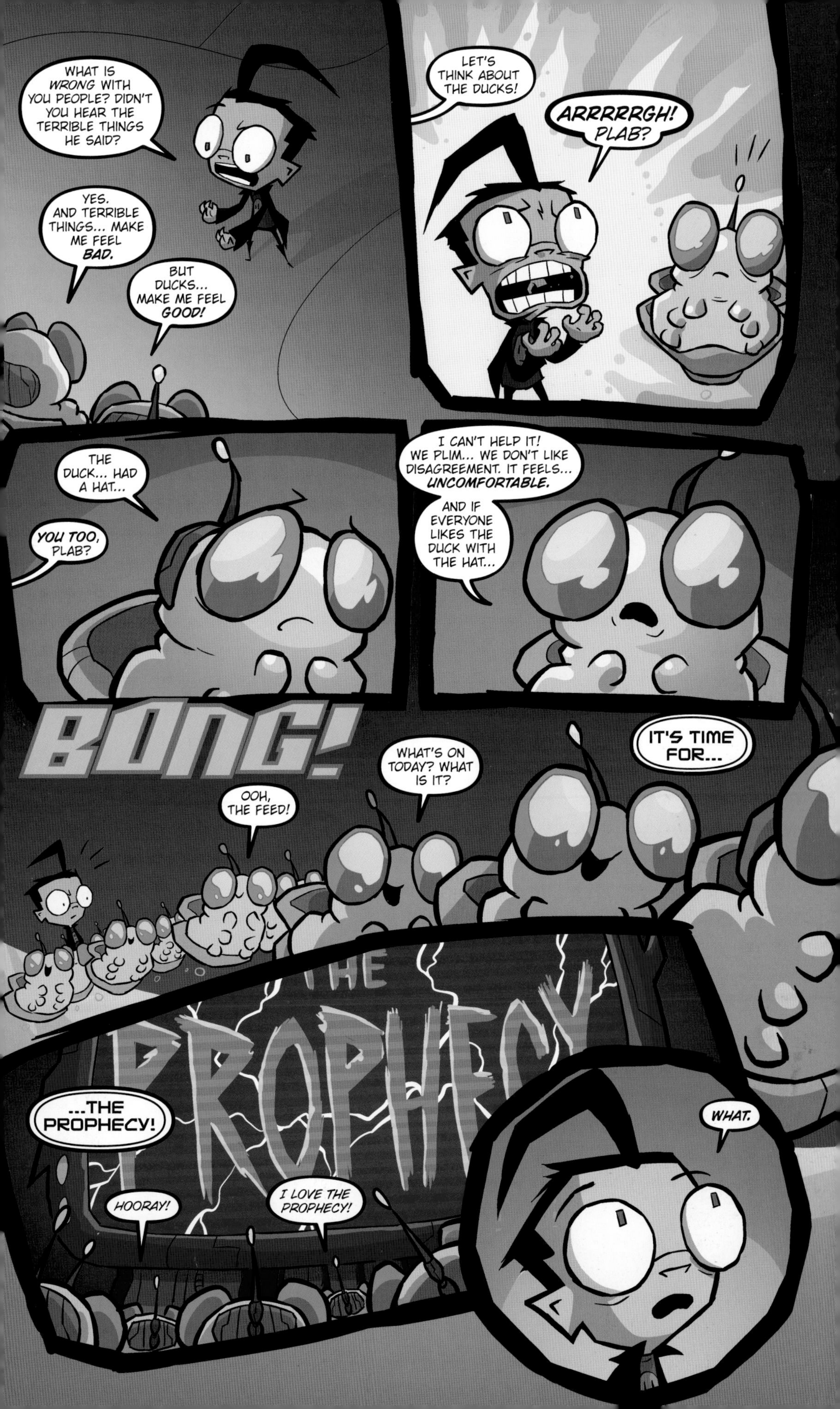
WHAT IS *WRONG* WITH YOU PEOPLE? DIDN'T YOU HEAR THE TERRIBLE THINGS HE SAID?
YES. AND TERRIBLE THINGS... MAKE ME FEEL ***BAD.***
BUT DUCKS... MAKE ME FEEL ***GOOD!***
LET'S THINK ABOUT THE DUCKS!
ARRRRRGH! *PLAB?*
THE DUCK... HAD A HAT...
YOU TOO, PLAB?
I CAN'T HELP IT! WE PLIM... WE DON'T LIKE DISAGREEMENT. IT FEELS... ***UNCOMFORTABLE.***
AND IF EVERYONE LIKES THE DUCK WITH THE HAT...
BONG!
OOH, THE FEED!
WHAT'S ON TODAY? WHAT IS IT?
IT'S TIME FOR...
THE PROPHECY
...THE PROPHECY!
HOORAY!
I LOVE THE PROPHECY!
WHAT.

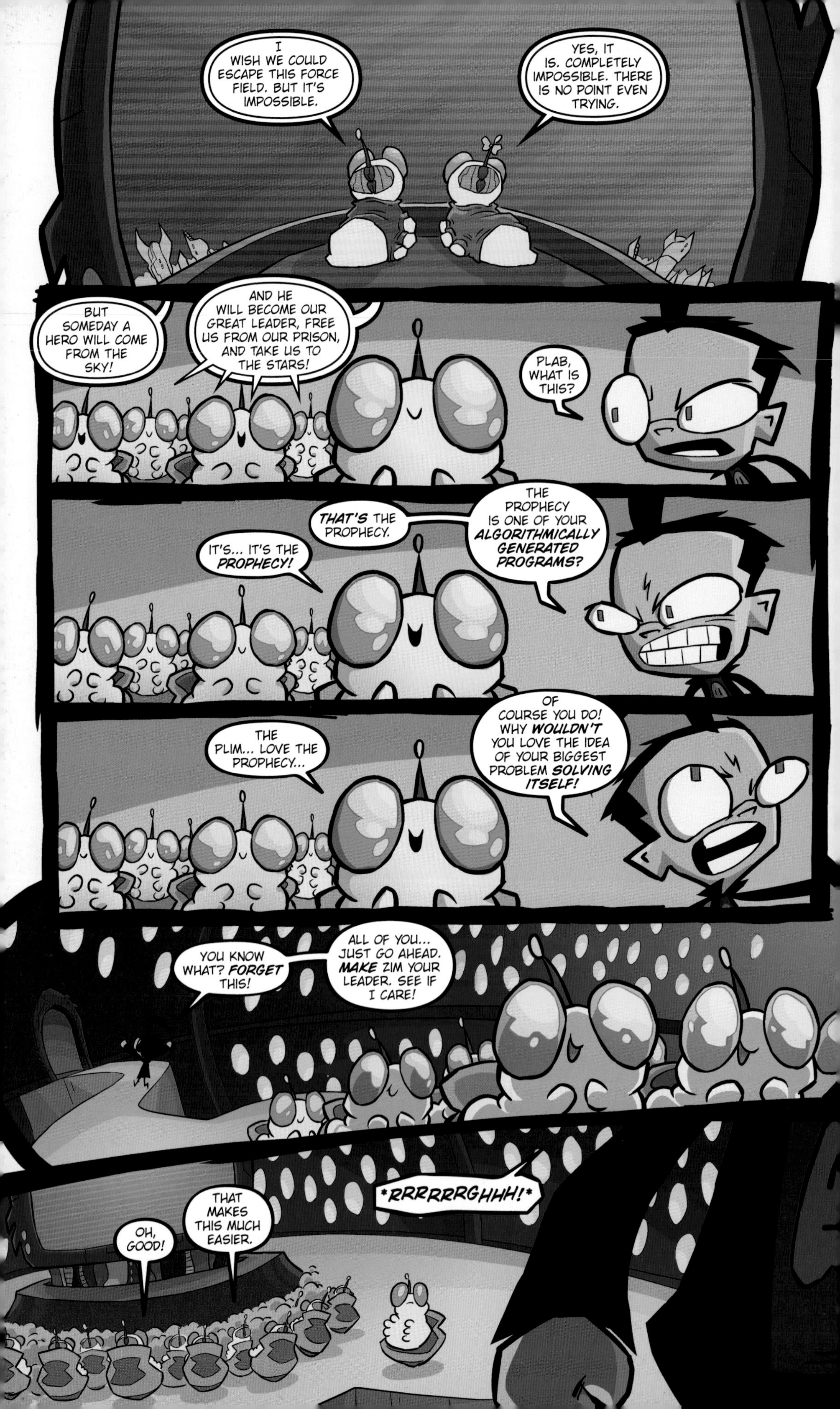
I WISH WE COULD ESCAPE THIS FORCE FIELD. BUT IT'S IMPOSSIBLE.
YES, IT IS. COMPLETELY IMPOSSIBLE. THERE IS NO POINT EVEN TRYING.
BUT SOMEDAY A HERO WILL COME FROM THE SKY!
AND HE WILL BECOME OUR GREAT LEADER, FREE US FROM OUR PRISON, AND TAKE US TO THE STARS!
PLAB, WHAT IS THIS?
IT'S... IT'S THE PROPHECY!
THAT'S THE PROPHECY.
THE PROPHECY IS ONE OF YOUR ALGORITHMICALLY GENERATED PROGRAMS?
THE PLIM... LOVE THE PROPHECY...
OF COURSE YOU DO! WHY WOULDN'T YOU LOVE THE IDEA OF YOUR BIGGEST PROBLEM SOLVING ITSELF!
YOU KNOW WHAT? FORGET THIS!
ALL OF YOU... JUST GO AHEAD. MAKE ZIM YOUR LEADER. SEE IF I CARE!
RRRRRRGHHH!
OH, GOOD!
THAT MAKES THIS MUCH EASIER.

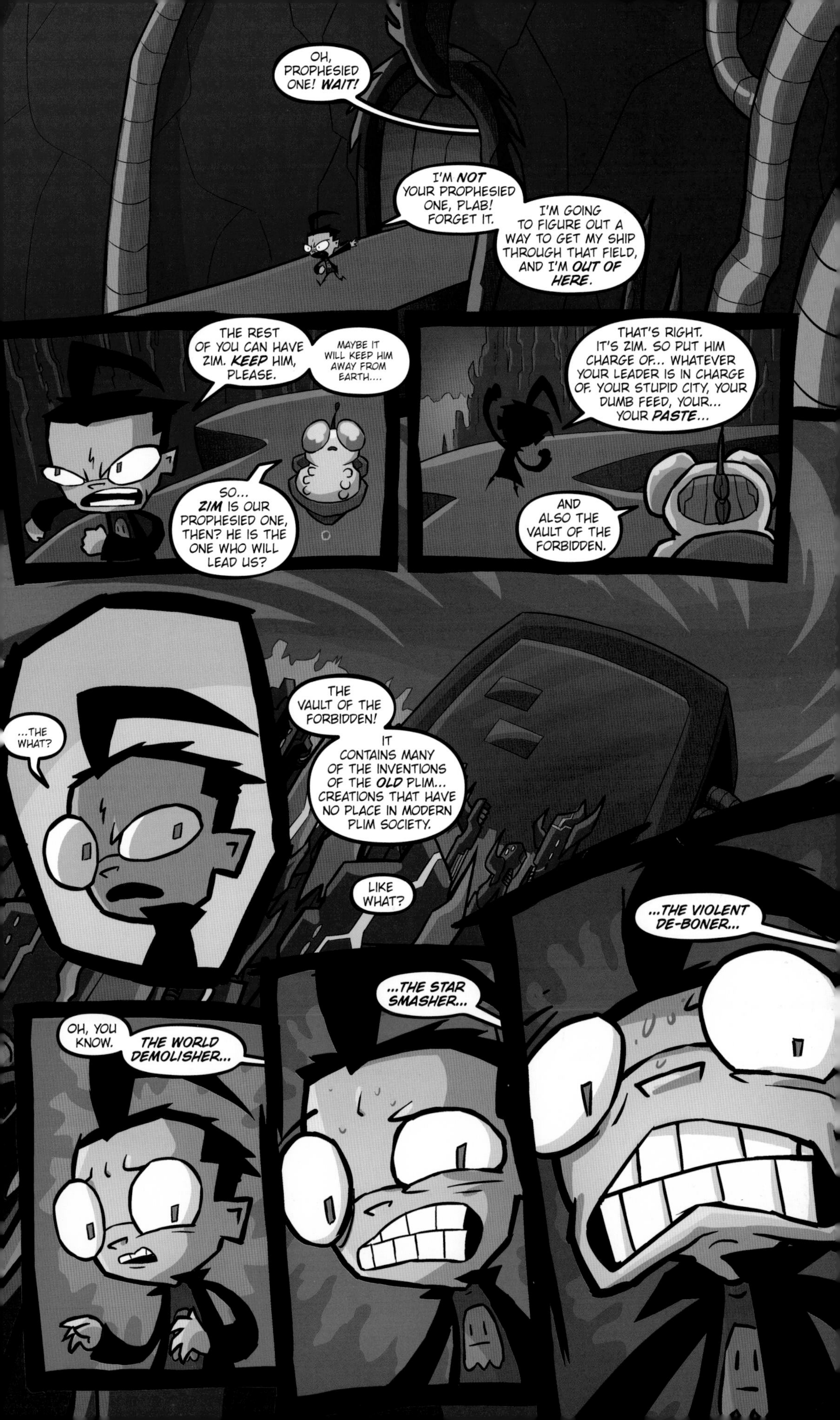

OH, PROPHESIED ONE! WAIT!
I'M NOT YOUR PROPHESIED ONE, PLAB! FORGET IT.
I'M GOING TO FIGURE OUT A WAY TO GET MY SHIP THROUGH THAT FIELD, AND I'M OUT OF HERE.
THE REST OF YOU CAN HAVE ZIM. KEEP HIM, PLEASE.
MAYBE IT WILL KEEP HIM AWAY FROM EARTH....
SO... ZIM IS OUR PROPHESIED ONE, THEN? HE IS THE ONE WHO WILL LEAD US?
THAT'S RIGHT. IT'S ZIM. SO PUT HIM CHARGE OF... WHATEVER YOUR LEADER IS IN CHARGE OF. YOUR STUPID CITY, YOUR DUMB FEED, YOUR... YOUR PASTE...
AND ALSO THE VAULT OF THE FORBIDDEN.
...THE WHAT?
THE VAULT OF THE FORBIDDEN!
IT CONTAINS MANY OF THE INVENTIONS OF THE OLD PLIM... CREATIONS THAT HAVE NO PLACE IN MODERN PLIM SOCIETY.
LIKE WHAT?
OH, YOU KNOW.
THE WORLD DEMOLISHER...
...THE STAR SMASHER...
...THE VIOLENT DE-BONER...

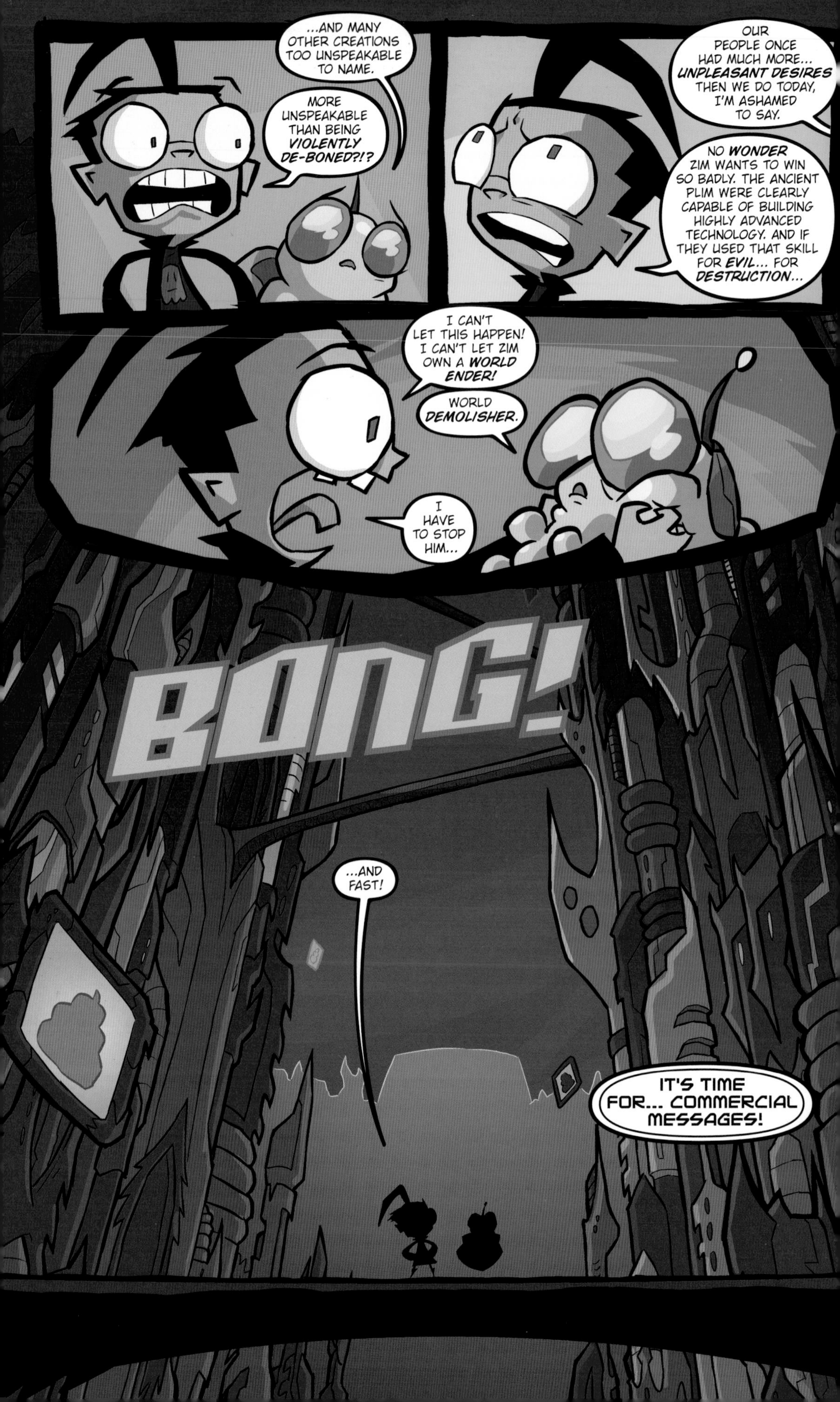
...AND MANY OTHER CREATIONS TOO UNSPEAKABLE TO NAME.
MORE UNSPEAKABLE THAN BEING VIOLENTLY DE-BONED?!?
OUR PEOPLE ONCE HAD MUCH MORE... UNPLEASANT DESIRES THEN WE DO TODAY, I'M ASHAMED TO SAY.
NO WONDER ZIM WANTS TO WIN SO BADLY. THE ANCIENT PLIM WERE CLEARLY CAPABLE OF BUILDING HIGHLY ADVANCED TECHNOLOGY. AND IF THEY USED THAT SKILL FOR EVIL... FOR DESTRUCTION...
I CAN'T LET THIS HAPPEN! I CAN'T LET ZIM OWN A WORLD ENDER!
WORLD DEMOLISHER.
I HAVE TO STOP HIM...
BONG!
...AND FAST!
IT'S TIME FOR... COMMERCIAL MESSAGES!

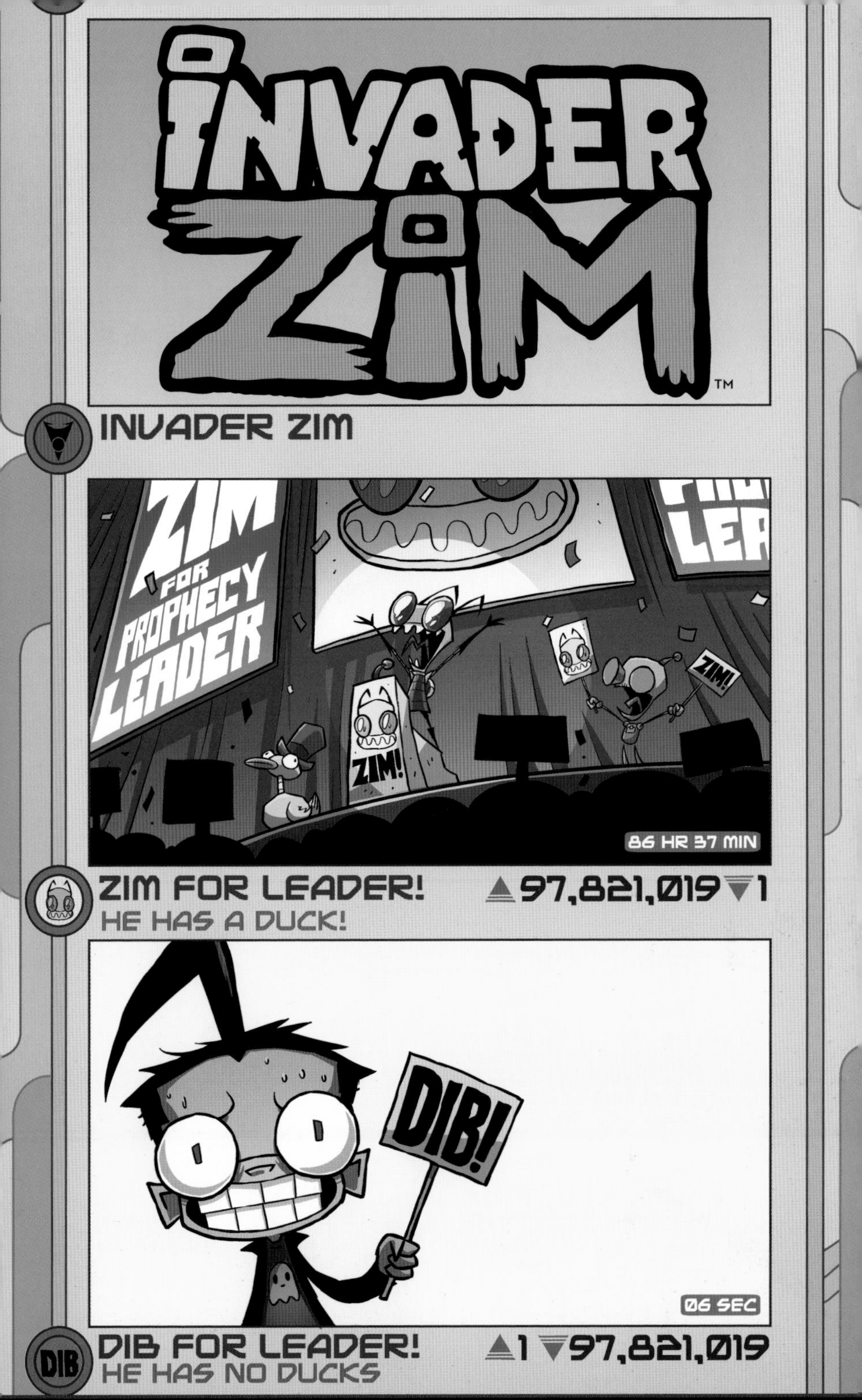
INVADER ZIM
TM
INVADER ZIM
ZIM FOR PROPHECY LEADER
ZIM!
ZIM!
86 HR 37 MIN
ZIM FOR LEADER!
HE HAS A DUCK!
97,821,019
1
DIB!
06 SEC
DIB
DIB FOR LEADER!
HE HAS NO DUCKS
1
97,821,019

CHAPTER: 2

illustration by WARREN WUCINICH with FRED C. STRESING

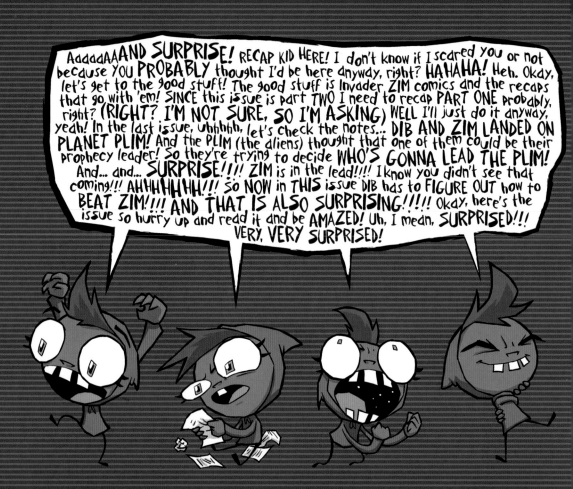

AaaaaAAAND SURPRISE! RECAP KID HERE! I don't know if I scared you or not because YOU PROBABLY thought I'd be here anyway, right? HAHAHA! Heh. Okay, let's get to the good stuff! The good stuff is Invader ZIM comics and the recaps that go with 'em! SINCE this issue is part TWO I need to recap PART ONE probably, right? (RIGHT? I'M NOT SURE, SO I'M ASKING) WELL I'll just do it anyway, yeah! In the last issue, uhhhhh, let's check the notes... DIB AND ZIM LANDED ON PLANET PLIM! And the PLIM (the aliens) thought that one of them could be their prophecy leader! So they're trying to decide WHO'S GONNA LEAD THE PLIM! And... and... SURPRISE!!!! ZIM is in the lead!!!! I know you didn't see that coming!!! AHHHHHHH!!! So NOW in THIS issue DIB has to FIGURE OUT how to BEAT ZIM!!!! AND THAT IS ALSO SURPRISING!!!!! Okay, here's the issue so hurry up and read it and be AMAZED! Uh, I mean, SURPRISED!!! VERY, VERY SURPRISED!

Recap Kid illustrated, colored, and lettered by

WARREN WUCINICH

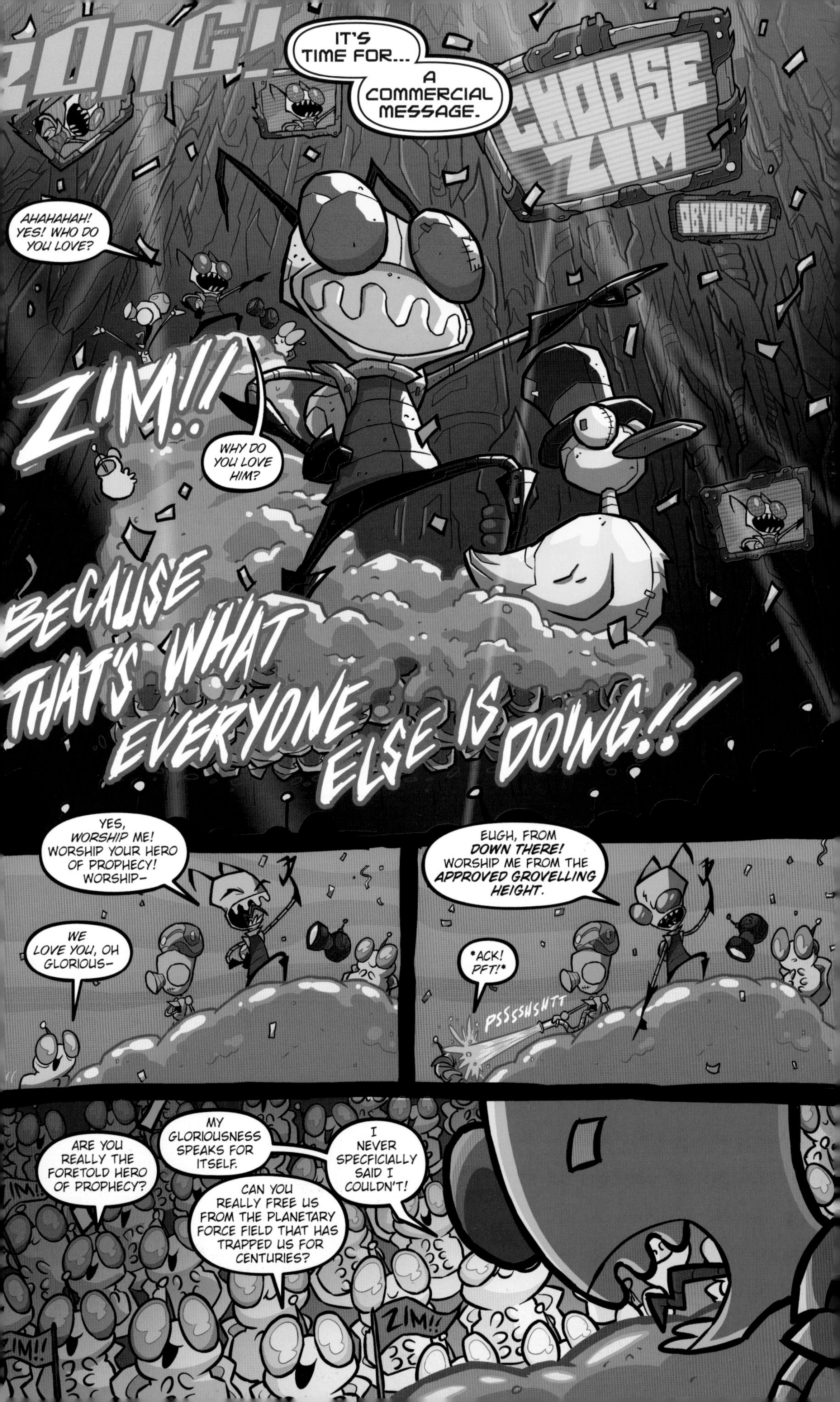
ZONG!
IT'S TIME FOR...
A COMMERCIAL MESSAGE.
CHOOSE ZIM
OBVIOUSLY
AHAHAHAH! YES! WHO DO YOU LOVE?
ZIM!!
WHY DO YOU LOVE HIM?
BECAUSE THAT'S WHAT EVERYONE ELSE IS DOING!!!
YES, WORSHIP ME! WORSHIP YOUR HERO OF PROPHECY! WORSHIP-
WE LOVE YOU, OH GLORIOUS-
EUGH, FROM DOWN THERE! WORSHIP ME FROM THE APPROVED GROVELLING HEIGHT.
ACK! PFT!
PSSSSHSHTT
ARE YOU REALLY THE FORETOLD HERO OF PROPHECY?
MY GLORIOUSNESS SPEAKS FOR ITSELF.
CAN YOU REALLY FREE US FROM THE PLANETARY FORCE FIELD THAT HAS TRAPPED US FOR CENTURIES?
I NEVER SPECFICIALLY SAID I COULDN'T!
ZIM!!
ZIM!!
ZIM!!

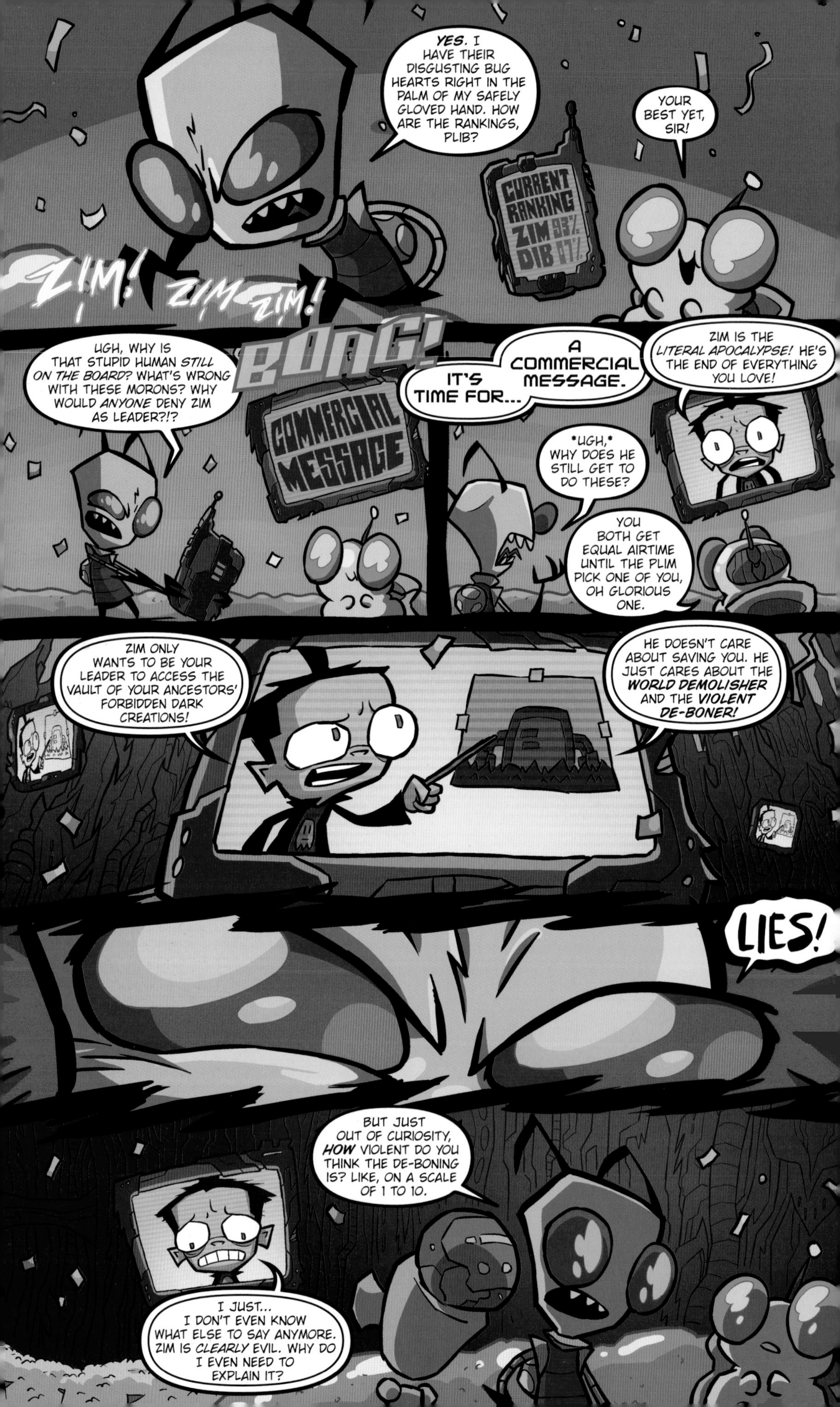

YES. I HAVE THEIR DISGUSTING BUG HEARTS RIGHT IN THE PALM OF MY SAFELY GLOVED HAND. HOW ARE THE RANKINGS, PLIB?
YOUR BEST YET, SIR!
CURRENT RANKING ZIM 93% DIB 07%
ZIM! ZIM! ZIM!
BONG!
UGH, WHY IS THAT STUPID HUMAN STILL ON THE BOARD? WHAT'S WRONG WITH THESE MORONS? WHY WOULD ANYONE DENY ZIM AS LEADER?!?
COMMERCIAL MESSAGE
IT'S TIME FOR...
A COMMERCIAL MESSAGE.
ZIM IS THE LITERAL APOCALYPSE! HE'S THE END OF EVERYTHING YOU LOVE!
UGH, WHY DOES HE STILL GET TO DO THESE?
YOU BOTH GET EQUAL AIRTIME UNTIL THE PLIM PICK ONE OF YOU, OH GLORIOUS ONE.
ZIM ONLY WANTS TO BE YOUR LEADER TO ACCESS THE VAULT OF YOUR ANCESTORS' FORBIDDEN DARK CREATIONS!
HE DOESN'T CARE ABOUT SAVING YOU. HE JUST CARES ABOUT THE WORLD DEMOLISHER AND THE VIOLENT DE-BONER!
LIES!
BUT JUST OUT OF CURIOSITY, HOW VIOLENT DO YOU THINK THE DE-BONING IS? LIKE, ON A SCALE OF 1 TO 10.
I JUST... I DON'T EVEN KNOW WHAT ELSE TO SAY ANYMORE. ZIM IS CLEARLY EVIL. WHY DO I EVEN NEED TO EXPLAIN IT?

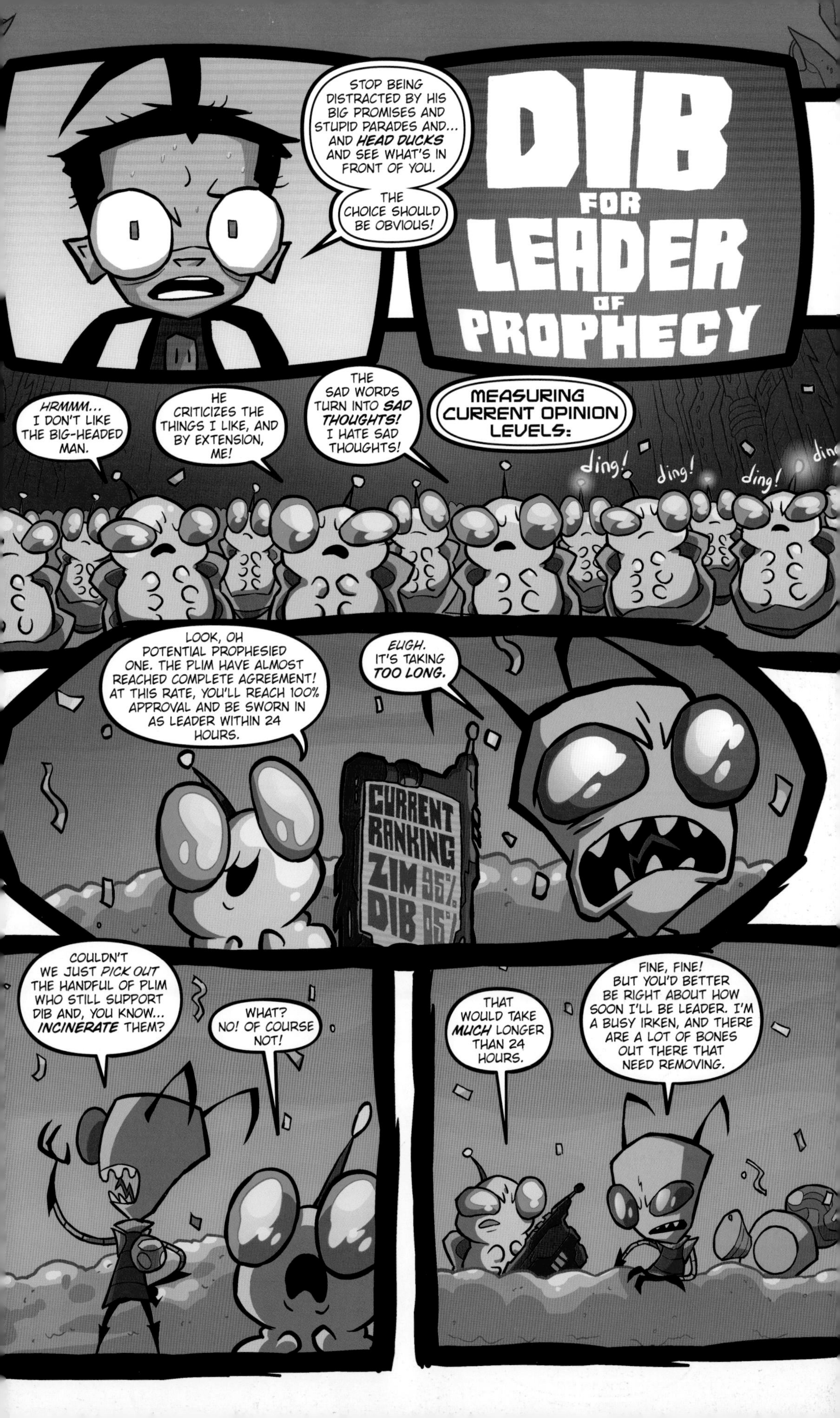
STOP BEING DISTRACTED BY HIS BIG PROMISES AND STUPID PARADES AND... AND *HEAD DUCKS* AND SEE WHAT'S IN FRONT OF YOU.
THE CHOICE SHOULD BE OBVIOUS!
DIB FOR LEADER OF PROPHECY
HRMMM... I DON'T LIKE THE BIG-HEADED MAN.
HE CRITICIZES THE THINGS I LIKE, AND BY EXTENSION, ME!
THE SAD WORDS TURN INTO *SAD THOUGHTS!* I HATE SAD THOUGHTS!
MEASURING CURRENT OPINION LEVELS:
ding! ding! ding!
LOOK, OH POTENTIAL PROPHESIED ONE. THE PLIM HAVE ALMOST REACHED COMPLETE AGREEMENT! AT THIS RATE, YOU'LL REACH 100% APPROVAL AND BE SWORN IN AS LEADER WITHIN 24 HOURS.
EUGH. IT'S TAKING **TOO LONG.**
CURRENT RANKING
ZIM 95%
DIB
COULDN'T WE JUST *PICK OUT* THE HANDFUL OF PLIM WHO STILL SUPPORT DIB AND, YOU KNOW... *INCINERATE* THEM?
WHAT? NO! OF COURSE NOT!
THAT WOULD TAKE *MUCH* LONGER THAN 24 HOURS.
FINE, FINE! BUT YOU'D BETTER BE RIGHT ABOUT HOW SOON I'LL BE LEADER. I'M A BUSY IRKEN, AND THERE ARE A LOT OF BONES OUT THERE THAT NEED REMOVING.

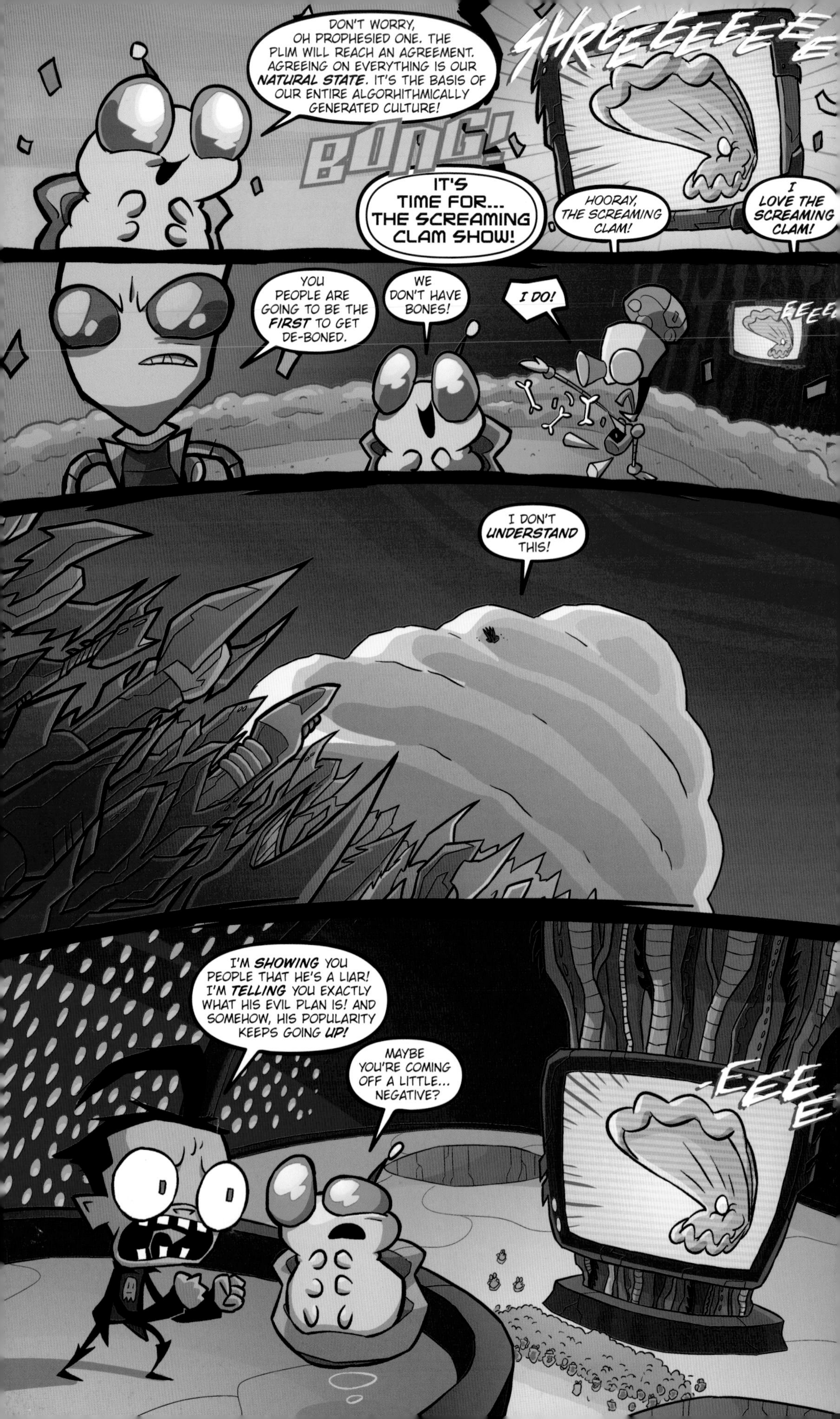
DON'T WORRY, OH PROPHESIED ONE. THE PLIM WILL REACH AN AGREEMENT. AGREEING ON EVERYTHING IS OUR NATURAL STATE. IT'S THE BASIS OF OUR ENTIRE ALGORHITHMICALLY GENERATED CULTURE!
SHREEEEEEEEE
BONG!
IT'S TIME FOR... THE SCREAMING CLAM SHOW!
HOORAY, THE SCREAMING CLAM!
I LOVE THE SCREAMING CLAM!
YOU PEOPLE ARE GOING TO BE THE FIRST TO GET DE-BONED.
WE DON'T HAVE BONES!
I DO!
-EEEE
I DON'T UNDERSTAND THIS!
I'M SHOWING YOU PEOPLE THAT HE'S A LIAR! I'M TELLING YOU EXACTLY WHAT HIS EVIL PLAN IS! AND SOMEHOW, HIS POPULARITY KEEPS GOING UP!
MAYBE YOU'RE COMING OFF A LITTLE... NEGATIVE?
-EEEE

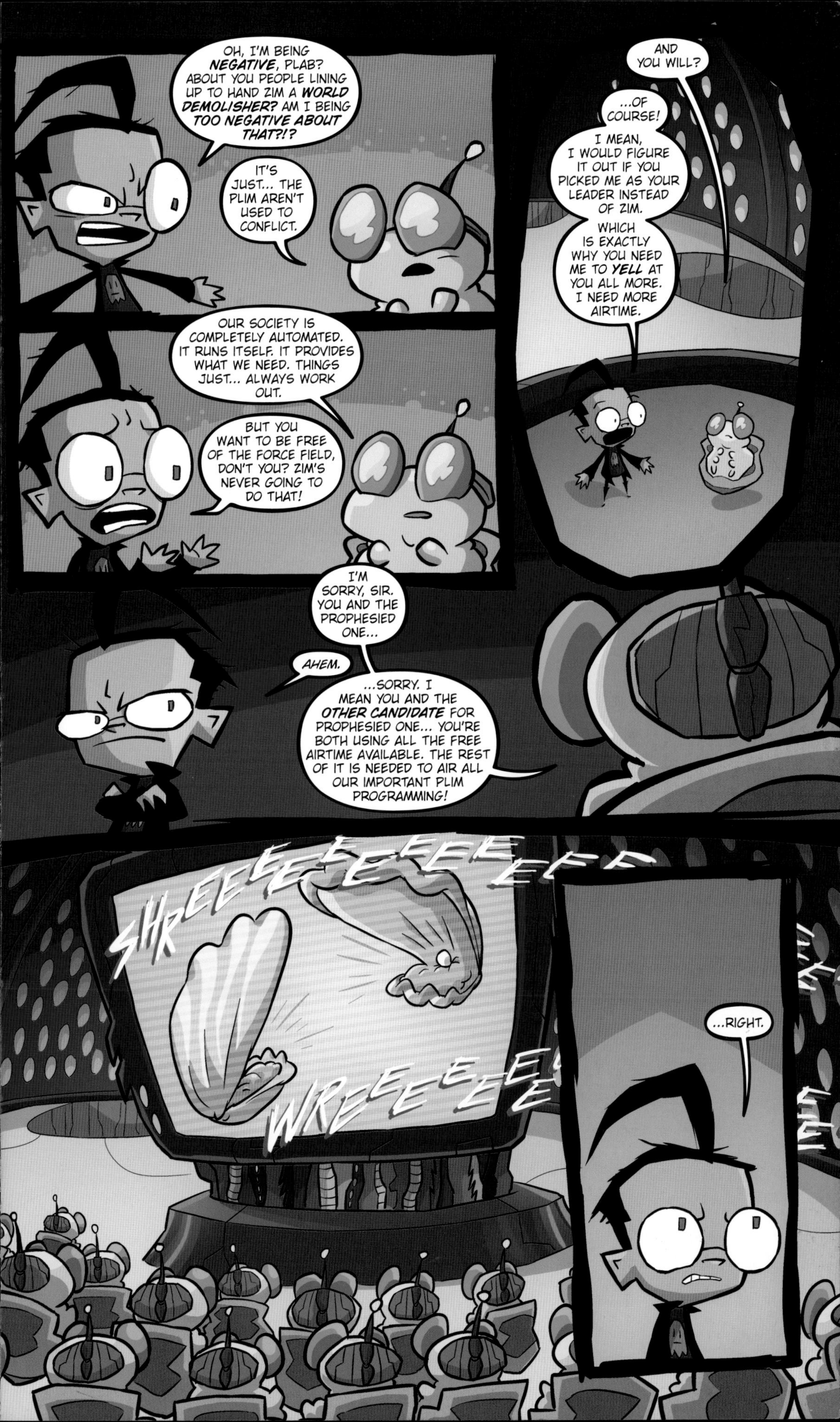
OH, I'M BEING NEGATIVE, PLAB? ABOUT YOU PEOPLE LINING UP TO HAND ZIM A WORLD DEMOLISHER? AM I BEING TOO NEGATIVE ABOUT THAT?!?
IT'S JUST... THE PLIM AREN'T USED TO CONFLICT.
OUR SOCIETY IS COMPLETELY AUTOMATED. IT RUNS ITSELF. IT PROVIDES WHAT WE NEED. THINGS JUST... ALWAYS WORK OUT.
BUT YOU WANT TO BE FREE OF THE FORCE FIELD, DON'T YOU? ZIM'S NEVER GOING TO DO THAT!
AND YOU WILL?
...OF COURSE!
I MEAN, I WOULD FIGURE IT OUT IF YOU PICKED ME AS YOUR LEADER INSTEAD OF ZIM.
WHICH IS EXACTLY WHY YOU NEED ME TO YELL AT YOU ALL MORE. I NEED MORE AIRTIME.
I'M SORRY, SIR. YOU AND THE PROPHESIED ONE...
AHEM.
...SORRY. I MEAN YOU AND THE OTHER CANDIDATE FOR PROPHESIED ONE... YOU'RE BOTH USING ALL THE FREE AIRTIME AVAILABLE. THE REST OF IT IS NEEDED TO AIR ALL OUR IMPORTANT PLIM PROGRAMMING!
SHREEEEEEEEEEEEE
WREEEEEEEE
...RIGHT.

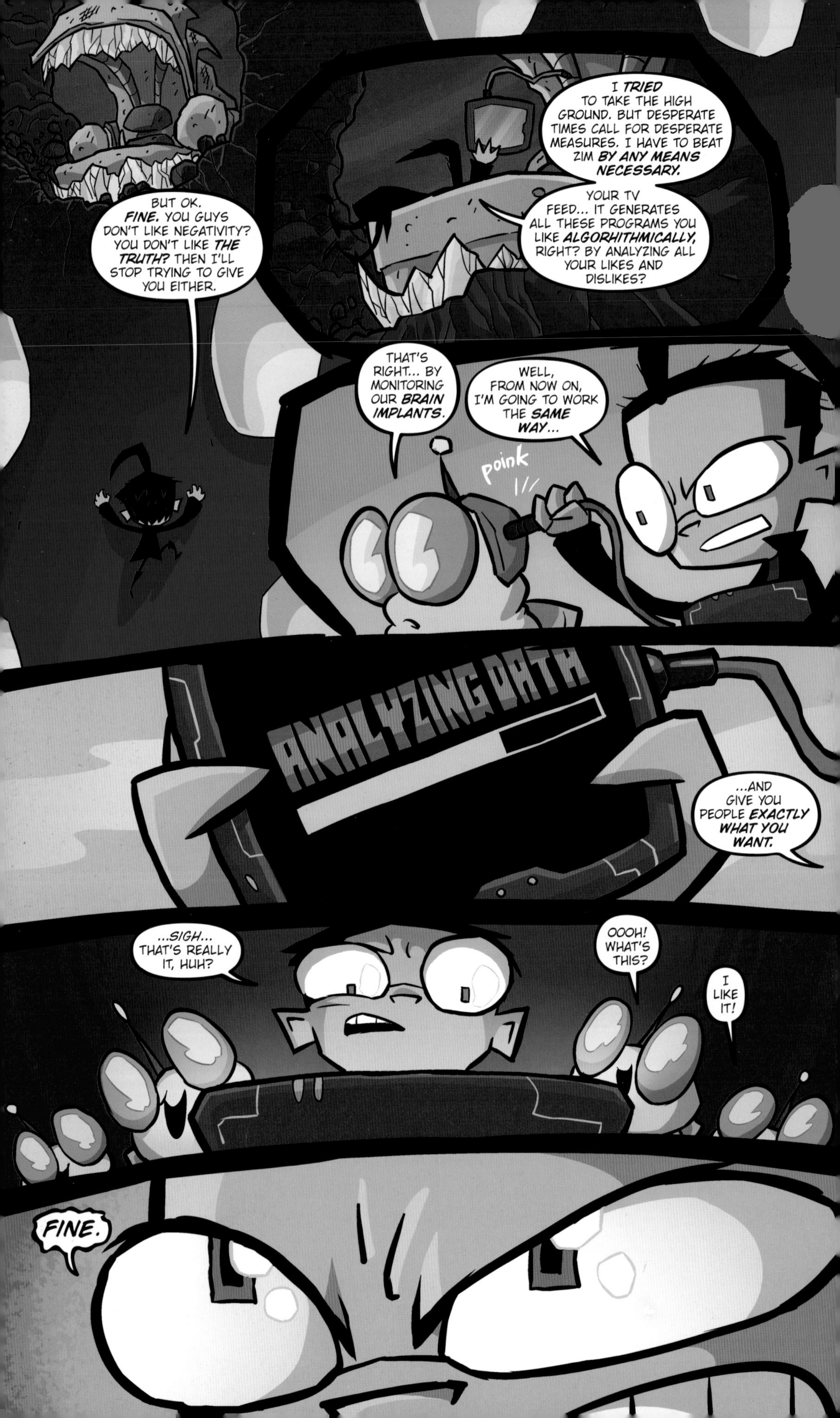

I TRIED TO TAKE THE HIGH GROUND. BUT DESPERATE TIMES CALL FOR DESPERATE MEASURES. I HAVE TO BEAT ZIM BY ANY MEANS NECESSARY.
BUT OK. FINE. YOU GUYS DON'T LIKE NEGATIVITY? YOU DON'T LIKE THE TRUTH? THEN I'LL STOP TRYING TO GIVE YOU EITHER.
YOUR TV FEED... IT GENERATES ALL THESE PROGRAMS YOU LIKE ALGORHITHMICALLY, RIGHT? BY ANALYZING ALL YOUR LIKES AND DISLIKES?
THAT'S RIGHT... BY MONITORING OUR BRAIN IMPLANTS.
WELL, FROM NOW ON, I'M GOING TO WORK THE SAME WAY...
poink
ANALYZING DATA
...AND GIVE YOU PEOPLE EXACTLY WHAT YOU WANT.
...SIGH... THAT'S REALLY IT, HUH?
OOOH! WHAT'S THIS?
I LIKE IT!
FINE.

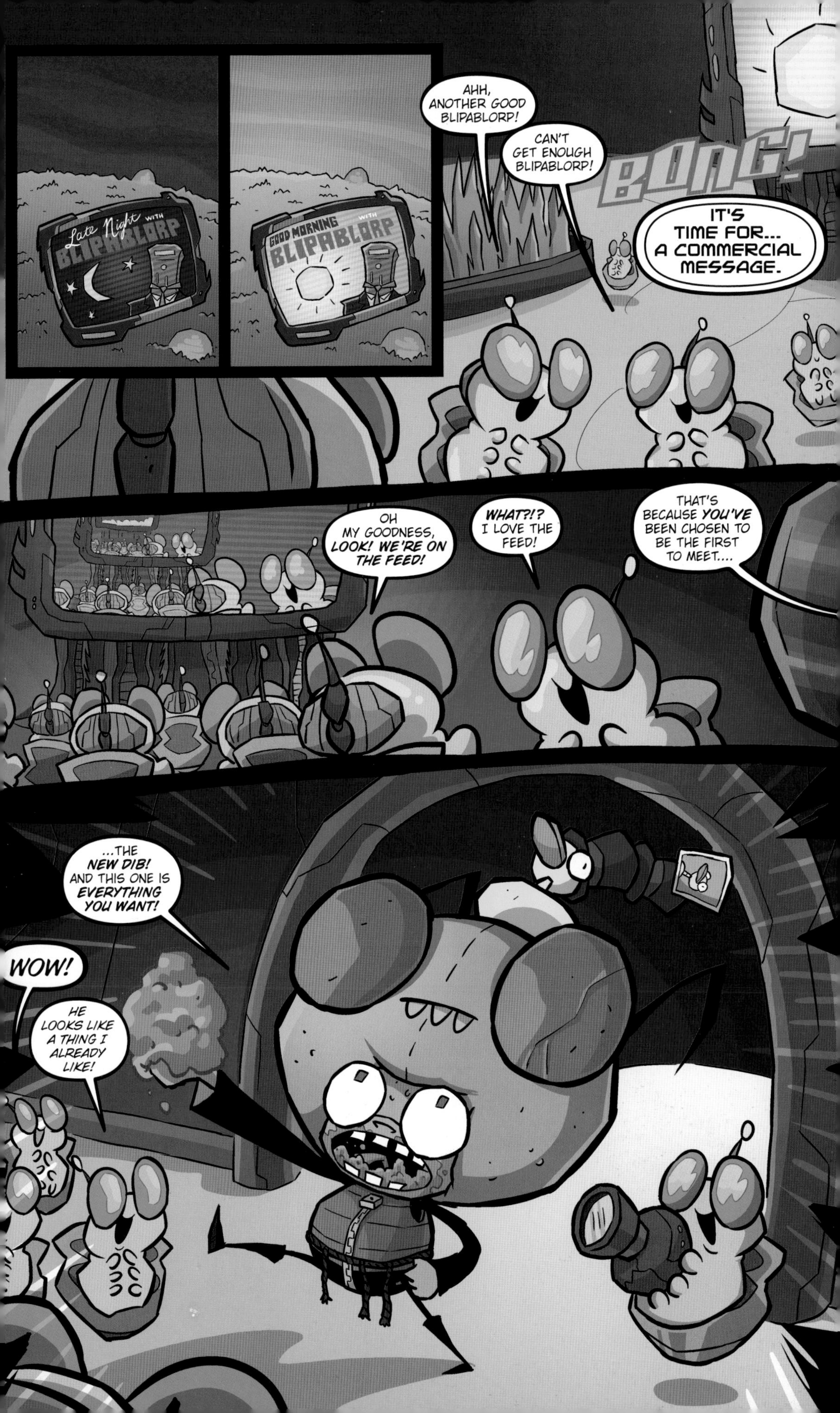
Late Night WITH BLIPABLORP
GOOD MORNING WITH BLIPABLORP
AHH, ANOTHER GOOD BLIPABLORP!
CAN'T GET ENOUGH BLIPABLORP!
BONG!
IT'S TIME FOR... A COMMERCIAL MESSAGE.
OH MY GOODNESS, LOOK! WE'RE ON THE FEED!
WHAT?!? I LOVE THE FEED!
THAT'S BECAUSE YOU'VE BEEN CHOSEN TO BE THE FIRST TO MEET....
...THE NEW DIB! AND THIS ONE IS EVERYTHING YOU WANT!
WOW!
HE LOOKS LIKE A THING I ALREADY LIKE!

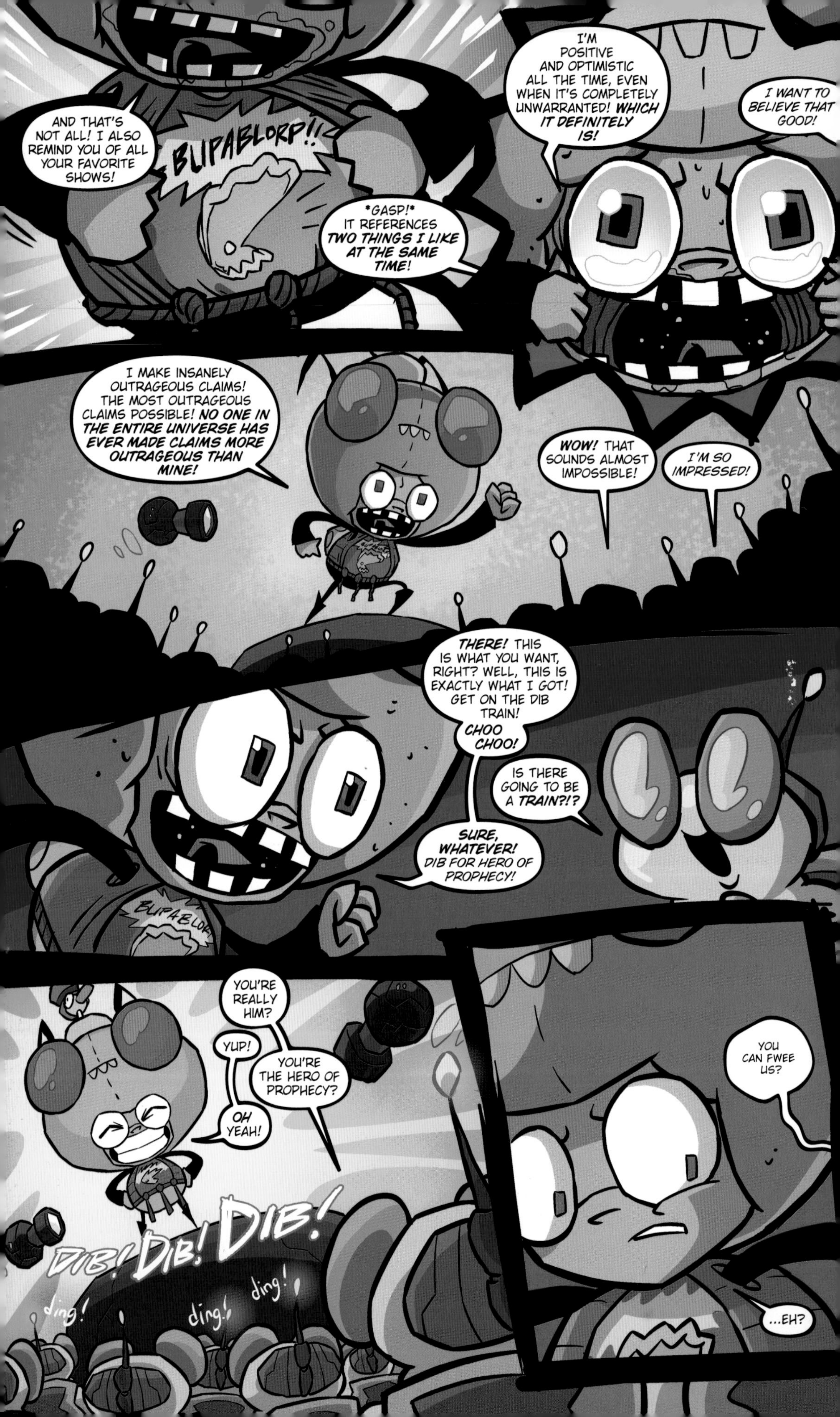
AND THAT'S NOT ALL! I ALSO REMIND YOU OF ALL YOUR FAVORITE SHOWS!
BLIPABLORP!!
GASP! IT REFERENCES TWO THINGS I LIKE AT THE SAME TIME!
I'M POSITIVE AND OPTIMISTIC ALL THE TIME, EVEN WHEN IT'S COMPLETELY UNWARRANTED! WHICH IT DEFINITELY IS!
I WANT TO BELIEVE THAT GOOD!
I MAKE INSANELY OUTRAGEOUS CLAIMS! THE MOST OUTRAGEOUS CLAIMS POSSIBLE! NO ONE IN THE ENTIRE UNIVERSE HAS EVER MADE CLAIMS MORE OUTRAGEOUS THAN MINE!
WOW! THAT SOUNDS ALMOST IMPOSSIBLE!
I'M SO IMPRESSED!
THERE! THIS IS WHAT YOU WANT, RIGHT? WELL, THIS IS EXACTLY WHAT I GOT! GET ON THE DIB TRAIN!
CHOO CHOO!
IS THERE GOING TO BE A TRAIN?!?
SURE, WHATEVER! DIB FOR HERO OF PROPHECY!
YOU'RE REALLY HIM?
YUP!
YOU'RE THE HERO OF PROPHECY?
OH YEAH!
DIB! DIB! DIB!
ding!
ding!
ding!
YOU CAN FWEE US?
...EH?

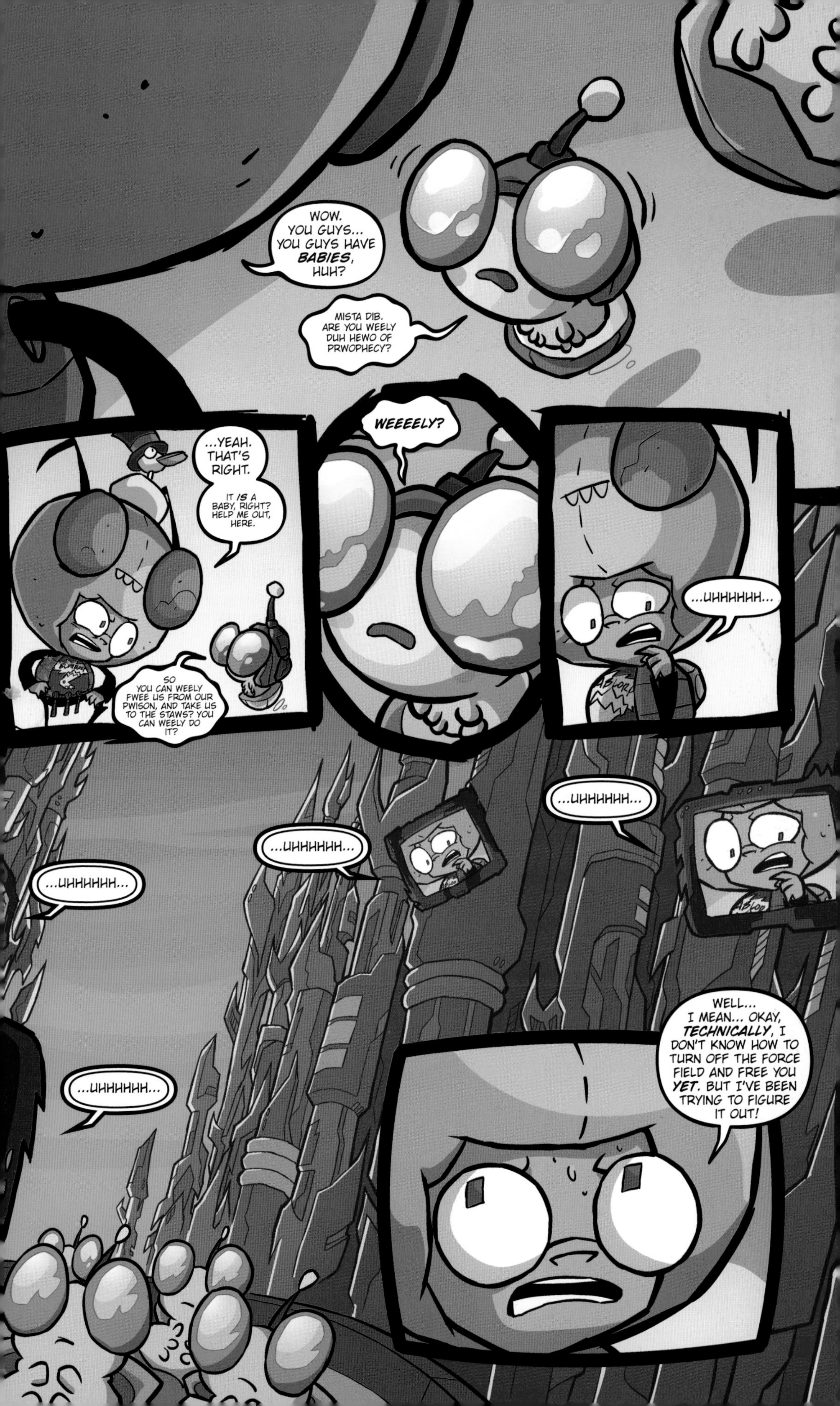
WOW. YOU GUYS... YOU GUYS HAVE BABIES, HUH?
MISTA DIB. ARE YOU WEELY DUH HEWO OF PRWOPHECY?
...YEAH. THAT'S RIGHT.
IT IS A BABY, RIGHT? HELP ME OUT, HERE.
SO YOU CAN WEELY FWEE US FROM OUR PWISON, AND TAKE US TO THE STAWS? YOU CAN WEELY DO IT?
WEEEELY?
...UHHHHHH...
...UHHHHHH...
...UHHHHHH...
...UHHHHHH...
...UHHHHHH...
WELL... I MEAN... OKAY, TECHNICALLY, I DON'T KNOW HOW TO TURN OFF THE FORCE FIELD AND FREE YOU YET. BUT I'VE BEEN TRYING TO FIGURE IT OUT!

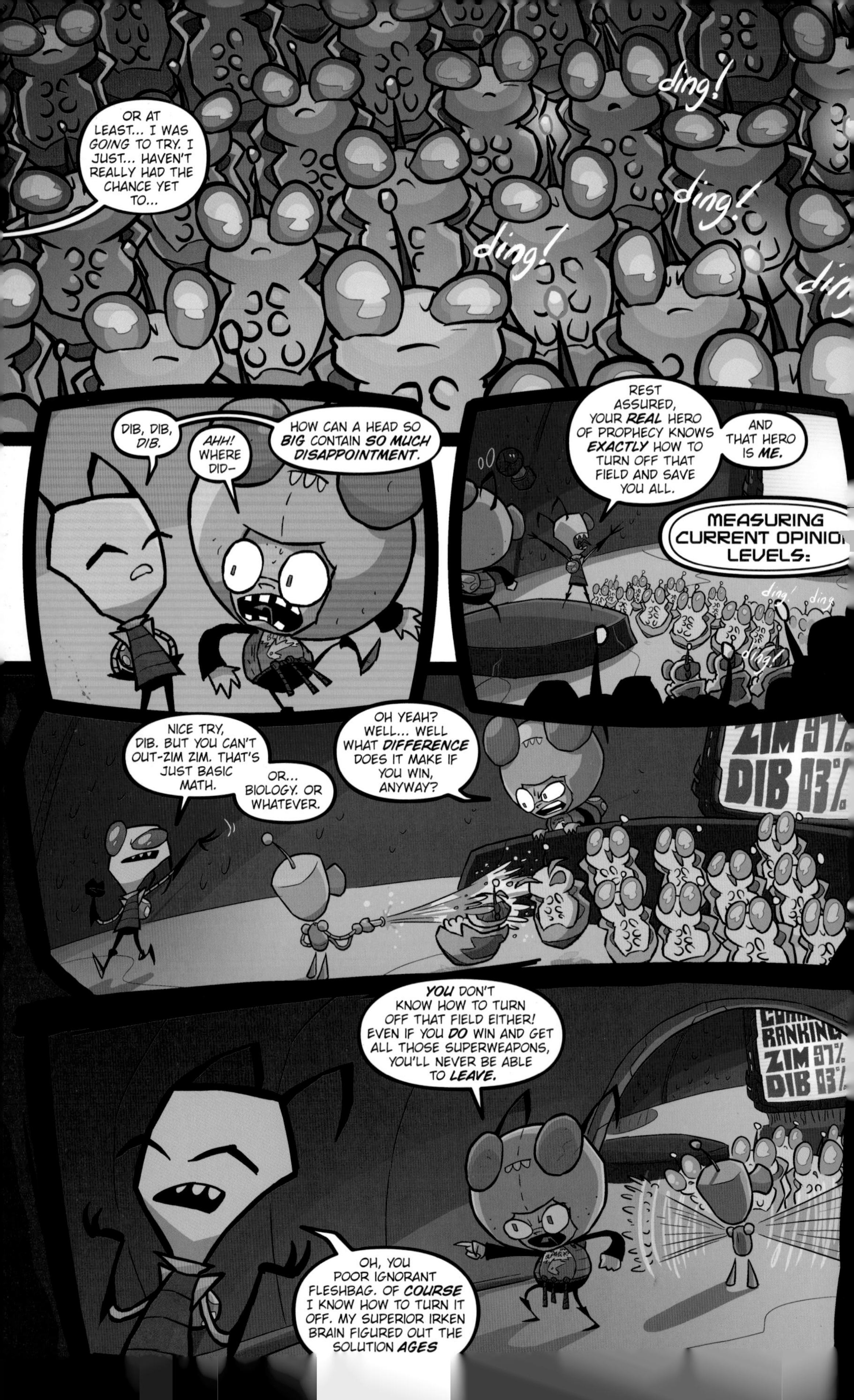
OR AT LEAST... I WAS GOING TO TRY. I JUST... HAVEN'T REALLY HAD THE CHANCE YET TO...
ding!
ding!
ding!
DIB, DIB, DIB.
AHH! WHERE DID-
HOW CAN A HEAD SO BIG CONTAIN SO MUCH DISAPPOINTMENT.
REST ASSURED, YOUR REAL HERO OF PROPHECY KNOWS EXACTLY HOW TO TURN OFF THAT FIELD AND SAVE YOU ALL.
AND THAT HERO IS ME.
MEASURING CURRENT OPINIO LEVELS:
NICE TRY, DIB. BUT YOU CAN'T OUT-ZIM ZIM. THAT'S JUST BASIC MATH.
OR... BIOLOGY. OR WHATEVER.
OH YEAH? WELL... WELL WHAT DIFFERENCE DOES IT MAKE IF YOU WIN, ANYWAY?
ZIM 97%
DIB 03%
YOU DON'T KNOW HOW TO TURN OFF THAT FIELD EITHER! EVEN IF YOU DO WIN AND GET ALL THOSE SUPERWEAPONS, YOU'LL NEVER BE ABLE TO LEAVE.
RANKING
ZIM 97%
DIB 03%
OH, YOU POOR IGNORANT FLESHBAG. OF COURSE I KNOW HOW TO TURN IT OFF. MY SUPERIOR IRKEN BRAIN FIGURED OUT THE SOLUTION AGES

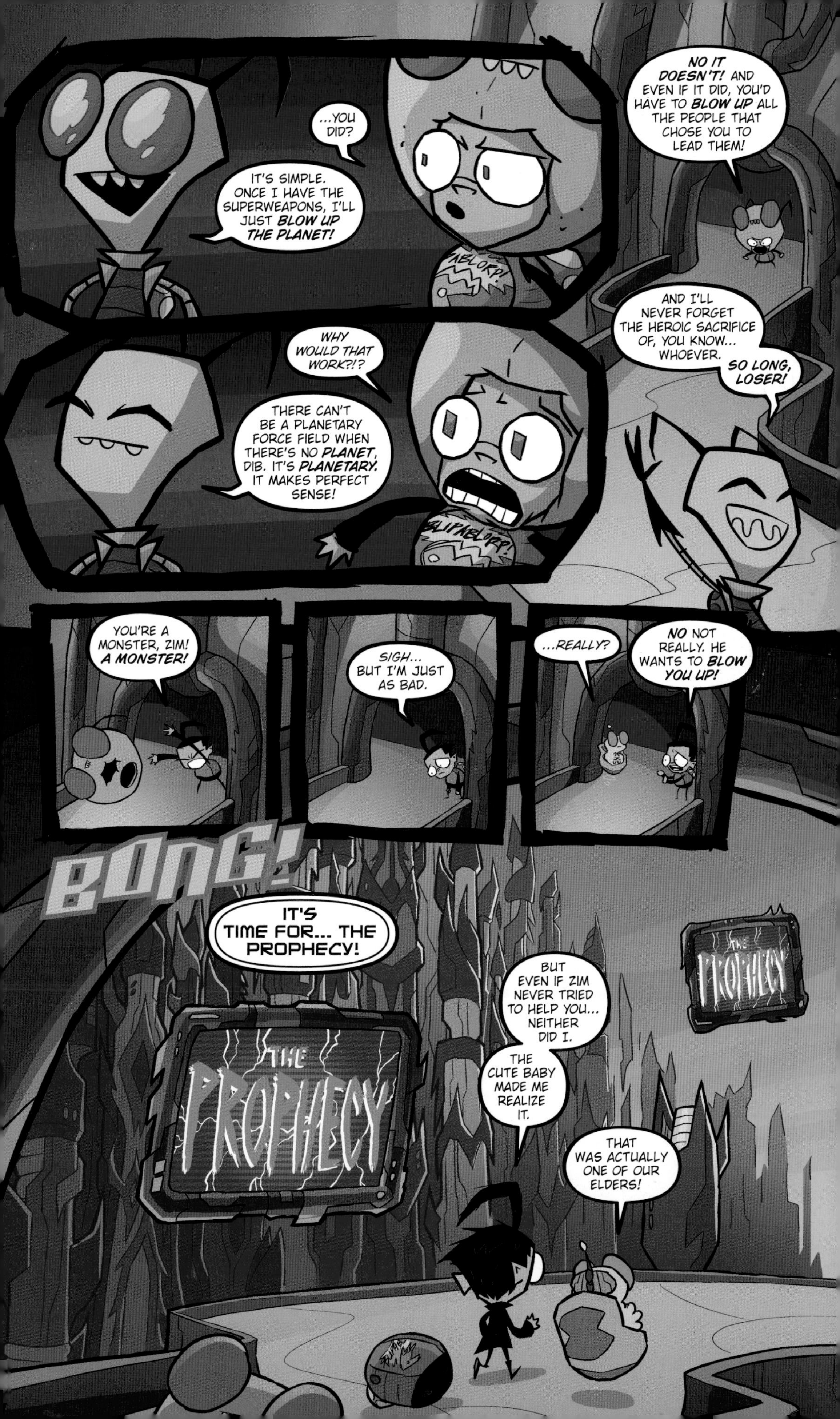
...YOU DID?
IT'S SIMPLE. ONCE I HAVE THE SUPERWEAPONS, I'LL JUST **BLOW UP THE PLANET!**
NO IT DOESN'T! AND EVEN IF IT DID, YOU'D HAVE TO **BLOW UP** ALL THE PEOPLE THAT CHOSE YOU TO LEAD THEM!
BLORP!
WHY WOULD THAT WORK?!?
THERE CAN'T BE A PLANETARY FORCE FIELD WHEN THERE'S NO **PLANET**, DIB. IT'S **PLANETARY.** IT MAKES PERFECT SENSE!
SLIPABLORP!
AND I'LL NEVER FORGET THE HEROIC SACRIFICE OF, YOU KNOW... WHOEVER.
SO LONG, LOSER!
YOU'RE A MONSTER, ZIM! **A MONSTER!**
SIGH... BUT I'M JUST AS BAD.
...REALLY?
NO NOT REALLY. HE WANTS TO **BLOW YOU UP!**
BONG!
IT'S TIME FOR... THE PROPHECY!
THE PROPHECY
THE PROPHECY
BUT EVEN IF ZIM NEVER TRIED TO HELP YOU... NEITHER DID I.
THE CUTE BABY MADE ME REALIZE IT.
THAT WAS ACTUALLY ONE OF OUR ELDERS!

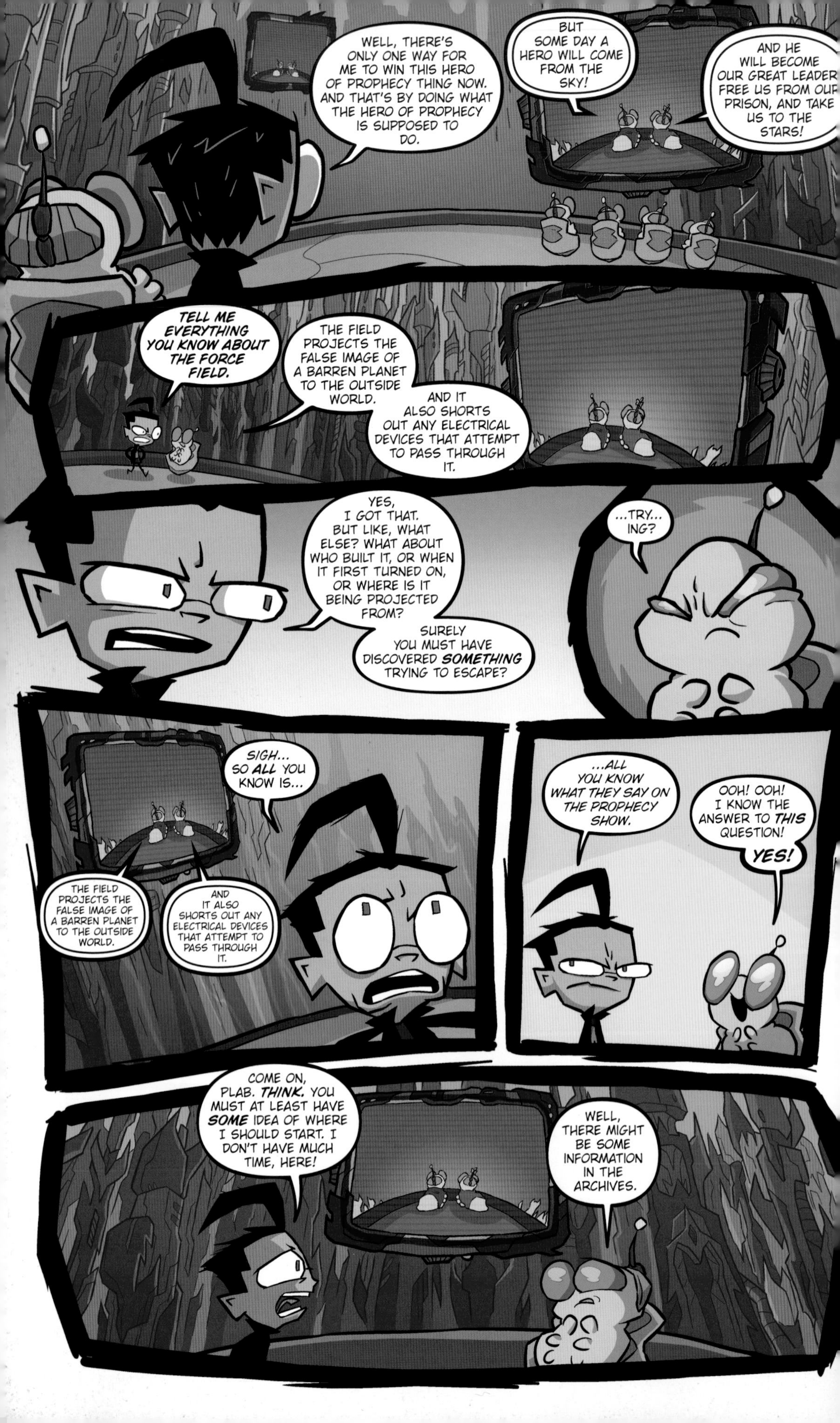
WELL, THERE'S ONLY ONE WAY FOR ME TO WIN THIS HERO OF PROPHECY THING NOW. AND THAT'S BY DOING WHAT THE HERO OF PROPHECY IS SUPPOSED TO DO.
BUT SOME DAY A HERO WILL COME FROM THE SKY!
AND HE WILL BECOME OUR GREAT LEADER FREE US FROM OUR PRISON, AND TAKE US TO THE STARS!
TELL ME EVERYTHING YOU KNOW ABOUT THE FORCE FIELD.
THE FIELD PROJECTS THE FALSE IMAGE OF A BARREN PLANET TO THE OUTSIDE WORLD.
AND IT ALSO SHORTS OUT ANY ELECTRICAL DEVICES THAT ATTEMPT TO PASS THROUGH IT.
YES, I GOT THAT. BUT LIKE, WHAT ELSE? WHAT ABOUT WHO BUILT IT, OR WHEN IT FIRST TURNED ON, OR WHERE IS IT BEING PROJECTED FROM?
SURELY YOU MUST HAVE DISCOVERED SOMETHING TRYING TO ESCAPE?
...TRY... ING?
SIGH... SO ALL YOU KNOW IS...
THE FIELD PROJECTS THE FALSE IMAGE OF A BARREN PLANET TO THE OUTSIDE WORLD.
AND IT ALSO SHORTS OUT ANY ELECTRICAL DEVICES THAT ATTEMPT TO PASS THROUGH IT.
...ALL YOU KNOW WHAT THEY SAY ON THE PROPHECY SHOW.
OOH! OOH! I KNOW THE ANSWER TO THIS QUESTION!
YES!
COME ON, PLAB. THINK. YOU MUST AT LEAST HAVE SOME IDEA OF WHERE I SHOULD START. I DON'T HAVE MUCH TIME, HERE!
WELL, THERE MIGHT BE SOME INFORMATION IN THE ARCHIVES.

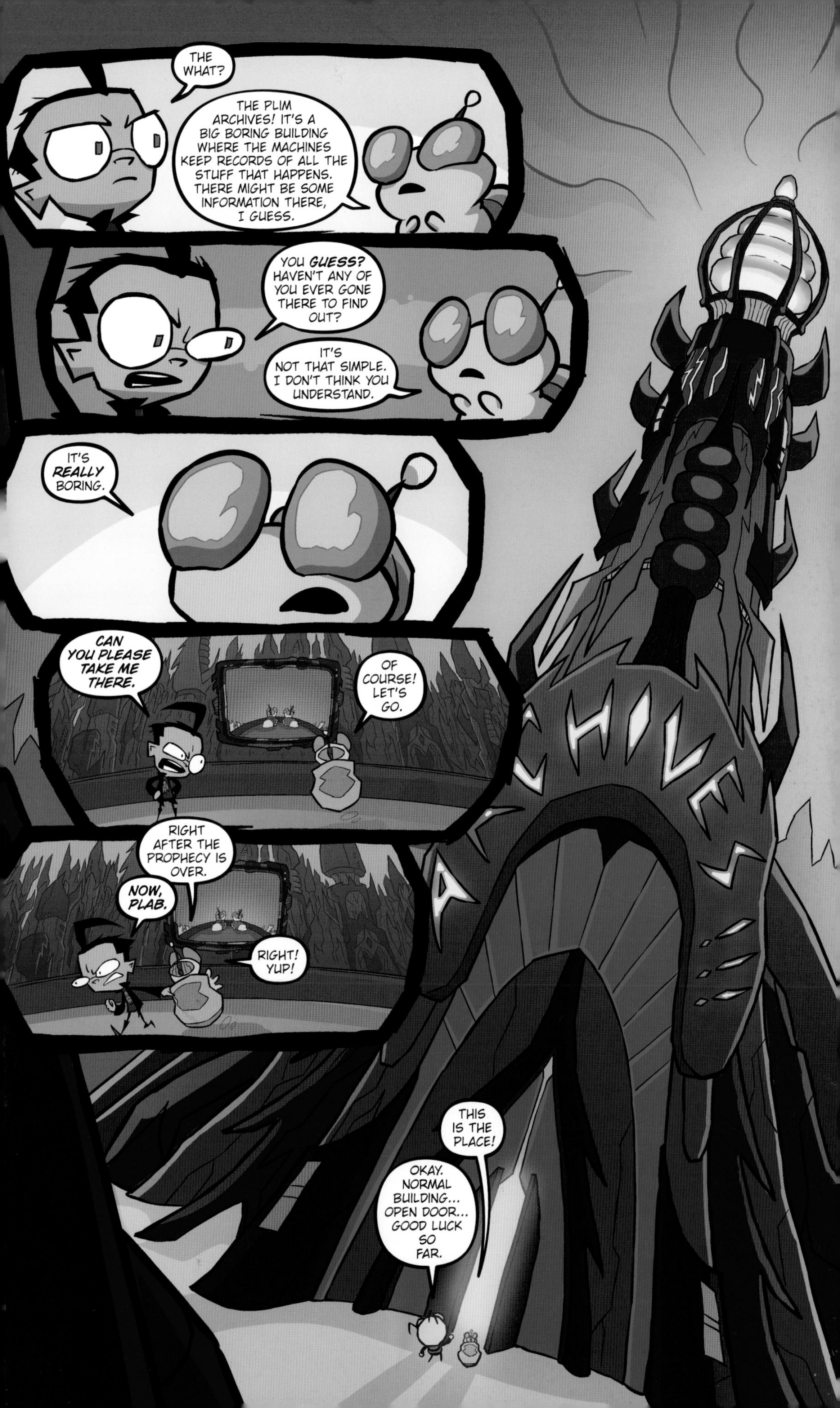
THE WHAT?
THE PLIM ARCHIVES! IT'S A BIG BORING BUILDING WHERE THE MACHINES KEEP RECORDS OF ALL THE STUFF THAT HAPPENS. THERE MIGHT BE SOME INFORMATION THERE, I GUESS.
YOU **GUESS?** HAVEN'T ANY OF YOU EVER GONE THERE TO FIND OUT?
IT'S NOT THAT SIMPLE. I DON'T THINK YOU UNDERSTAND.
IT'S **REALLY** BORING.
CAN YOU PLEASE TAKE ME THERE.
OF COURSE! LET'S GO.
RIGHT AFTER THE PROPHECY IS OVER.
NOW, PLAB.
RIGHT! YUP!
ARCHIVES
THIS IS THE PLACE!
OKAY. NORMAL BUILDING... OPEN DOOR... GOOD LUCK SO FAR.

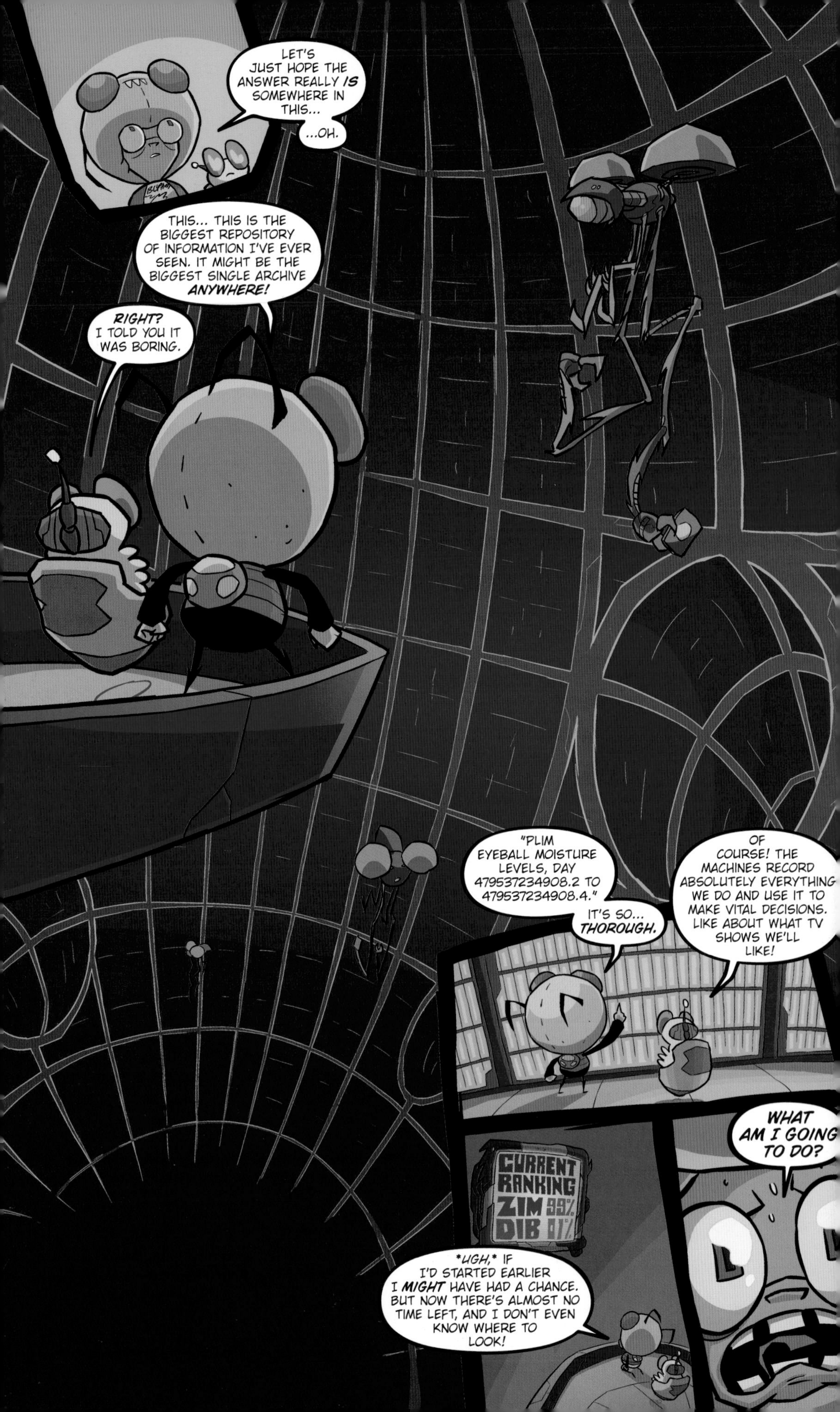

LET'S JUST HOPE THE ANSWER REALLY *IS* SOMEWHERE IN THIS...
...OH.
THIS... THIS IS THE BIGGEST REPOSITORY OF INFORMATION I'VE EVER SEEN. IT MIGHT BE THE BIGGEST SINGLE ARCHIVE ***ANYWHERE!***
RIGHT? I TOLD YOU IT WAS BORING.
"PLIM EYEBALL MOISTURE LEVELS, DAY 479537234908.2 TO 479537234908.4."
IT'S SO... ***THOROUGH.***
OF COURSE! THE MACHINES RECORD ABSOLUTELY EVERYTHING WE DO AND USE IT TO MAKE VITAL DECISIONS. LIKE ABOUT WHAT TV SHOWS WE'LL LIKE!
CURRENT RANKING
ZIM 99%
DIB 01%
UGH, IF I'D STARTED EARLIER I ***MIGHT*** HAVE HAD A CHANCE. BUT NOW THERE'S ALMOST NO TIME LEFT, AND I DON'T EVEN KNOW WHERE TO LOOK!
WHAT AM I GOING TO DO?

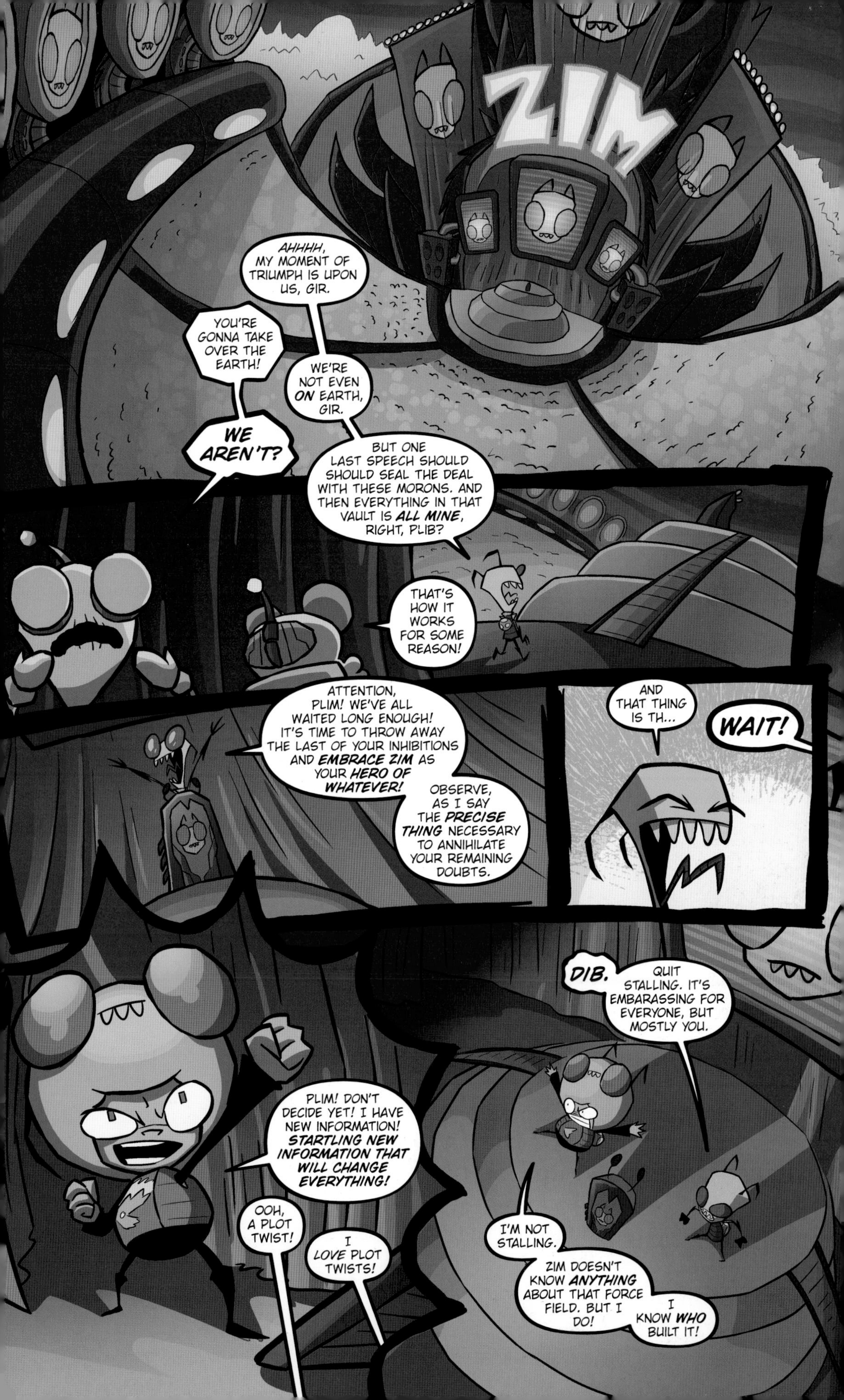
ZIM
AHHHH, MY MOMENT OF TRIUMPH IS UPON US, GIR.
YOU'RE GONNA TAKE OVER THE EARTH!
WE'RE NOT EVEN ON EARTH, GIR.
WE AREN'T?
BUT ONE LAST SPEECH SHOULD SHOULD SEAL THE DEAL WITH THESE MORONS. AND THEN EVERYTHING IN THAT VAULT IS ALL MINE, RIGHT, PLIB?
THAT'S HOW IT WORKS FOR SOME REASON!
ATTENTION, PLIM! WE'VE ALL WAITED LONG ENOUGH! IT'S TIME TO THROW AWAY THE LAST OF YOUR INHIBITIONS AND EMBRACE ZIM AS YOUR HERO OF WHATEVER!
OBSERVE, AS I SAY THE PRECISE THING NECESSARY TO ANNIHILATE YOUR REMAINING DOUBTS.
AND THAT THING IS TH...
WAIT!
PLIM! DON'T DECIDE YET! I HAVE NEW INFORMATION! STARTLING NEW INFORMATION THAT WILL CHANGE EVERYTHING!
DIB.
QUIT STALLING. IT'S EMBARASSING FOR EVERYONE, BUT MOSTLY YOU.
OOH, A PLOT TWIST!
I LOVE PLOT TWISTS!
I'M NOT STALLING.
ZIM DOESN'T KNOW ANYTHING ABOUT THAT FORCE FIELD. BUT I DO!
I KNOW WHO BUILT IT!

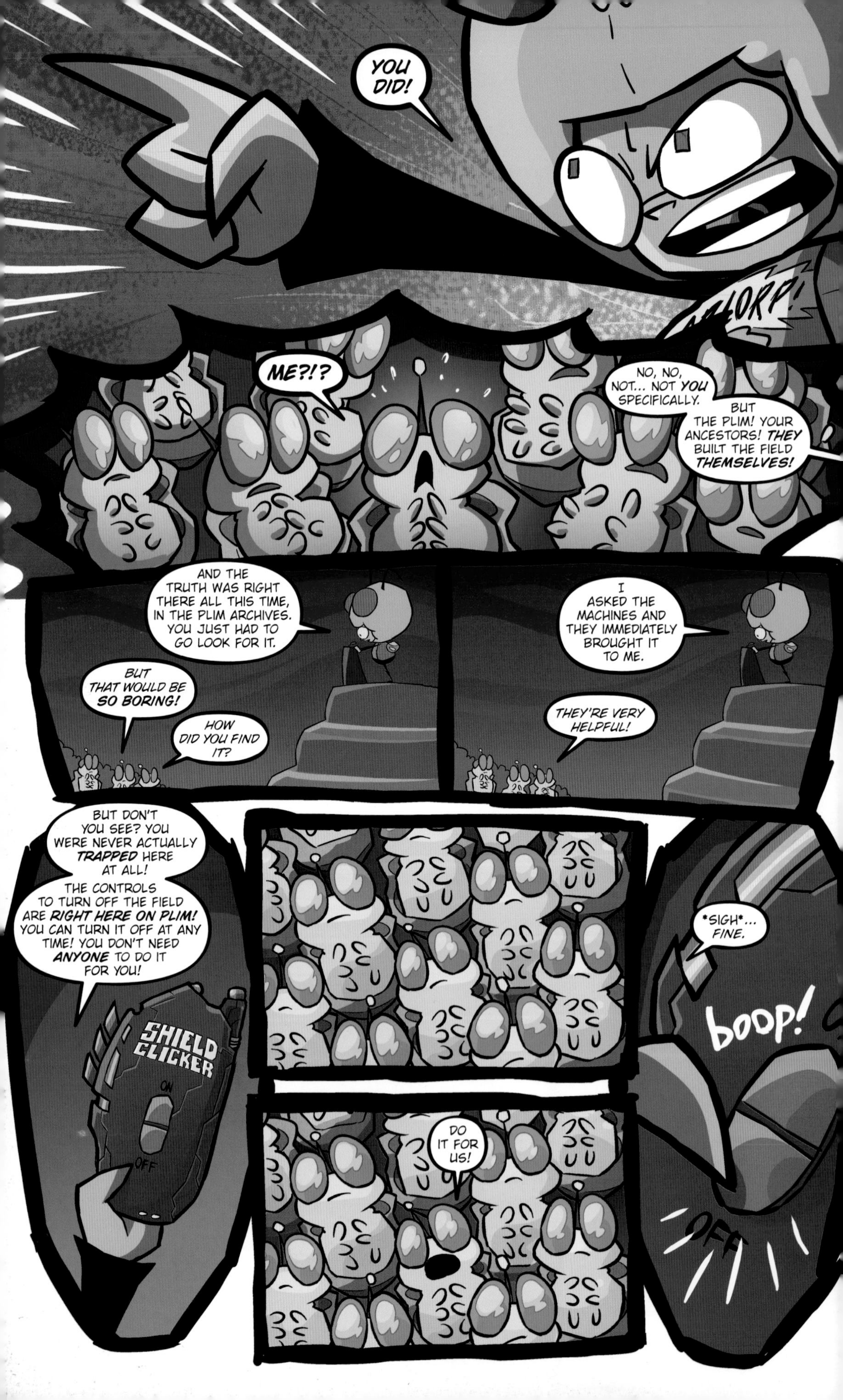
YOU DID!
SHLORP!
ME?!?
NO, NO, NOT... NOT YOU SPECIFICALLY.
BUT THE PLIM! YOUR ANCESTORS! THEY BUILT THE FIELD THEMSELVES!
AND THE TRUTH WAS RIGHT THERE ALL THIS TIME, IN THE PLIM ARCHIVES. YOU JUST HAD TO GO LOOK FOR IT.
BUT THAT WOULD BE SO BORING!
HOW DID YOU FIND IT?
I ASKED THE MACHINES AND THEY IMMEDIATELY BROUGHT IT TO ME.
THEY'RE VERY HELPFUL!
BUT DON'T YOU SEE? YOU WERE NEVER ACTUALLY TRAPPED HERE AT ALL!
THE CONTROLS TO TURN OFF THE FIELD ARE RIGHT HERE ON PLIM! YOU CAN TURN IT OFF AT ANY TIME! YOU DON'T NEED ANYONE TO DO IT FOR YOU!
SHIELD CLICKER
ON
OFF
DO IT FOR US!
SIGH... FINE.
boop!
OFF

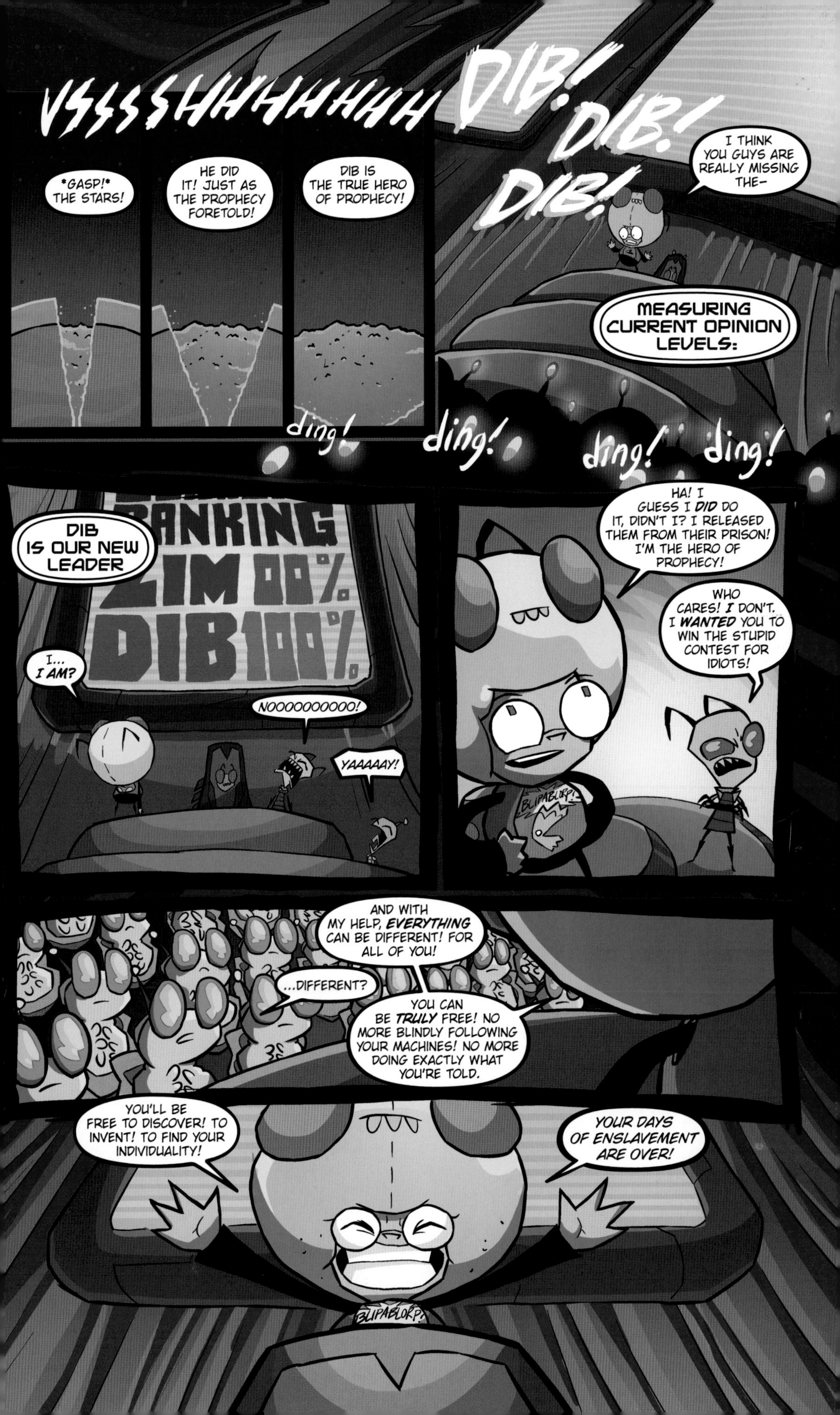

VSSSSHHHHHHHH
GASP! THE STARS!
HE DID IT! JUST AS THE PROPHECY FORETOLD!
DIB IS THE TRUE HERO OF PROPHECY!
DIB! DIB! DIB!
I THINK YOU GUYS ARE REALLY MISSING THE-
MEASURING CURRENT OPINION LEVELS:
ding! ding! ding! ding!
DIB IS OUR NEW LEADER
ANKING
ZIM 00%
DIB 100%
I... I AM?
NOOOOOOOOOO!
YAAAAAY!
HA! I GUESS I DID DO IT, DIDN'T I? I RELEASED THEM FROM THEIR PRISON! I'M THE HERO OF PROPHECY!
WHO CARES! I DON'T. I WANTED YOU TO WIN THE STUPID CONTEST FOR IDIOTS!
BLIPABLORP!
AND WITH MY HELP, EVERYTHING CAN BE DIFFERENT! FOR ALL OF YOU!
...DIFFERENT?
YOU CAN BE TRULY FREE! NO MORE BLINDLY FOLLOWING YOUR MACHINES! NO MORE DOING EXACTLY WHAT YOU'RE TOLD.
YOU'LL BE FREE TO DISCOVER! TO INVENT! TO FIND YOUR INDIVIDUALITY!
YOUR DAYS OF ENSLAVEMENT ARE OVER!
BLIPABLORP!

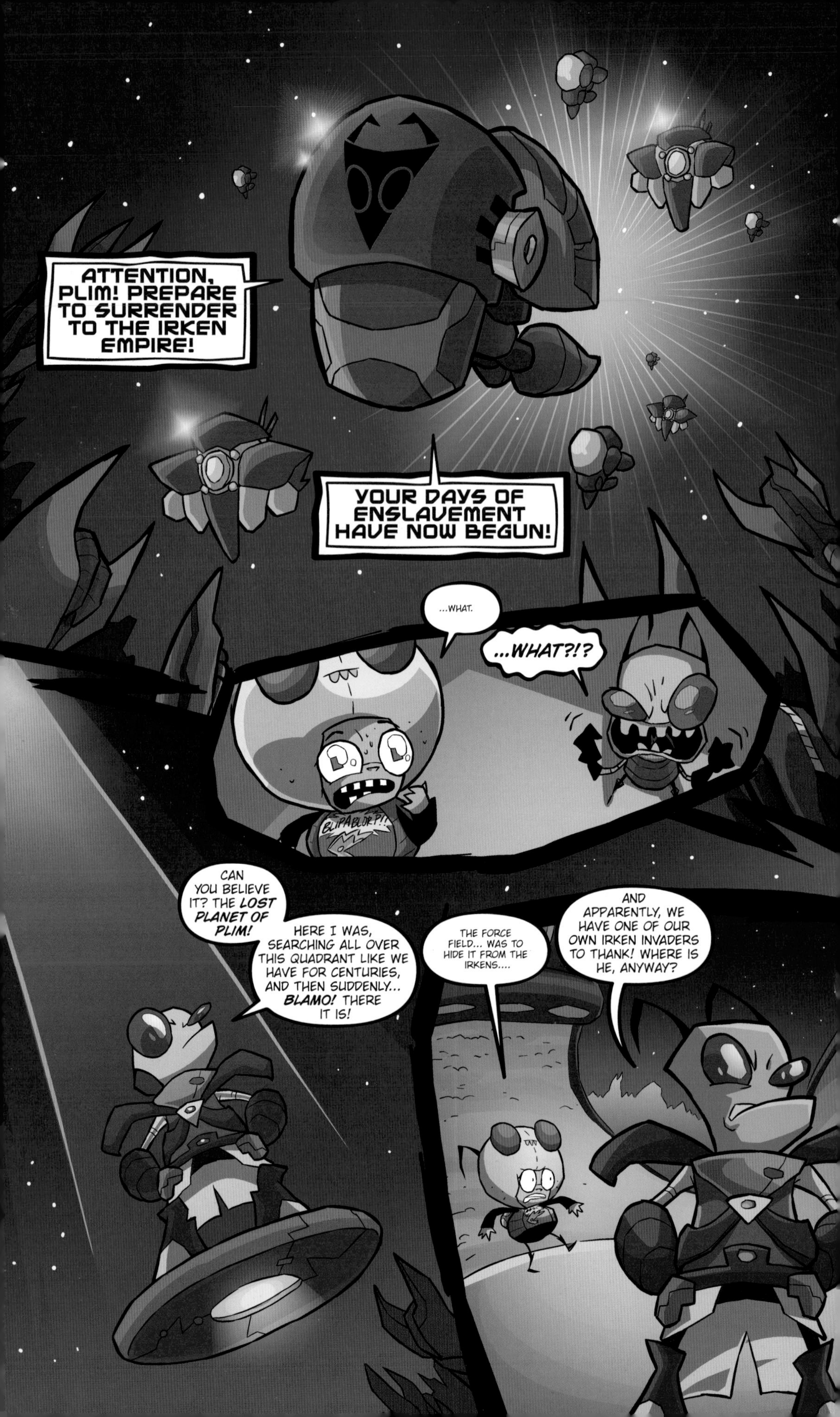
ATTENTION, PLIM! PREPARE TO SURRENDER TO THE IRKEN EMPIRE!
YOUR DAYS OF ENSLAVEMENT HAVE NOW BEGUN!
...WHAT.
...WHAT?!?
BLIPABLORP?!
CAN YOU BELIEVE IT? THE LOST PLANET OF PLIM!
HERE I WAS, SEARCHING ALL OVER THIS QUADRANT LIKE WE HAVE FOR CENTURIES, AND THEN SUDDENLY... BLAMO! THERE IT IS!
THE FORCE FIELD... WAS TO HIDE IT FROM THE IRKENS....
AND APPARENTLY, WE HAVE ONE OF OUR OWN IRKEN INVADERS TO THANK! WHERE IS HE, ANYWAY?

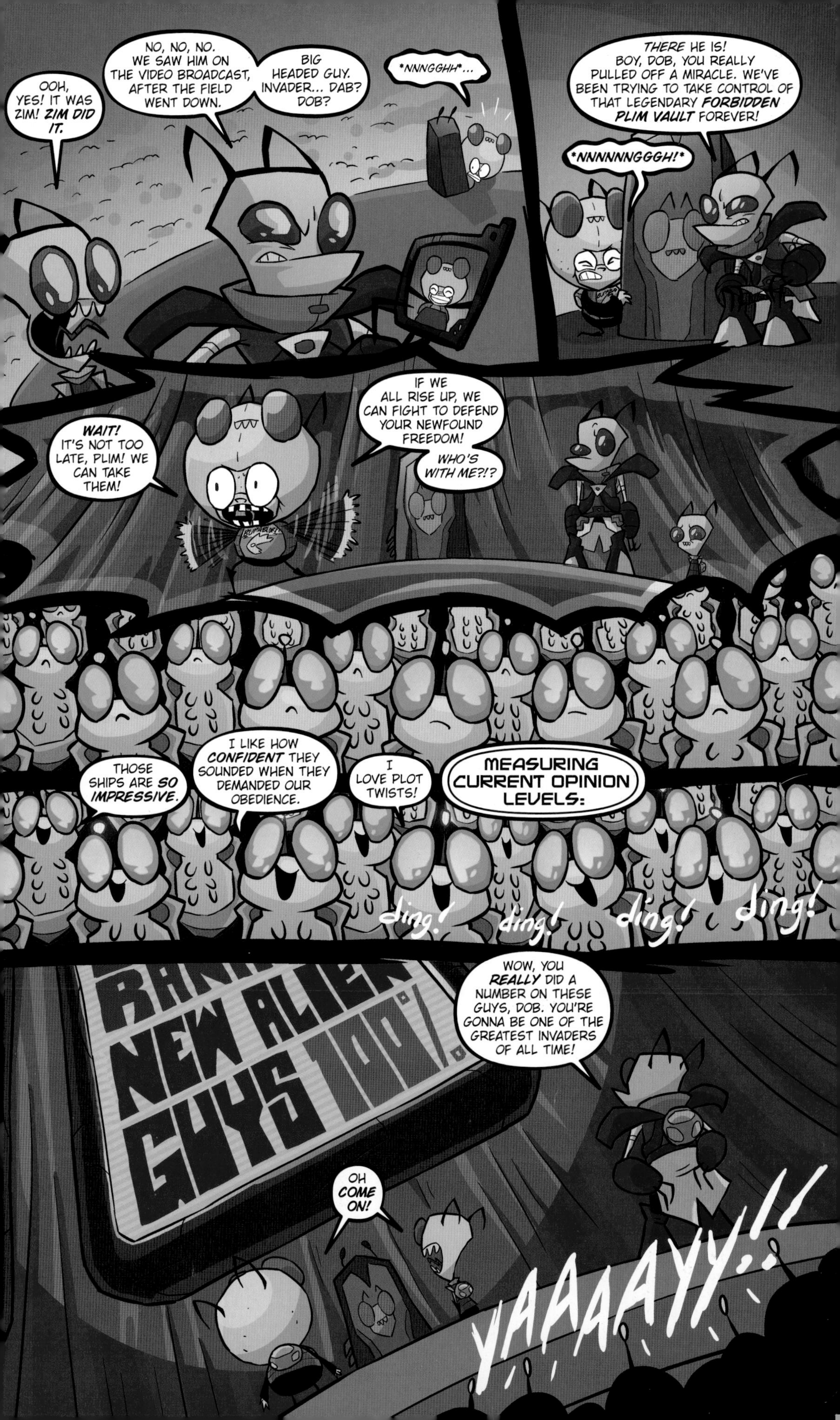
OOH, YES! IT WAS ZIM! ZIM DID IT.
NO, NO, NO. WE SAW HIM ON THE VIDEO BROADCAST, AFTER THE FIELD WENT DOWN.
BIG HEADED GUY. INVADER... DAB? DOB?
NNNGGHH...
THERE HE IS! BOY, DOB, YOU REALLY PULLED OFF A MIRACLE. WE'VE BEEN TRYING TO TAKE CONTROL OF THAT LEGENDARY FORBIDDEN PLIM VAULT FOREVER!
NNNNNNGGGH!
WAIT! IT'S NOT TOO LATE, PLIM! WE CAN TAKE THEM!
IF WE ALL RISE UP, WE CAN FIGHT TO DEFEND YOUR NEWFOUND FREEDOM!
WHO'S WITH ME?!?
THOSE SHIPS ARE SO IMPRESSIVE.
I LIKE HOW CONFIDENT THEY SOUNDED WHEN THEY DEMANDED OUR OBEDIENCE.
I LOVE PLOT TWISTS!
MEASURING CURRENT OPINION LEVELS:
ding! ding! ding! ding!
NEW ALIEN GUYS 100%
WOW, YOU REALLY DID A NUMBER ON THESE GUYS, DOB. YOU'RE GONNA BE ONE OF THE GREATEST INVADERS OF ALL TIME!
OH COME ON!
YAAAAYY!!

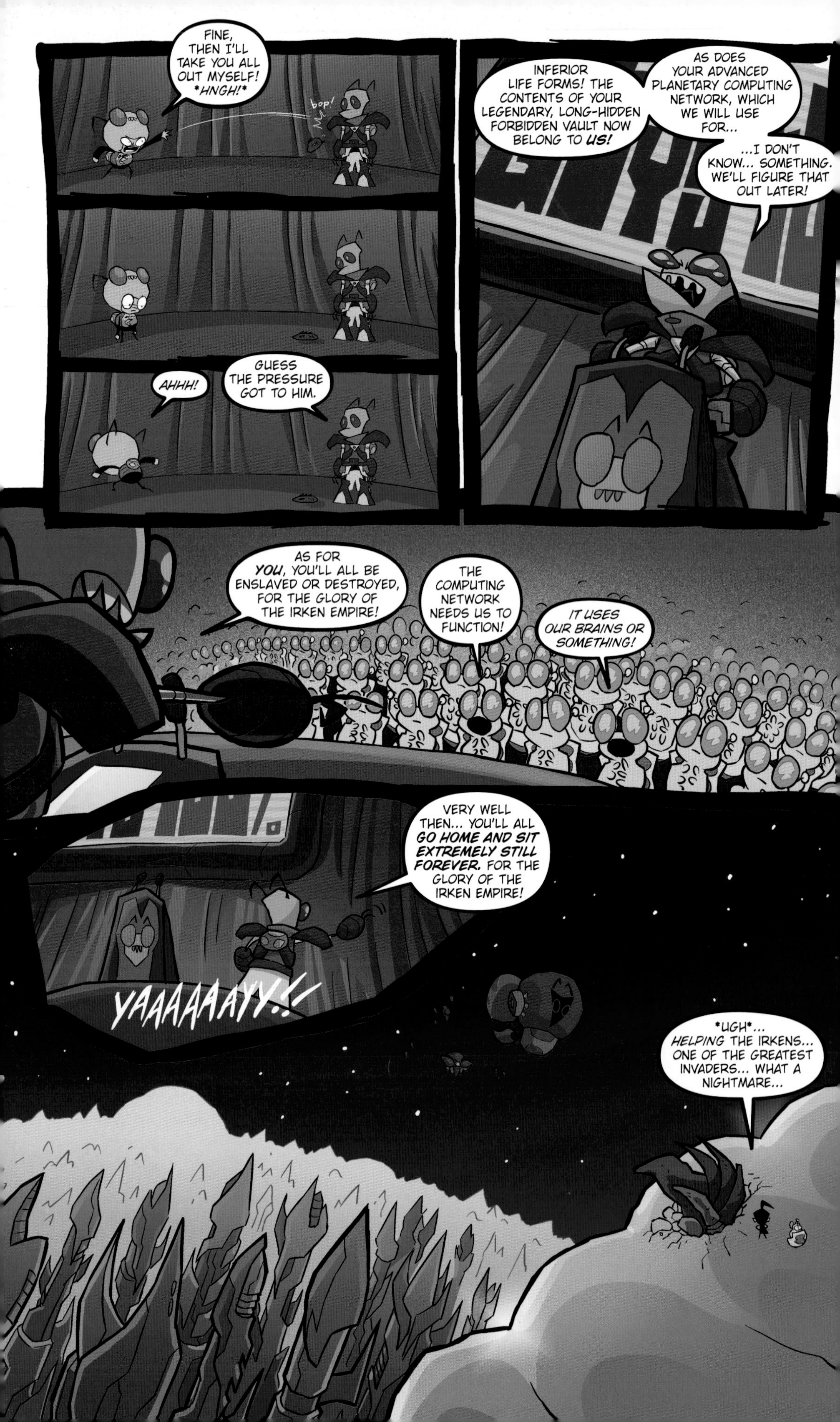
FINE, THEN I'LL TAKE YOU ALL OUT MYSELF! *HNGH!*
bop!
INFERIOR LIFE FORMS! THE CONTENTS OF YOUR LEGENDARY, LONG-HIDDEN FORBIDDEN VAULT NOW BELONG TO US!
AS DOES YOUR ADVANCED PLANETARY COMPUTING NETWORK, WHICH WE WILL USE FOR...
...I DON'T KNOW... SOMETHING. WE'LL FIGURE THAT OUT LATER!
AHHH!
GUESS THE PRESSURE GOT TO HIM.
AS FOR YOU, YOU'LL ALL BE ENSLAVED OR DESTROYED, FOR THE GLORY OF THE IRKEN EMPIRE!
THE COMPUTING NETWORK NEEDS US TO FUNCTION!
IT USES OUR BRAINS OR SOMETHING!
VERY WELL THEN... YOU'LL ALL GO HOME AND SIT EXTREMELY STILL FOREVER. FOR THE GLORY OF THE IRKEN EMPIRE!
YAAAAAAYY!!
UGH... HELPING THE IRKENS... ONE OF THE GREATEST INVADERS... WHAT A NIGHTMARE...

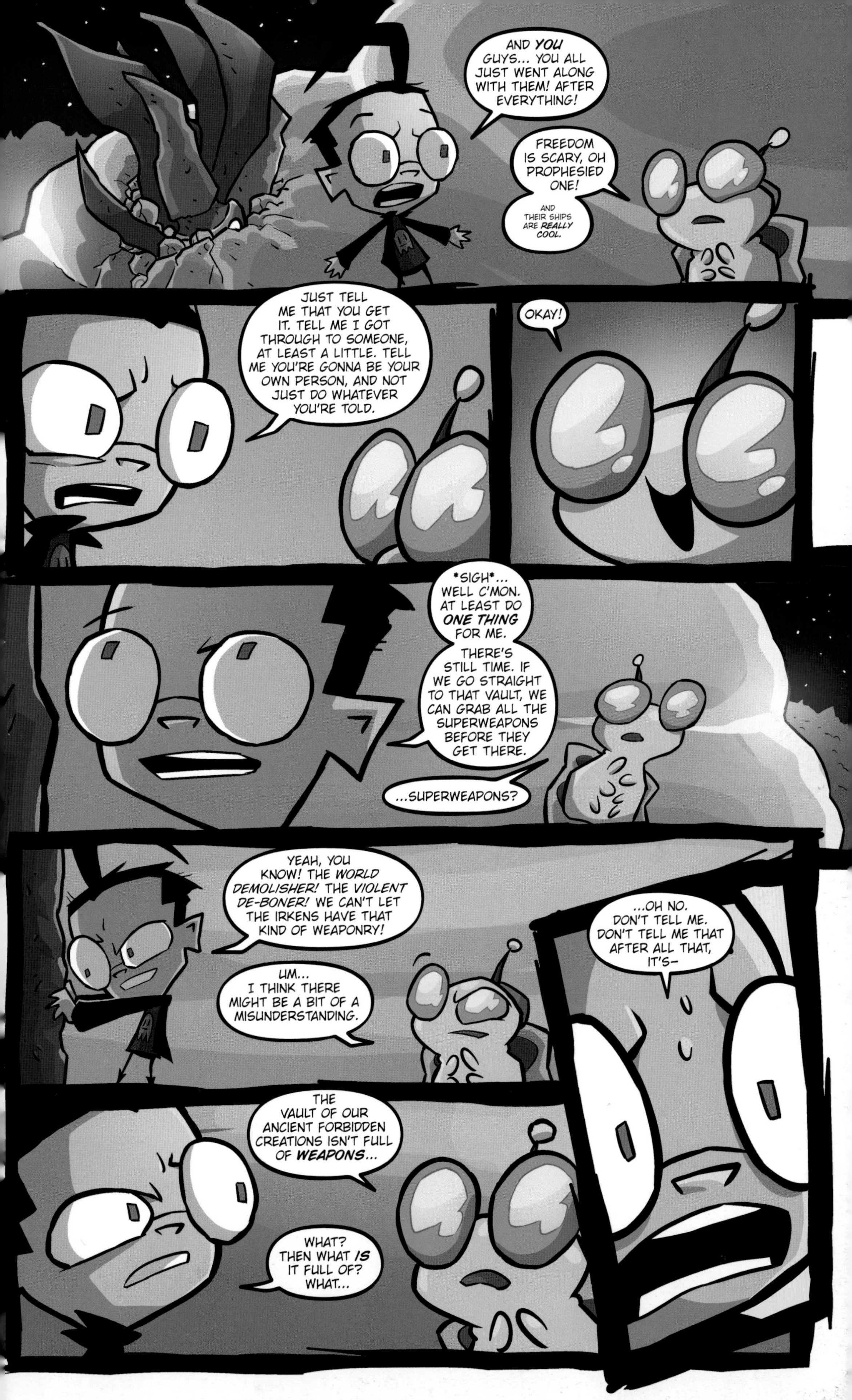
AND YOU GUYS... YOU ALL JUST WENT ALONG WITH THEM! AFTER EVERYTHING!
FREEDOM IS SCARY, OH PROPHESIED ONE!
AND THEIR SHIPS ARE REALLY COOL.
JUST TELL ME THAT YOU GET IT. TELL ME I GOT THROUGH TO SOMEONE, AT LEAST A LITTLE. TELL ME YOU'RE GONNA BE YOUR OWN PERSON, AND NOT JUST DO WHATEVER YOU'RE TOLD.
OKAY!
SIGH... WELL C'MON. AT LEAST DO ONE THING FOR ME.
THERE'S STILL TIME. IF WE GO STRAIGHT TO THAT VAULT, WE CAN GRAB ALL THE SUPERWEAPONS BEFORE THEY GET THERE.
...SUPERWEAPONS?
YEAH, YOU KNOW! THE WORLD DEMOLISHER! THE VIOLENT DE-BONER! WE CAN'T LET THE IRKENS HAVE THAT KIND OF WEAPONRY!
UM... I THINK THERE MIGHT BE A BIT OF A MISUNDERSTANDING.
THE VAULT OF OUR ANCIENT FORBIDDEN CREATIONS ISN'T FULL OF WEAPONS...
WHAT? THEN WHAT IS IT FULL OF? WHAT...
...OH NO. DON'T TELL ME. DON'T TELL ME THAT AFTER ALL THAT, IT'S–

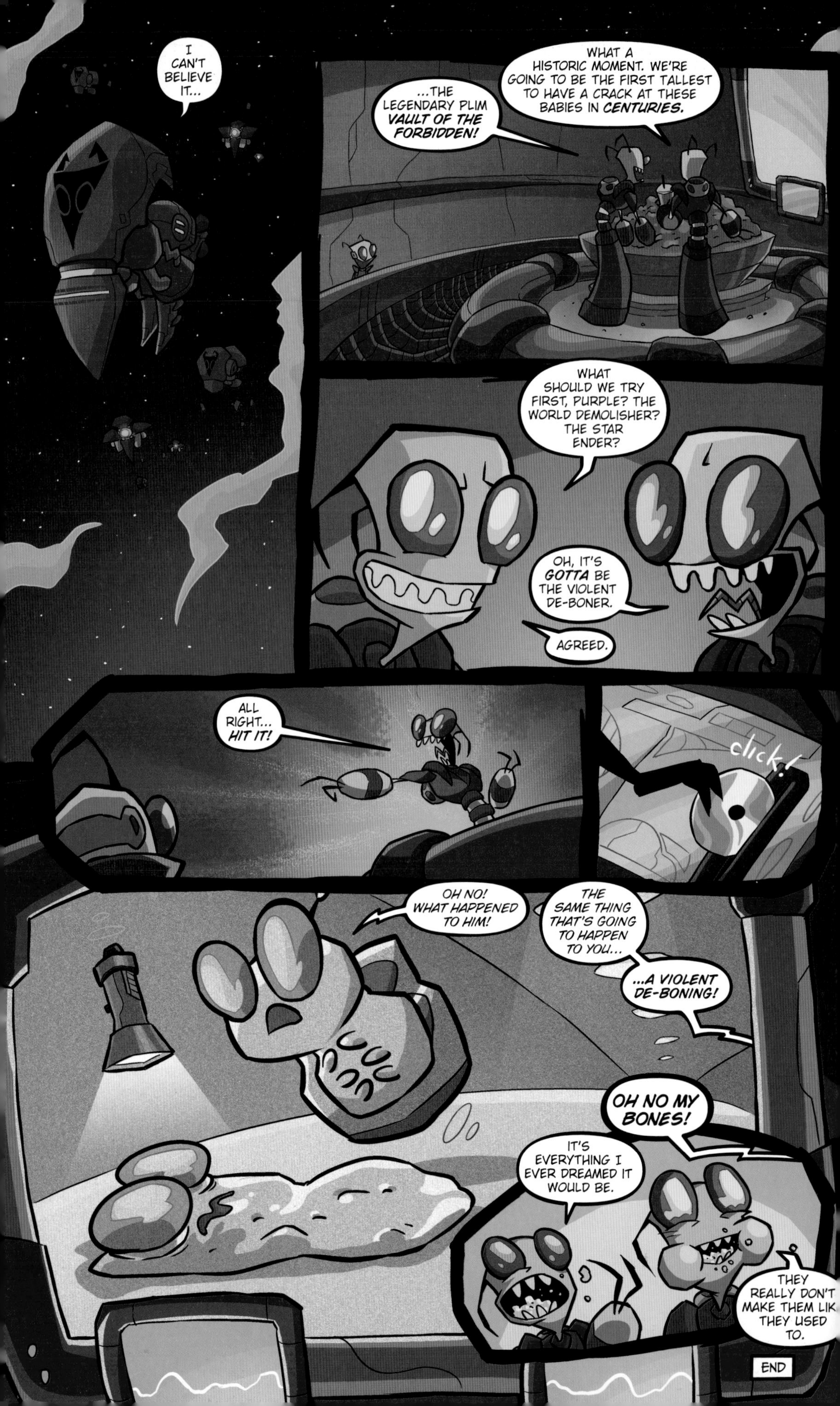
I CAN'T BELIEVE IT...
...THE LEGENDARY PLIM VAULT OF THE FORBIDDEN!
WHAT A HISTORIC MOMENT. WE'RE GOING TO BE THE FIRST TALLEST TO HAVE A CRACK AT THESE BABIES IN CENTURIES.
WHAT SHOULD WE TRY FIRST, PURPLE? THE WORLD DEMOLISHER? THE STAR ENDER?
OH, IT'S GOTTA BE THE VIOLENT DE-BONER.
AGREED.
ALL RIGHT... HIT IT!
click!
OH NO! WHAT HAPPENED TO HIM!
THE SAME THING THAT'S GOING TO HAPPEN TO YOU...
...A VIOLENT DE-BONING!
OH NO MY BONES!
IT'S EVERYTHING I EVER DREAMED IT WOULD BE.
THEY REALLY DON'T MAKE THEM LIK THEY USED TO.
END

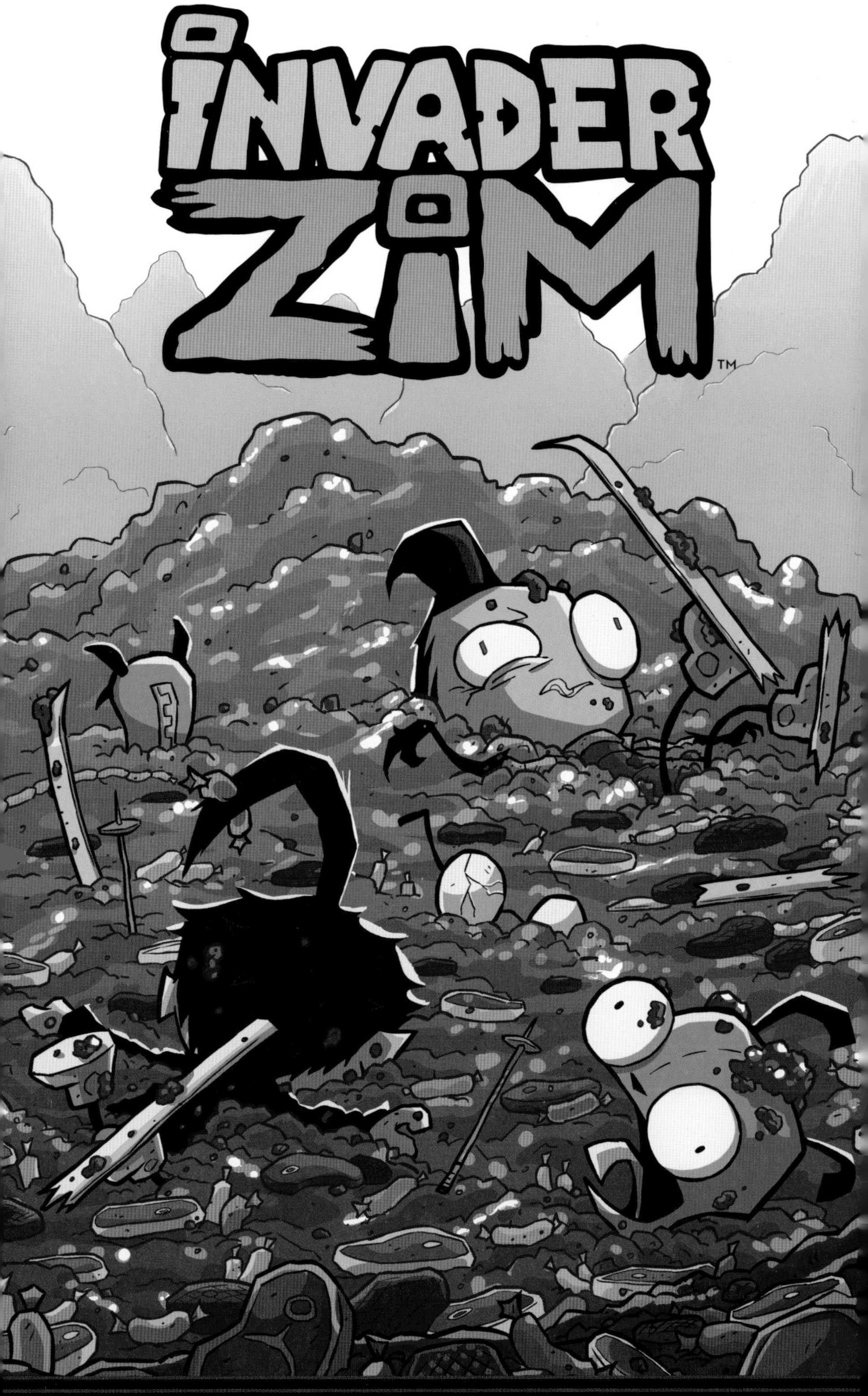
INVADER ZIM™

CHAPTER: 3

illustration by WARREN WUCINICH with FRED C. STRESING

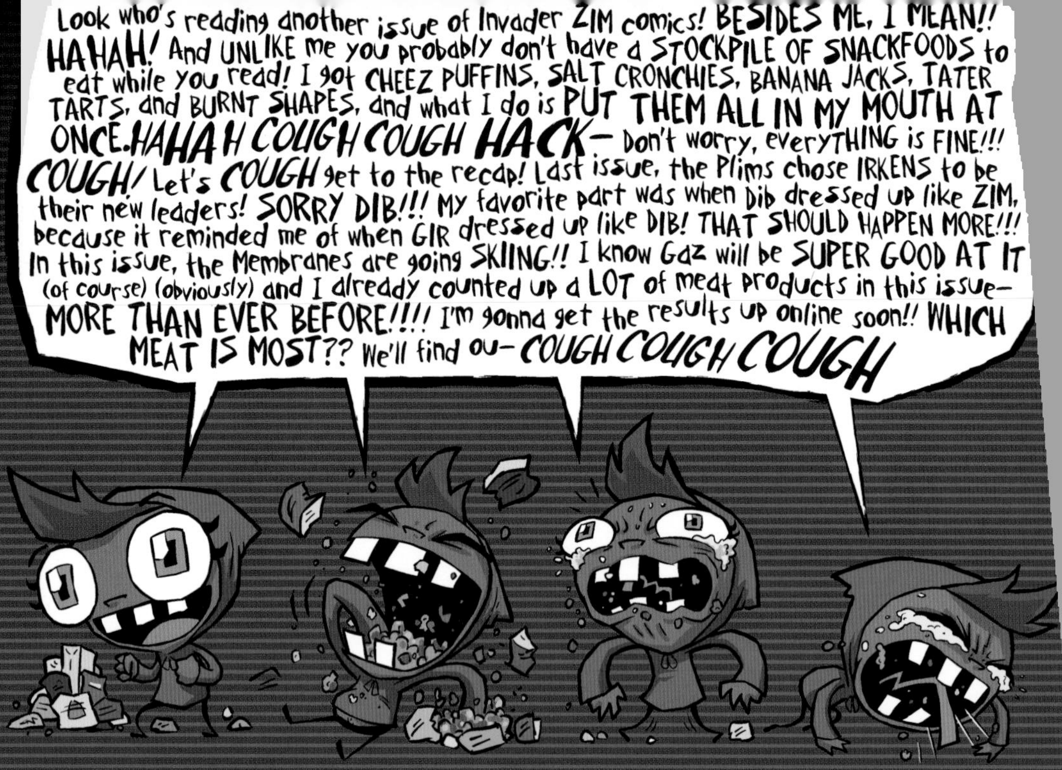
Look who's reading another issue of Invader ZIM comics! BESIDES ME, I MEAN!! HAHAH! And UNLIKE me you probably don't have a STOCKPILE OF SNACKFOODS to eat while you read! I got CHEEZ PUFFINS, SALT CRONCHIES, BANANA JACKS, TATER TARTS, and BURNT SHAPES, and what I do is PUT THEM ALL IN MY MOUTH AT ONCE. HAHAHAH COUGH COUGH HACK— Don't worry, everyTHING is FINE!!! COUGH! Let's COUGH get to the recap! Last issue, the Plims chose IRKENS to be their new leaders! SORRY DIB!!! My favorite part was when Dib dressed up like ZIM, because it reminded me of when GIR dressed up like DIB! THAT SHOULD HAPPEN MORE!!! In this issue, the Membranes are going SKIING!! I know Gaz will be SUPER GOOD AT IT (of course) (obviously) and I already counted up a LOT of meat products in this issue— MORE THAN EVER BEFORE!!!! I'm gonna get the results up online soon!! WHICH MEAT IS MOST?? We'll find ou— COUGH COUGH COUGH

Recap Kid illustrated, colored, and lettered by

WARREN WUCINICH

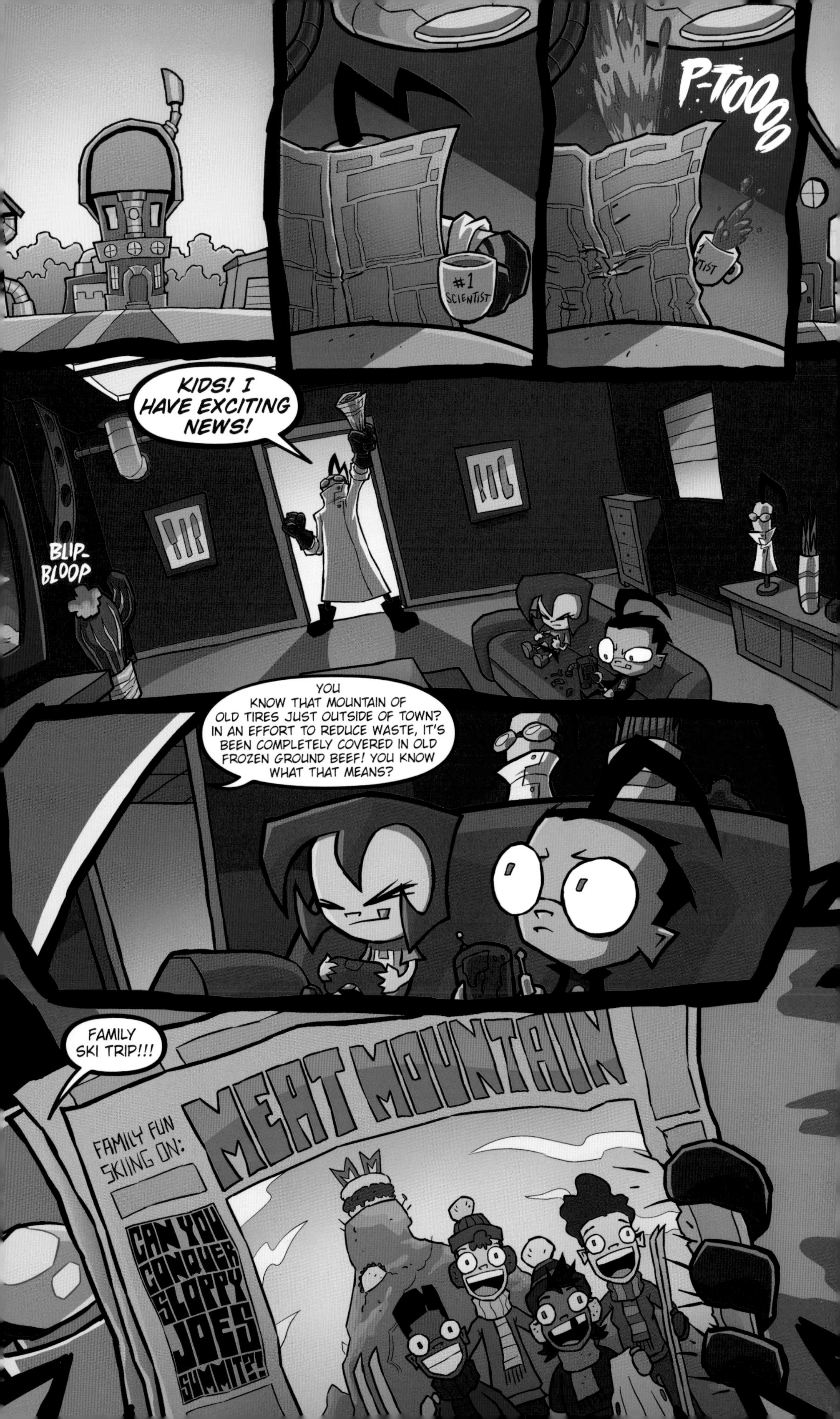

#1 SCIENTIST
P-TOOOO
KIDS! I HAVE EXCITING NEWS!
BLIP-BLOOP
YOU KNOW THAT MOUNTAIN OF OLD TIRES JUST OUTSIDE OF TOWN? IN AN EFFORT TO REDUCE WASTE, IT'S BEEN COMPLETELY COVERED IN OLD FROZEN GROUND BEEF! YOU KNOW WHAT THAT MEANS?
FAMILY SKI TRIP!!!
FAMILY FUN SKIING ON: MEAT MOUNTAIN
CAN YOU CONQUER SLOPPY JOES SUMMIT?!

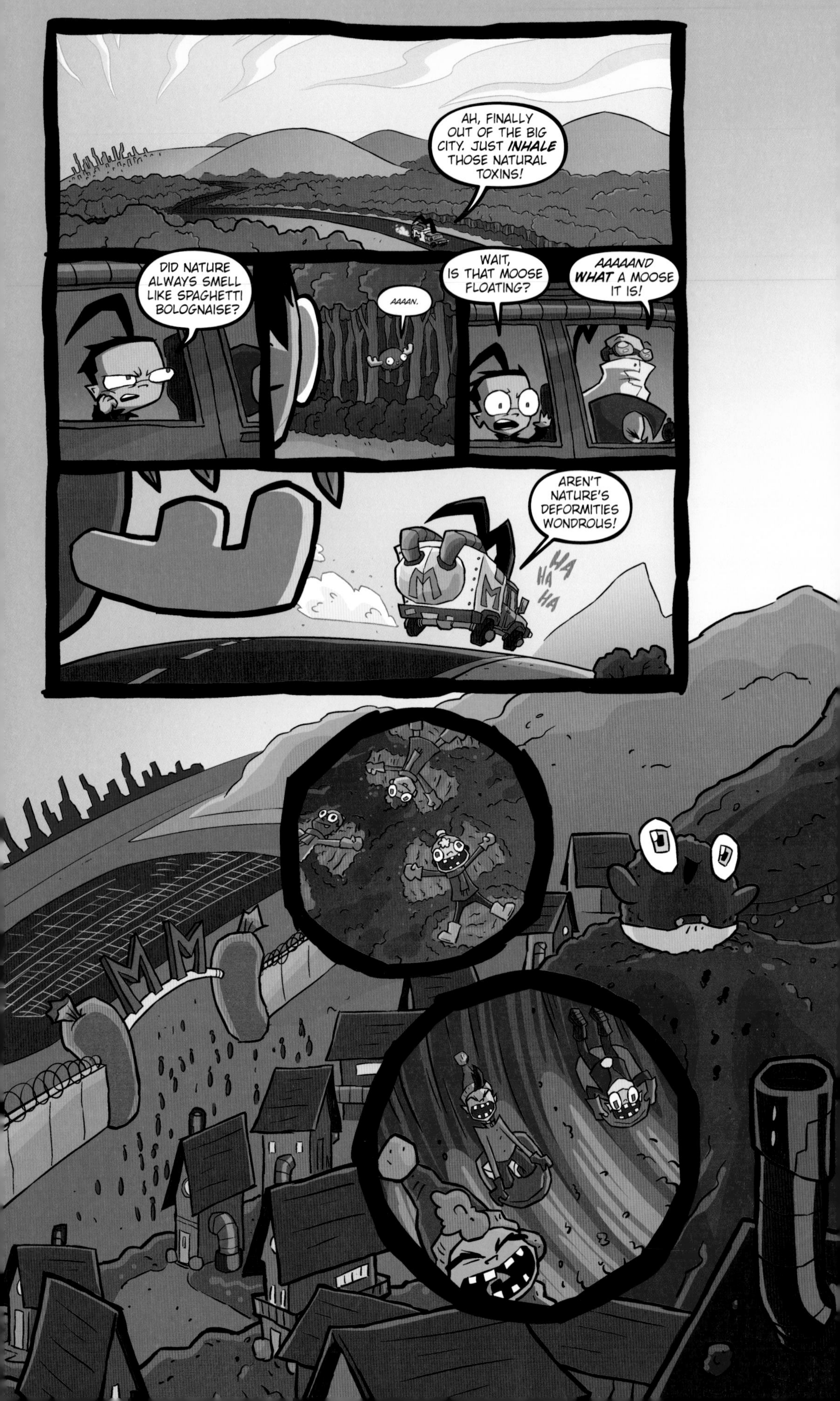
AH, FINALLY OUT OF THE BIG CITY. JUST INHALE THOSE NATURAL TOXINS!
DID NATURE ALWAYS SMELL LIKE SPAGHETTI BOLOGNAISE?
AAAAN.
WAIT, IS THAT MOOSE FLOATING?
AAAAAND WHAT A MOOSE IT IS!
AREN'T NATURE'S DEFORMITIES WONDROUS!
HA HA HA HA

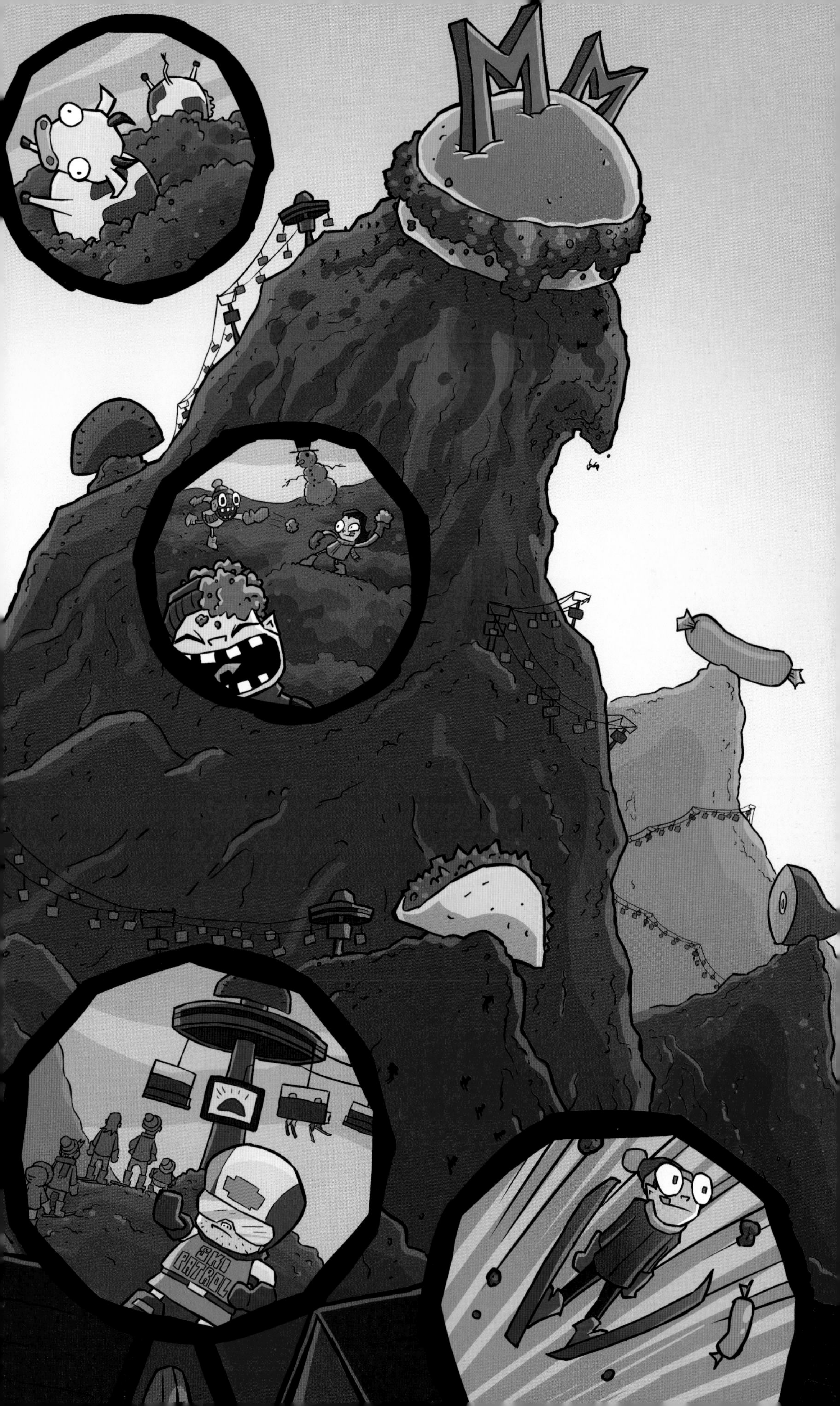
MM
SKI PATROL

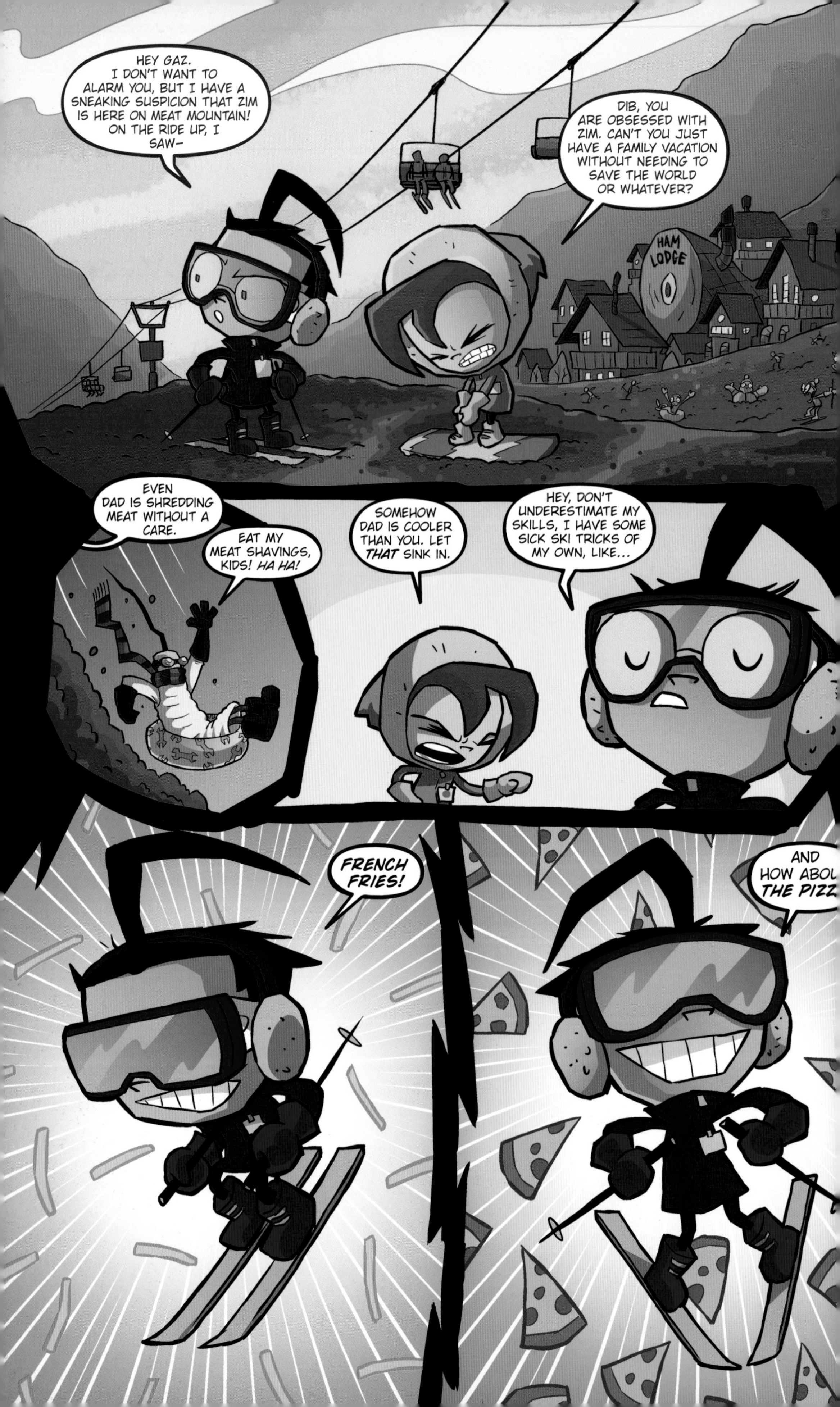
HEY GAZ. I DON'T WANT TO ALARM YOU, BUT I HAVE A SNEAKING SUSPICION THAT ZIM IS HERE ON MEAT MOUNTAIN! ON THE RIDE UP, I SAW–
DIB, YOU ARE OBSESSED WITH ZIM. CAN'T YOU JUST HAVE A FAMILY VACATION WITHOUT NEEDING TO SAVE THE WORLD OR WHATEVER?
HAM LODGE
EVEN DAD IS SHREDDING MEAT WITHOUT A CARE.
EAT MY MEAT SHAVINGS, KIDS! *HA HA!*
SOMEHOW DAD IS COOLER THAN YOU. LET *THAT* SINK IN.
HEY, DON'T UNDERESTIMATE MY SKILLS, I HAVE SOME SICK SKI TRICKS OF MY OWN, LIKE...
FRENCH FRIES!
AND HOW ABOU *THE PIZZ*

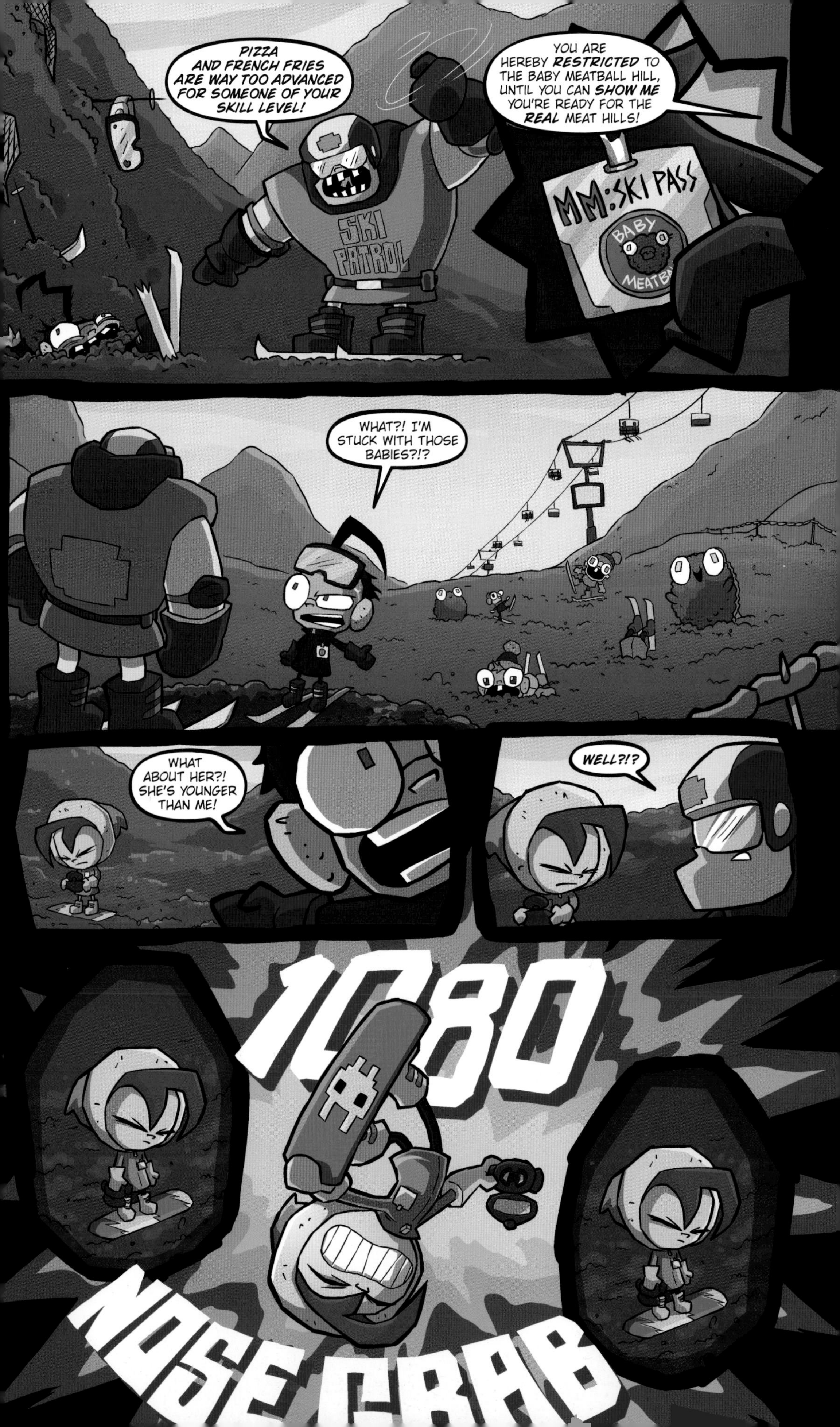
PIZZA AND FRENCH FRIES ARE WAY TOO ADVANCED FOR SOMEONE OF YOUR SKILL LEVEL!
YOU ARE HEREBY RESTRICTED TO THE BABY MEATBALL HILL, UNTIL YOU CAN SHOW ME YOU'RE READY FOR THE REAL MEAT HILLS!
SKI PATROL
MM:SKI PASS
BABY MEATBA
WHAT?! I'M STUCK WITH THOSE BABIES?!?
WHAT ABOUT HER?! SHE'S YOUNGER THAN ME!
WELL?!?
1080
NOSE GRAB

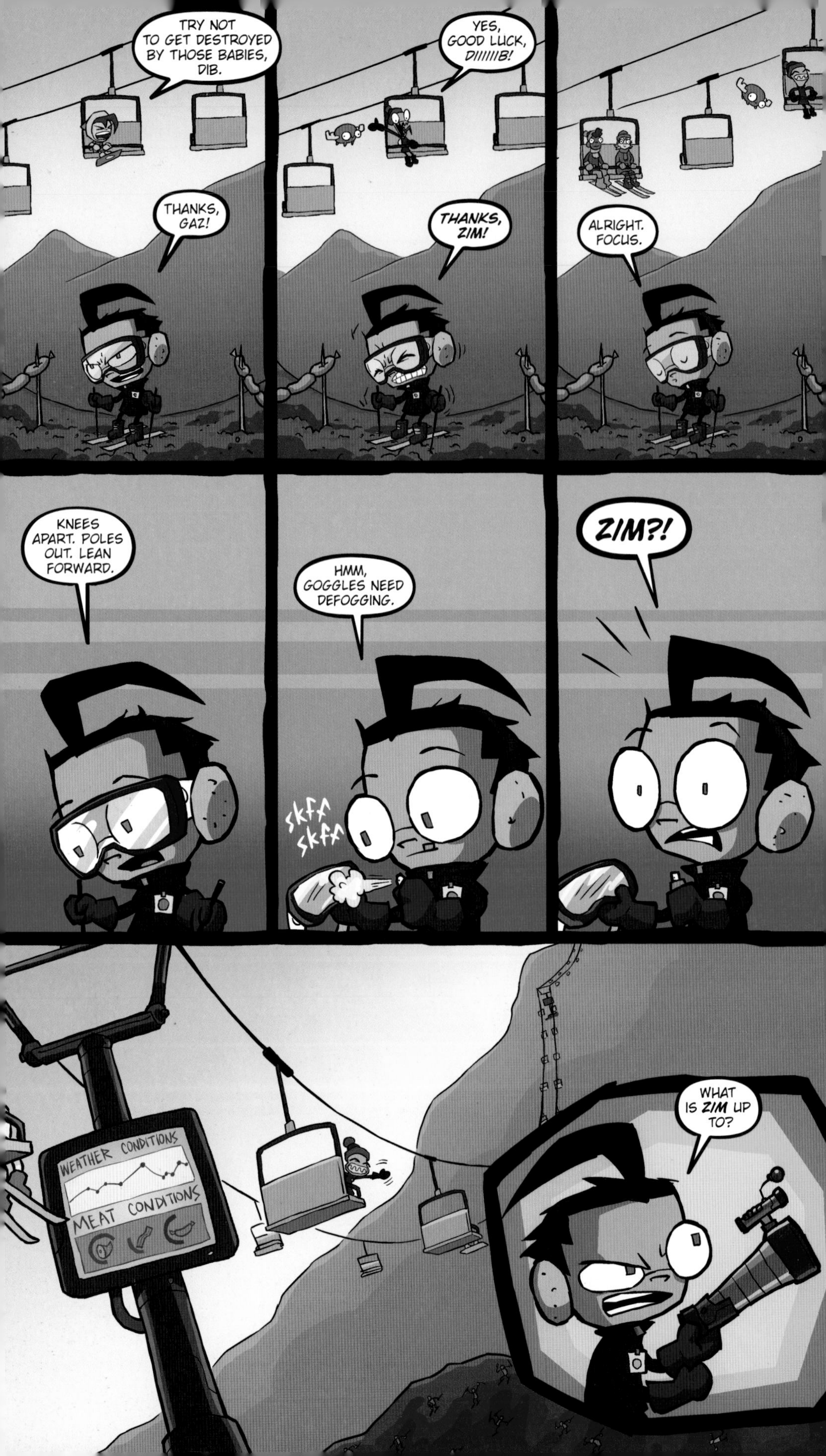
TRY NOT TO GET DESTROYED BY THOSE BABIES, DIB.
THANKS, GAZ!
YES, GOOD LUCK, DIIIIIIB!
THANKS, ZIM!
ALRIGHT. FOCUS.
KNEES APART. POLES OUT. LEAN FORWARD.
HMM, GOGGLES NEED DEFOGGING.
SKFF SKFF
ZIM?!
WEATHER CONDITIONS
MEAT CONDITIONS
WHAT IS ZIM UP TO?

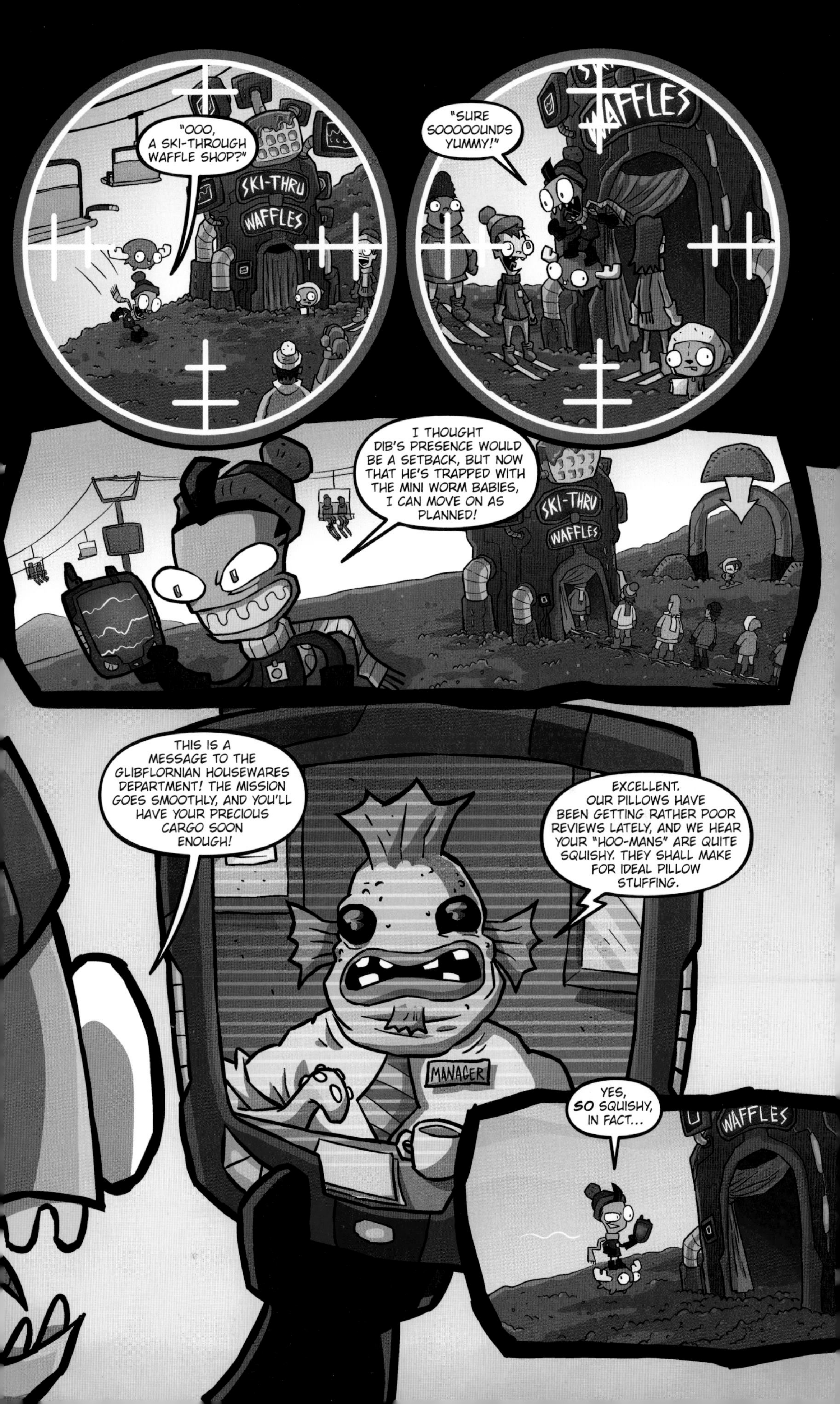
"OOO, A SKI-THROUGH WAFFLE SHOP?"
SKI-THRU
WAFFLES
"SURE SOOOOOUNDS YUMMY!"
WAFFLES
I THOUGHT DIB'S PRESENCE WOULD BE A SETBACK, BUT NOW THAT HE'S TRAPPED WITH THE MINI WORM BABIES, I CAN MOVE ON AS PLANNED!
SKI-THRU
WAFFLES
THIS IS A MESSAGE TO THE GLIBFLORNIAN HOUSEWARES DEPARTMENT! THE MISSION GOES SMOOTHLY, AND YOU'LL HAVE YOUR PRECIOUS CARGO SOON ENOUGH!
EXCELLENT. OUR PILLOWS HAVE BEEN GETTING RATHER POOR REVIEWS LATELY, AND WE HEAR YOUR "HOO-MANS" ARE QUITE SQUISHY. THEY SHALL MAKE FOR IDEAL PILLOW STUFFING.
MANAGER
YES, **SO** SQUISHY, IN FACT...
WAFFLES

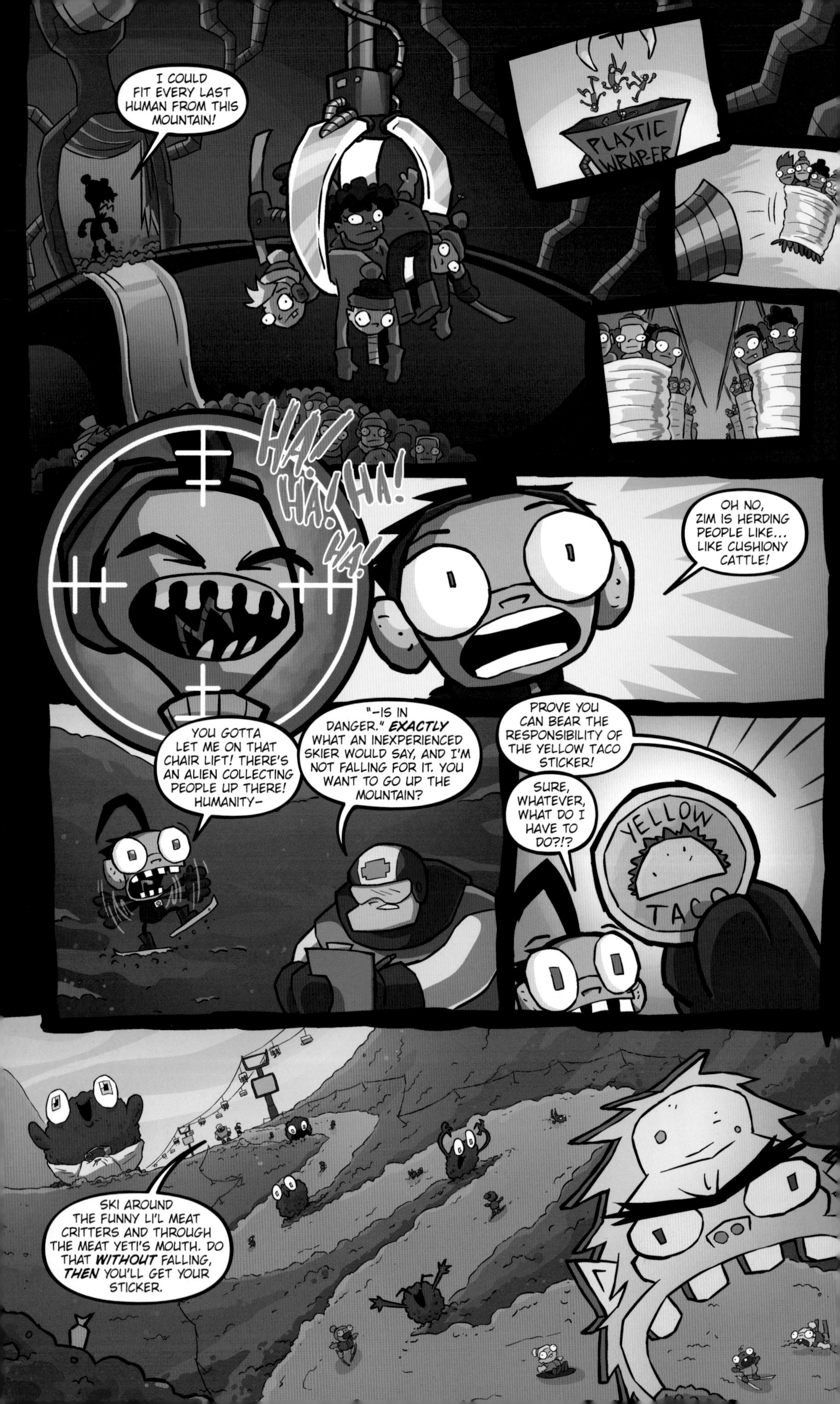
I COULD FIT EVERY LAST HUMAN FROM THIS MOUNTAIN!
PLASTIC WRAP-ER
HA! HA! HA! HA!
OH NO, ZIM IS HERDING PEOPLE LIKE... LIKE CUSHIONY CATTLE!
YOU GOTTA LET ME ON THAT CHAIR LIFT! THERE'S AN ALIEN COLLECTING PEOPLE UP THERE! HUMANITY-
"-IS IN DANGER." ***EXACTLY*** WHAT AN INEXPERIENCED SKIER WOULD SAY, AND I'M NOT FALLING FOR IT. YOU WANT TO GO UP THE MOUNTAIN?
PROVE YOU CAN BEAR THE RESPONSIBILITY OF THE YELLOW TACO STICKER!
SURE, WHATEVER, WHAT DO I HAVE TO DO?!?
YELLOW TACO
SKI AROUND THE FUNNY LI'L MEAT CRITTERS AND THROUGH THE MEAT YETI'S MOUTH. DO THAT ***WITHOUT*** FALLING, ***THEN*** YOU'LL GET YOUR STICKER.

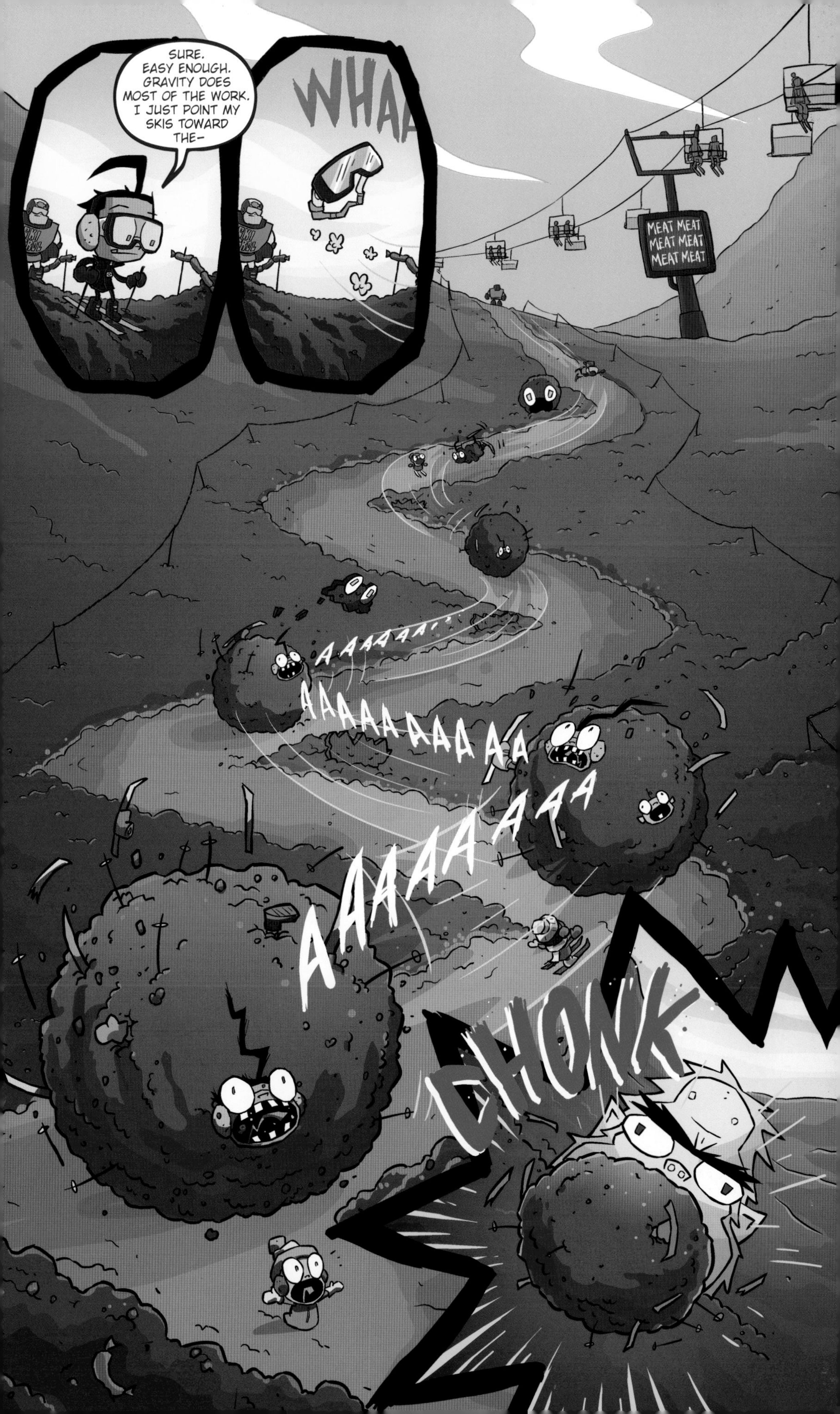
SURE. EASY ENOUGH. GRAVITY DOES MOST OF THE WORK. I JUST POINT MY SKIS TOWARD THE–
WHAA
MEAT MEAT MEAT MEAT MEAT MEAT
AAAAAAA
AAAAAAAAAAAAAAAAAAA
CHONK

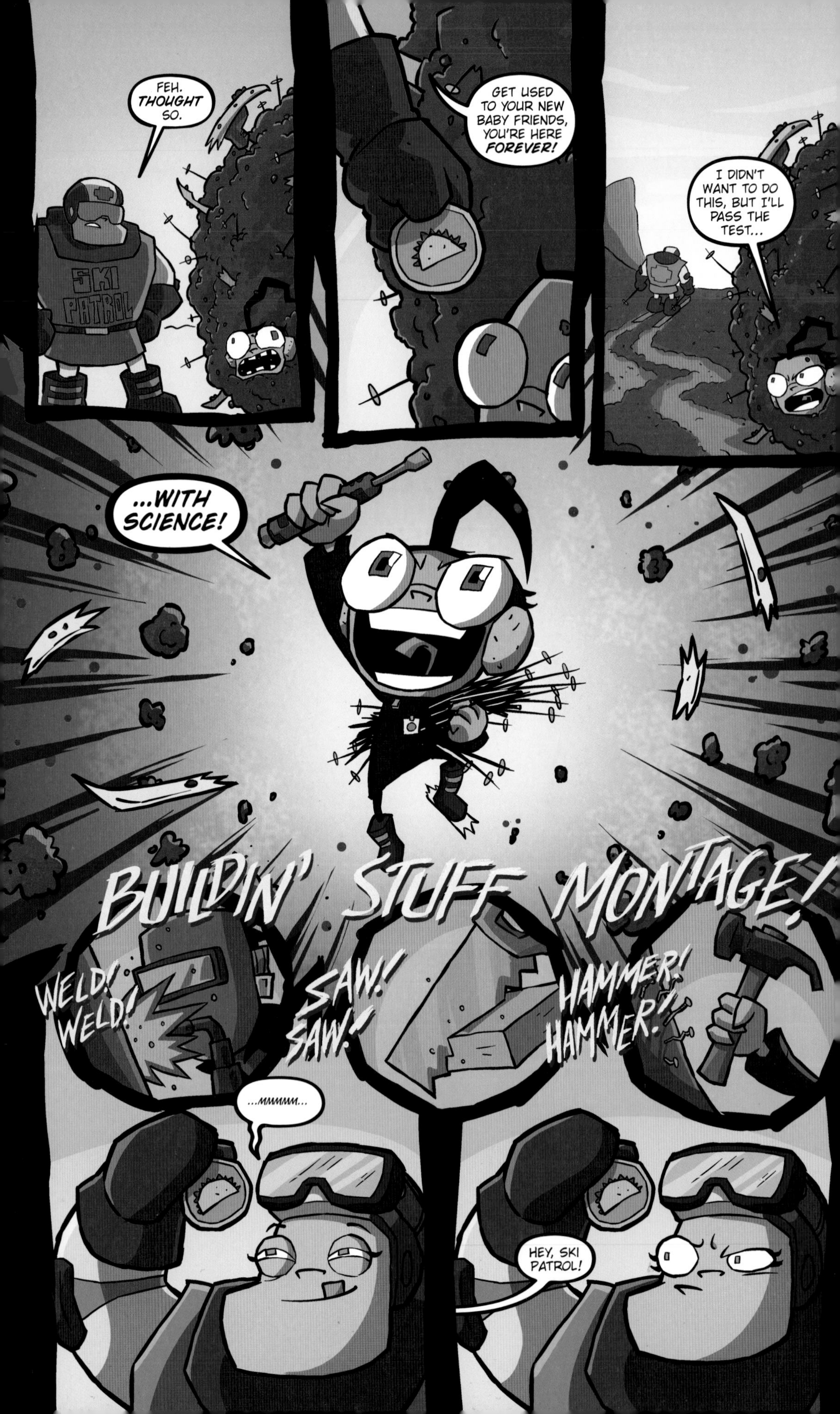
FEH. THOUGHT SO.
GET USED TO YOUR NEW BABY FRIENDS, YOU'RE HERE FOREVER!
I DIDN'T WANT TO DO THIS, BUT I'LL PASS THE TEST...
...WITH SCIENCE!
BUILDIN' STUFF MONTAGE!
WELD! WELD!
SAW! SAW!
HAMMER! HAMMER!
...MMMMM...
HEY, SKI PATROL!

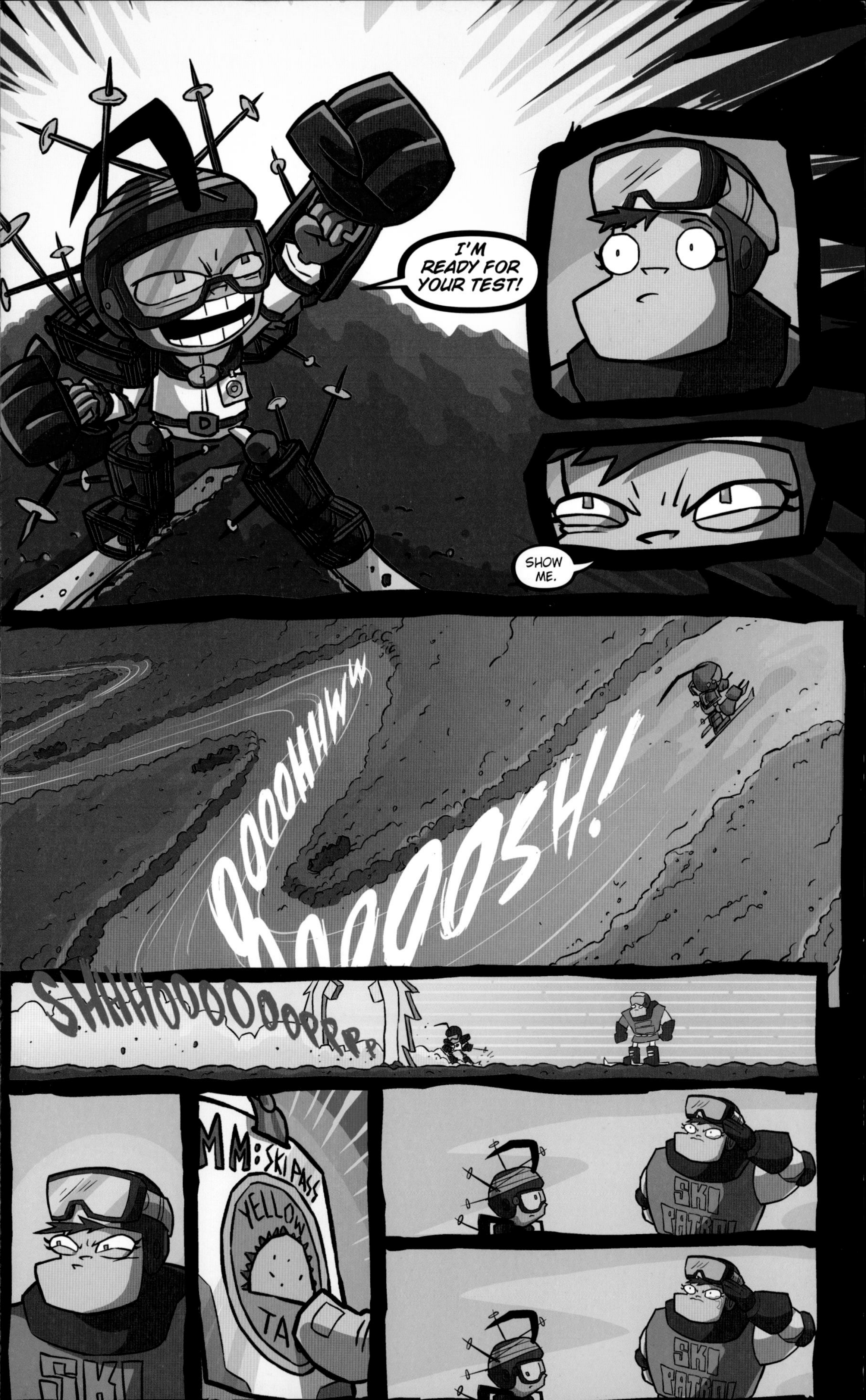
I'M READY FOR YOUR TEST!
SHOW ME.
SHOOOOOOOOSH!
SHHHOOOOOOOOPPRRP
MM: SKI PASS
YELLOW
TA
SKI
SKI PATROL
SKI PATROL

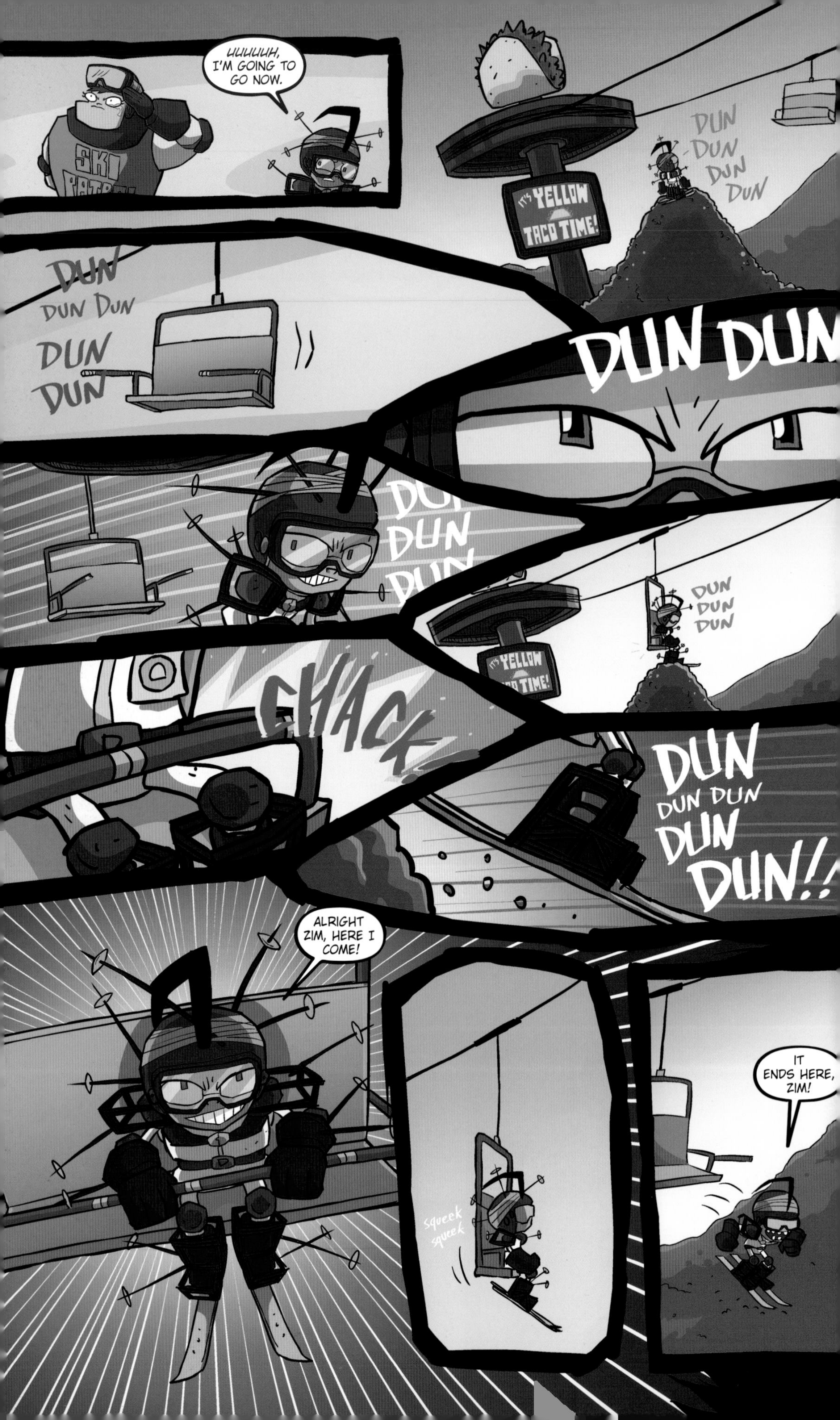
UHHHHH, I'M GOING TO GO NOW.
SKI PATROL
IT'S YELLOW TACO TIME!
DUN DUN DUN DUN
DUN DUN DUN DUN DUN
DUN DUN
DUN DUN DUN
DUN DUN DUN
IT'S YELLOW TACO TIME!
CHACK
DUN DUN DUN DUN DUN!!
ALRIGHT ZIM, HERE I COME!
squeek squeek
IT ENDS HERE, ZIM!

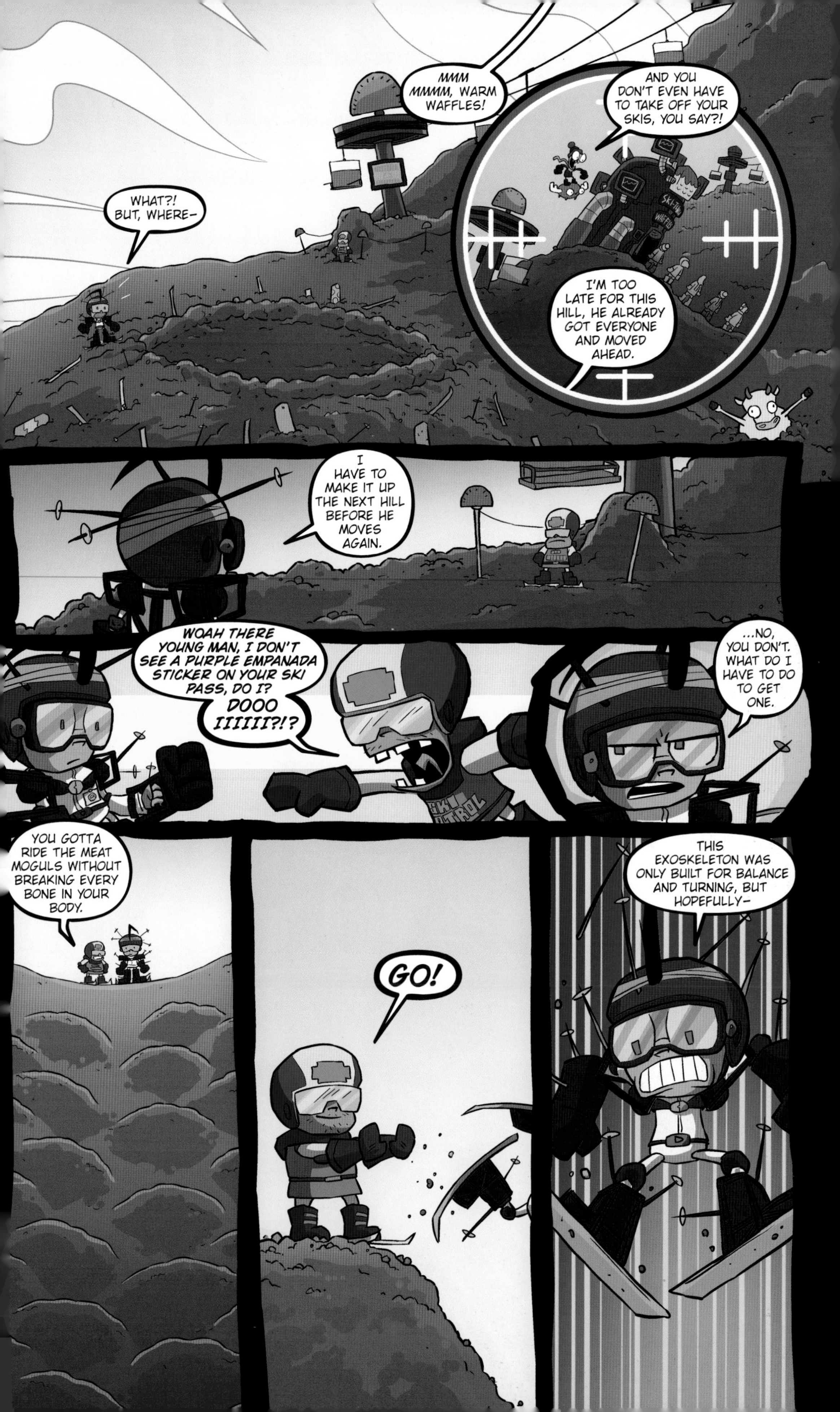
MMM MMMM, WARM WAFFLES!
AND YOU DON'T EVEN HAVE TO TAKE OFF YOUR SKIS, YOU SAY?!
WHAT?! BUT, WHERE-
I'M TOO LATE FOR THIS HILL, HE ALREADY GOT EVERYONE AND MOVED AHEAD.
I HAVE TO MAKE IT UP THE NEXT HILL BEFORE HE MOVES AGAIN.
WOAH THERE YOUNG MAN, I DON'T SEE A PURPLE EMPANADA STICKER ON YOUR SKI PASS, DO I?
DOOO IIIIII?!?
...NO, YOU DON'T. WHAT DO I HAVE TO DO TO GET ONE.
YOU GOTTA RIDE THE MEAT MOGULS WITHOUT BREAKING EVERY BONE IN YOUR BODY.
GO!
THIS EXOSKELETON WAS ONLY BUILT FOR BALANCE AND TURNING, BUT HOPEFULLY-

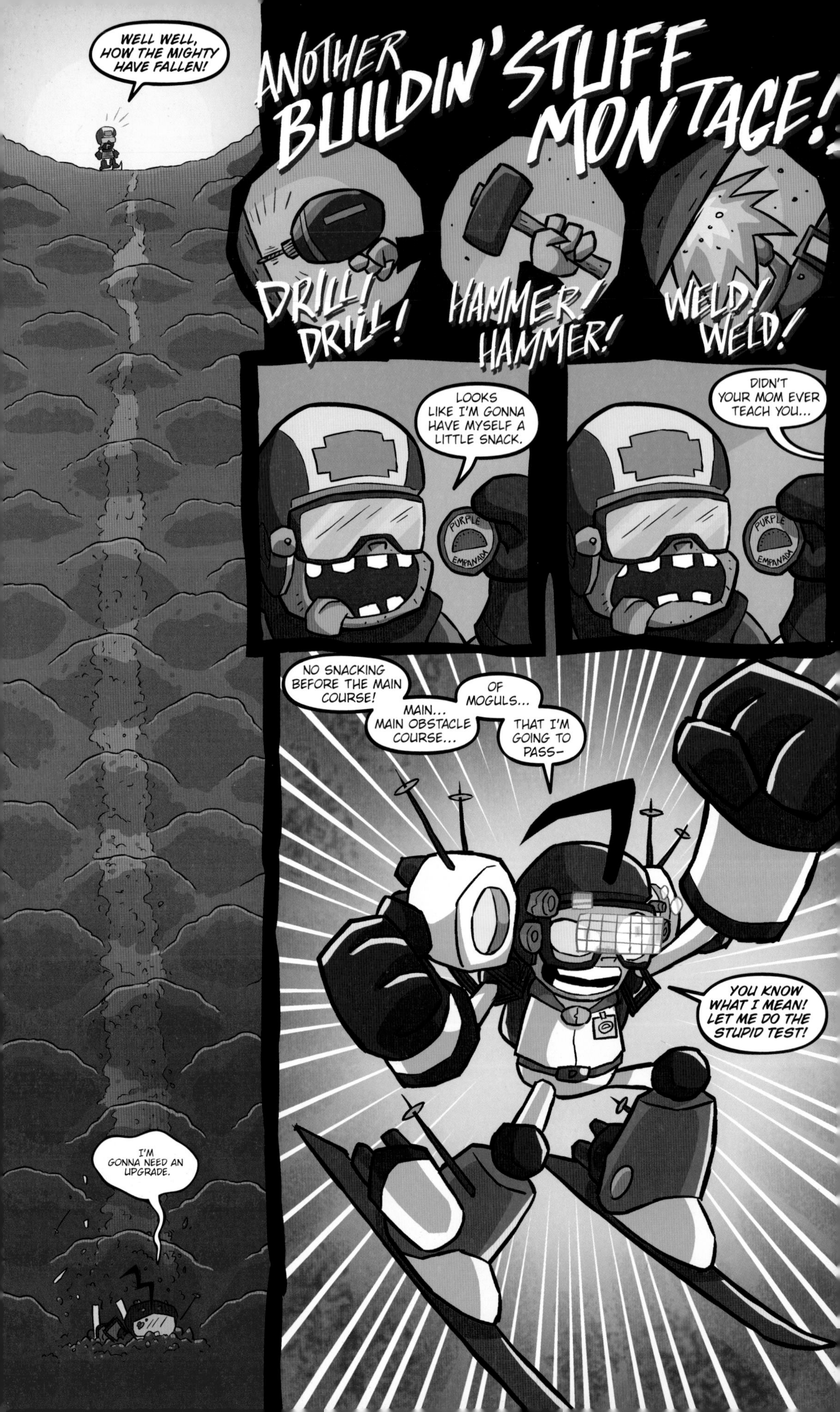
WELL WELL, HOW THE MIGHTY HAVE FALLEN!
I'M GONNA NEED AN UPGRADE.
ANOTHER BUILDIN' STUFF MONTAGE!
DRILL! DRILL!
HAMMER! HAMMER!
WELD! WELD!
LOOKS LIKE I'M GONNA HAVE MYSELF A LITTLE SNACK.
PURPLE EMPANADA
DIDN'T YOUR MOM EVER TEACH YOU...
PURPLE EMPANADA
NO SNACKING BEFORE THE MAIN COURSE!
MAIN... MAIN OBSTACLE COURSE...
OF MOGULS...
THAT I'M GOING TO PASS-
YOU KNOW WHAT I MEAN! LET ME DO THE STUPID TEST!

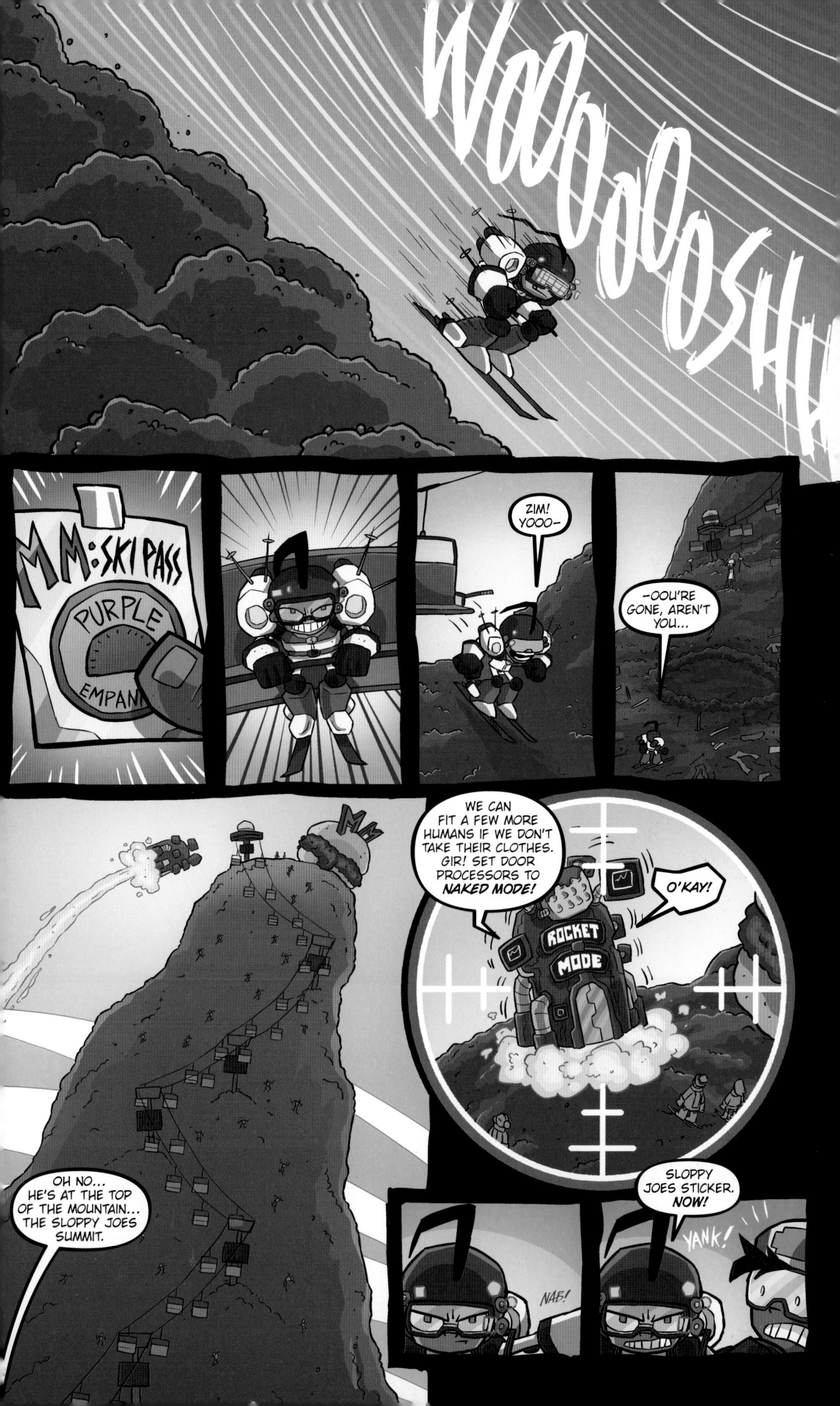
WOOOOOOOSHH
MM: SKI PASS
PURPLE
EMPANI
ZIM! YOOO-
-OOU'RE GONE, AREN'T YOU...
WE CAN FIT A FEW MORE HUMANS IF WE DON'T TAKE THEIR CLOTHES. GIR! SET DOOR PROCESSORS TO **NAKED MODE!**
O'KAY!
ROCKET MODE
OH NO... HE'S AT THE TOP OF THE MOUNTAIN... THE SLOPPY JOES SUMMIT.
NAB!
SLOPPY JOES STICKER. **NOW!**
YANK!

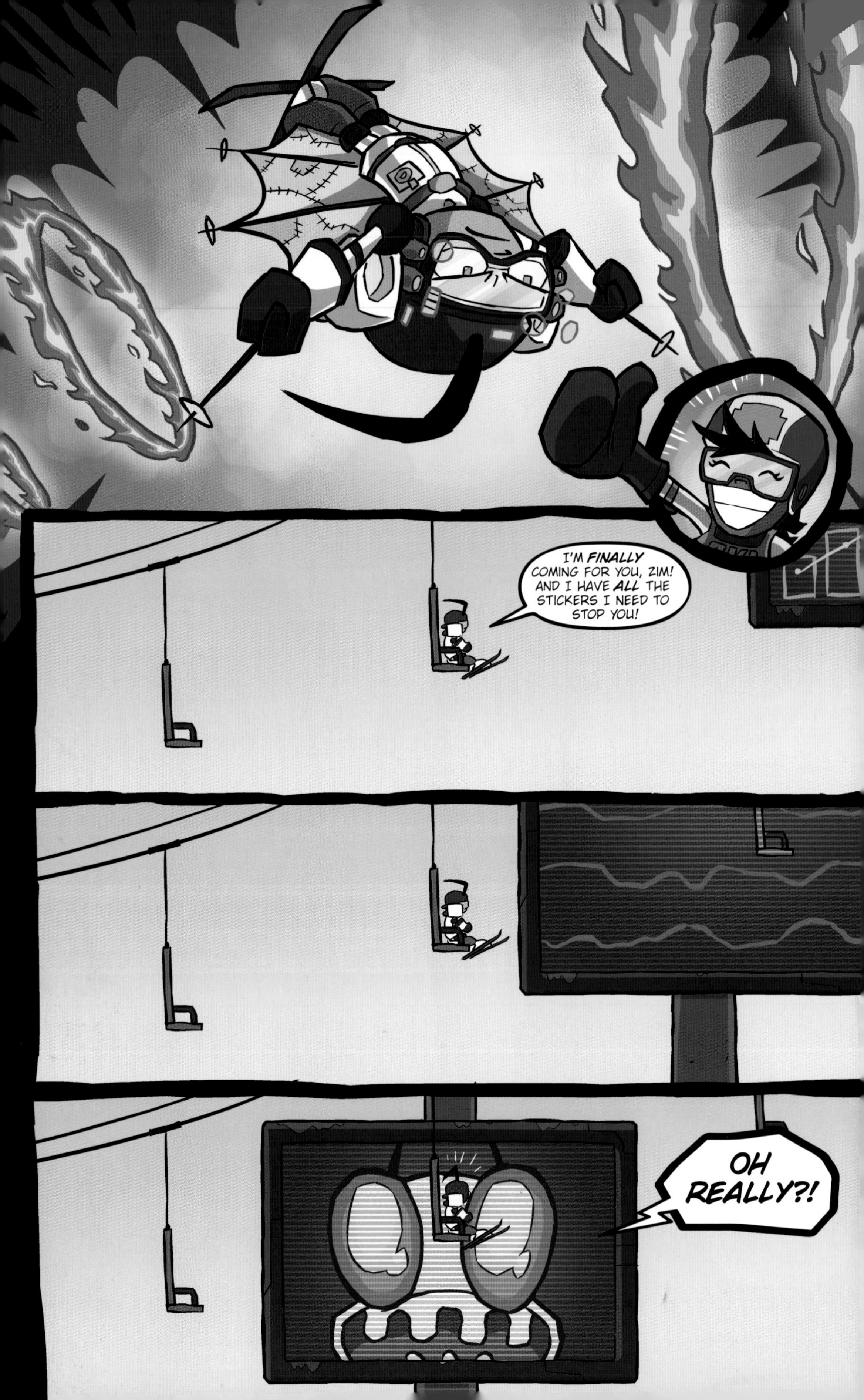
I'M FINALLY COMING FOR YOU, ZIM! AND I HAVE ALL THE STICKERS I NEED TO STOP YOU!
OH REALLY?!

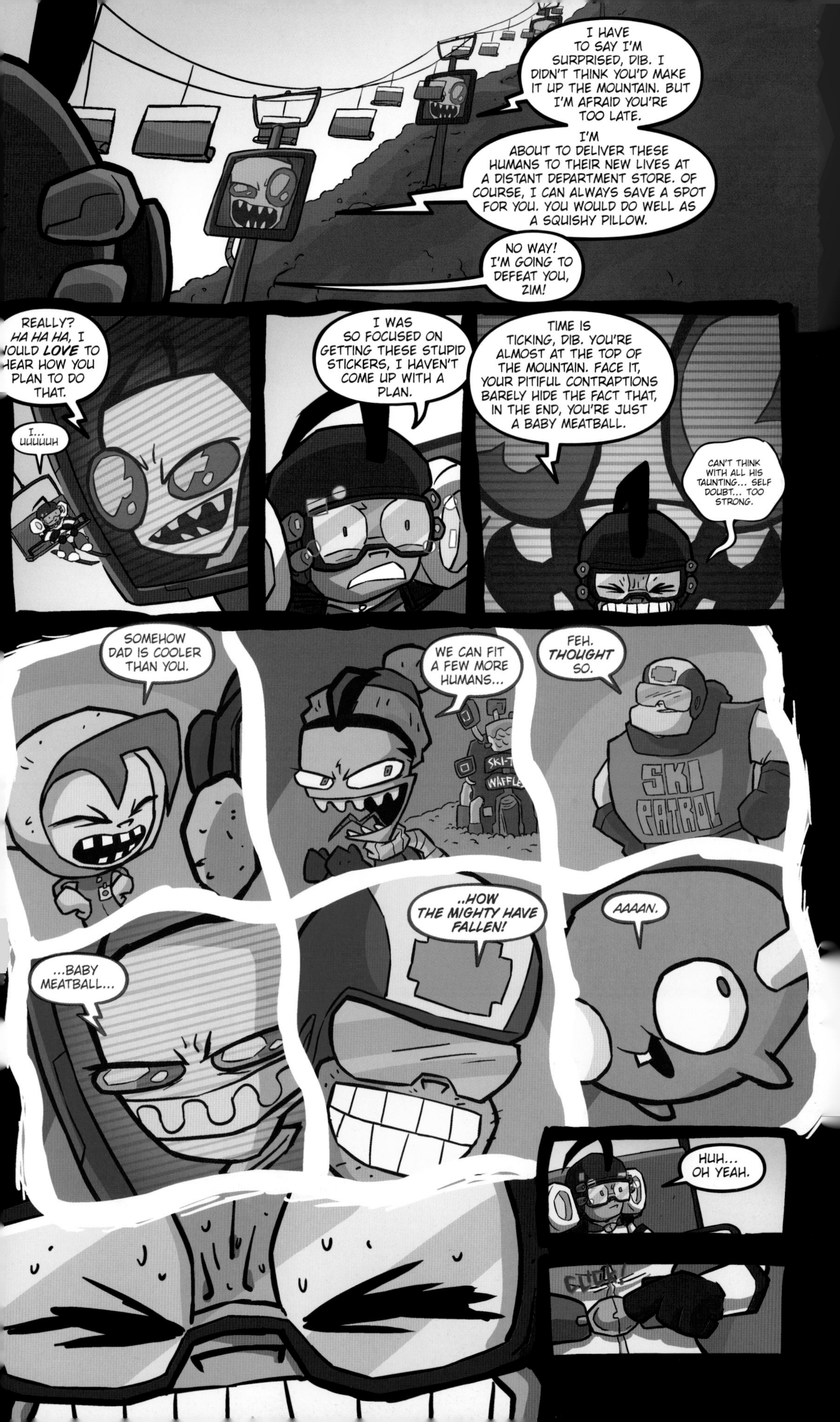
I HAVE TO SAY I'M SURPRISED, DIB. I DIDN'T THINK YOU'D MAKE IT UP THE MOUNTAIN. BUT I'M AFRAID YOU'RE TOO LATE.
I'M ABOUT TO DELIVER THESE HUMANS TO THEIR NEW LIVES AT A DISTANT DEPARTMENT STORE. OF COURSE, I CAN ALWAYS SAVE A SPOT FOR YOU. YOU WOULD DO WELL AS A SQUISHY PILLOW.
NO WAY! I'M GOING TO DEFEAT YOU, ZIM!
REALLY? *HA HA HA*, I WOULD ***LOVE*** TO HEAR HOW YOU PLAN TO DO THAT.
I... UUUUUH
I WAS SO FOCUSED ON GETTING THESE STUPID STICKERS, I HAVEN'T COME UP WITH A PLAN.
TIME IS TICKING, DIB. YOU'RE ALMOST AT THE TOP OF THE MOUNTAIN. FACE IT, YOUR PITIFUL CONTRAPTIONS BARELY HIDE THE FACT THAT, IN THE END, YOU'RE JUST A BABY MEATBALL.
CAN'T THINK WITH ALL HIS TAUNTING... SELF DOUBT... TOO STRONG.
SOMEHOW DAD IS COOLER THAN YOU.
WE CAN FIT A FEW MORE HUMANS...
SKI-T
WAFFLE
FEH. ***THOUGHT*** SO.
SKI PATROL
...BABY MEATBALL...
..HOW THE MIGHTY HAVE FALLEN!
AAAAN.
HUH... OH YEAH.
CLICK!

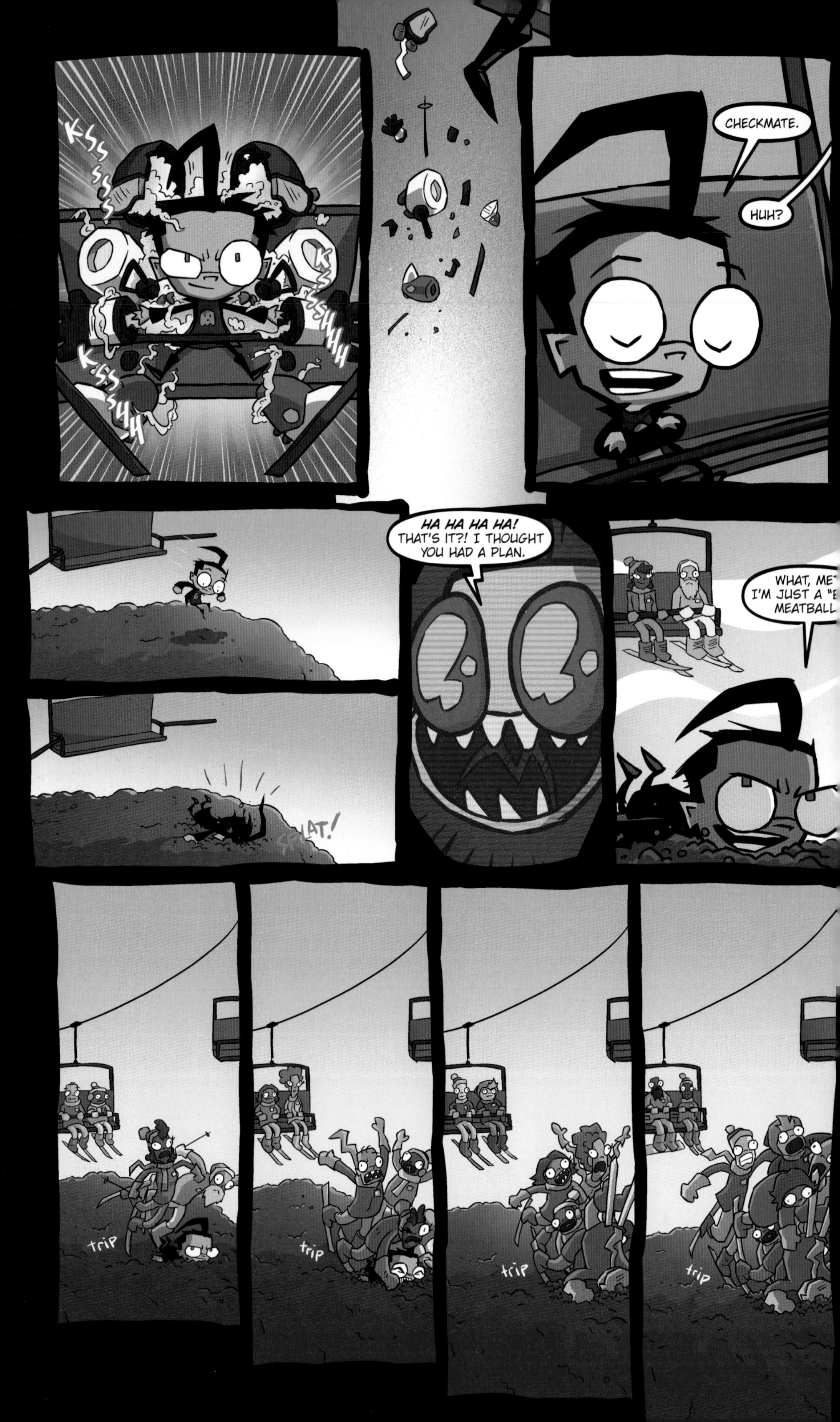
CHECKMATE.
HUH?
HA HA HA HA! THAT'S IT?! I THOUGHT YOU HAD A PLAN.
SPLAT!
WHAT, ME
I'M JUST A "
MEATBALL
trip
trip
trip
trip

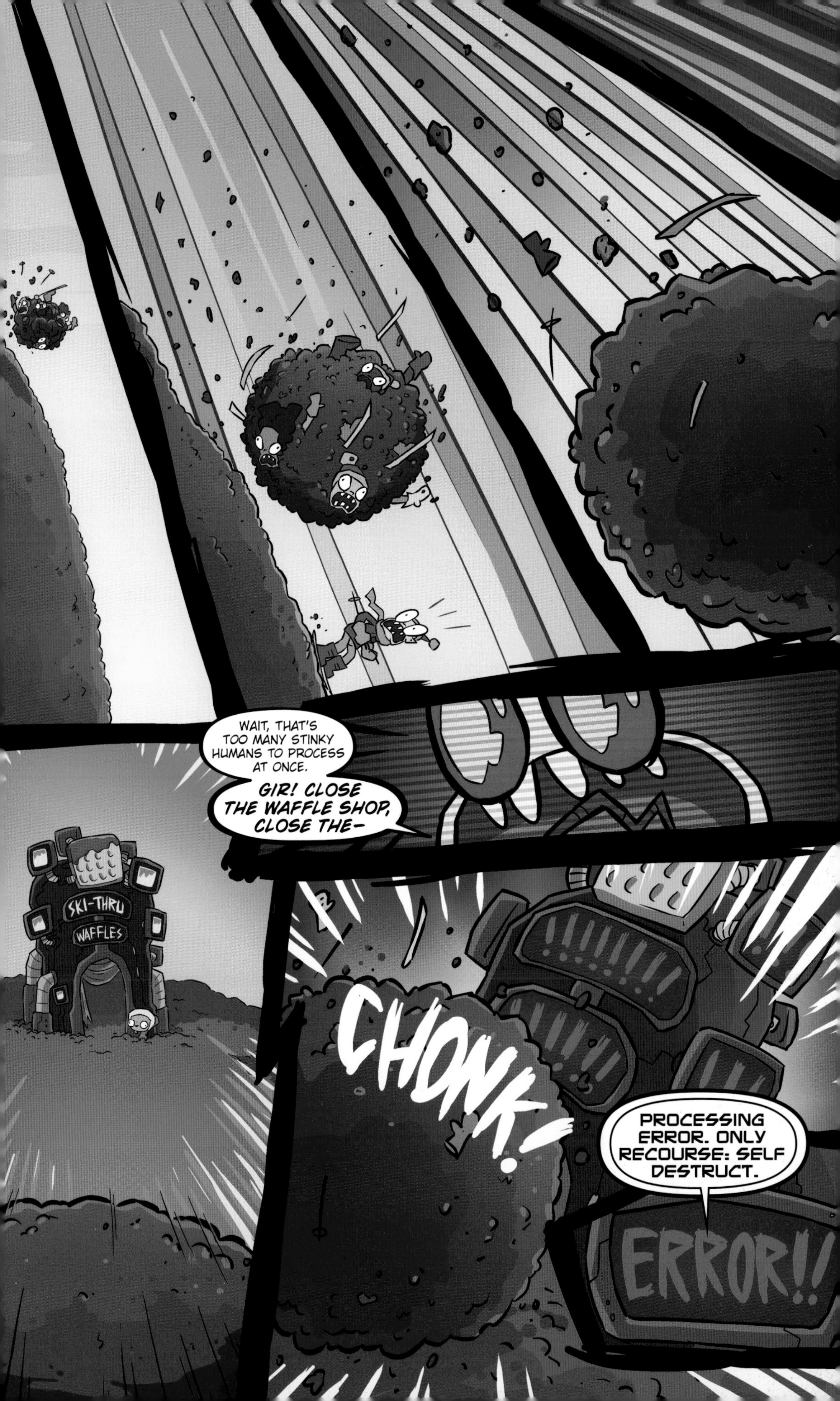

WAIT, THAT'S TOO MANY STINKY HUMANS TO PROCESS AT ONCE.
GIR! CLOSE THE WAFFLE SHOP, CLOSE THE-
SKI-THRU
WAFFLES
CHONK!
PROCESSING ERROR. ONLY RECOURSE: SELF DESTRUCT.
ERROR!!

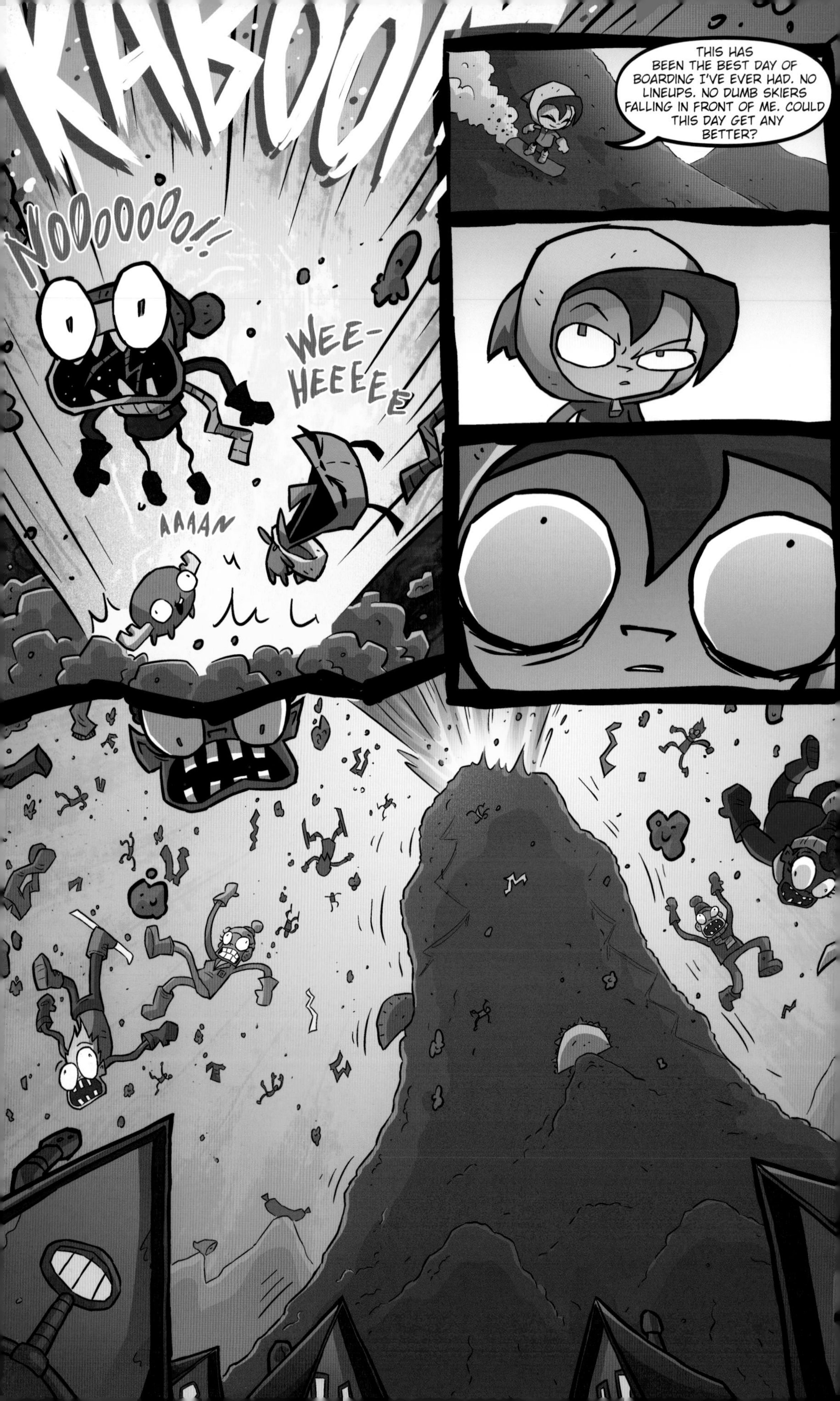
KABOOM
THIS HAS BEEN THE BEST DAY OF BOARDING I'VE EVER HAD. NO LINEUPS. NO DUMB SKIERS FALLING IN FRONT OF ME. COULD THIS DAY GET ANY BETTER?
NOOOOOOOO!!!
WEE-HEEEEEE
AAAAN

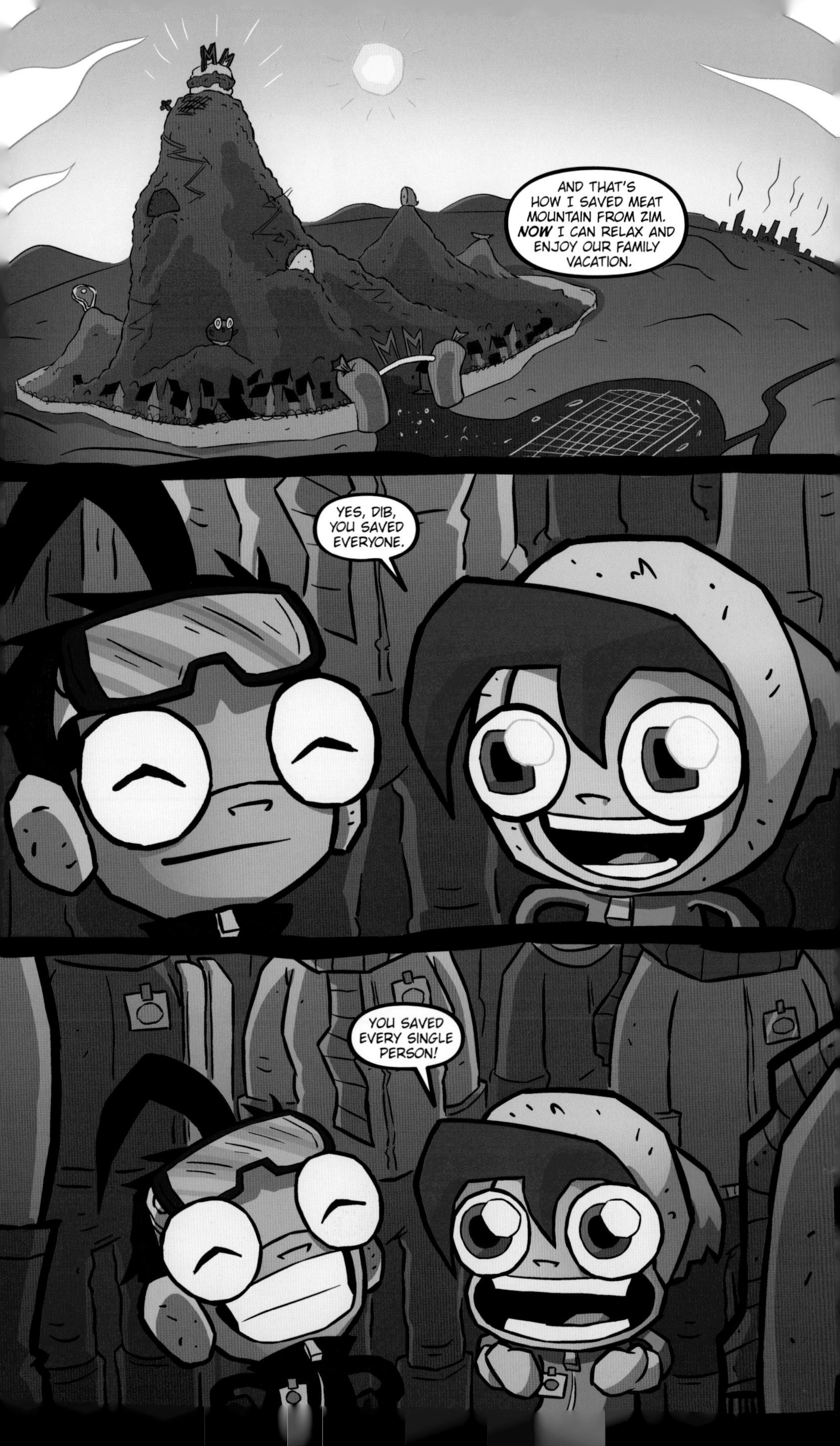

AND THAT'S HOW I SAVED MEAT MOUNTAIN FROM ZIM. **NOW** I CAN RELAX AND ENJOY OUR FAMILY VACATION.
YES, DIB, YOU SAVED EVERYONE.
YOU SAVED EVERY SINGLE PERSON!

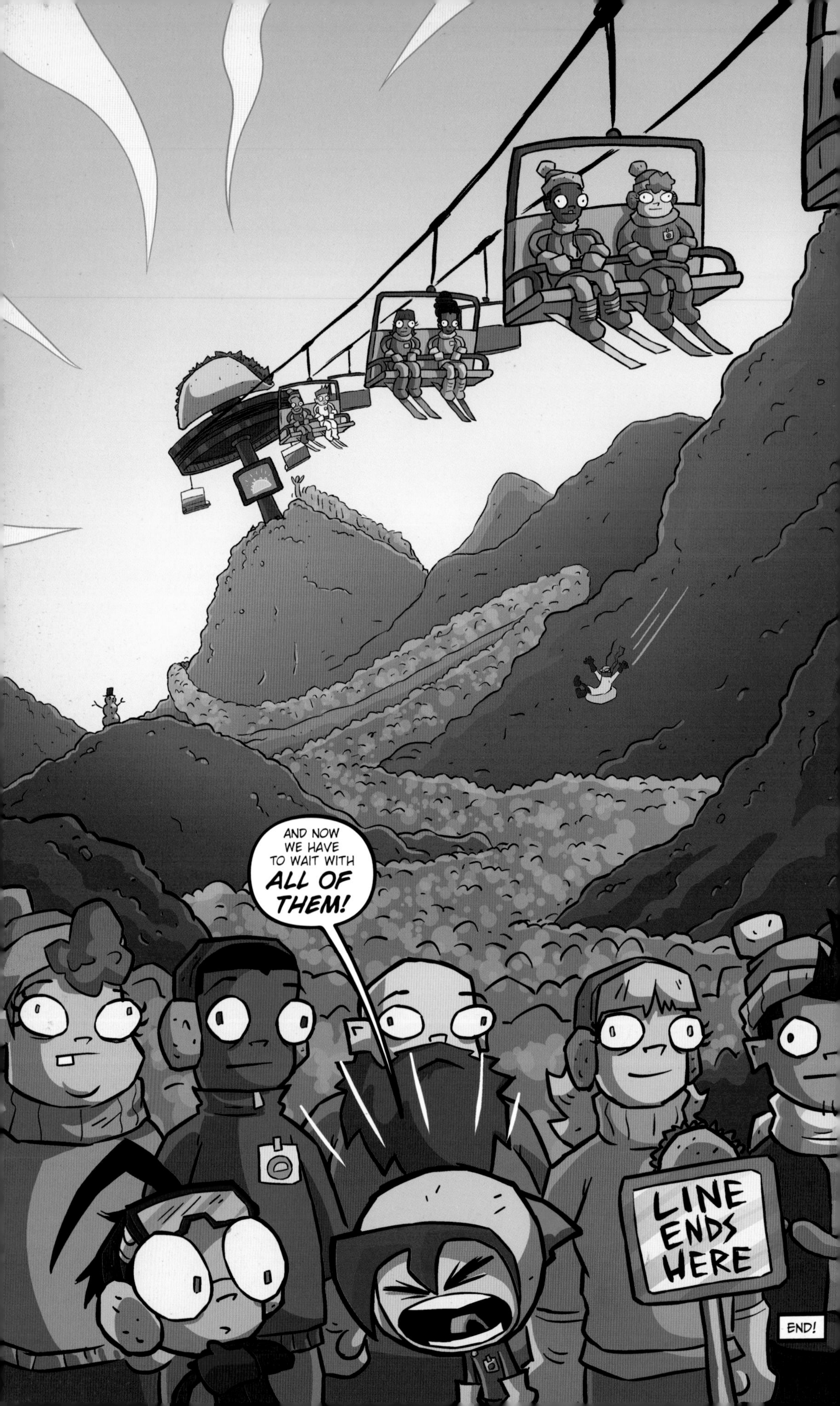
AND NOW WE HAVE TO WAIT WITH ALL OF THEM!
LINE ENDS HERE
END!

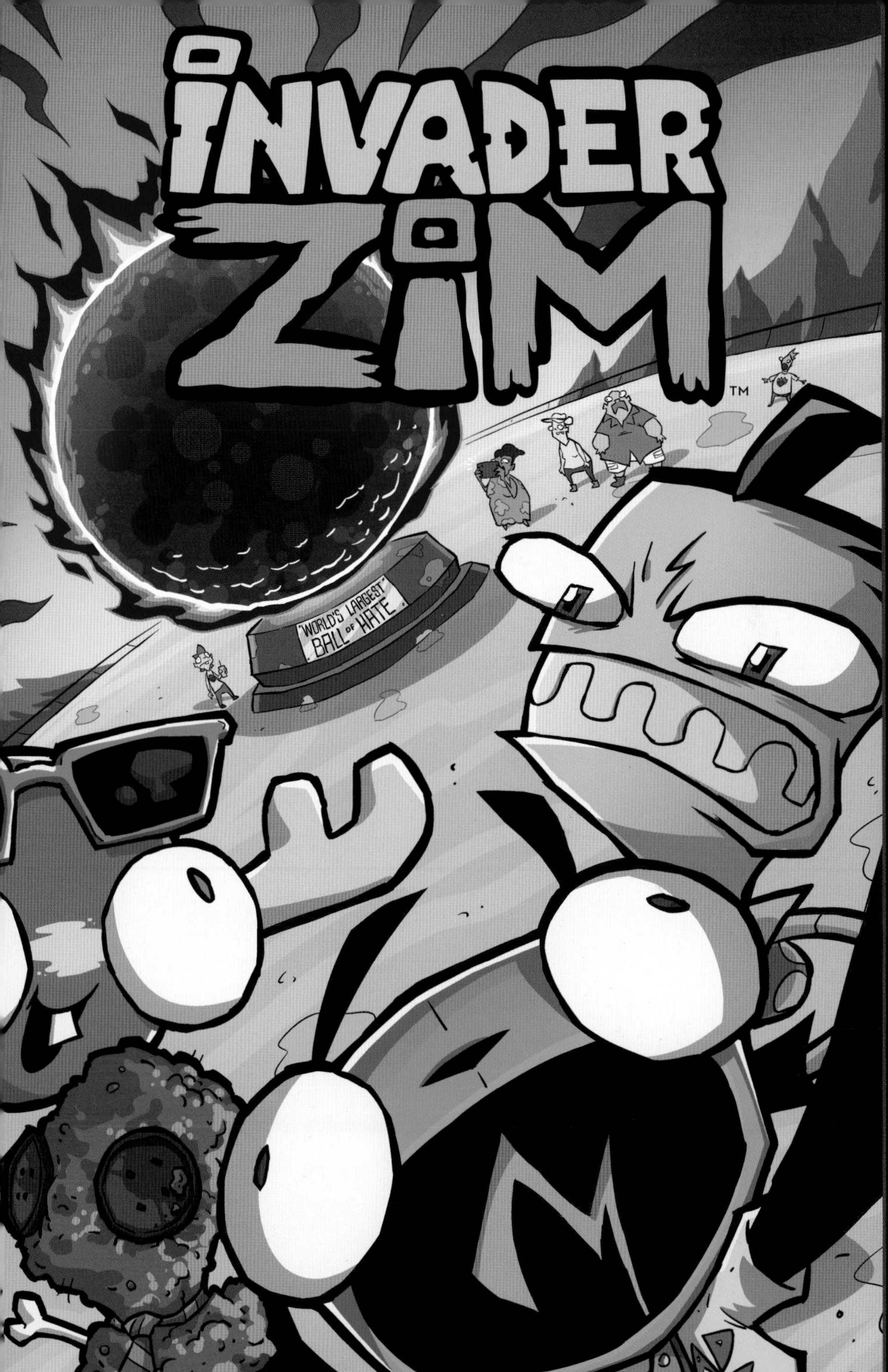
INVADER ZIM™
"WORLD'S LARGEST" BALL OF HATE

CHAPTER: 4

illustration by WARREN WUCINICH with FRED C. STRESING

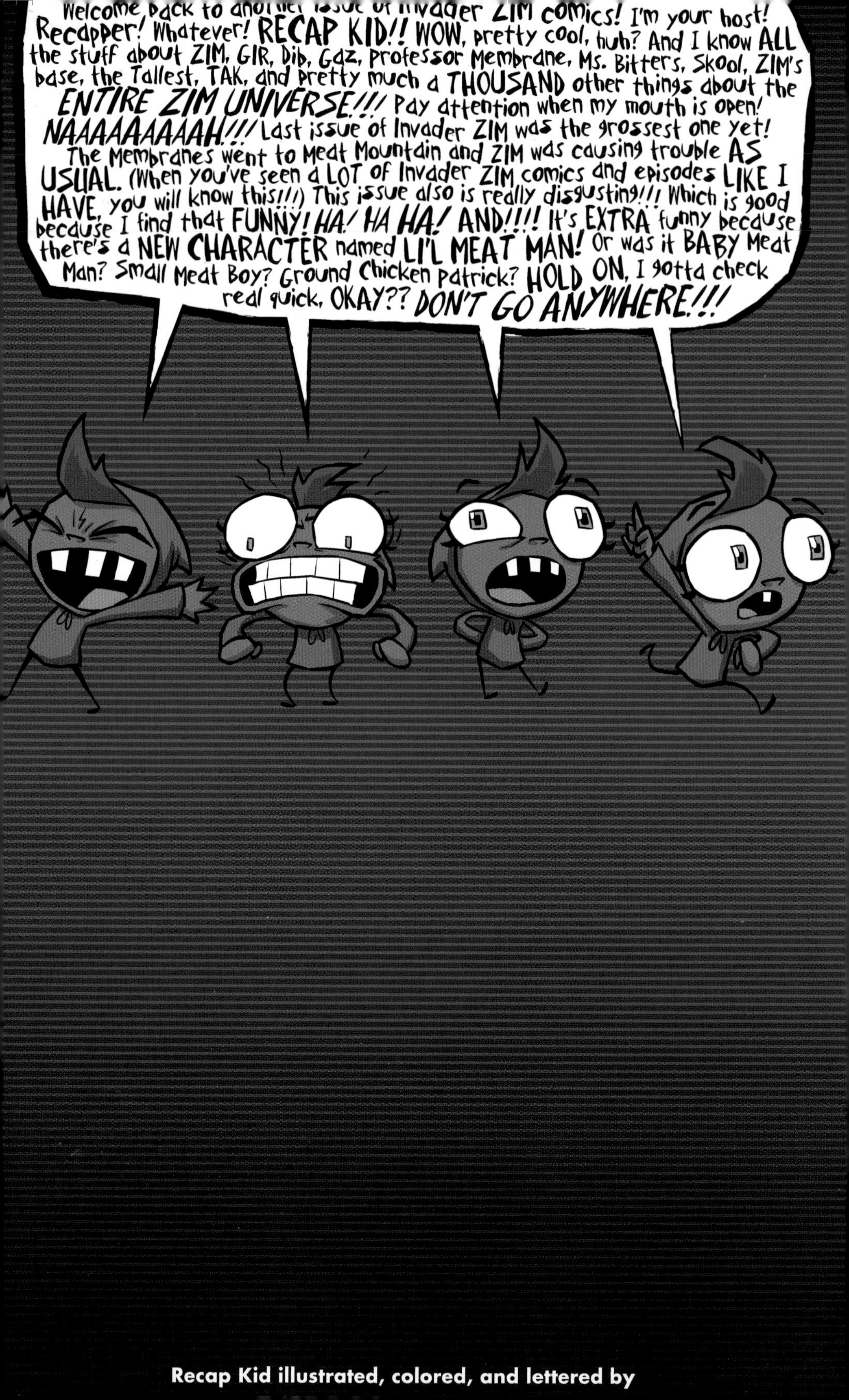
Welcome back to another issue of Invader ZIM comics! I'm your host! Recapper! Whatever! RECAP KID!! WOW, pretty cool, huh? And I know ALL the stuff about ZIM, GIR, Dib, Gaz, Professor Membrane, Ms. Bitters, Skool, ZIM's base, the Tallest, TAK, and pretty much a THOUSAND other things about the ENTIRE ZIM UNIVERSE!!! Pay attention when my mouth is open! NAAAAAAAAAH!!! Last issue of Invader ZIM was the grossest one yet! The Membranes went to Meat Mountain and ZIM was causing trouble AS USUAL. (When you've seen a LOT of Invader ZIM comics and episodes LIKE I HAVE, you will know this!!!) This issue also is really disgusting!!! Which is good because I find that FUNNY! HA! HA HA! AND!!!! It's EXTRA funny because there's a NEW CHARACTER named LI'L MEAT MAN! Or was it BABY Meat Man? Small Meat Boy? Ground Chicken Patrick? HOLD ON, I gotta check real quick, OKAY?? DON'T GO ANYWHERE!!!

Recap Kid illustrated, colored, and lettered by

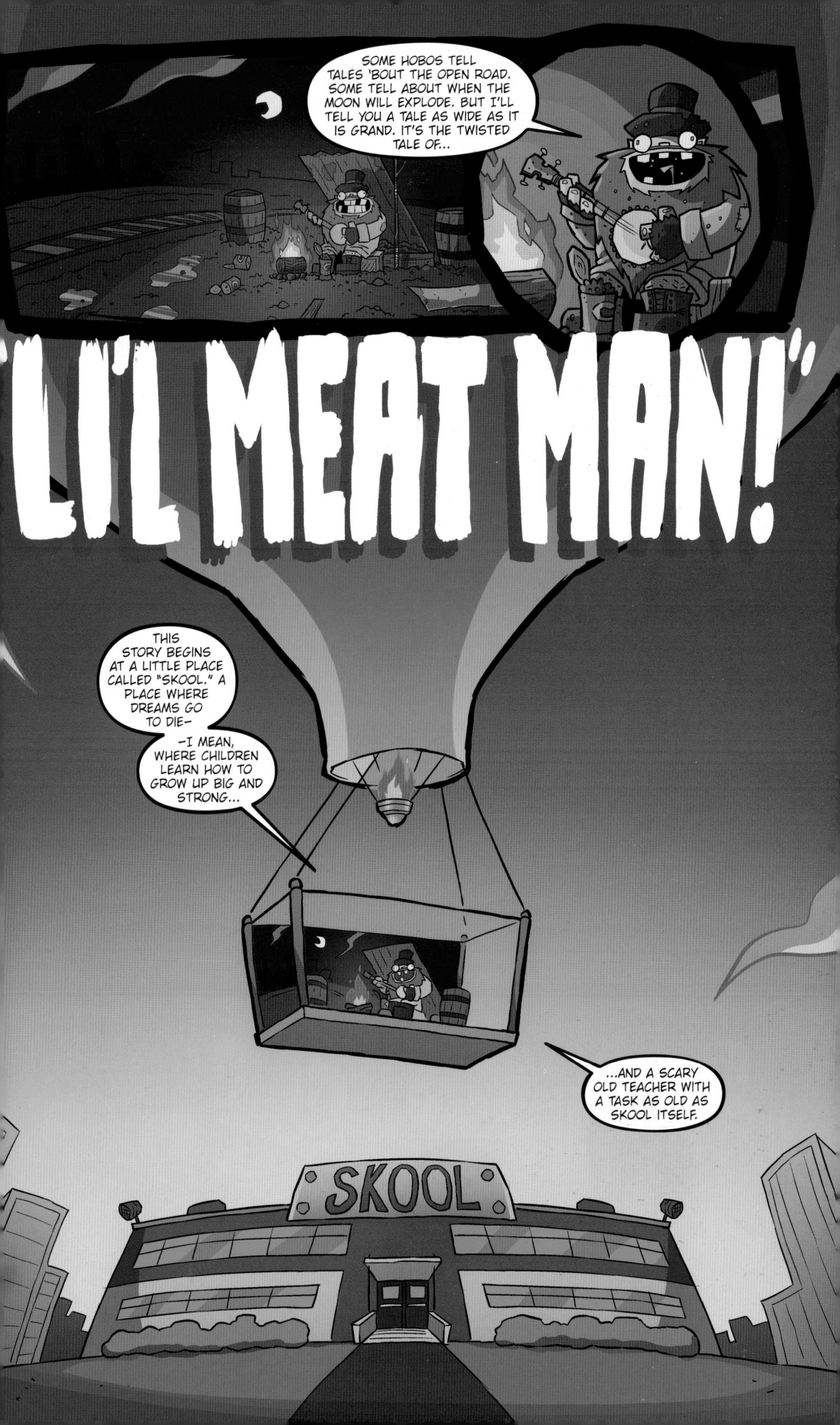
SOME HOBOS TELL TALES 'BOUT THE OPEN ROAD. SOME TELL ABOUT WHEN THE MOON WILL EXPLODE. BUT I'LL TELL YOU A TALE AS WIDE AS IT IS GRAND. IT'S THE TWISTED TALE OF...
"LI'L MEAT MAN!"
THIS STORY BEGINS AT A LITTLE PLACE CALLED "SKOOL." A PLACE WHERE DREAMS GO TO DIE–
–I MEAN, WHERE CHILDREN LEARN HOW TO GROW UP BIG AND STRONG...
...AND A SCARY OLD TEACHER WITH A TASK AS OLD AS SKOOL ITSELF.
SKOOL

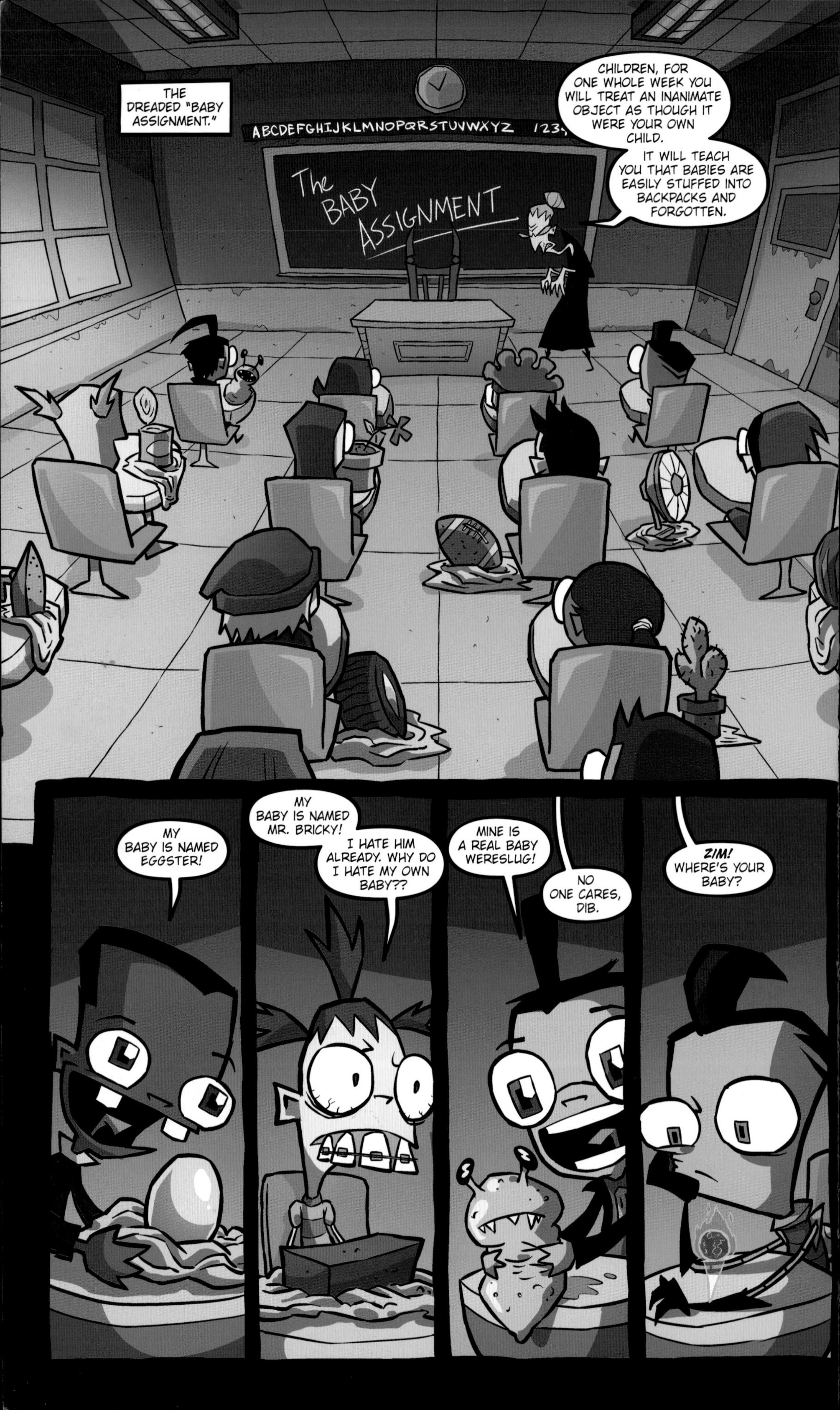
THE DREADED "BABY ASSIGNMENT."
ABCDEFGHIJKLMNOPQRSTUVWXYZ 1234
The BABY ASSIGNMENT
CHILDREN, FOR ONE WHOLE WEEK YOU WILL TREAT AN INANIMATE OBJECT AS THOUGH IT WERE YOUR OWN CHILD.
IT WILL TEACH YOU THAT BABIES ARE EASILY STUFFED INTO BACKPACKS AND FORGOTTEN.
MY BABY IS NAMED EGGSTER!
MY BABY IS NAMED MR. BRICKY!
I HATE HIM ALREADY. WHY DO I HATE MY OWN BABY??
MINE IS A REAL BABY WERESLUG!
NO ONE CARES, DIB.
ZIM! WHERE'S YOUR BABY?

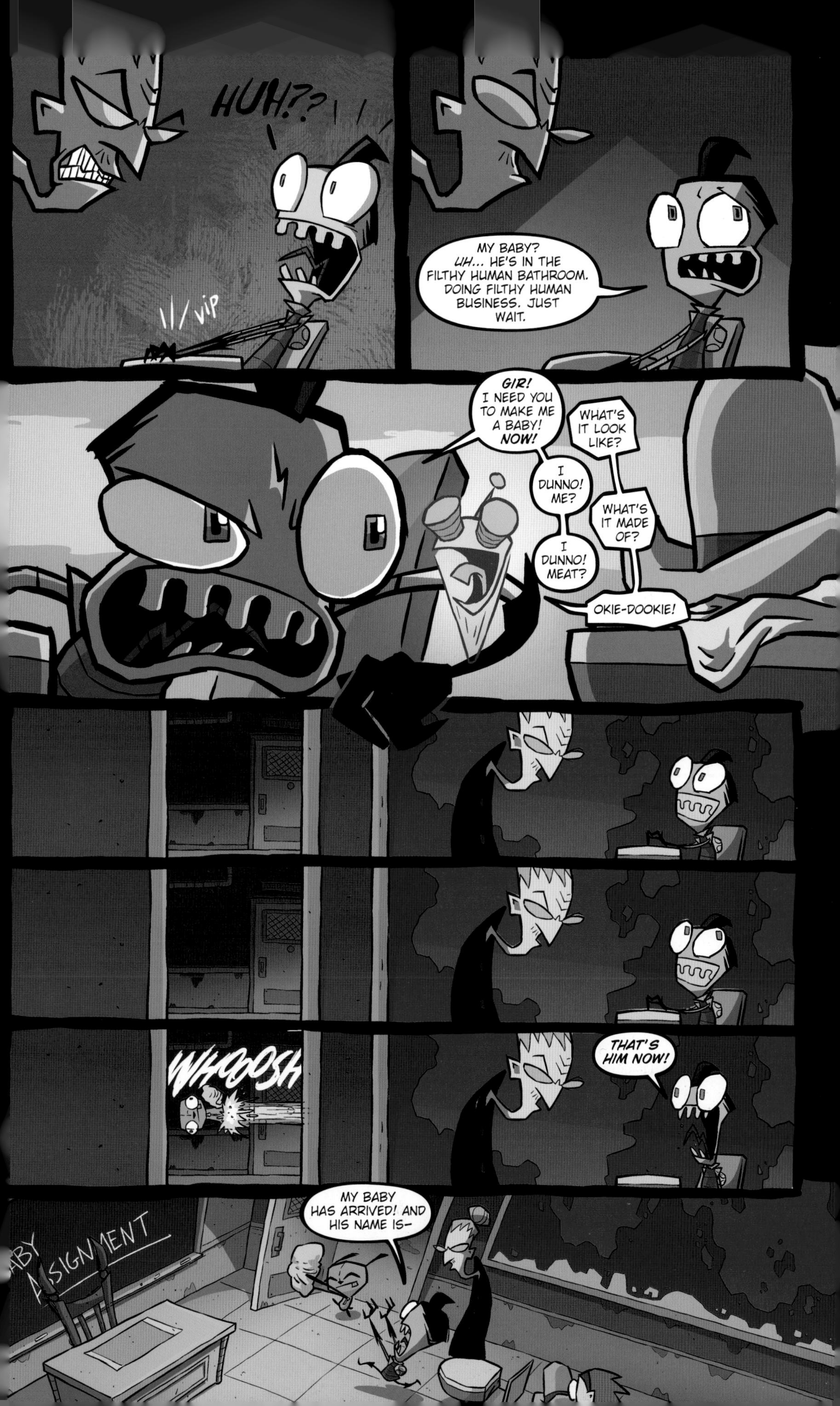
HUH!?
//vip
MY BABY? UH... HE'S IN THE FILTHY HUMAN BATHROOM. DOING FILTHY HUMAN BUSINESS. JUST WAIT.
GIR! I NEED YOU TO MAKE ME A BABY! NOW!
I DUNNO! ME?
WHAT'S IT LOOK LIKE?
WHAT'S IT MADE OF?
I DUNNO! MEAT?
OKIE-DOOKIE!
WHOOOSH
THAT'S HIM NOW!
MY BABY HAS ARRIVED! AND HIS NAME IS–
ASIGNMENT

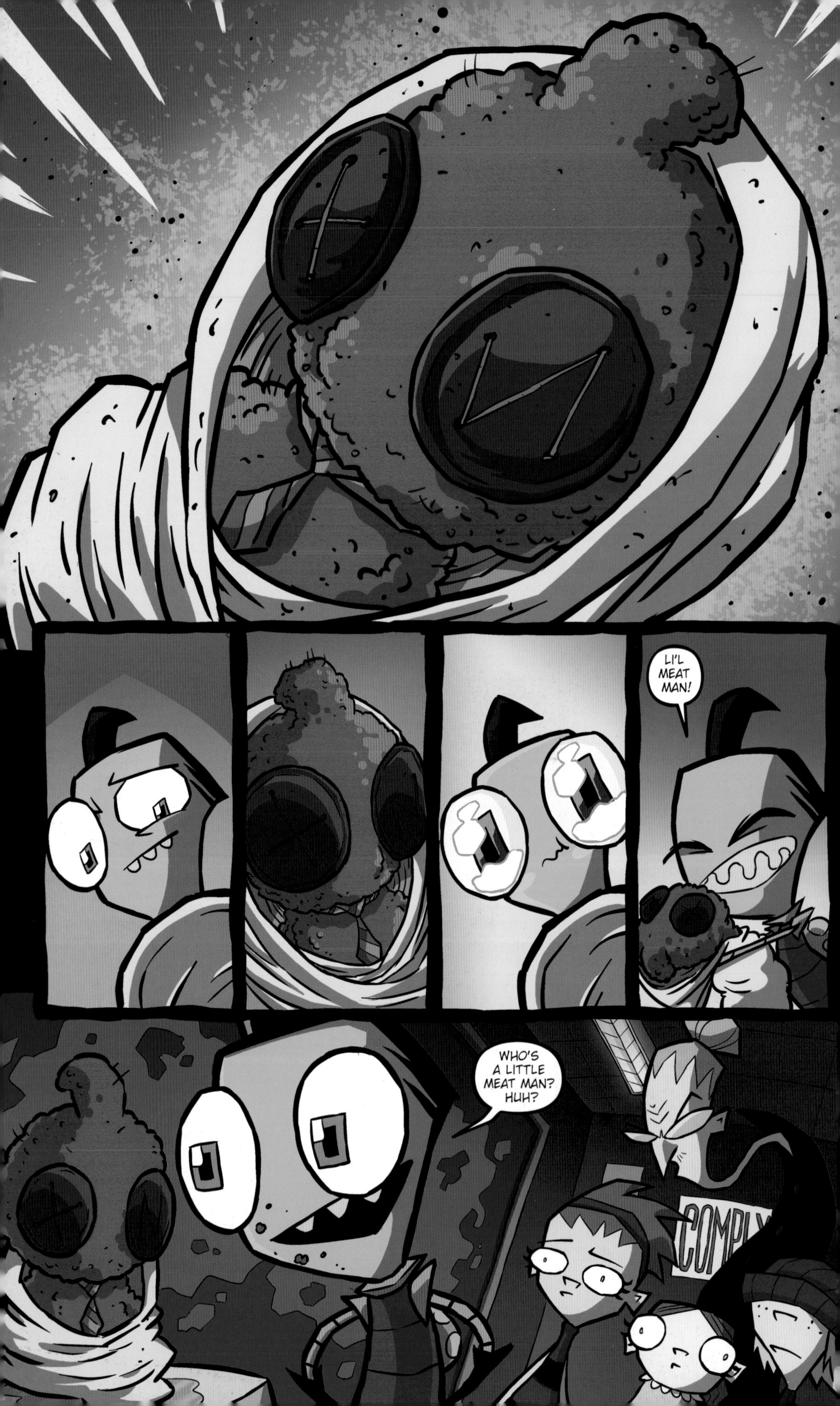
LI'L
MEAT
MAN!
WHO'S
A LITTLE
MEAT MAN?
HUH?
COMPLY

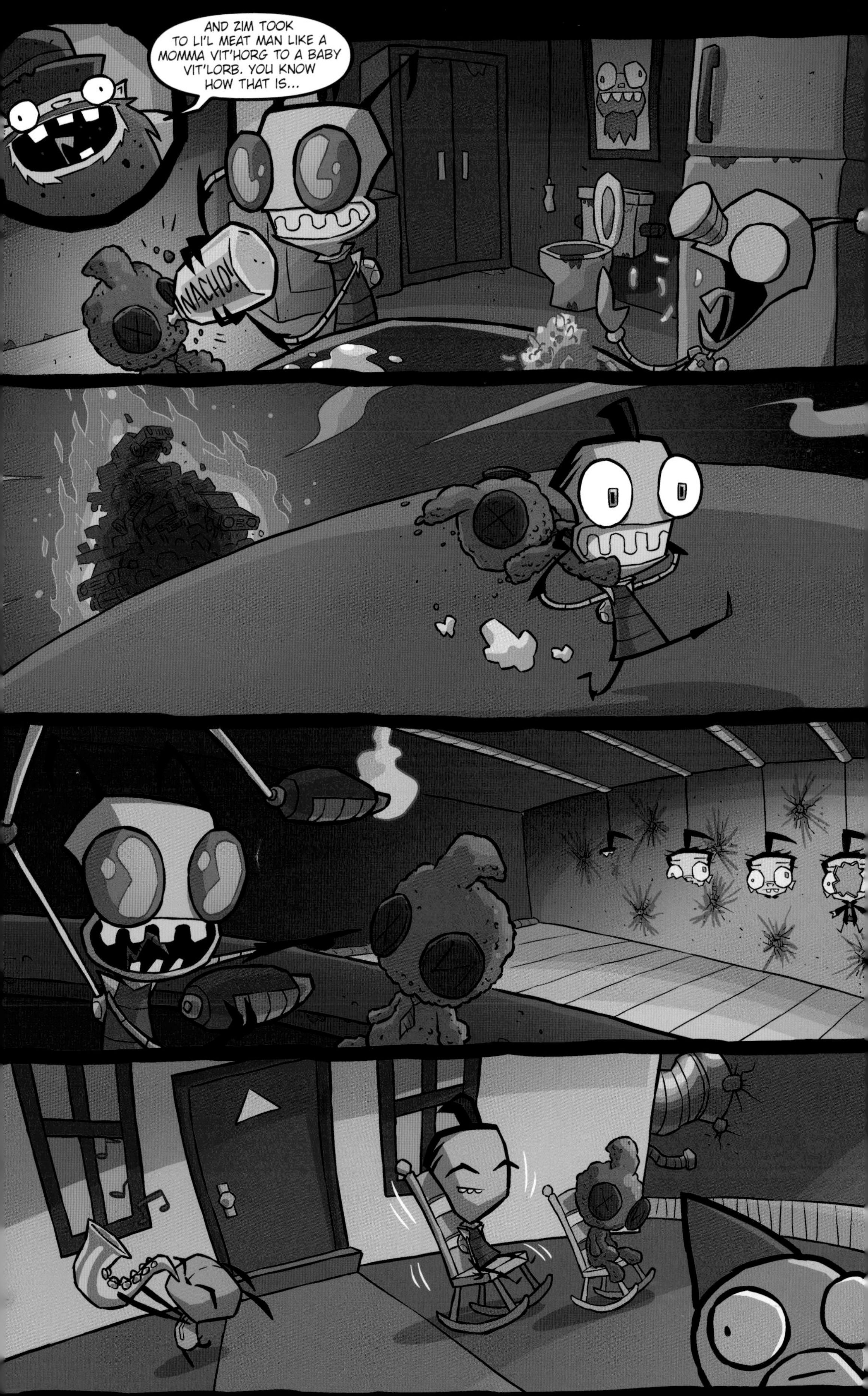
AND ZIM TOOK TO LI'L MEAT MAN LIKE A MOMMA VIT'HORG TO A BABY VIT'LORB. YOU KNOW HOW THAT IS...
NACHO!

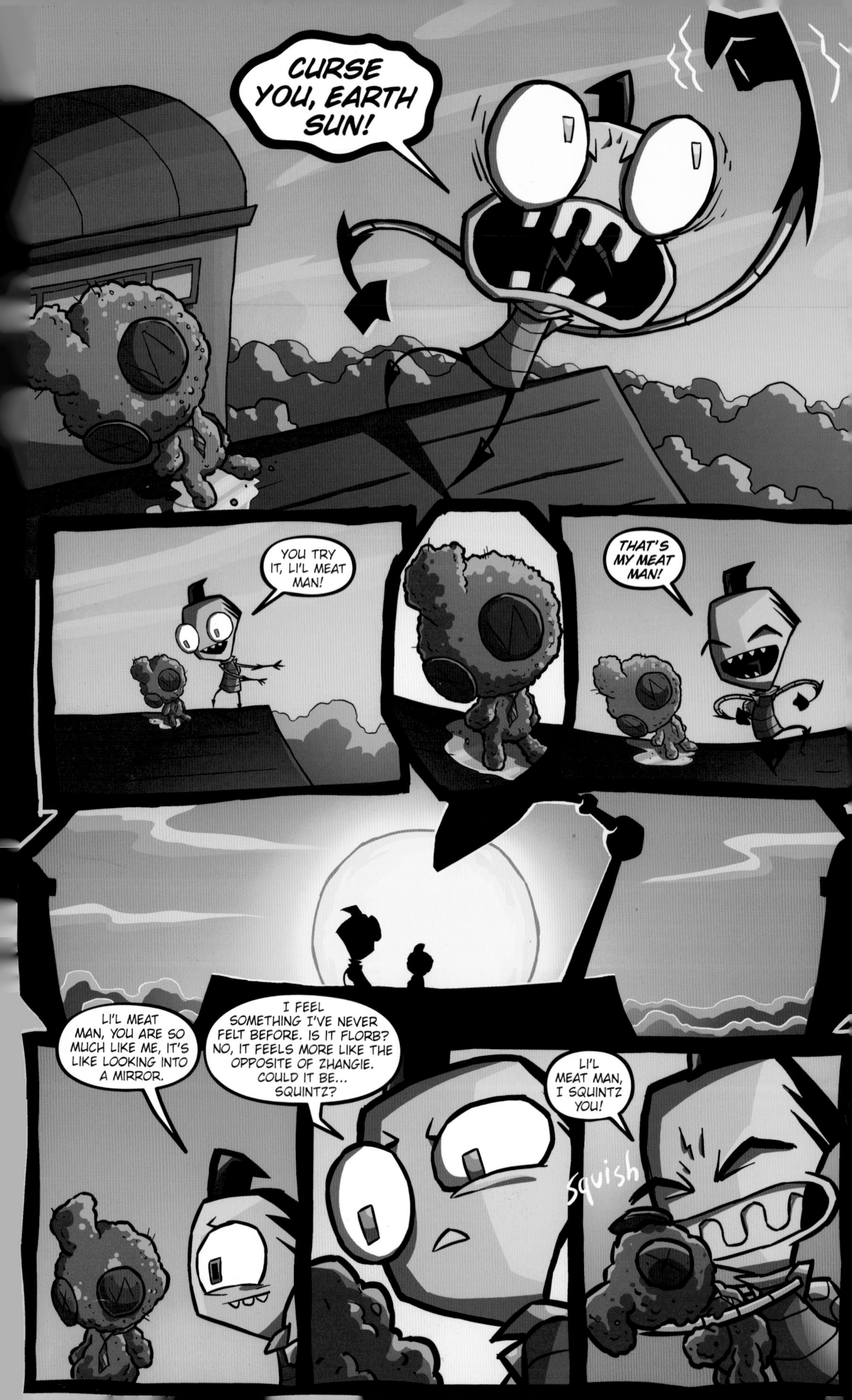
CURSE YOU, EARTH SUN!
YOU TRY IT, LI'L MEAT MAN!
THAT'S MY MEAT MAN!
LI'L MEAT MAN, YOU ARE SO MUCH LIKE ME, IT'S LIKE LOOKING INTO A MIRROR.
I FEEL SOMETHING I'VE NEVER FELT BEFORE. IS IT FLORB? NO, IT FEELS MORE LIKE THE OPPOSITE OF ZHANGIE. COULD IT BE... SQUINTZ?
LI'L MEAT MAN, I SQUINTZ YOU!
squish

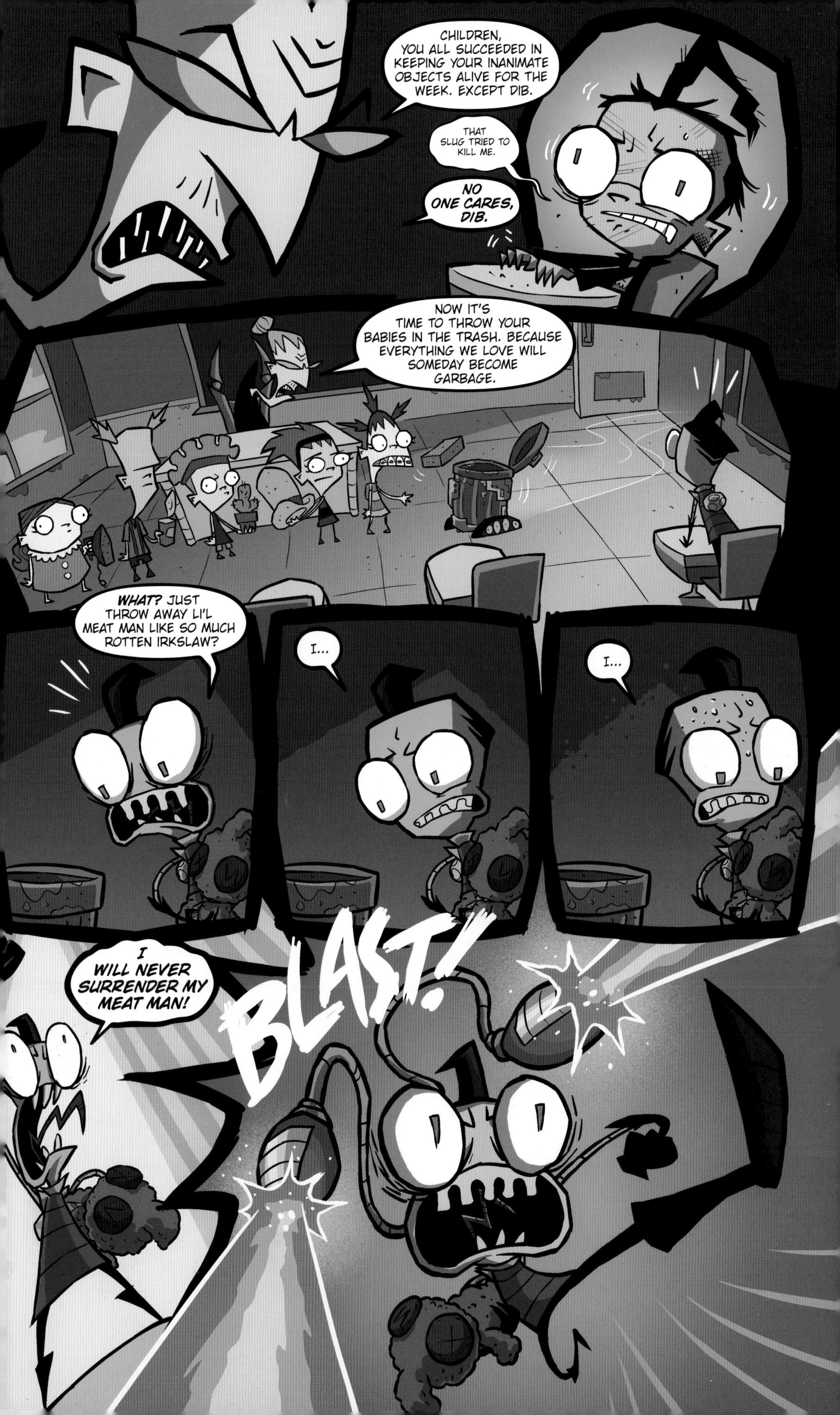
CHILDREN, YOU ALL SUCCEEDED IN KEEPING YOUR INANIMATE OBJECTS ALIVE FOR THE WEEK. EXCEPT DIB.
THAT SLUG TRIED TO KILL ME.
NO ONE CARES, DIB.
NOW IT'S TIME TO THROW YOUR BABIES IN THE TRASH. BECAUSE EVERYTHING WE LOVE WILL SOMEDAY BECOME GARBAGE.
WHAT? JUST THROW AWAY LI'L MEAT MAN LIKE SO MUCH ROTTEN IRKSLAW?
I...
I...
I WILL NEVER SURRENDER MY MEAT MAN!
BLAST!

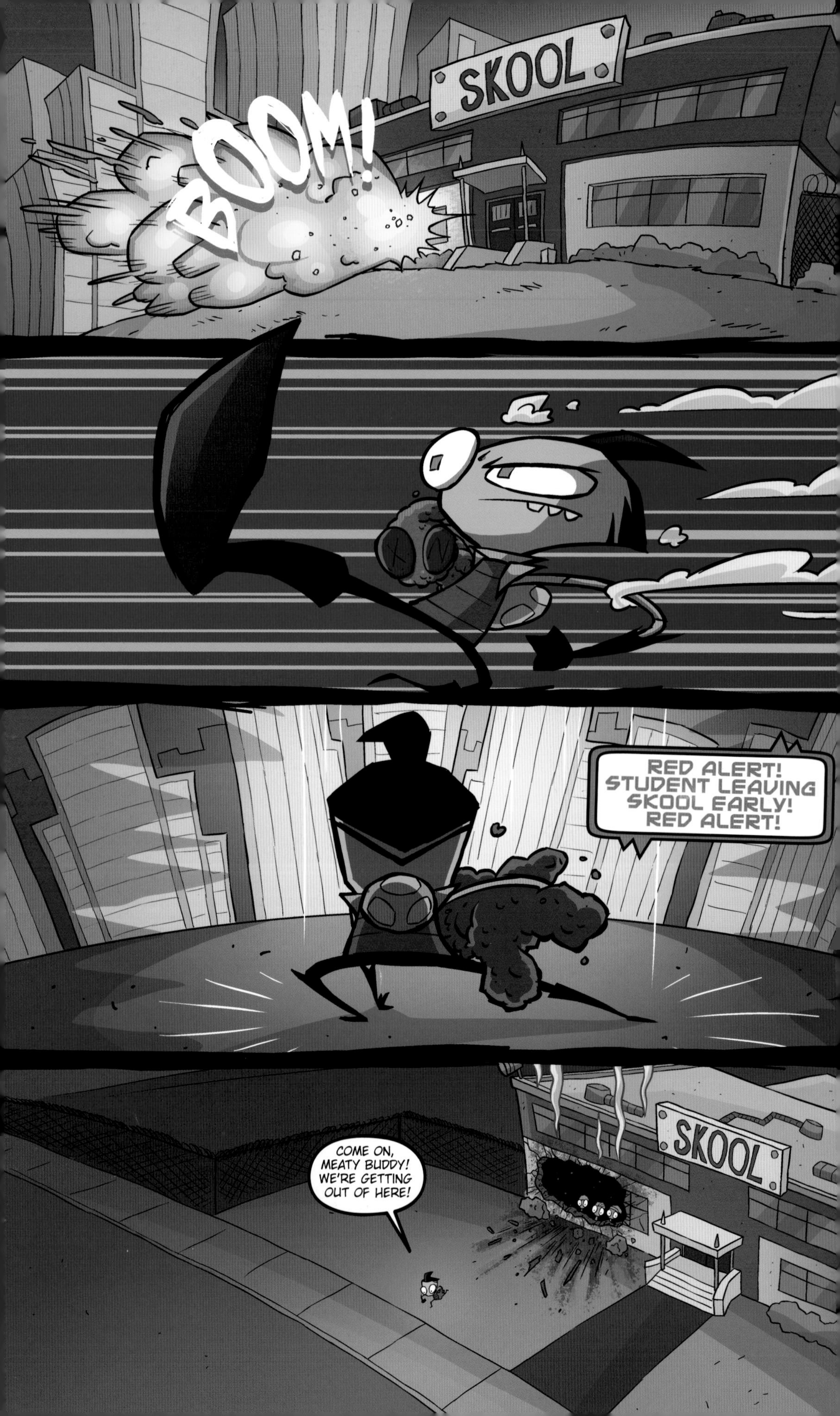
SKOOL
BOOM!
RED ALERT! STUDENT LEAVING SKOOL EARLY! RED ALERT!
SKOOL
COME ON, MEATY BUDDY! WE'RE GETTING OUT OF HERE!

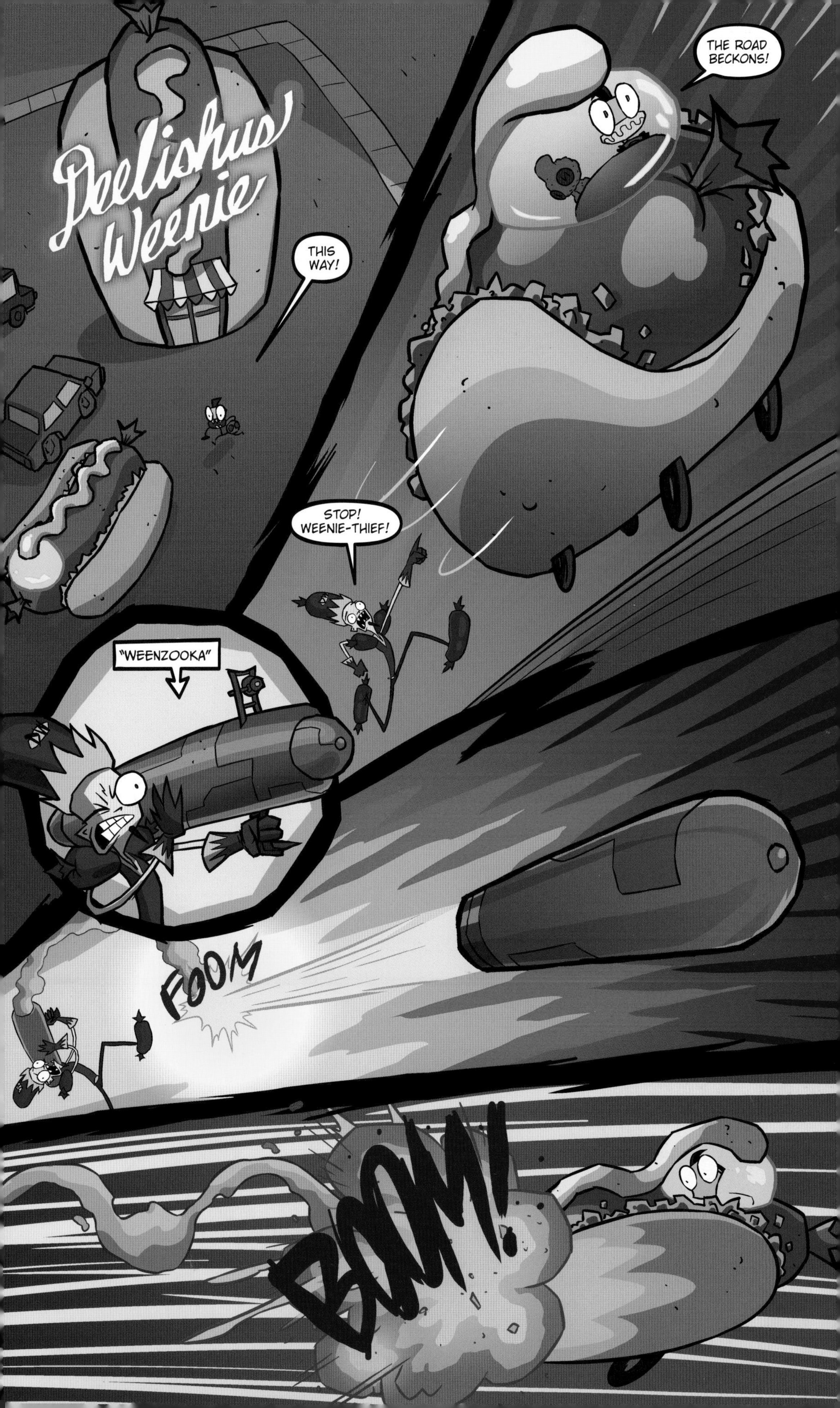
Deelishus Weenie
THIS WAY!
THE ROAD BECKONS!
STOP! WEENIE-THIEF!
"WEENZOOKA"
FOOM
BOOM!

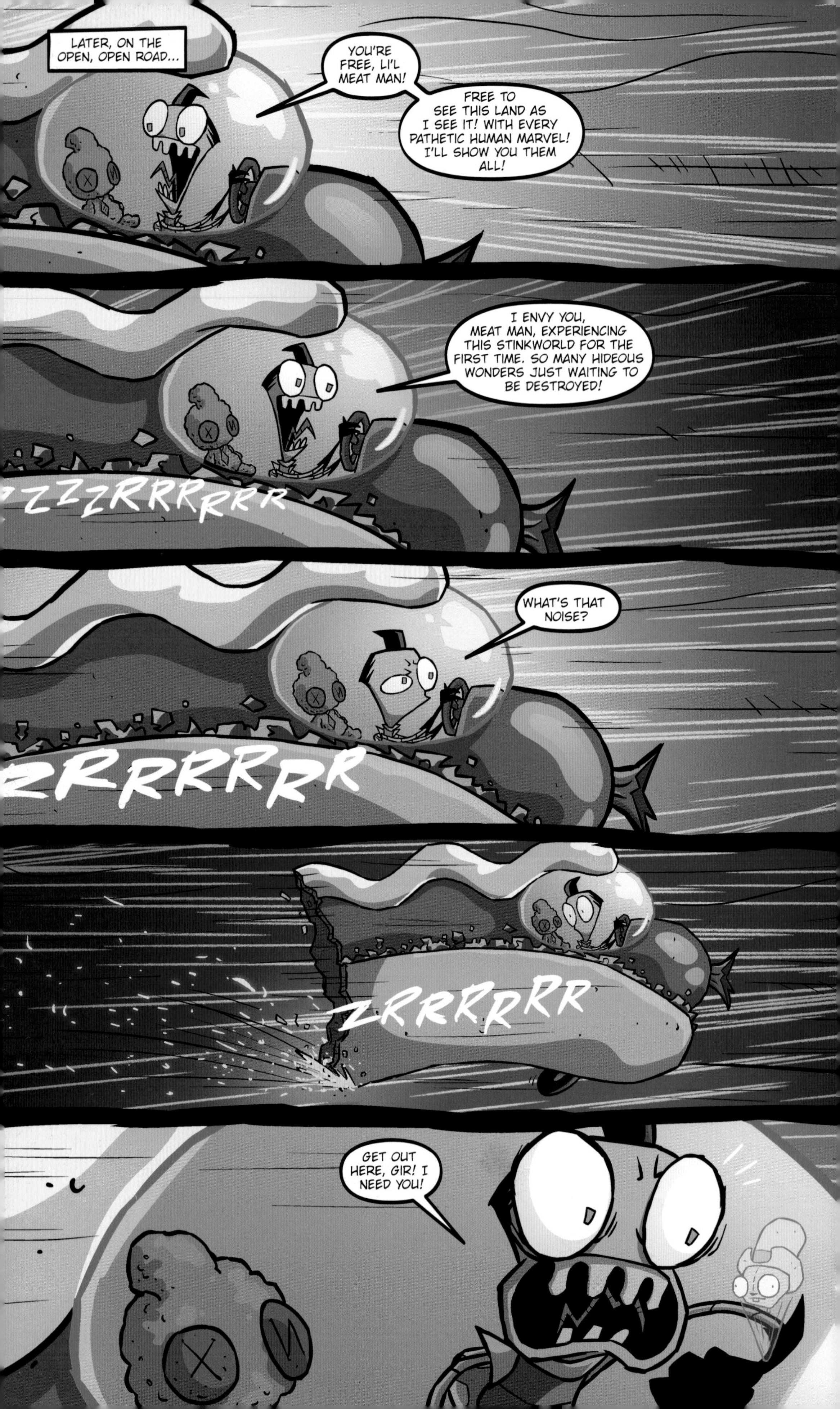

LATER, ON THE OPEN, OPEN ROAD...
YOU'RE FREE, LI'L MEAT MAN!
FREE TO SEE THIS LAND AS I SEE IT! WITH EVERY PATHETIC HUMAN MARVEL! I'LL SHOW YOU THEM ALL!
I ENVY YOU, MEAT MAN, EXPERIENCING THIS STINKWORLD FOR THE FIRST TIME. SO MANY HIDEOUS WONDERS JUST WAITING TO BE DESTROYED!
ZZZZRRRRRRR
WHAT'S THAT NOISE?
RRRRRRR
ZRRRRRRR
GET OUT HERE, GIR! I NEED YOU!

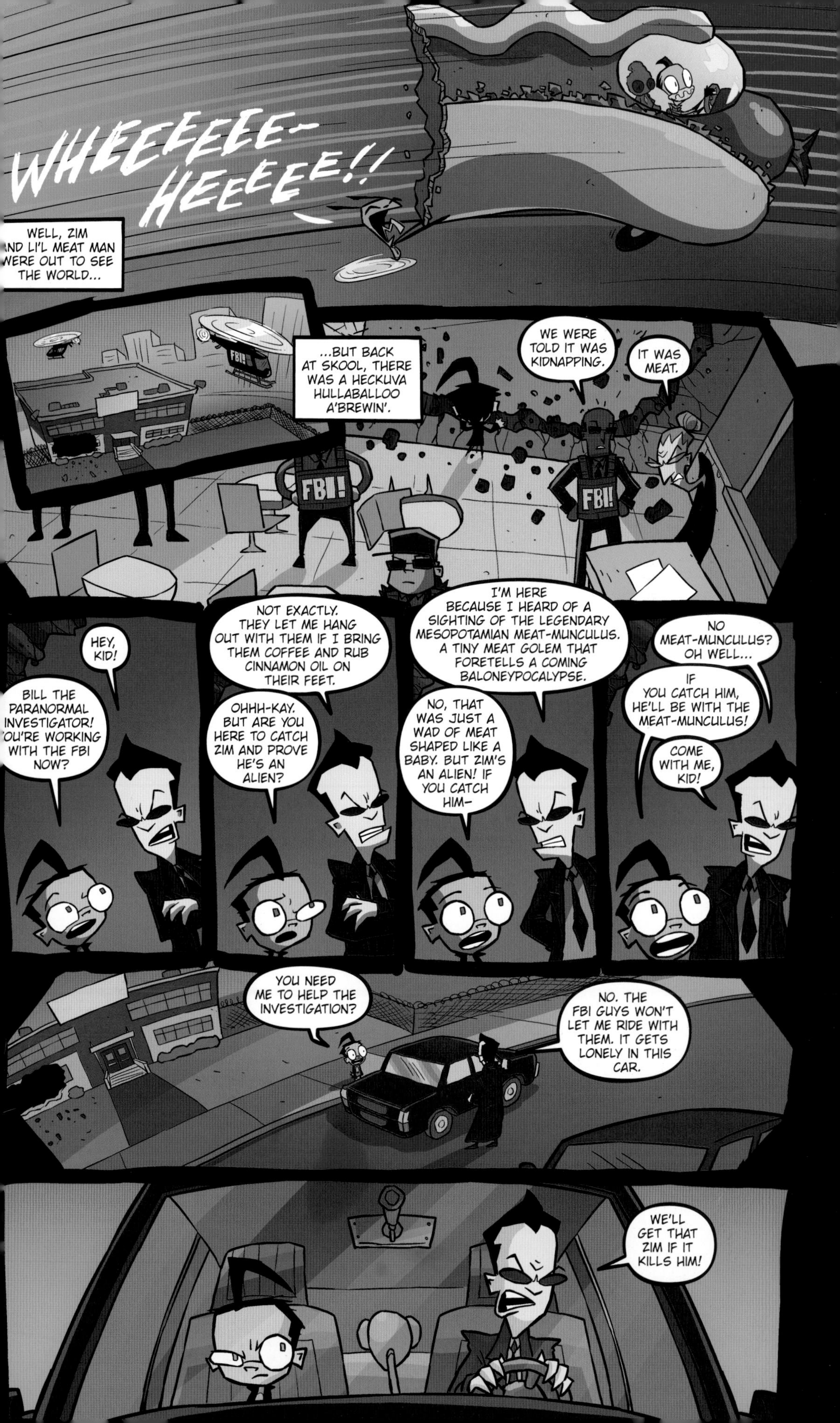
WHEEEEEE-HEEEEEE!!
WELL, ZIM AND LI'L MEAT MAN WERE OUT TO SEE THE WORLD...
...BUT BACK AT SKOOL, THERE WAS A HECKUVA HULLABALLOO A'BREWIN'.
WE WERE TOLD IT WAS KIDNAPPING.
IT WAS MEAT.
FBI!
FBI!
HEY, KID!
BILL THE PARANORMAL INVESTIGATOR! YOU'RE WORKING WITH THE FBI NOW?
NOT EXACTLY. THEY LET ME HANG OUT WITH THEM IF I BRING THEM COFFEE AND RUB CINNAMON OIL ON THEIR FEET.
OHHH-KAY. BUT ARE YOU HERE TO CATCH ZIM AND PROVE HE'S AN ALIEN?
I'M HERE BECAUSE I HEARD OF A SIGHTING OF THE LEGENDARY MESOPOTAMIAN MEAT-MUNCULUS. A TINY MEAT GOLEM THAT FORETELLS A COMING BALONEYPOCALYPSE.
NO, THAT WAS JUST A WAD OF MEAT SHAPED LIKE A BABY. BUT ZIM'S AN ALIEN! IF YOU CATCH HIM-
NO MEAT-MUNCULUS? OH WELL...
IF YOU CATCH HIM, HE'LL BE WITH THE MEAT-MUNCULUS!
COME WITH ME, KID!
YOU NEED ME TO HELP THE INVESTIGATION?
NO. THE FBI GUYS WON'T LET ME RIDE WITH THEM. IT GETS LONELY IN THIS CAR.
WE'LL GET THAT ZIM IF IT KILLS HIM!

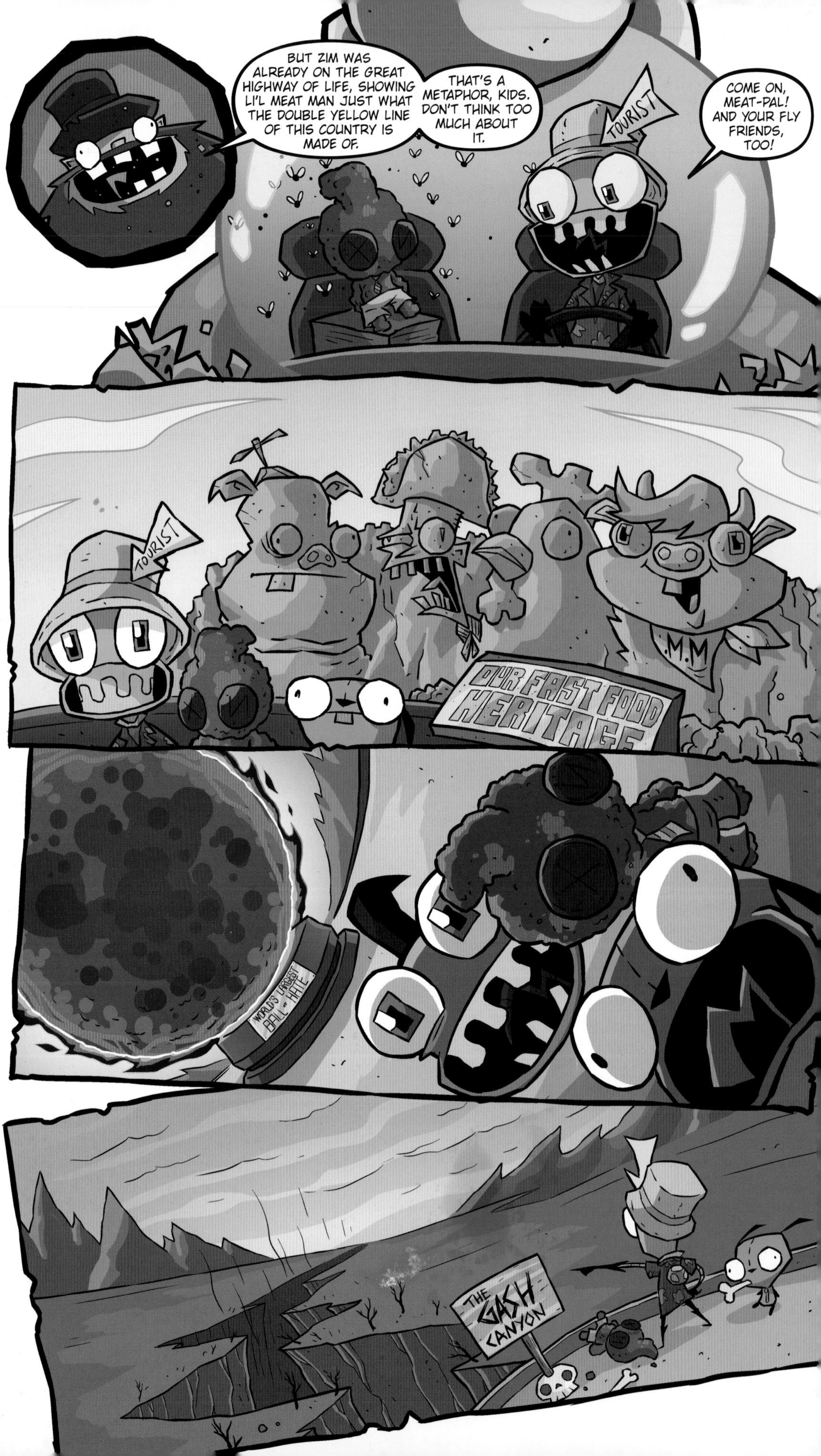

BUT ZIM WAS ALREADY ON THE GREAT HIGHWAY OF LIFE, SHOWING LI'L MEAT MAN JUST WHAT THE DOUBLE YELLOW LINE OF THIS COUNTRY IS MADE OF.
THAT'S A METAPHOR, KIDS. DON'T THINK TOO MUCH ABOUT IT.
TOURIST
COME ON, MEAT-PAL! AND YOUR FLY FRIENDS, TOO!
TOURIST
M.M
OUR FAST FOOD HERITAGE
WORLD'S LARGEST BALL o' HATE
THE GASH CANYON

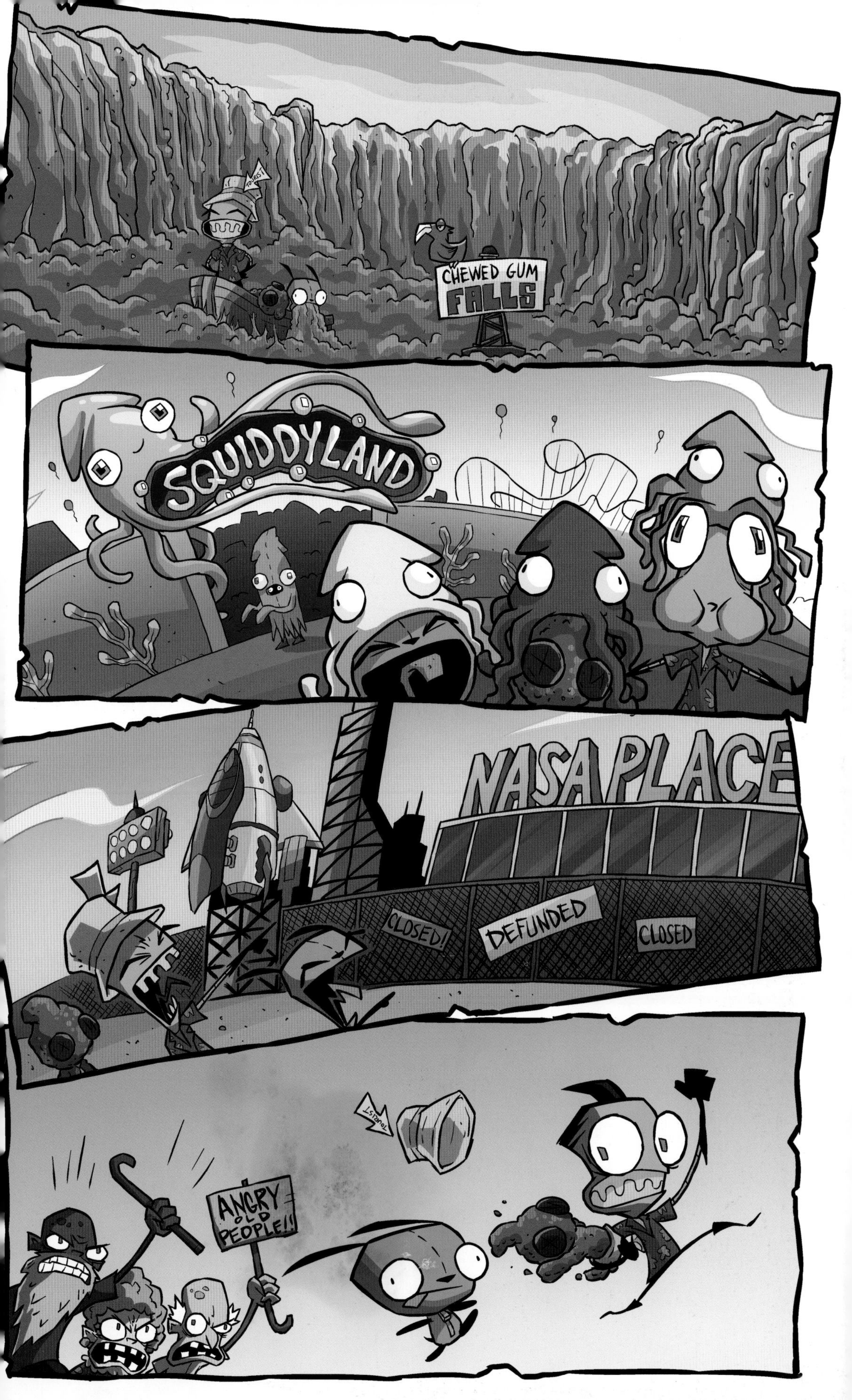
TOURIST
CHEWED GUM
FALLS
SQUIDDYLAND
NASA PLACE
CLOSED!
DEFUNDED
CLOSED
TOURIST
ANGRY OLD PEOPLE!!

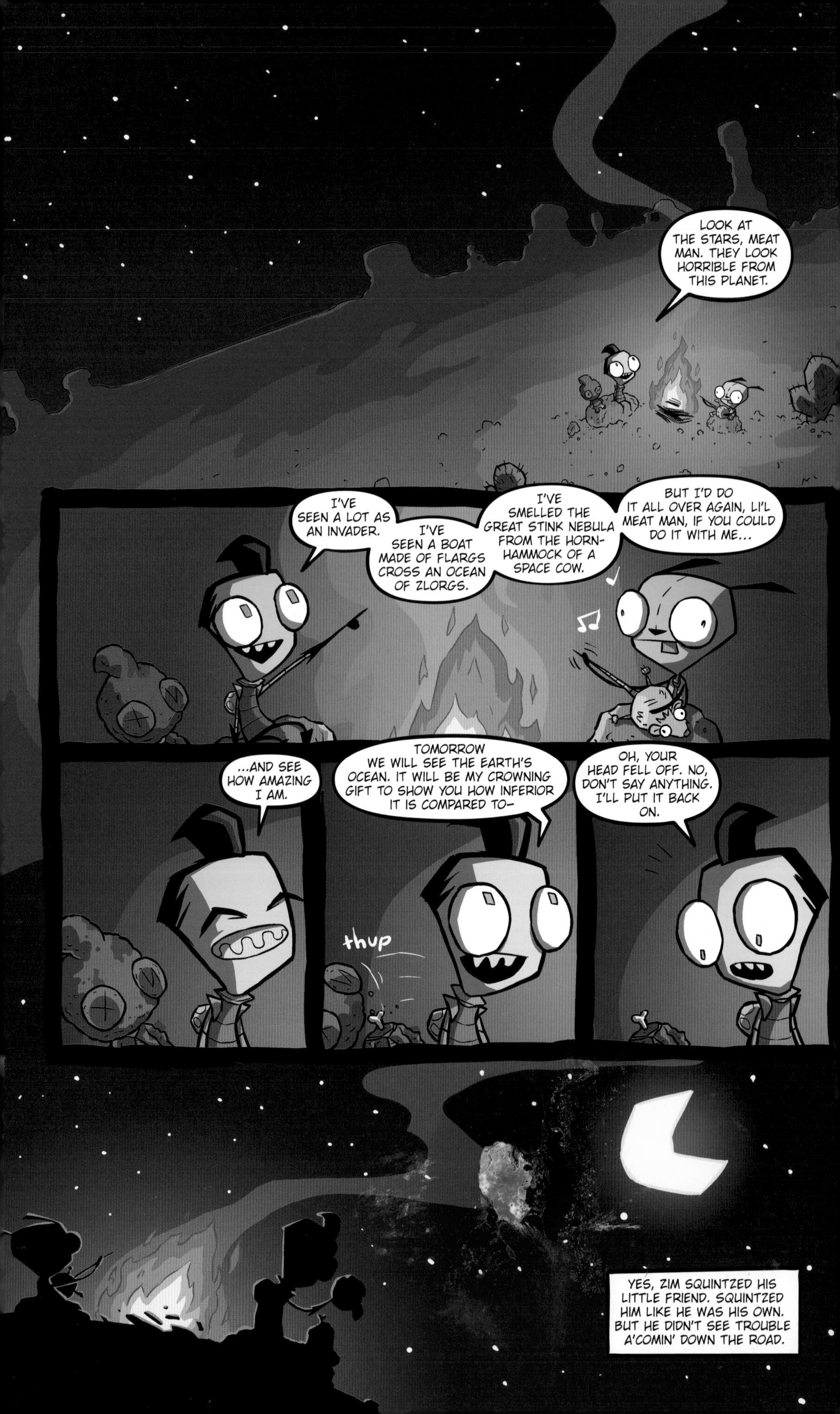
LOOK AT THE STARS, MEAT MAN. THEY LOOK HORRIBLE FROM THIS PLANET.
I'VE SEEN A LOT AS AN INVADER.
I'VE SEEN A BOAT MADE OF FLARGS CROSS AN OCEAN OF ZLORGS.
I'VE SMELLED THE GREAT STINK NEBULA FROM THE HORN-HAMMOCK OF A SPACE COW.
BUT I'D DO IT ALL OVER AGAIN, LI'L MEAT MAN, IF YOU COULD DO IT WITH ME...
...AND SEE HOW AMAZING I AM.
TOMORROW WE WILL SEE THE EARTH'S OCEAN. IT WILL BE MY CROWNING GIFT TO SHOW YOU HOW INFERIOR IT IS COMPARED TO-
thup
OH, YOUR HEAD FELL OFF. NO, DON'T SAY ANYTHING. I'LL PUT IT BACK ON.
YES, ZIM SQUINTZED HIS LITTLE FRIEND. SQUINTZED HIM LIKE HE WAS HIS OWN. BUT HE DIDN'T SEE TROUBLE A'COMIN' DOWN THE ROAD.

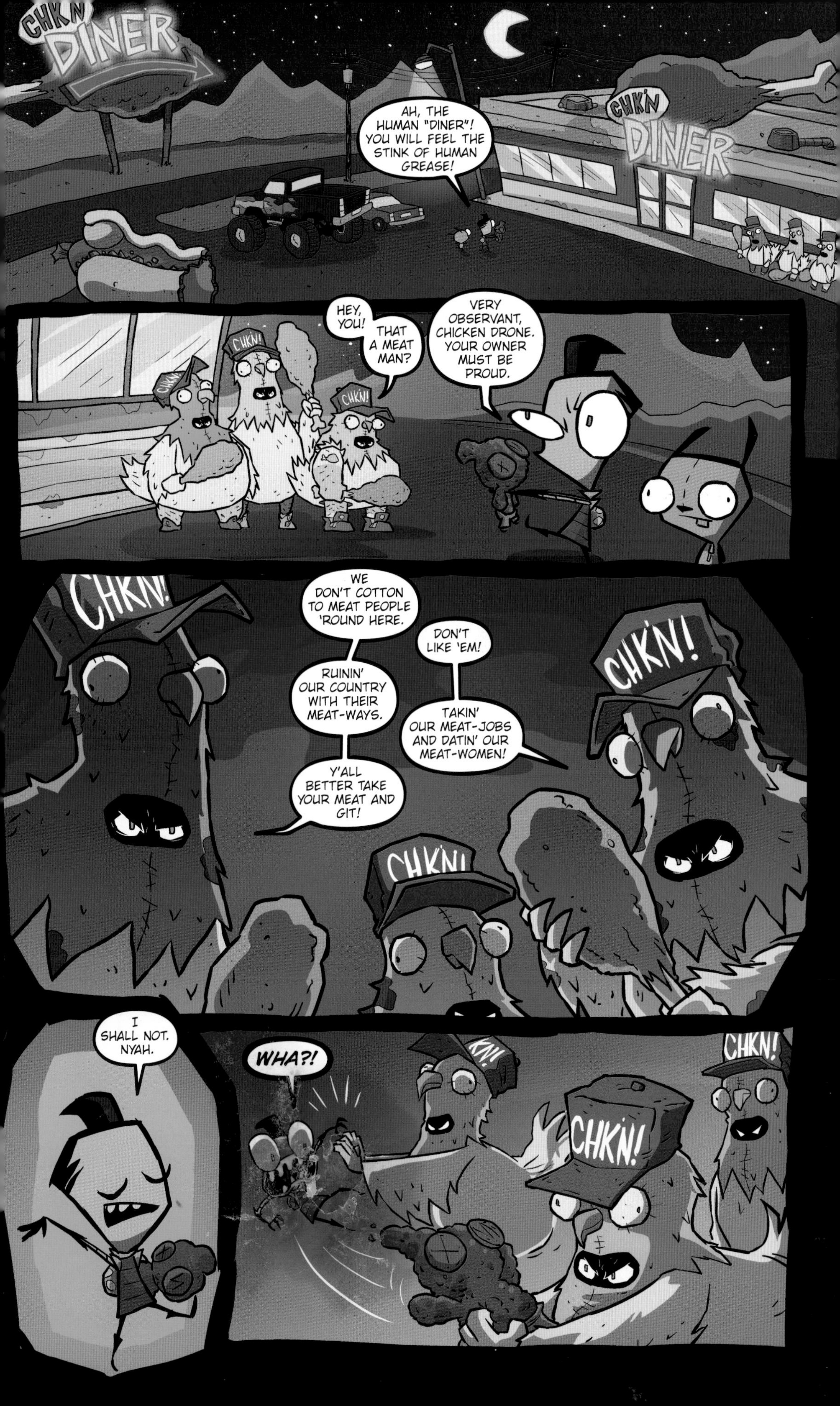
CHK'N DINER
AH, THE HUMAN "DINER"! YOU WILL FEEL THE STINK OF HUMAN GREASE!
CHK'N DINER
HEY, YOU!
THAT A MEAT MAN?
VERY OBSERVANT, CHICKEN DRONE. YOUR OWNER MUST BE PROUD.
WE DON'T COTTON TO MEAT PEOPLE 'ROUND HERE.
RUININ' OUR COUNTRY WITH THEIR MEAT-WAYS.
Y'ALL BETTER TAKE YOUR MEAT AND GIT!
DON'T LIKE 'EM!
TAKIN' OUR MEAT-JOBS AND DATIN' OUR MEAT-WOMEN!
I SHALL NOT. NYAH.
WHA?!
CHK'N!

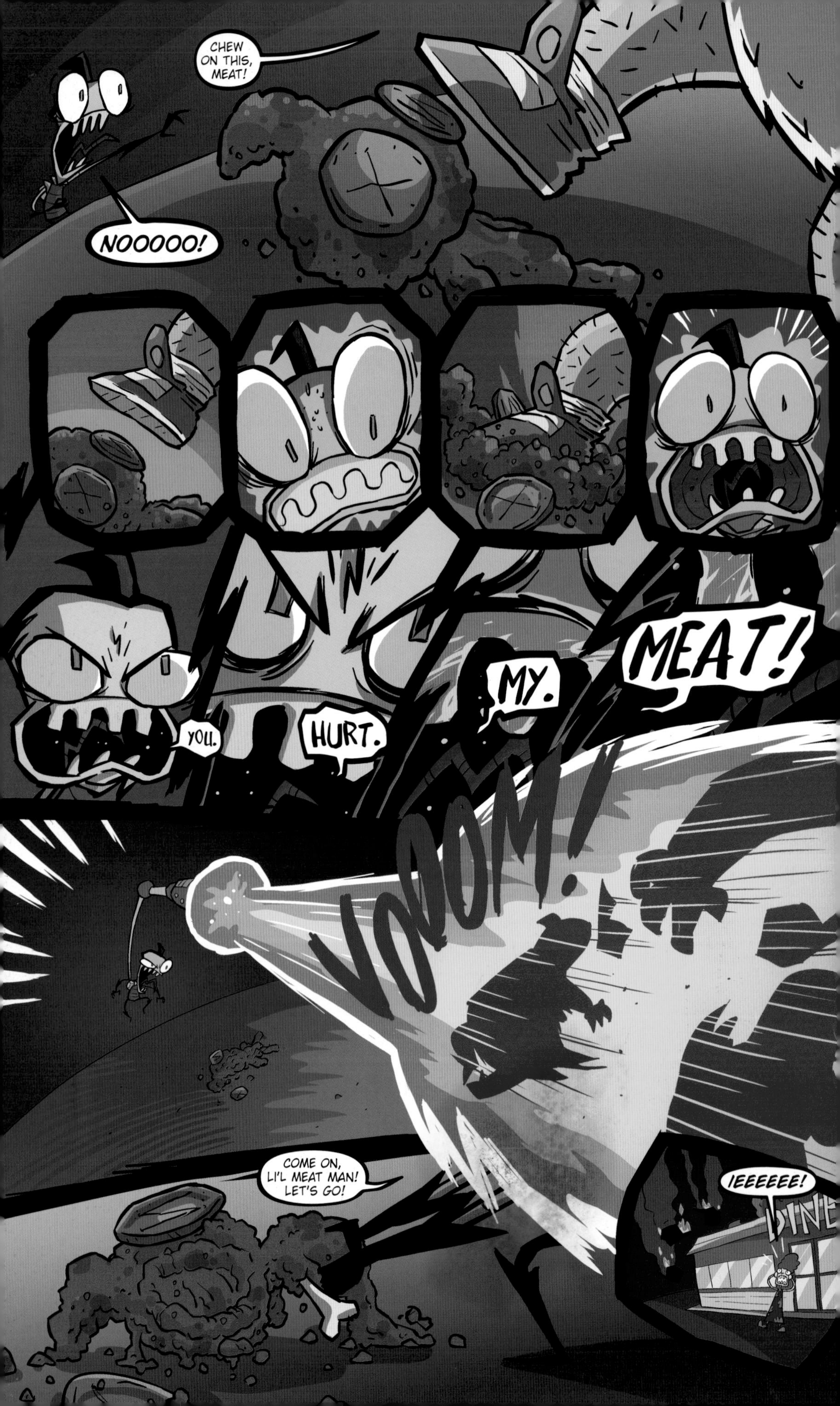
CHEW ON THIS, MEAT!
NOOOOO!
YOU.
HURT.
MY.
MEAT!
VOOOM!
COME ON, LI'L MEAT MAN! LET'S GO!
IEEEEEE!

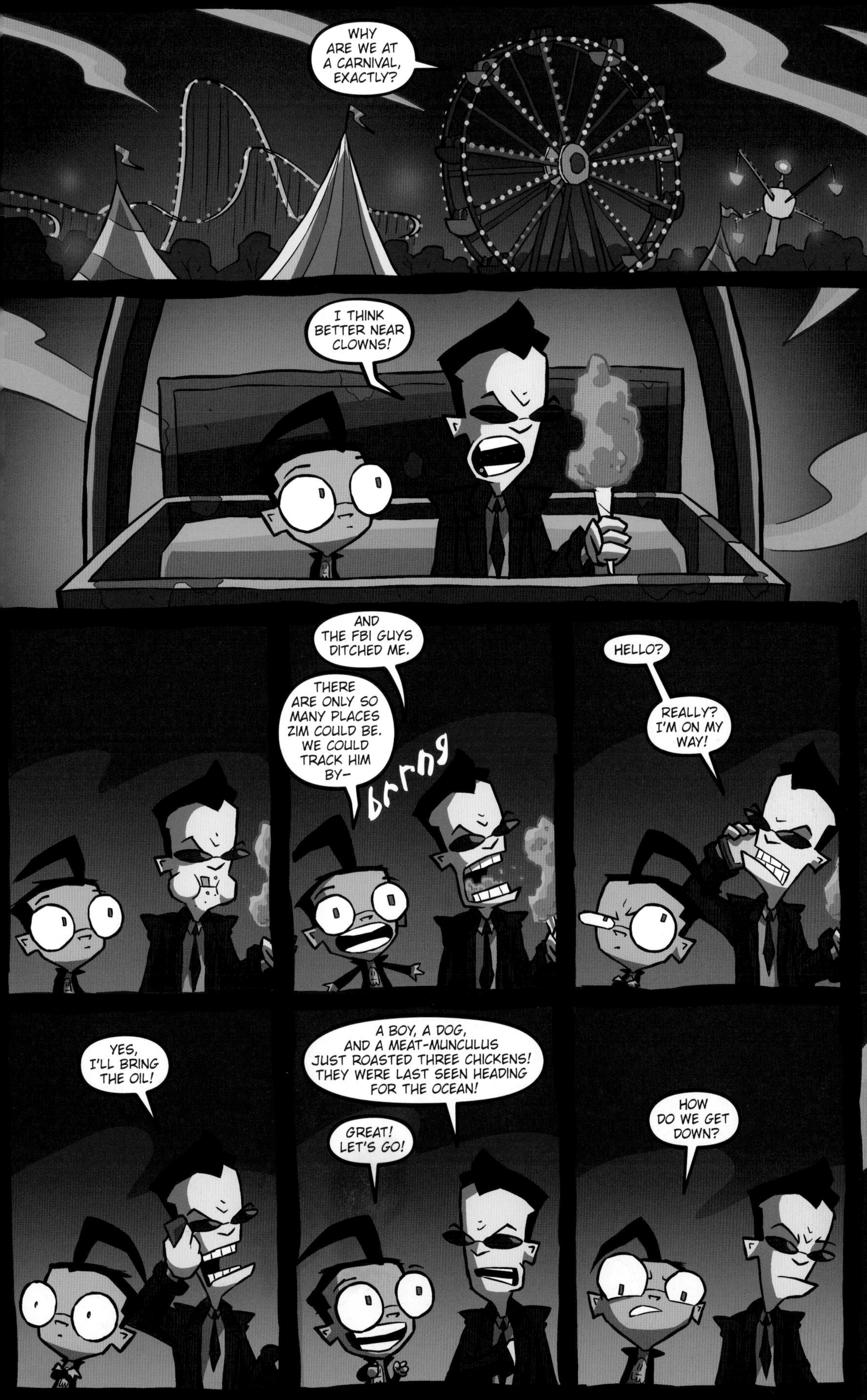

WHY ARE WE AT A CARNIVAL, EXACTLY?
I THINK BETTER NEAR CLOWNS!
AND THE FBI GUYS DITCHED ME.
THERE ARE ONLY SO MANY PLACES ZIM COULD BE. WE COULD TRACK HIM BY–
brrng
HELLO?
REALLY? I'M ON MY WAY!
YES, I'LL BRING THE OIL!
A BOY, A DOG, AND A MEAT-MUNCULUS JUST ROASTED THREE CHICKENS! THEY WERE LAST SEEN HEADING FOR THE OCEAN!
GREAT! LET'S GO!
HOW DO WE GET DOWN?

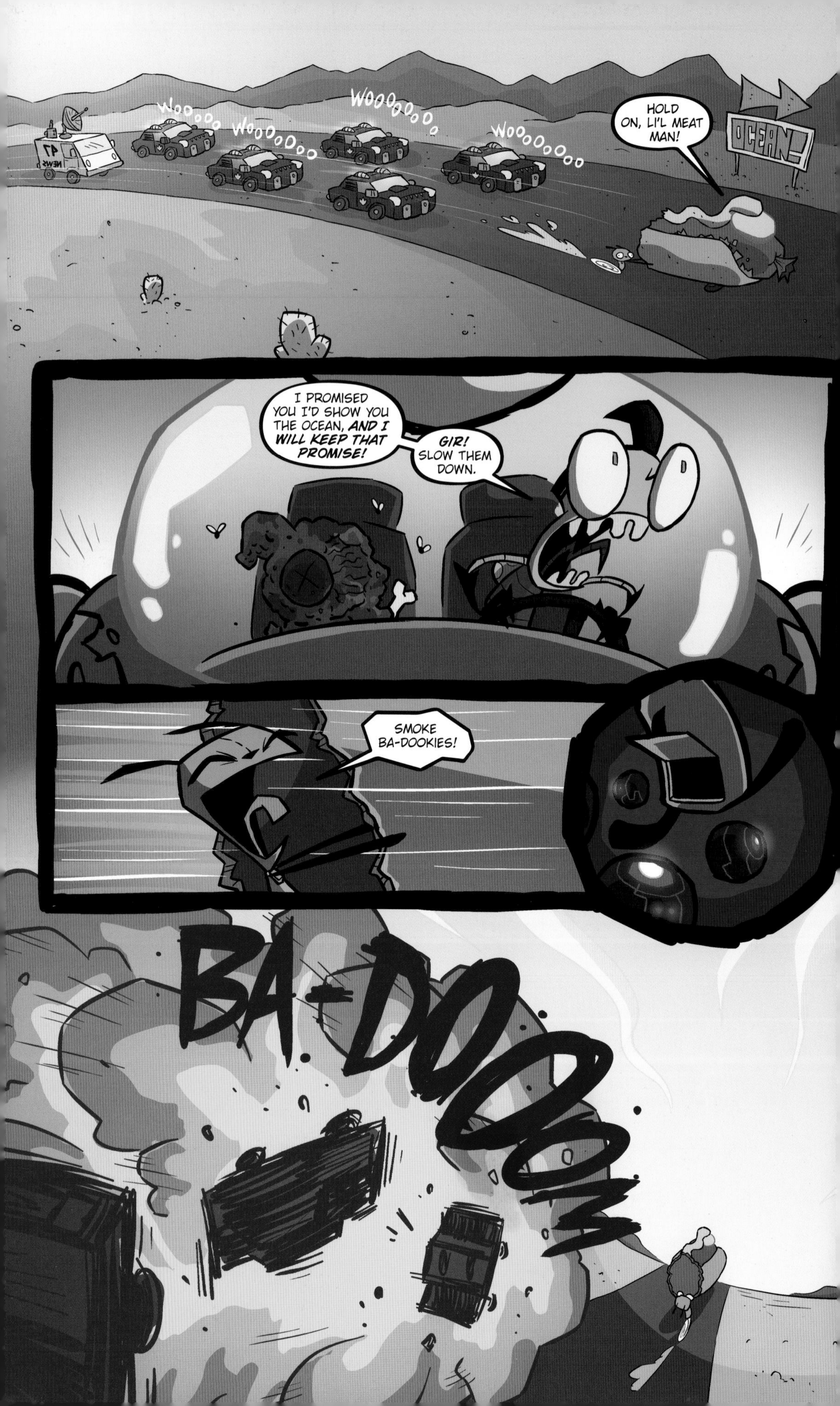

WOOOOOO
WOOOOOOO
WOOOOOOOO
WOOOOOOOO
HOLD ON, LI'L MEAT MAN!
OCEAN!
47 NEWS
I PROMISED YOU I'D SHOW YOU THE OCEAN, AND I WILL KEEP THAT PROMISE!
GIR! SLOW THEM DOWN.
SMOKE BA-DOOKIES!
BA-DOOOOM

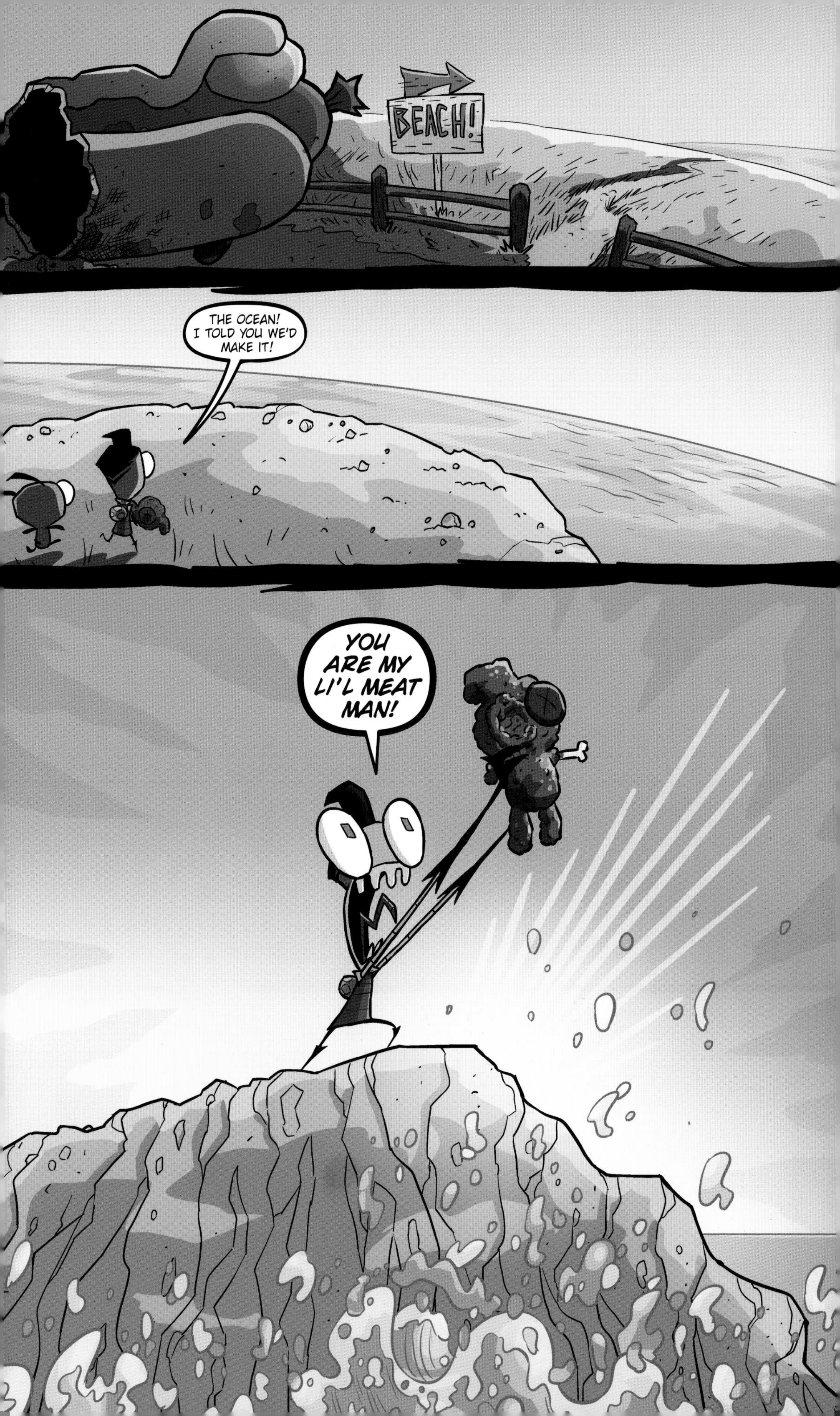
BEACH!
THE OCEAN! I TOLD YOU WE'D MAKE IT!
YOU ARE MY LI'L MEAT MAN!

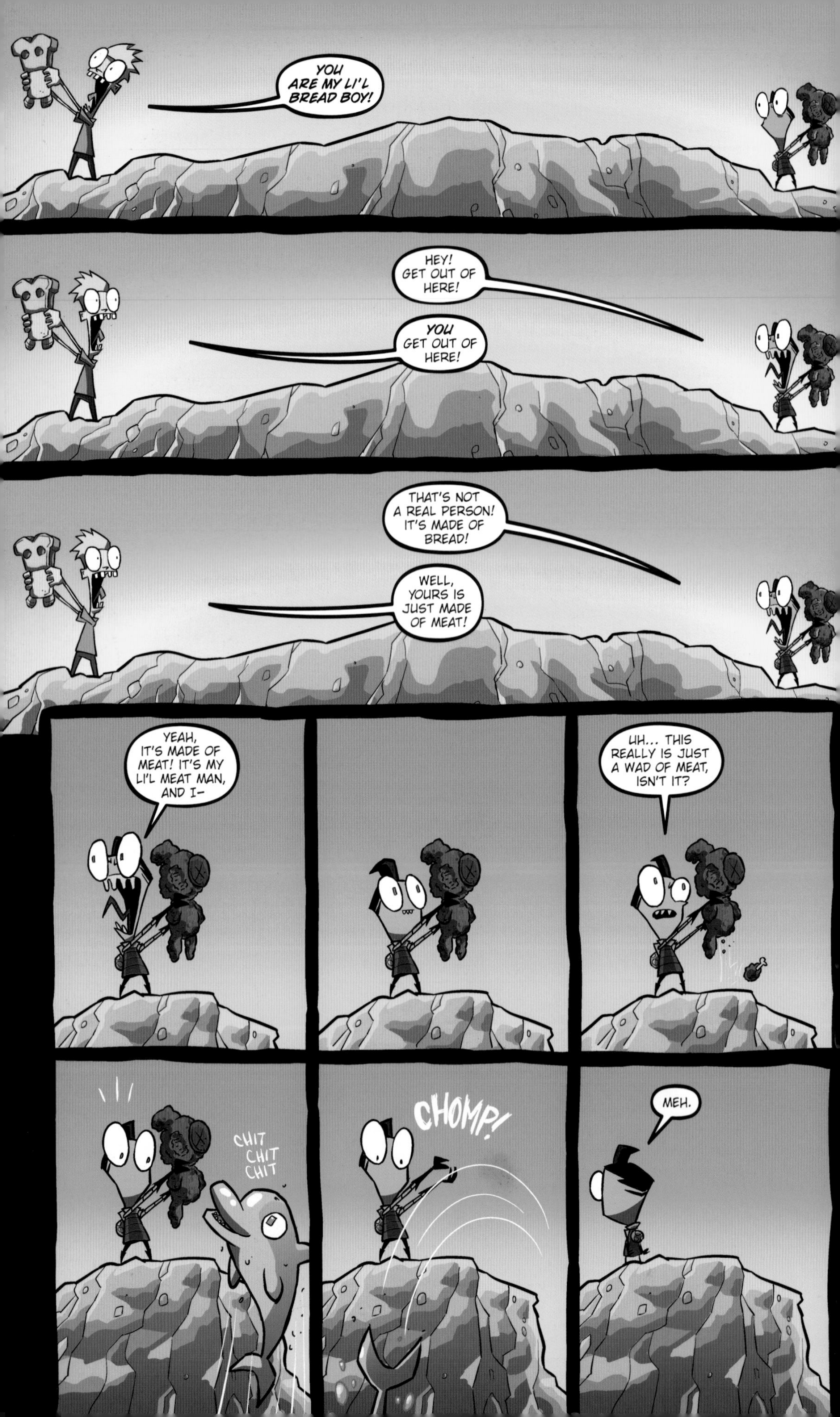
YOU ARE MY LI'L BREAD BOY!
HEY! GET OUT OF HERE!
YOU GET OUT OF HERE!
THAT'S NOT A REAL PERSON! IT'S MADE OF BREAD!
WELL, YOURS IS JUST MADE OF MEAT!
YEAH, IT'S MADE OF MEAT! IT'S MY LI'L MEAT MAN, AND I–
UH... THIS REALLY IS JUST A WAD OF MEAT, ISN'T IT?
CHIT CHIT CHIT
CHOMP!
MEH.

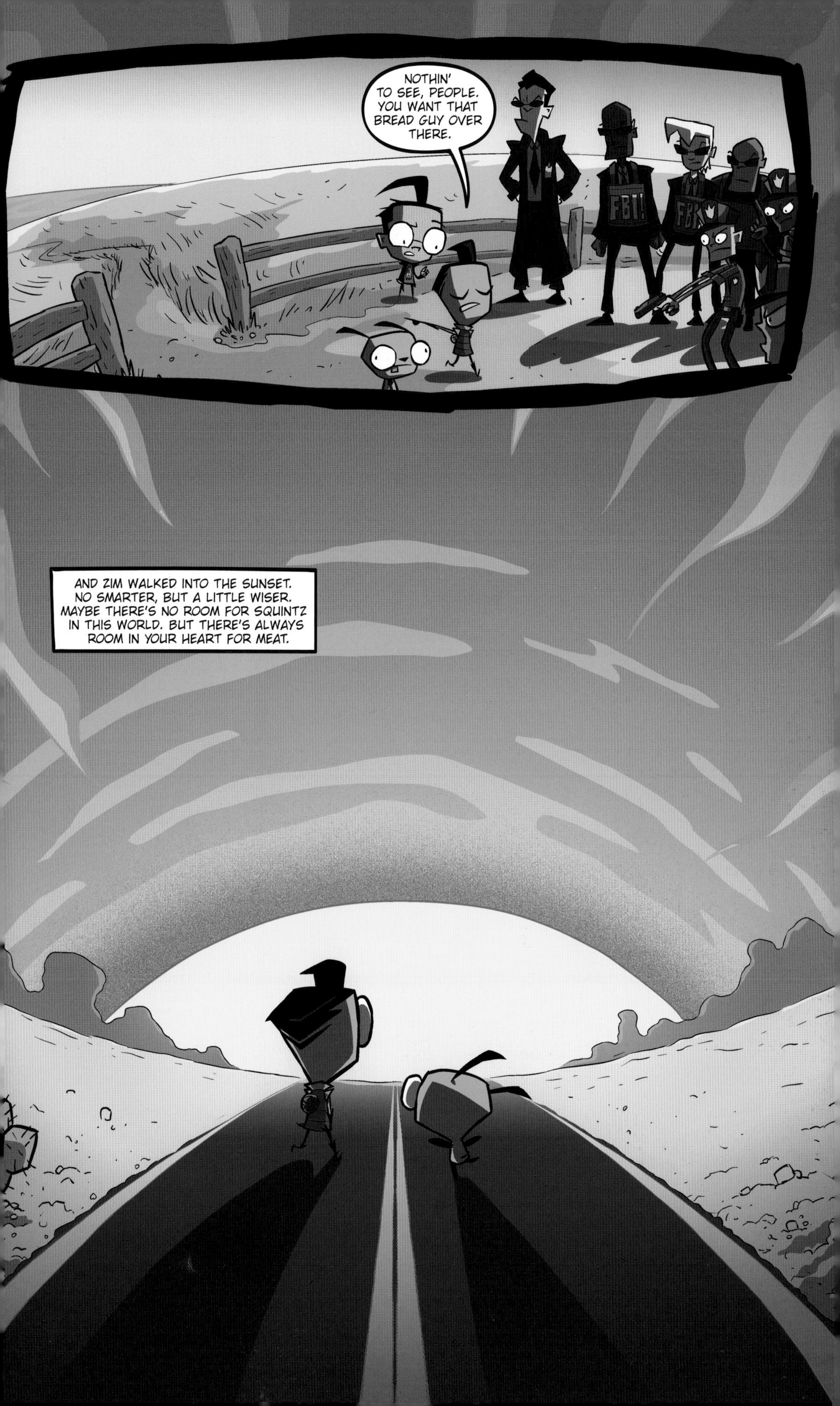
NOTHIN' TO SEE, PEOPLE. YOU WANT THAT BREAD GUY OVER THERE.
FBI!
FBI
AND ZIM WALKED INTO THE SUNSET. NO SMARTER, BUT A LITTLE WISER. MAYBE THERE'S NO ROOM FOR SQUINTZ IN THIS WORLD. BUT THERE'S ALWAYS ROOM IN YOUR HEART FOR MEAT.

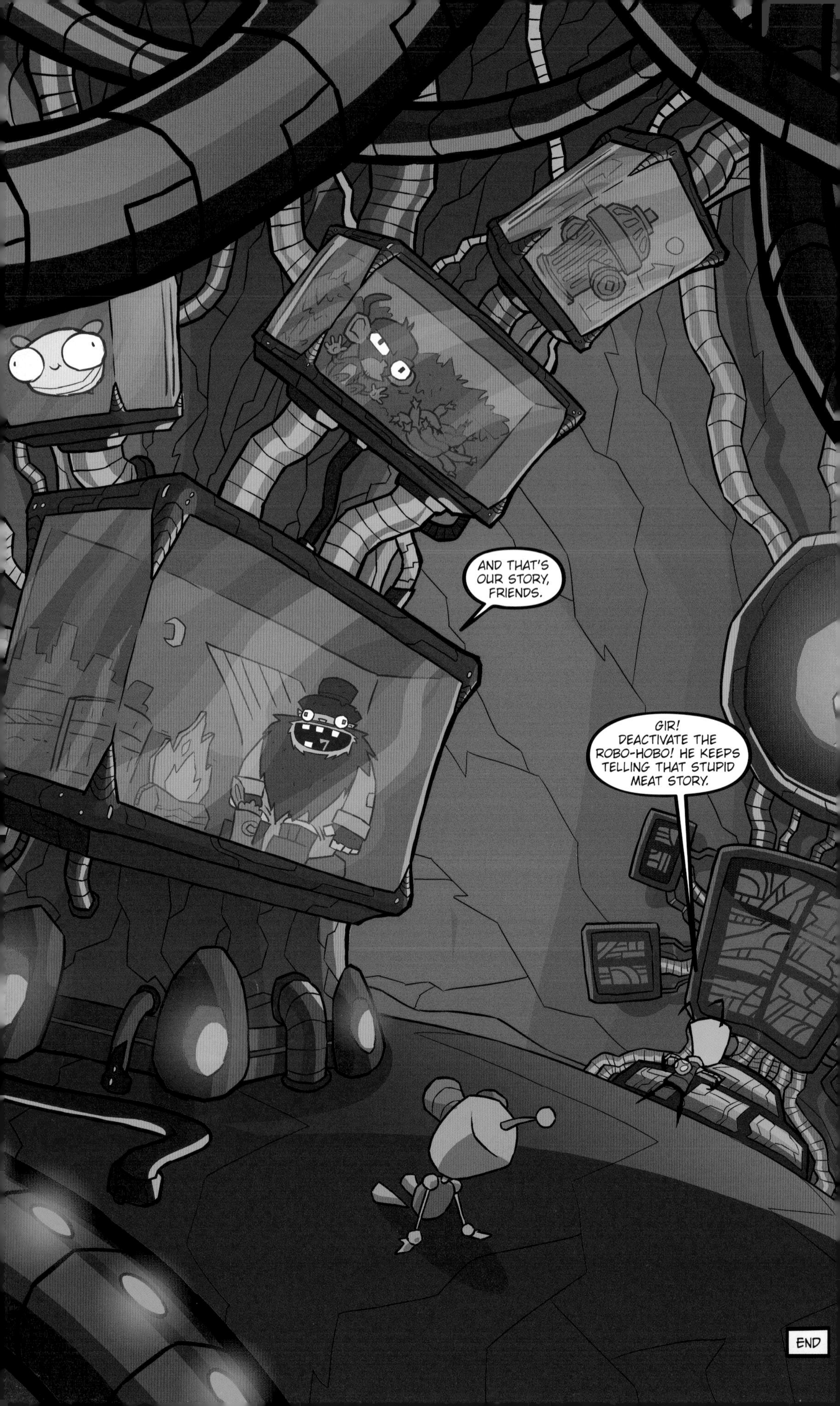
AND THAT'S OUR STORY, FRIENDS.
GIR! DEACTIVATE THE ROBO-HOBO! HE KEEPS TELLING THAT STUPID MEAT STORY.
END

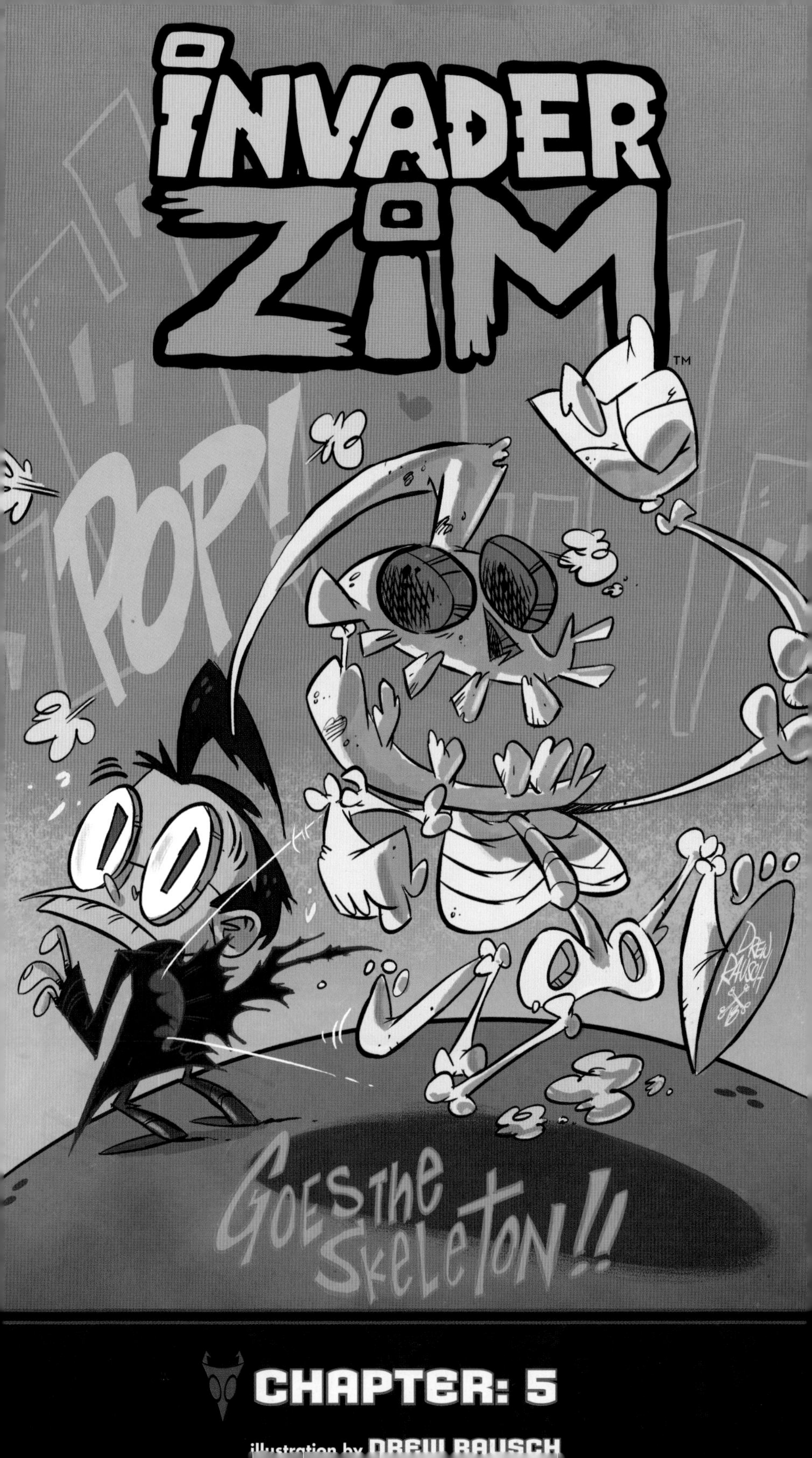
INVADER ZIM™
POP!
Goes the Skeleton!!
DREW RAUSCH

CHAPTER: 5

illustration by DREW RAUSCH

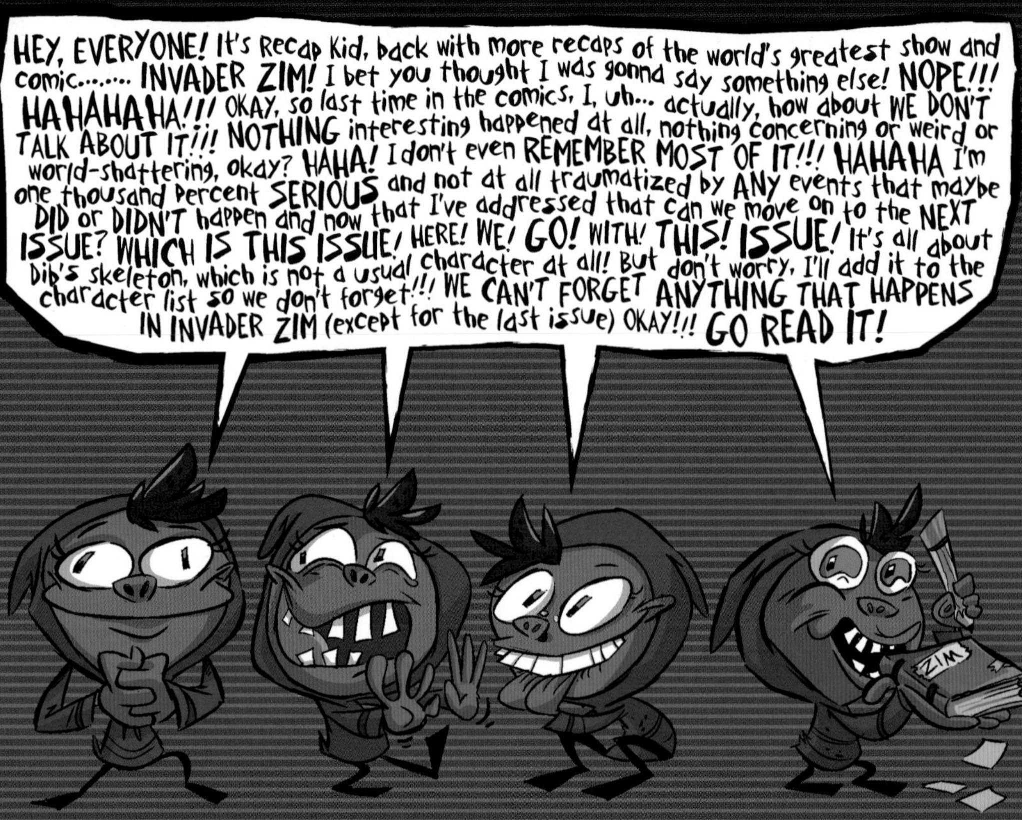
HEY, EVERYONE! It's Recap Kid, back with more recaps of the world's greatest show and comic........ INVADER ZIM! I bet you thought I was gonna say something else! NOPE!!! HAHAHAHA!!! OKAY, so last time in the comics, I, uh... actually, how about WE DON'T TALK ABOUT IT!!! NOTHING interesting happened at all, nothing concerning or weird or world-shattering, okay? HAHA! I don't even REMEMBER MOST OF IT!!! HAHAHA I'm one thousand percent SERIOUS and not at all traumatized by ANY events that maybe DID or DIDN'T happen and now that I've addressed that can we move on to the NEXT ISSUE? WHICH IS THIS ISSUE! HERE! WE! GO! WITH! THIS! ISSUE! It's all about Dib's skeleton, which is not a usual character at all! But don't worry, I'll add it to the character list so we don't forget!!! WE CAN'T FORGET ANYTHING THAT HAPPENS IN INVADER ZIM (except for the last issue) OKAY!!! GO READ IT!
ZIM

Recap Kid illustrated by **DREW RAUSCH**,
colored by **FRED C. STRESING**, and
lettered by **WARREN WUCINICH**

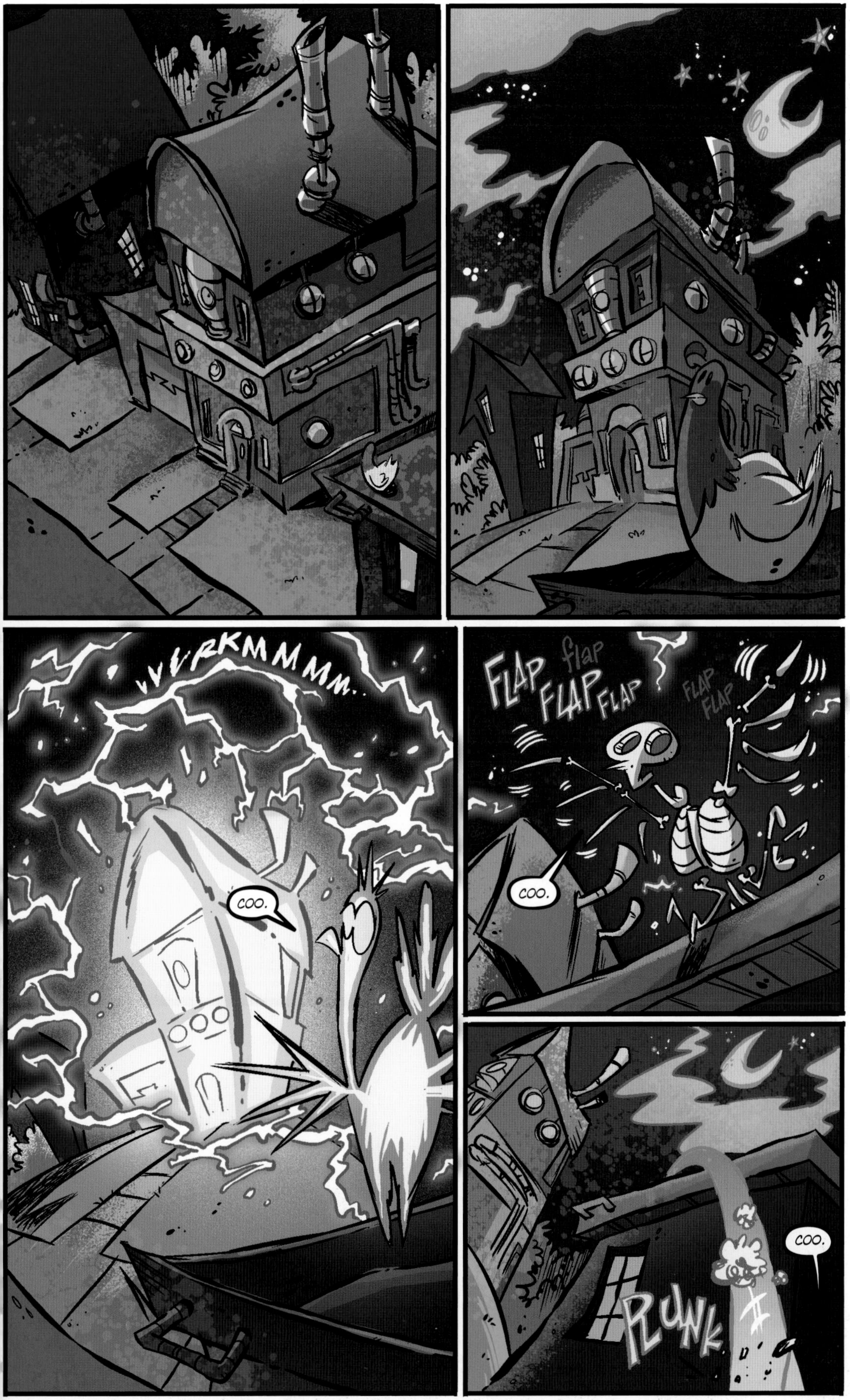
VVVRKMMMMM...
COO.
FLAP flap FLAP FLAP
FLAP FLAP
COO.
COO.
PLUNK

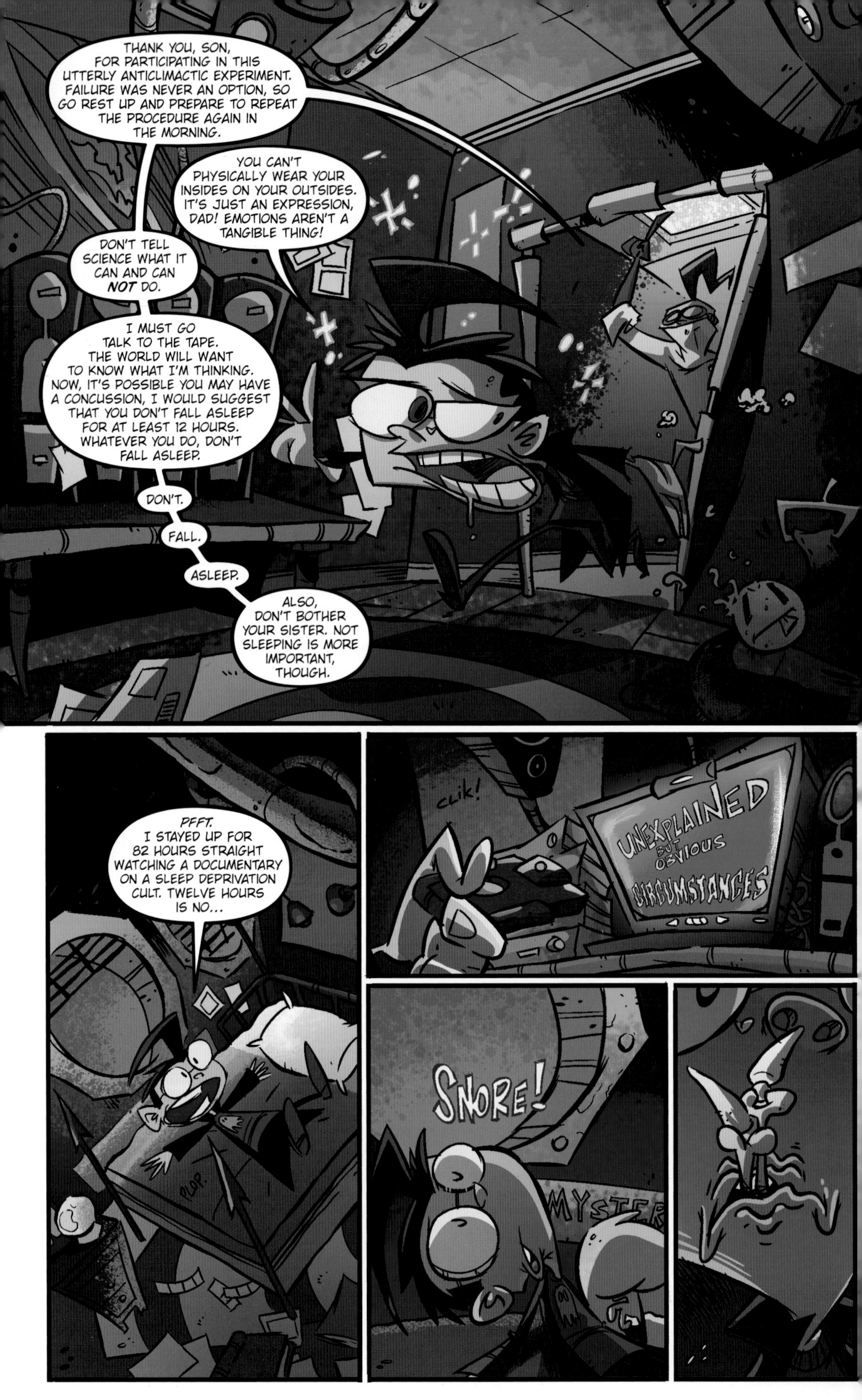
THANK YOU, SON, FOR PARTICIPATING IN THIS UTTERLY ANTICLIMACTIC EXPERIMENT. FAILURE WAS NEVER AN OPTION, SO GO REST UP AND PREPARE TO REPEAT THE PROCEDURE AGAIN IN THE MORNING.
YOU CAN'T PHYSICALLY WEAR YOUR INSIDES ON YOUR OUTSIDES. IT'S JUST AN EXPRESSION, DAD! EMOTIONS AREN'T A TANGIBLE THING!
DON'T TELL SCIENCE WHAT IT CAN AND CAN **NOT** DO.
I MUST GO TALK TO THE TAPE. THE WORLD WILL WANT TO KNOW WHAT I'M THINKING. NOW, IT'S POSSIBLE YOU MAY HAVE A CONCUSSION, I WOULD SUGGEST THAT YOU DON'T FALL ASLEEP FOR AT LEAST 12 HOURS. WHATEVER YOU DO, DON'T FALL ASLEEP.
DON'T.
FALL.
ASLEEP.
ALSO, DON'T BOTHER YOUR SISTER. NOT SLEEPING IS MORE IMPORTANT, THOUGH.
PFFT. I STAYED UP FOR 82 HOURS STRAIGHT WATCHING A DOCUMENTARY ON A SLEEP DEPRIVATION CULT. TWELVE HOURS IS NO...
PLOP.
CLIK!
UNEXPLAINED BUT OBVIOUS CIRCUMSTANCES
SNORE!
MYSTER

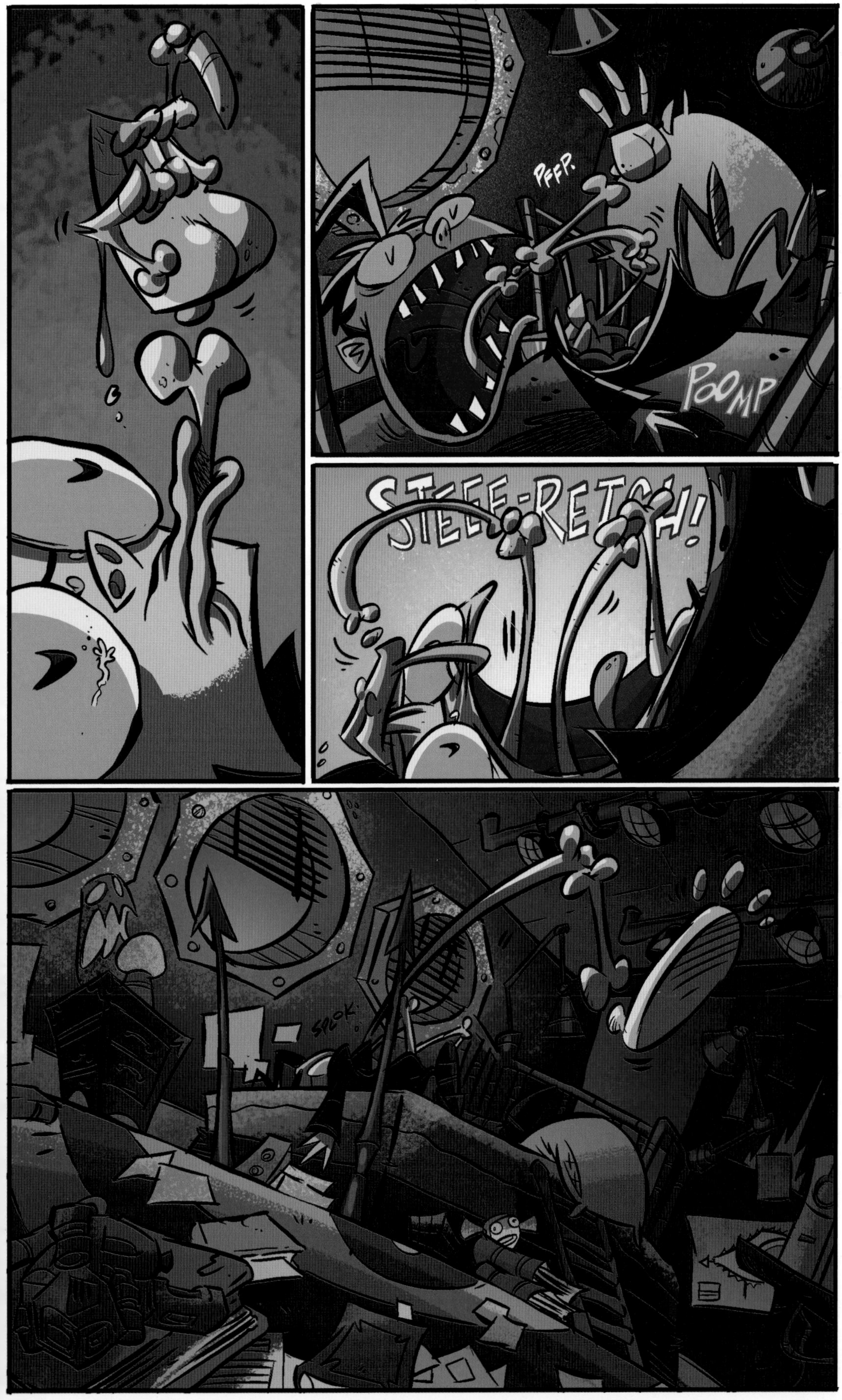
PFFP.
POOMP
STEEE-RETCH!
SPLOK.

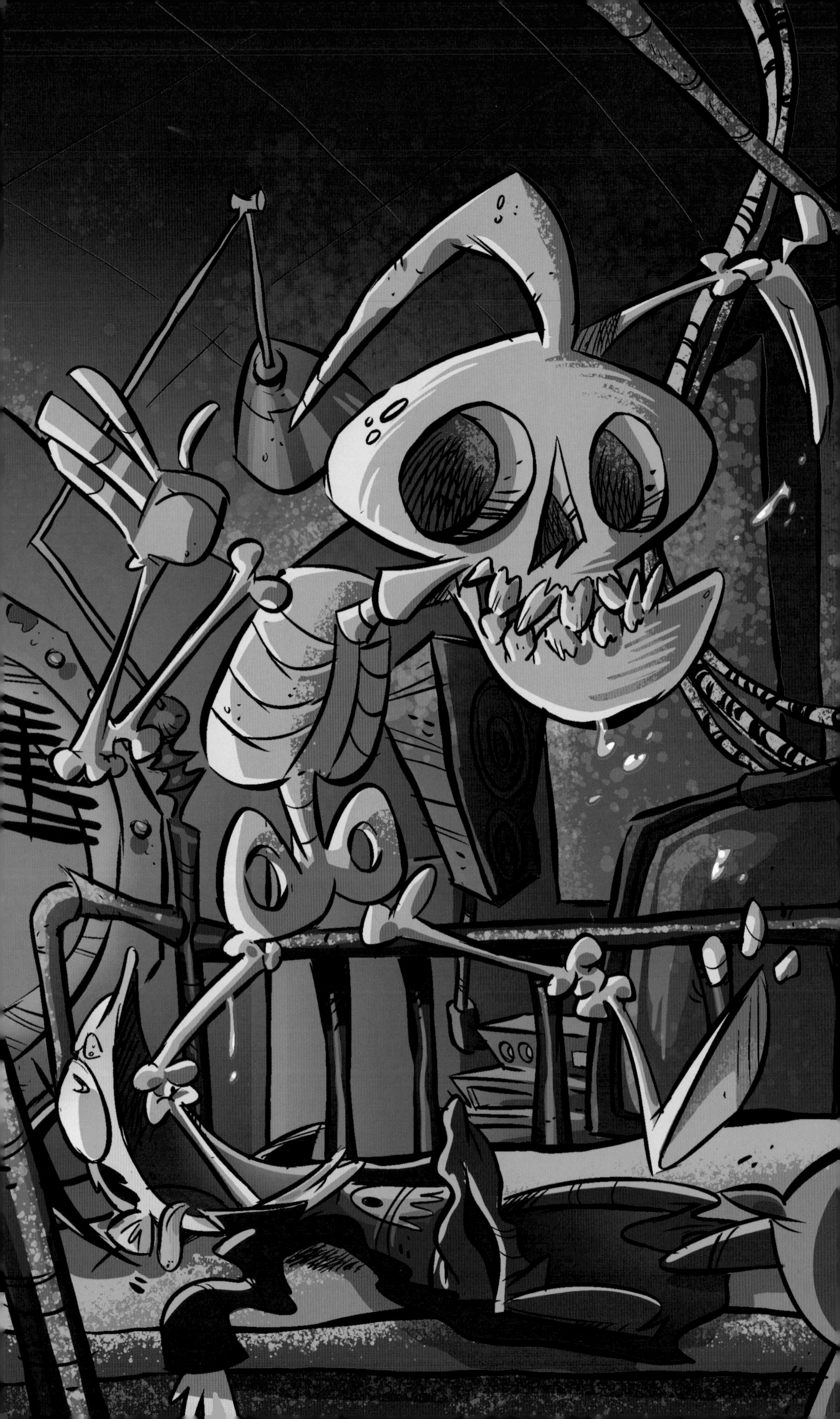

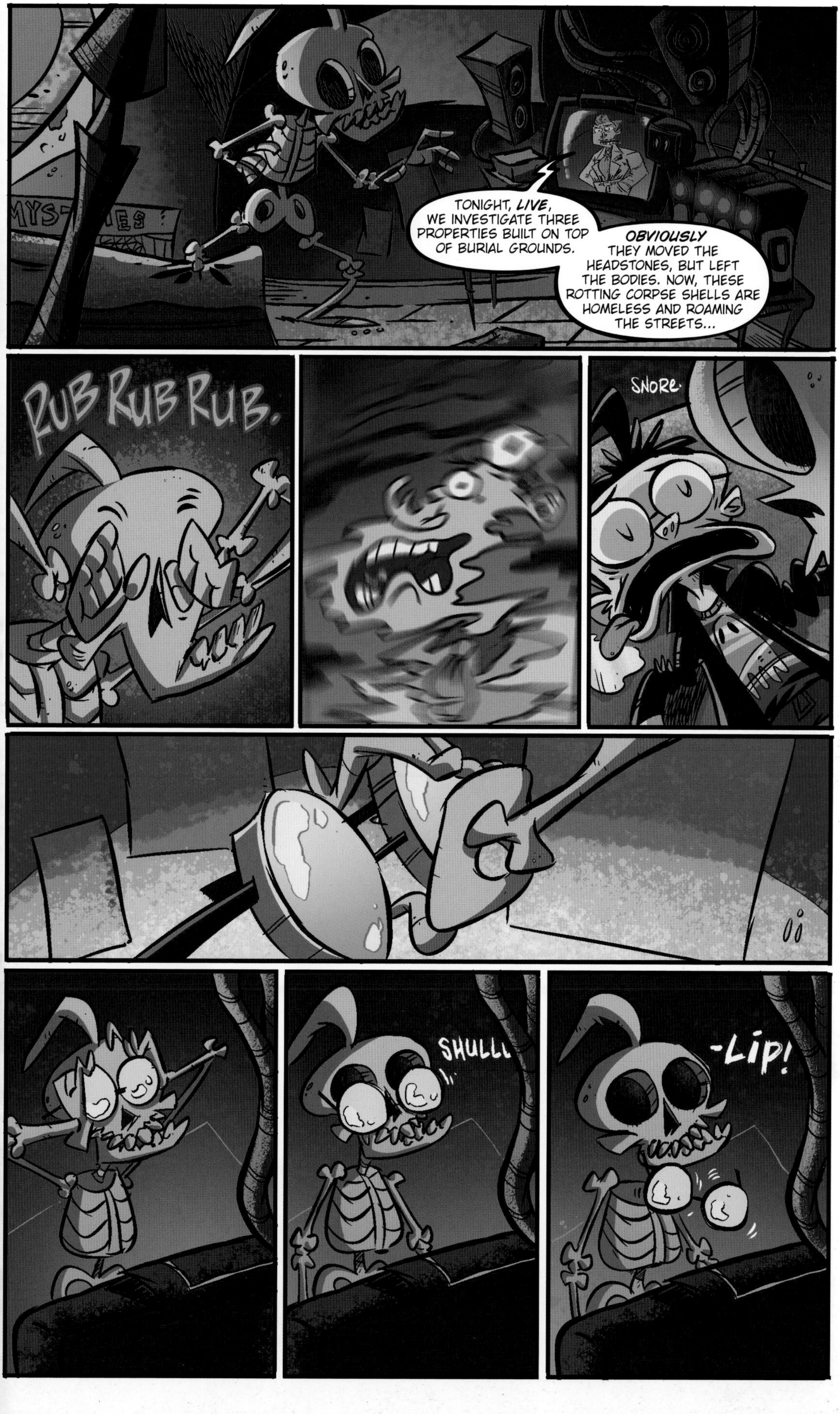
MYST IES
TONIGHT, LIVE, WE INVESTIGATE THREE PROPERTIES BUILT ON TOP OF BURIAL GROUNDS.
OBVIOUSLY THEY MOVED THE HEADSTONES, BUT LEFT THE BODIES. NOW, THESE ROTTING CORPSE SHELLS ARE HOMELESS AND ROAMING THE STREETS...
RUB RUB RUB.
SNORE.
SHULLL
-LIP!

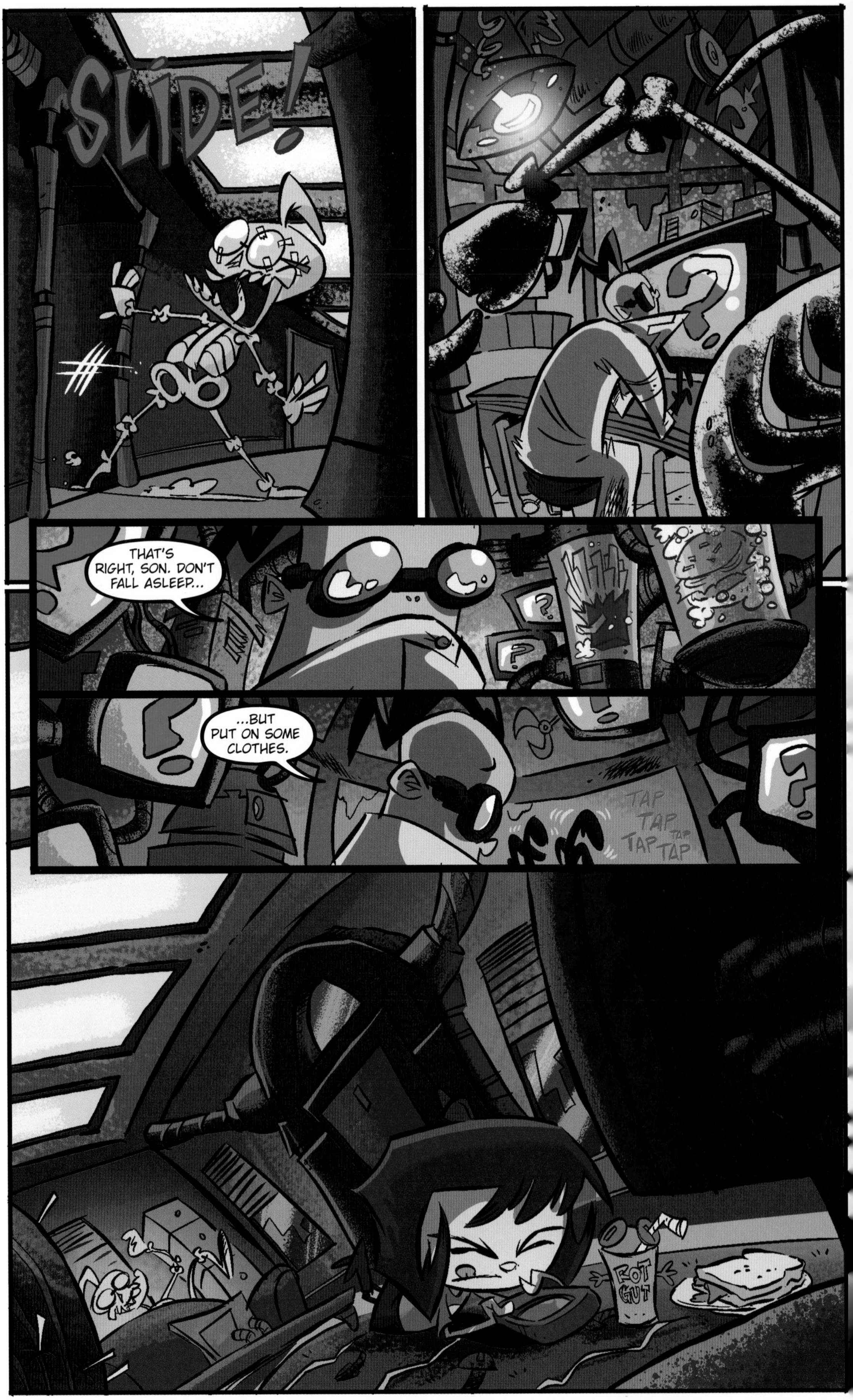
SLIDE!
THAT'S RIGHT, SON. DON'T FALL ASLEEP...
...BUT PUT ON SOME CLOTHES.
TAP TAP TAP TAP TAP TAP
ROT GUT

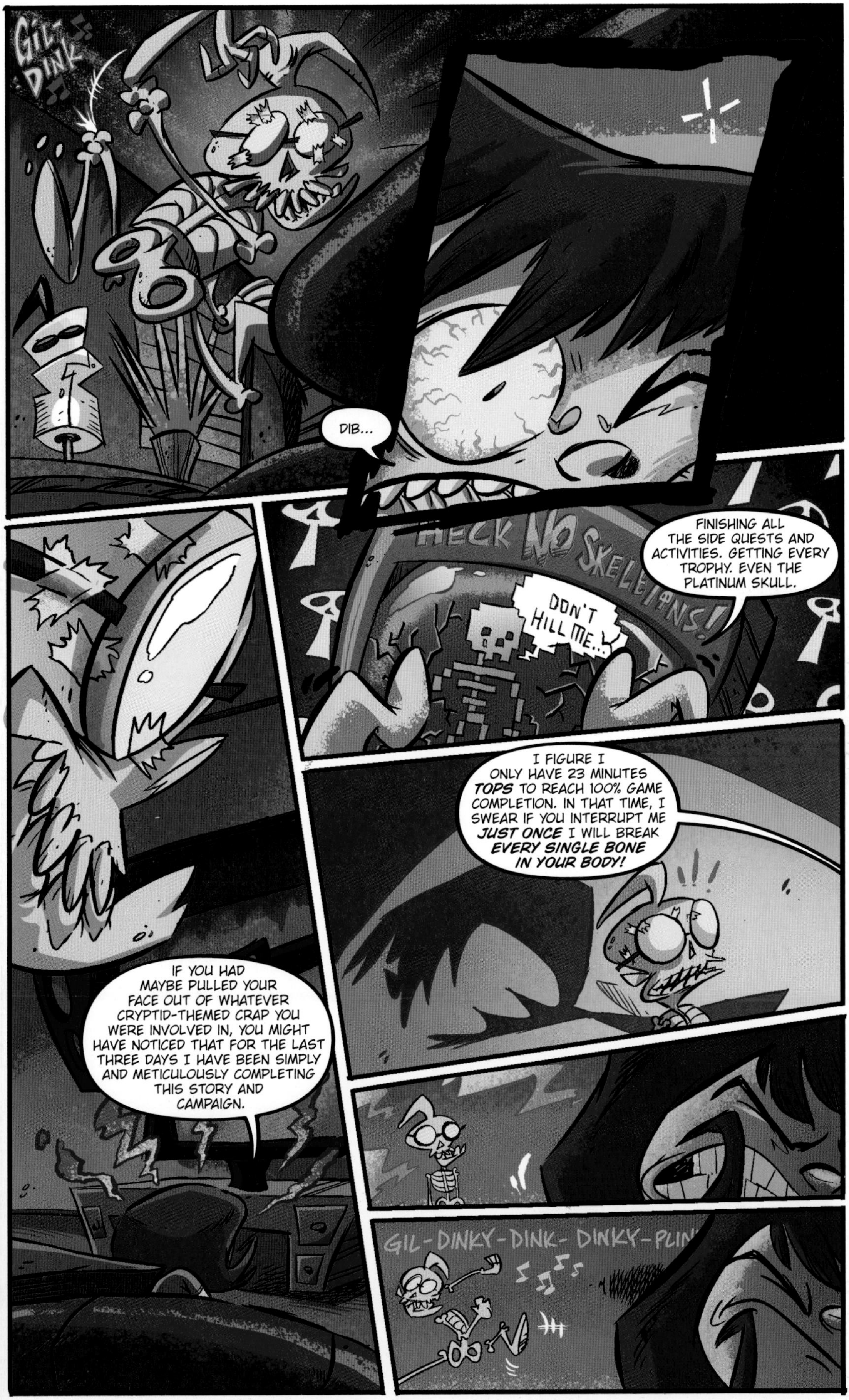
GIL-DINK
DIB...
HECK NO SKELETONS!
DON'T KILL ME...
FINISHING ALL THE SIDE QUESTS AND ACTIVITIES. GETTING EVERY TROPHY. EVEN THE PLATINUM SKULL.
IF YOU HAD MAYBE PULLED YOUR FACE OUT OF WHATEVER CRYPTID-THEMED CRAP YOU WERE INVOLVED IN, YOU MIGHT HAVE NOTICED THAT FOR THE LAST THREE DAYS I HAVE BEEN SIMPLY AND METICULOUSLY COMPLETING THIS STORY AND CAMPAIGN.
I FIGURE I ONLY HAVE 23 MINUTES TOPS TO REACH 100% GAME COMPLETION. IN THAT TIME, I SWEAR IF YOU INTERRUPT ME JUST ONCE I WILL BREAK EVERY SINGLE BONE IN YOUR BODY!
GIL-DINKY-DINK-DINKY-PLIN

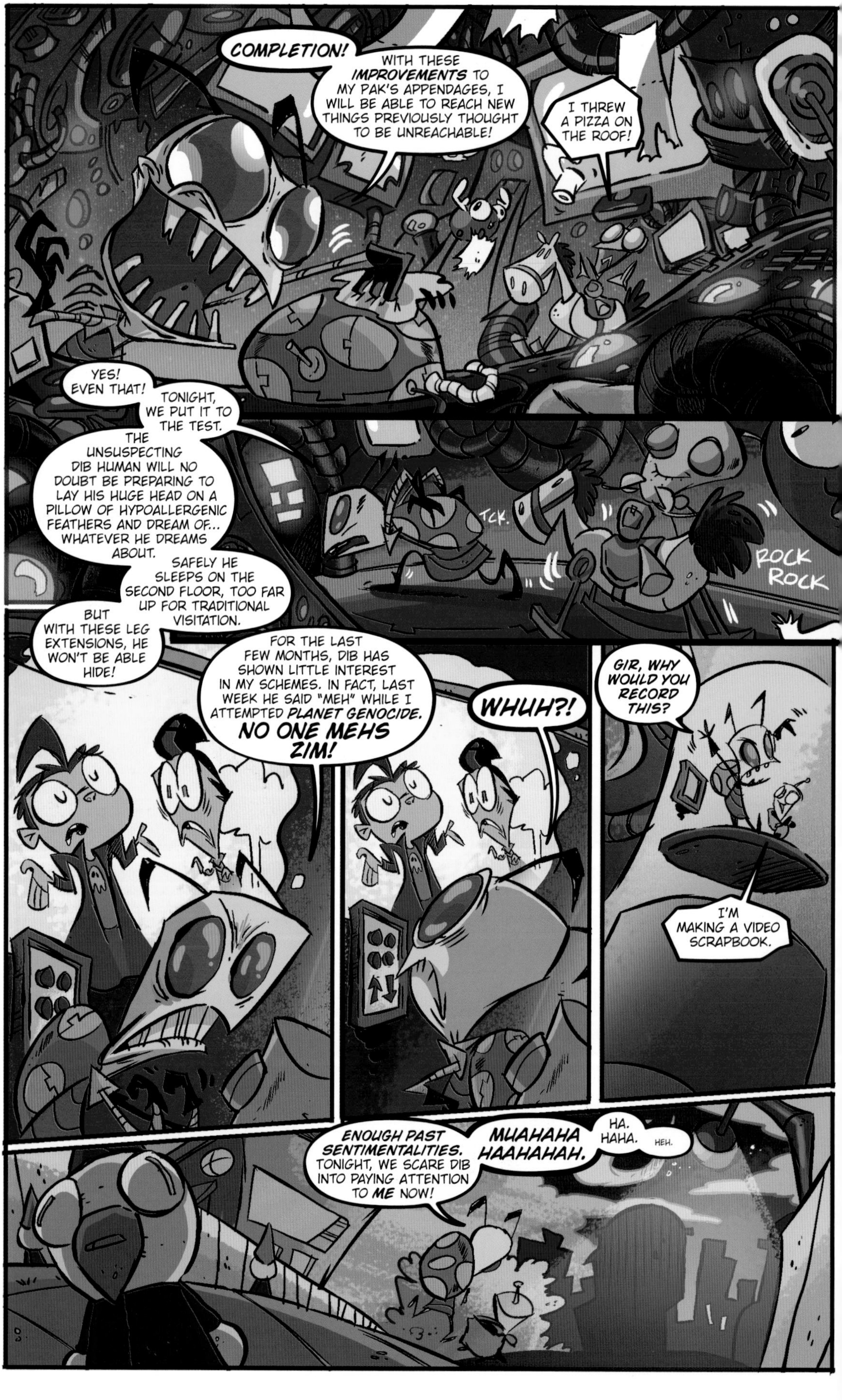

COMPLETION!
WITH THESE IMPROVEMENTS TO MY PAK'S APPENDAGES, I WILL BE ABLE TO REACH NEW THINGS PREVIOUSLY THOUGHT TO BE UNREACHABLE!
I THREW A PIZZA ON THE ROOF!
YES! EVEN THAT!
TONIGHT, WE PUT IT TO THE TEST.
THE UNSUSPECTING DIB HUMAN WILL NO DOUBT BE PREPARING TO LAY HIS HUGE HEAD ON A PILLOW OF HYPOALLERGENIC FEATHERS AND DREAM OF... WHATEVER HE DREAMS ABOUT.
SAFELY HE SLEEPS ON THE SECOND FLOOR, TOO FAR UP FOR TRADITIONAL VISITATION.
TCK.
ROCK ROCK
BUT WITH THESE LEG EXTENSIONS, HE WON'T BE ABLE HIDE!
FOR THE LAST FEW MONTHS, DIB HAS SHOWN LITTLE INTEREST IN MY SCHEMES. IN FACT, LAST WEEK HE SAID "MEH" WHILE I ATTEMPTED PLANET GENOCIDE. NO ONE MEHS ZIM!
WHUH?!
GIR, WHY WOULD YOU RECORD THIS?
I'M MAKING A VIDEO SCRAPBOOK.
ENOUGH PAST SENTIMENTALITIES. TONIGHT, WE SCARE DIB INTO PAYING ATTENTION TO ME NOW!
MUAHAHA HAAHAHAH.
HA. HAHA.
HEH.

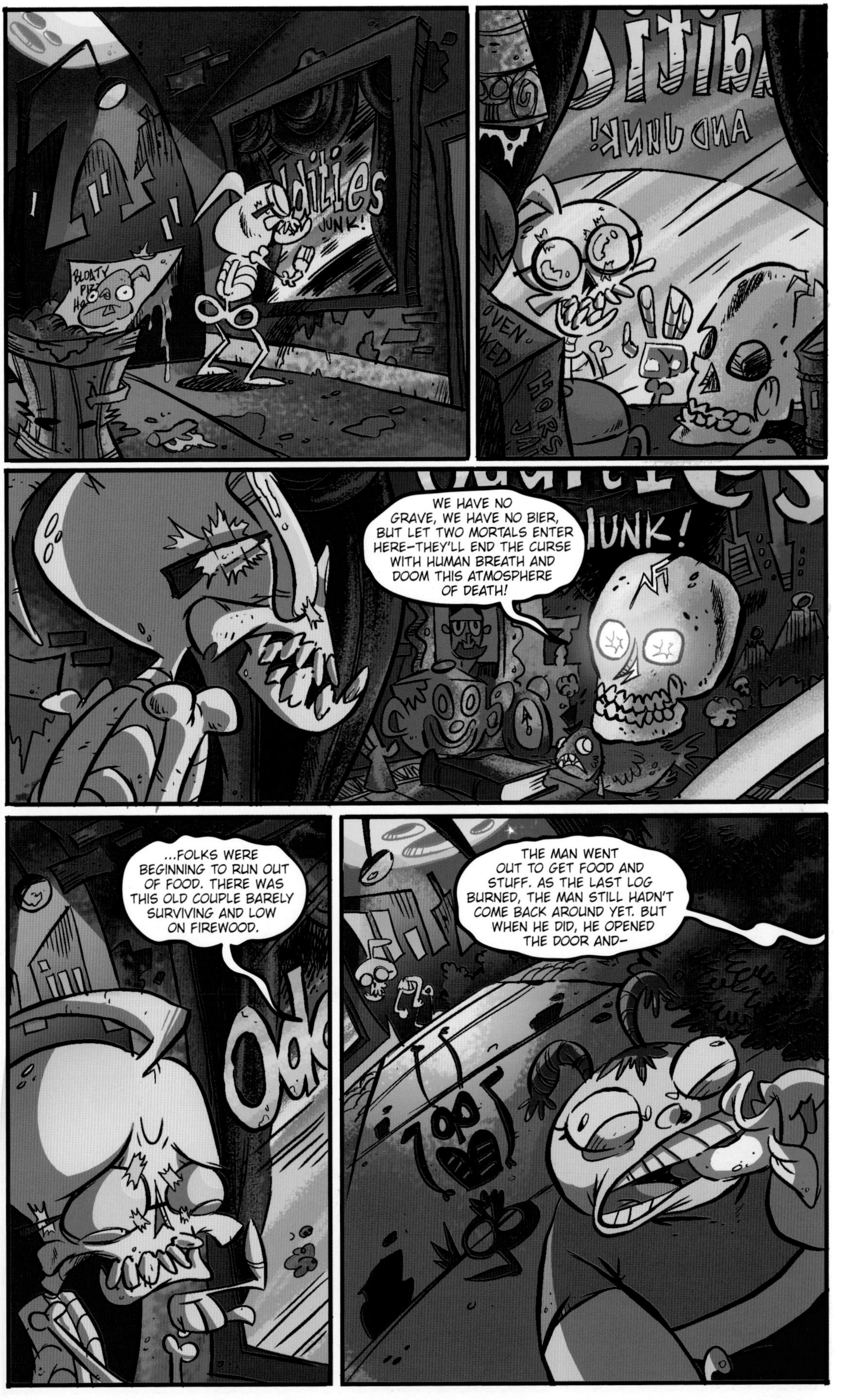

Oddities
JUNK!
BLOATY
AND JUNK!
OVEN
JUNK!
WE HAVE NO GRAVE, WE HAVE NO BIER, BUT LET TWO MORTALS ENTER HERE—THEY'LL END THE CURSE WITH HUMAN BREATH AND DOOM THIS ATMOSPHERE OF DEATH!
...FOLKS WERE BEGINNING TO RUN OUT OF FOOD. THERE WAS THIS OLD COUPLE BARELY SURVIVING AND LOW ON FIREWOOD.
THE MAN WENT OUT TO GET FOOD AND STUFF. AS THE LAST LOG BURNED, THE MAN STILL HADN'T COME BACK AROUND YET. BUT WHEN HE DID, HE OPENED THE DOOR AND—

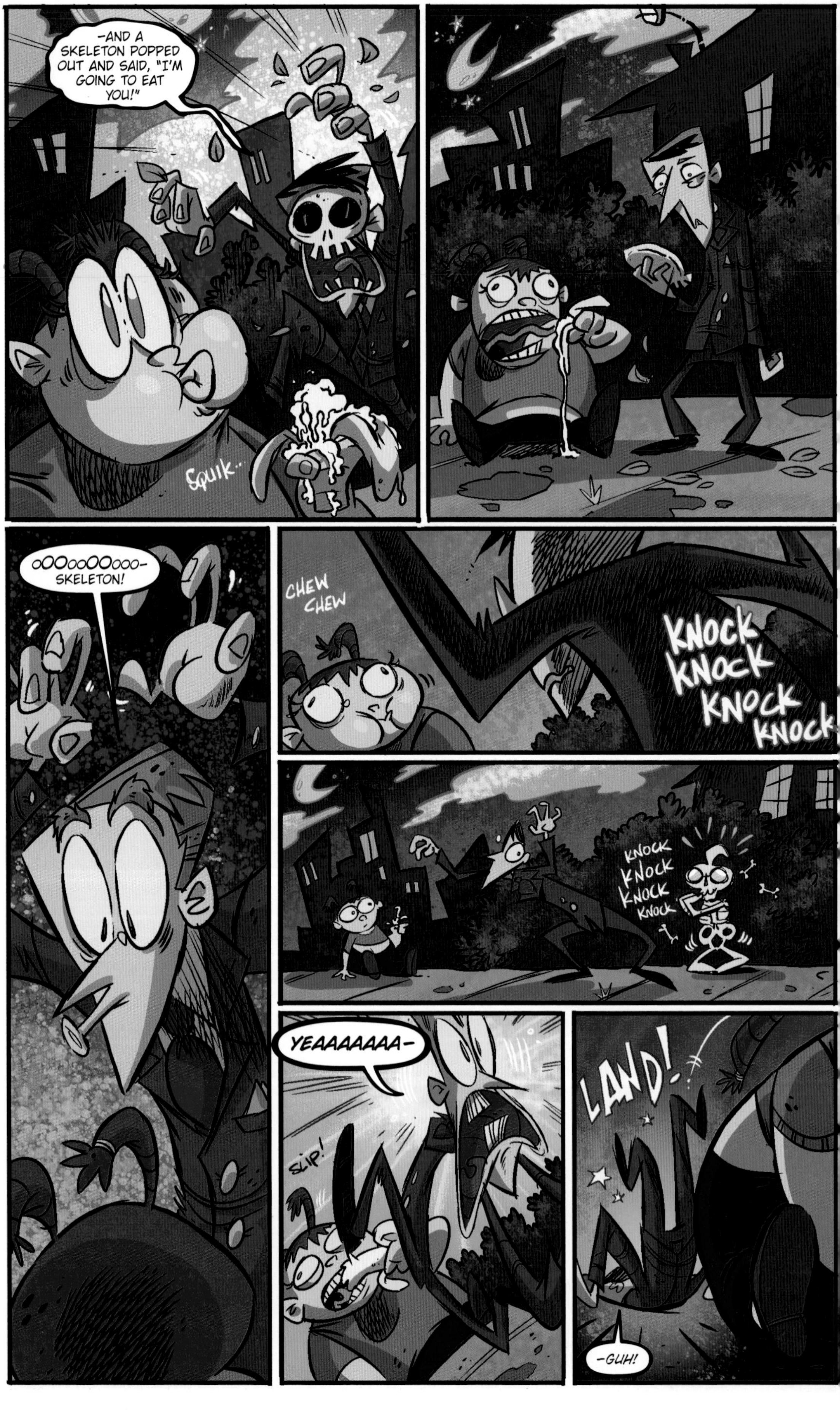
-AND A SKELETON POPPED OUT AND SAID, "I'M GOING TO EAT YOU!"
SQUIK..
oOOooOOooo- SKELETON!
CHEW CHEW
KNOCK KNOCK KNOCK KNOCK
KNOCK KNOCK KNOCK KNOCK
YEAAAAAAA-
SLIP!
LAND!
-GUH!

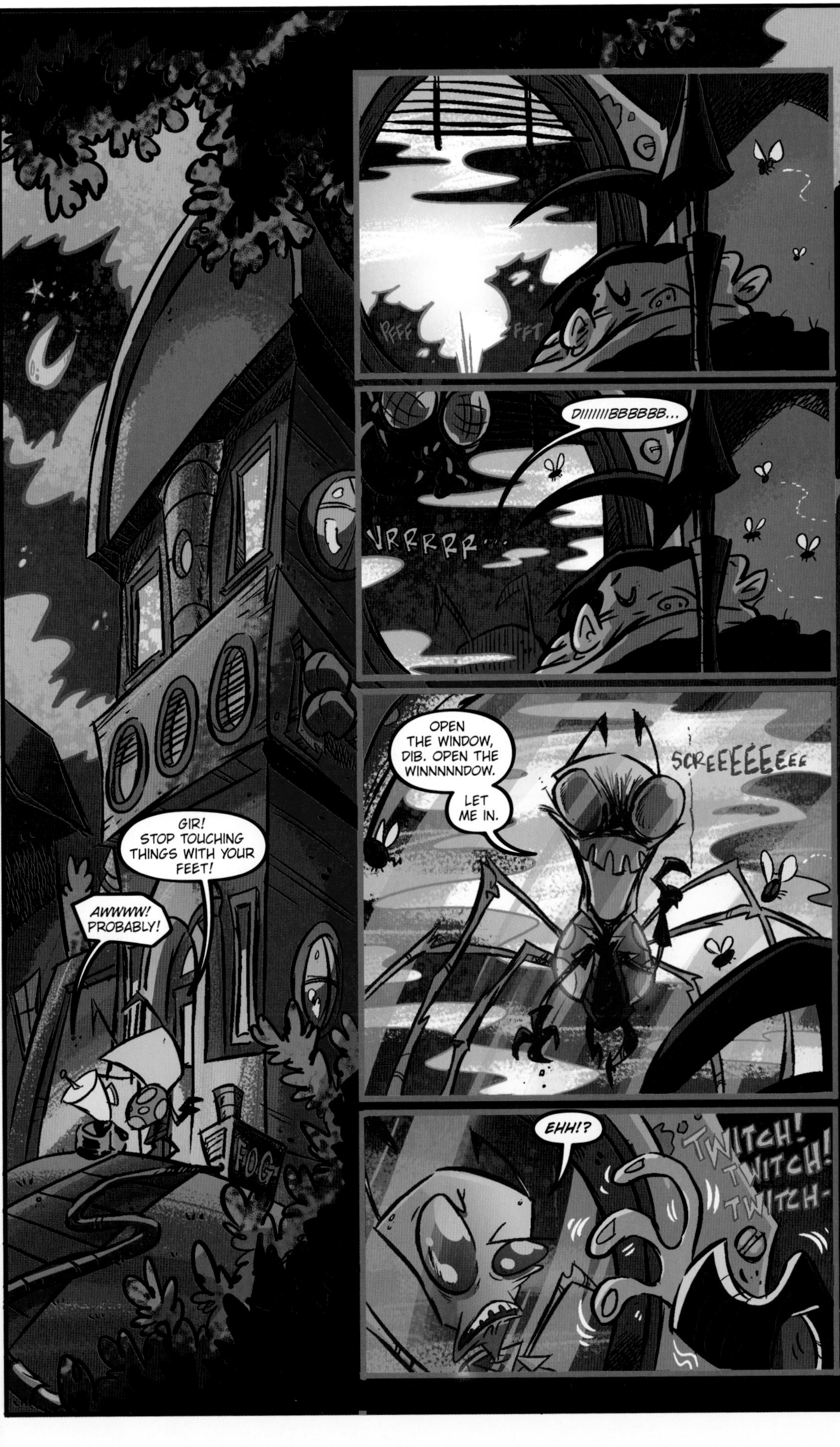

PFFF
FFT
DIIIIIIBBBBBB...
VRRRRR...
OPEN THE WINDOW, DIB. OPEN THE WINNNNNDOW.
LET ME IN.
SCREEEEEEeee
GIR! STOP TOUCHING THINGS WITH YOUR FEET!
AWWWW! PROBABLY!
FOG
EHH!?
TWITCH! TWITCH! TWITCH-

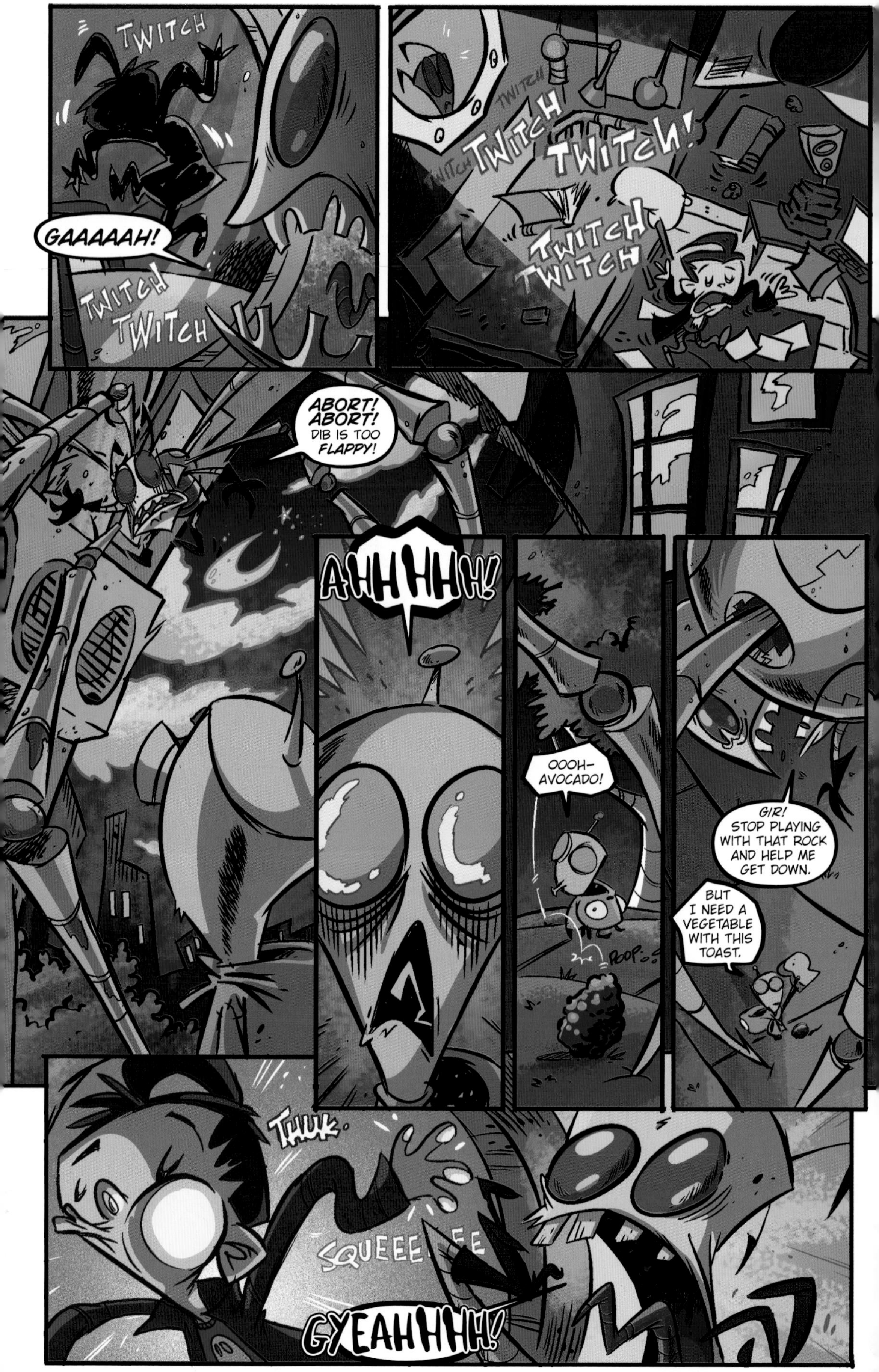
TWITCH
GAAAAAH!
TWITCH
TWITCH
TWITCH
TWITCH
TWITCH
TWITCH!
TWITCH
TWITCH
ABORT! ABORT! DIB IS TOO FLAPPY!
AHHHHH!
OOOH- AVOCADO!
POOP
GIR! STOP PLAYING WITH THAT ROCK AND HELP ME GET DOWN.
BUT I NEED A VEGETABLE WITH THIS TOAST.
THUK
SQUEEEEEE
GYEAHHHH!

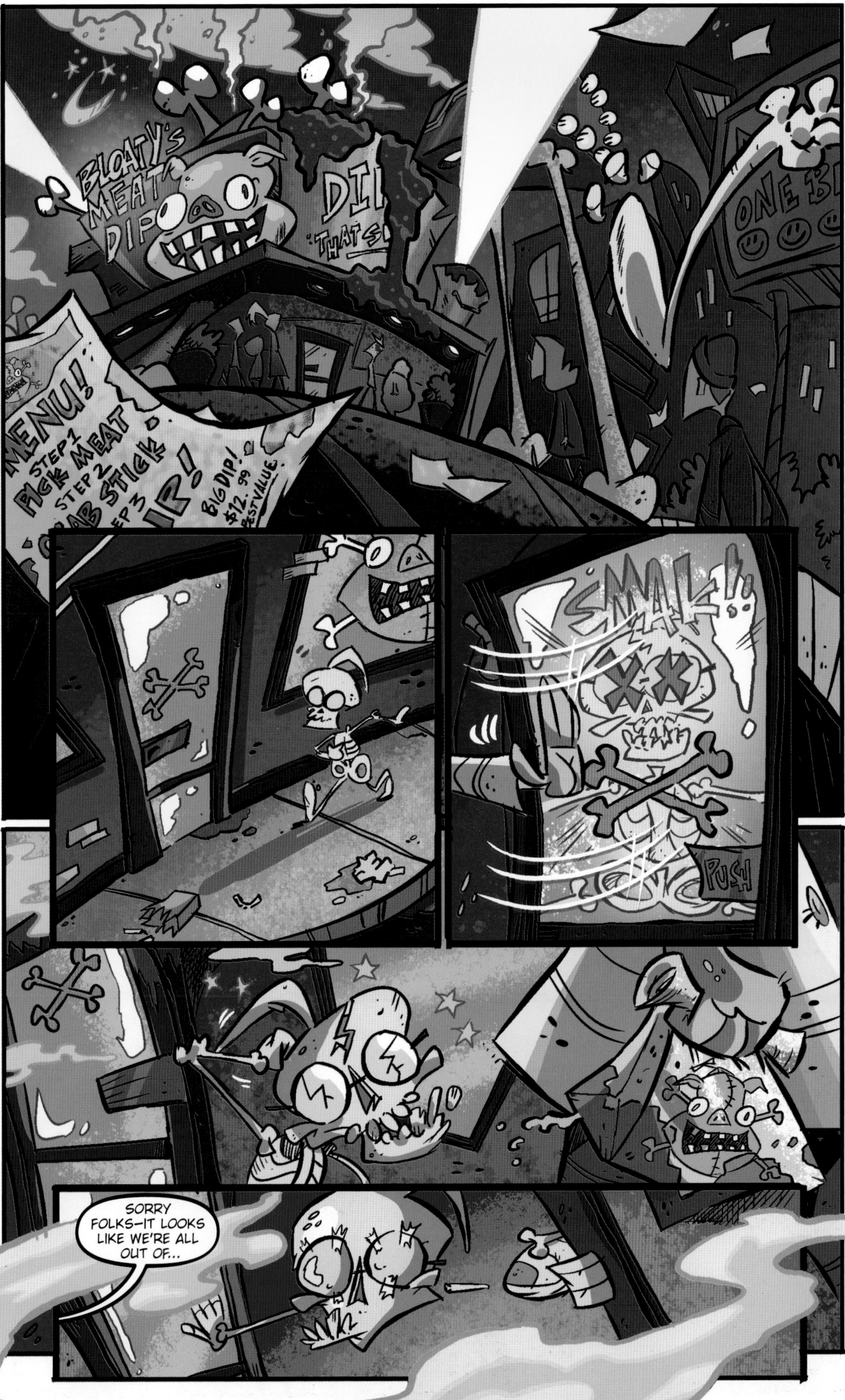

BLOATY'S MEAT DIP
MENU!
STEP 1 PICK MEAT
STEP 2
BIG DIP! $12.99 BEST VALUE
ONE
SMAK!
PUSH
SORRY FOLKS—IT LOOKS LIKE WE'RE ALL OUT OF...

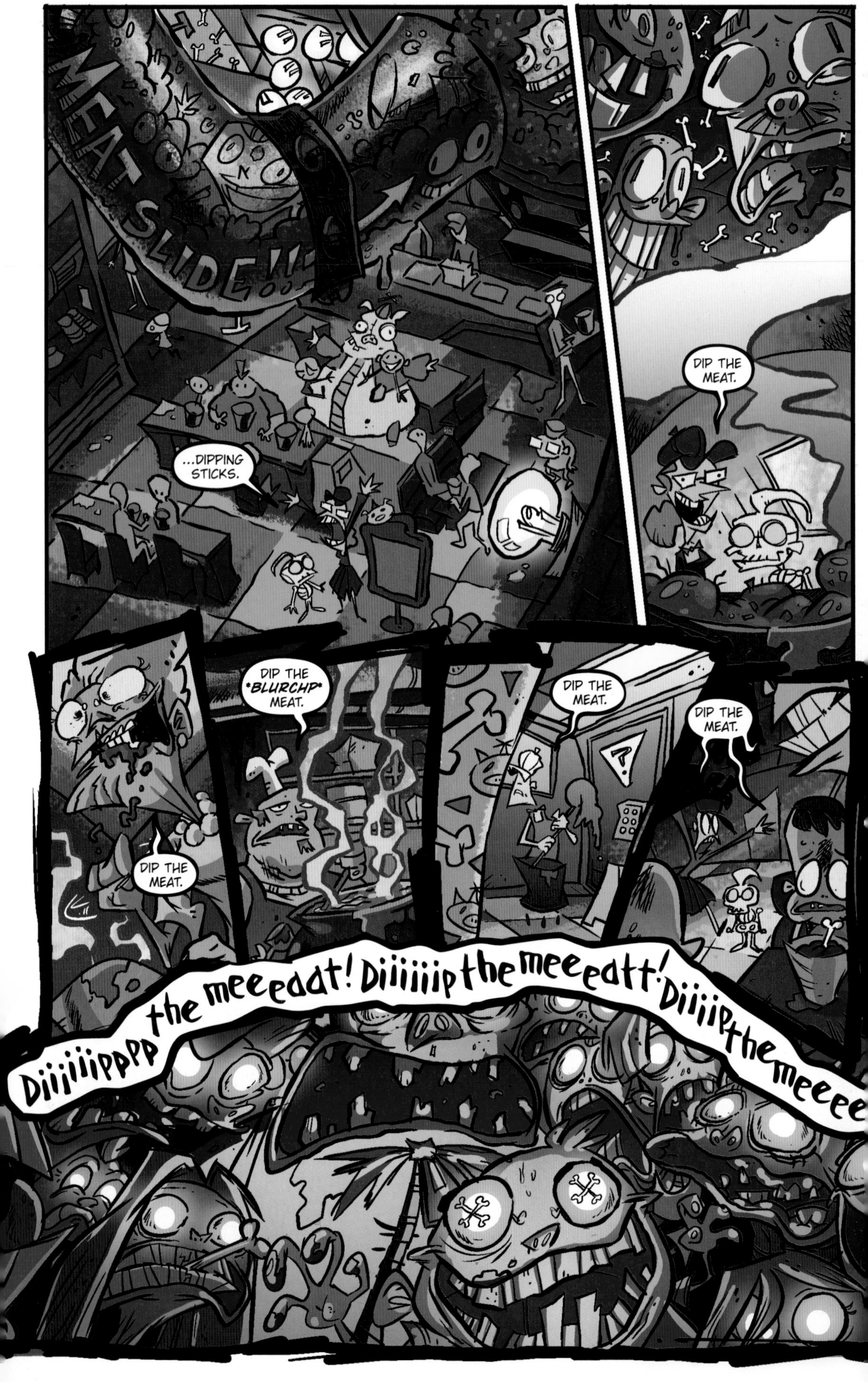

MEAT SLIDE!!!
...DIPPING STICKS.
DIP THE MEAT.
DIP THE MEAT.
DIP THE *BLURCHP* MEAT.
DIP THE MEAT.
DIP THE MEAT.
Diiiiiipppp the meeeaat! Diiiiiip the meeeatt! Diiiip the meeee

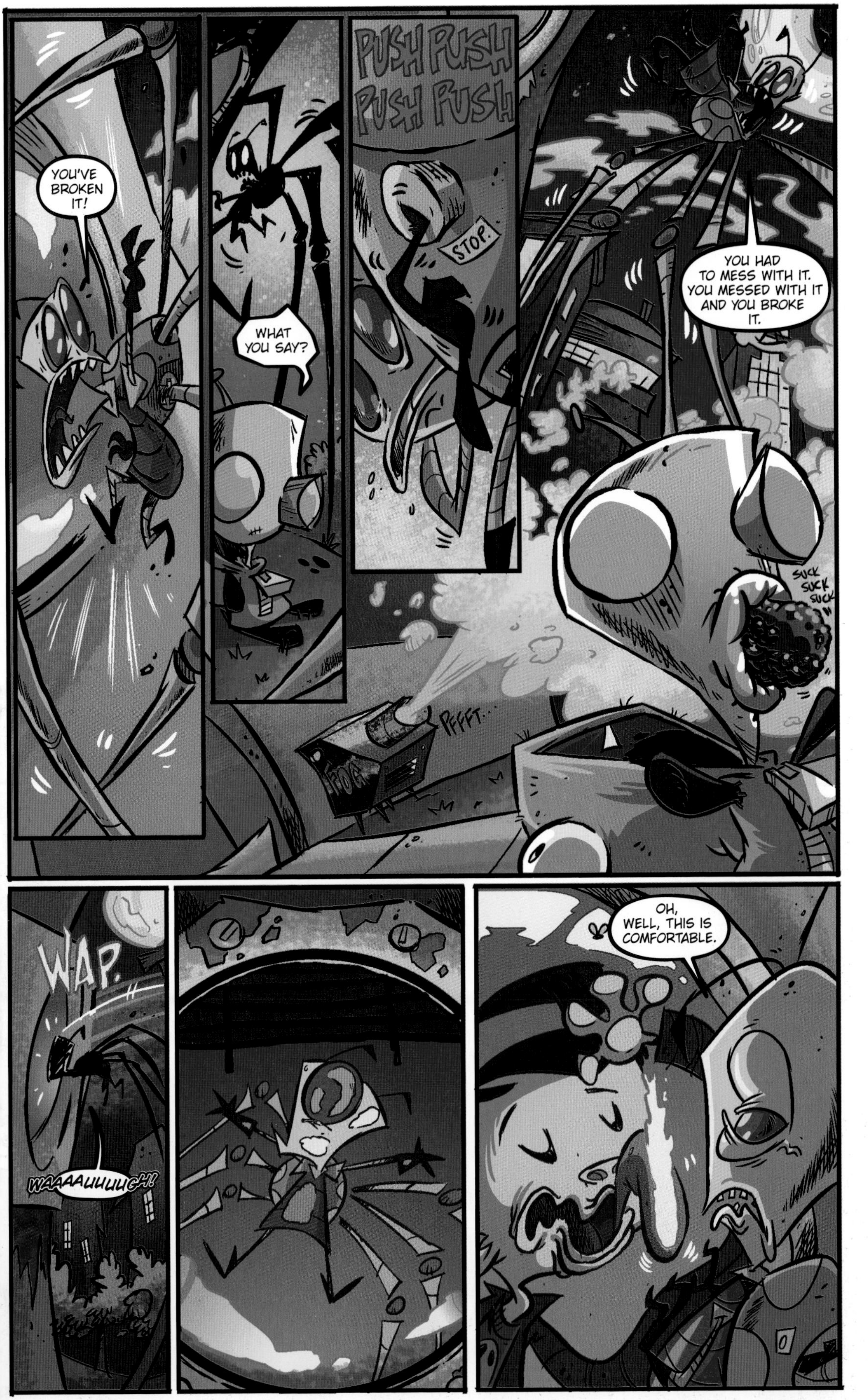

YOU'VE BROKEN IT!
WHAT YOU SAY?
PUSH PUSH PUSH PUSH
STOP.
YOU HAD TO MESS WITH IT. YOU MESSED WITH IT AND YOU BROKE IT.
SUCK SUCK SUCK
PFFFT...
FOG
WAP.
WAAAAUUUUGH!
OH, WELL, THIS IS COMFORTABLE.

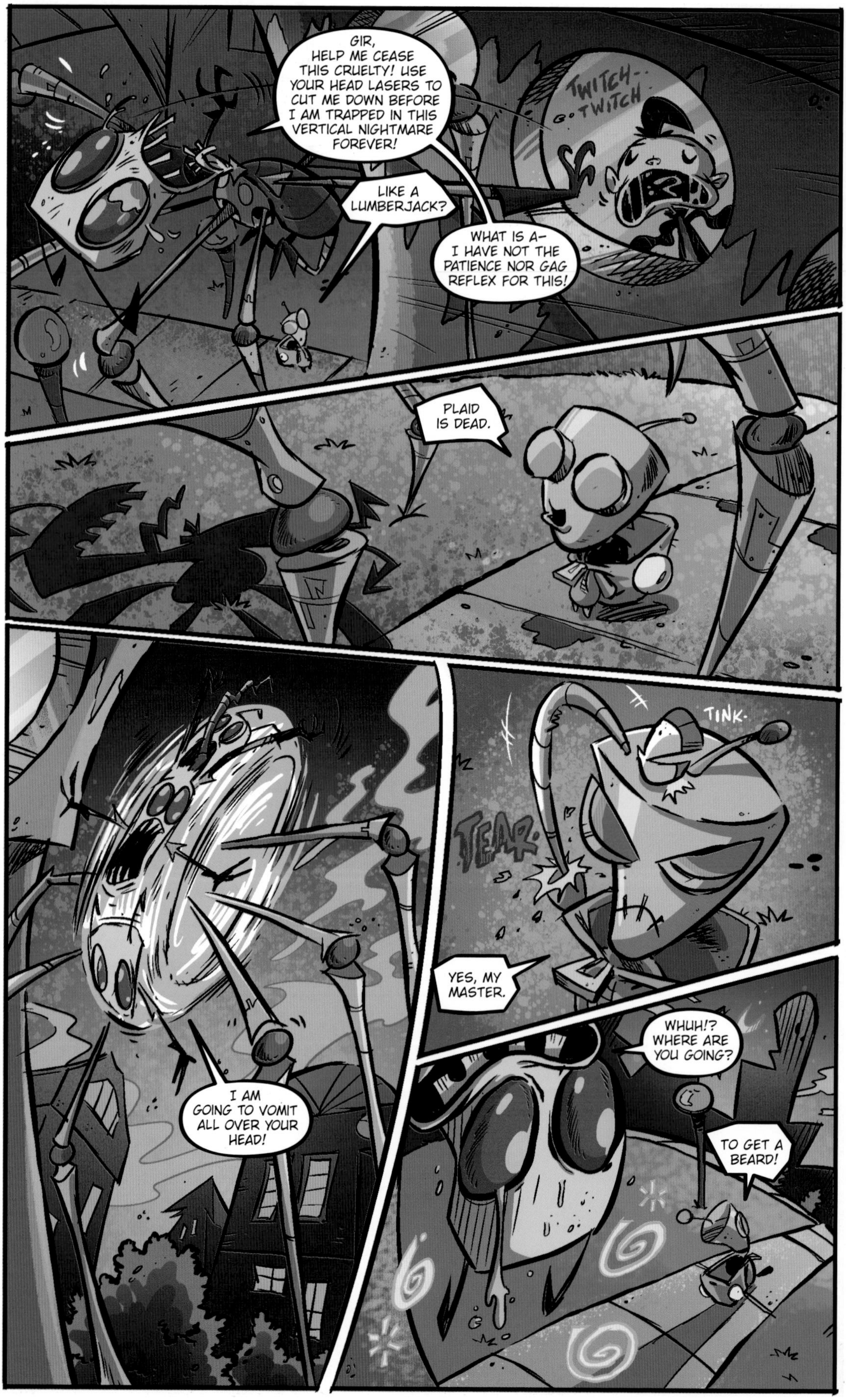
GIR, HELP ME CEASE THIS CRUELTY! USE YOUR HEAD LASERS TO CUT ME DOWN BEFORE I AM TRAPPED IN THIS VERTICAL NIGHTMARE FOREVER!
TWITCH-TWITCH
LIKE A LUMBERJACK?
WHAT IS A– I HAVE NOT THE PATIENCE NOR GAG REFLEX FOR THIS!
PLAID IS DEAD.
TINK.
TEAR
YES, MY MASTER.
I AM GOING TO VOMIT ALL OVER YOUR HEAD!
WHUH!? WHERE ARE YOU GOING?
TO GET A BEARD!

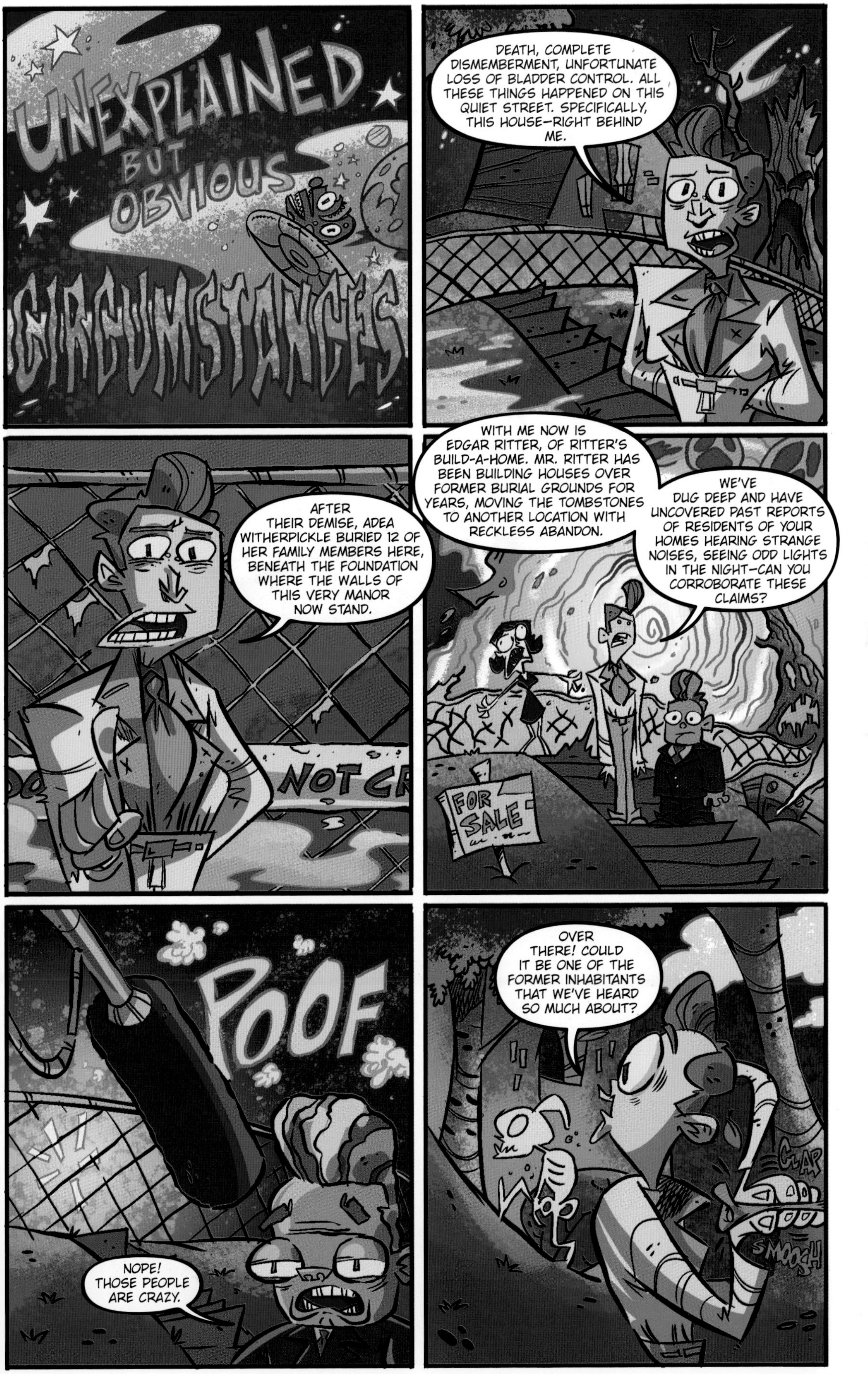
UNEXPLAINED BUT OBVIOUS CIRCUMSTANCES
DEATH, COMPLETE DISMEMBERMENT, UNFORTUNATE LOSS OF BLADDER CONTROL. ALL THESE THINGS HAPPENED ON THIS QUIET STREET. SPECIFICALLY, THIS HOUSE—RIGHT BEHIND ME.
AFTER THEIR DEMISE, ADEA WITHERPICKLE BURIED 12 OF HER FAMILY MEMBERS HERE, BENEATH THE FOUNDATION WHERE THE WALLS OF THIS VERY MANOR NOW STAND.
NOT CR
WITH ME NOW IS EDGAR RITTER, OF RITTER'S BUILD-A-HOME. MR. RITTER HAS BEEN BUILDING HOUSES OVER FORMER BURIAL GROUNDS FOR YEARS, MOVING THE TOMBSTONES TO ANOTHER LOCATION WITH RECKLESS ABANDON.
WE'VE DUG DEEP AND HAVE UNCOVERED PAST REPORTS OF RESIDENTS OF YOUR HOMES HEARING STRANGE NOISES, SEEING ODD LIGHTS IN THE NIGHT—CAN YOU CORROBORATE THESE CLAIMS?
FOR SALE
POOF
NOPE! THOSE PEOPLE ARE CRAZY.
OVER THERE! COULD IT BE ONE OF THE FORMER INHABITANTS THAT WE'VE HEARD SO MUCH ABOUT?
CLAP
SMOOCH

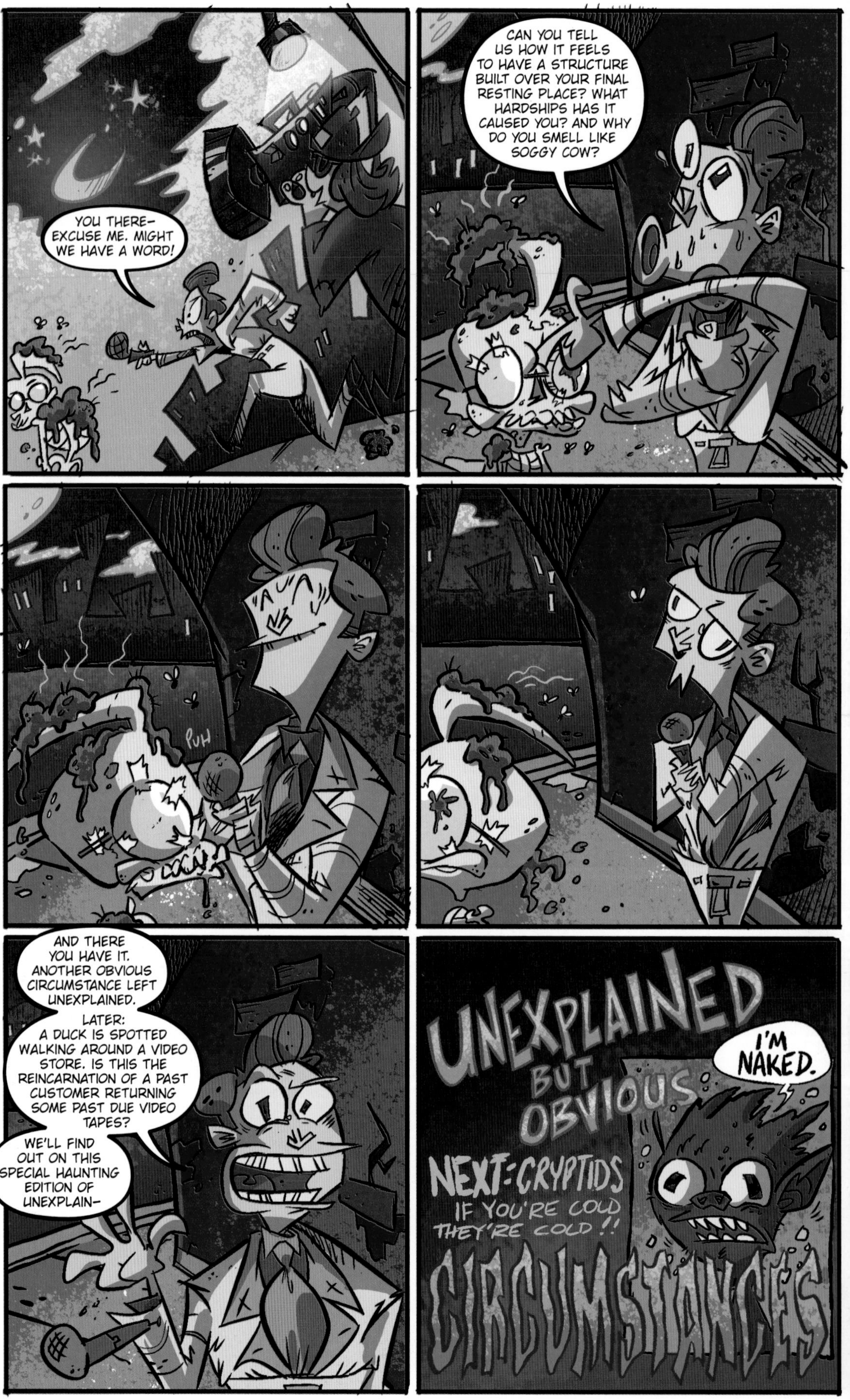
YOU THERE– EXCUSE ME. MIGHT WE HAVE A WORD!
CAN YOU TELL US HOW IT FEELS TO HAVE A STRUCTURE BUILT OVER YOUR FINAL RESTING PLACE? WHAT HARDSHIPS HAS IT CAUSED YOU? AND WHY DO YOU SMELL LIKE SOGGY COW?
PUH
AND THERE YOU HAVE IT. ANOTHER OBVIOUS CIRCUMSTANCE LEFT UNEXPLAINED.
LATER: A DUCK IS SPOTTED WALKING AROUND A VIDEO STORE. IS THIS THE REINCARNATION OF A PAST CUSTOMER RETURNING SOME PAST DUE VIDEO TAPES?
WE'LL FIND OUT ON THIS SPECIAL HAUNTING EDITION OF UNEXPLAIN–
UNEXPLAINED BUT OBVIOUS
NEXT: CRYPTIDS
IF YOU'RE COLD THEY'RE COLD!!
CIRCUMSTANCES
I'M NAKED.

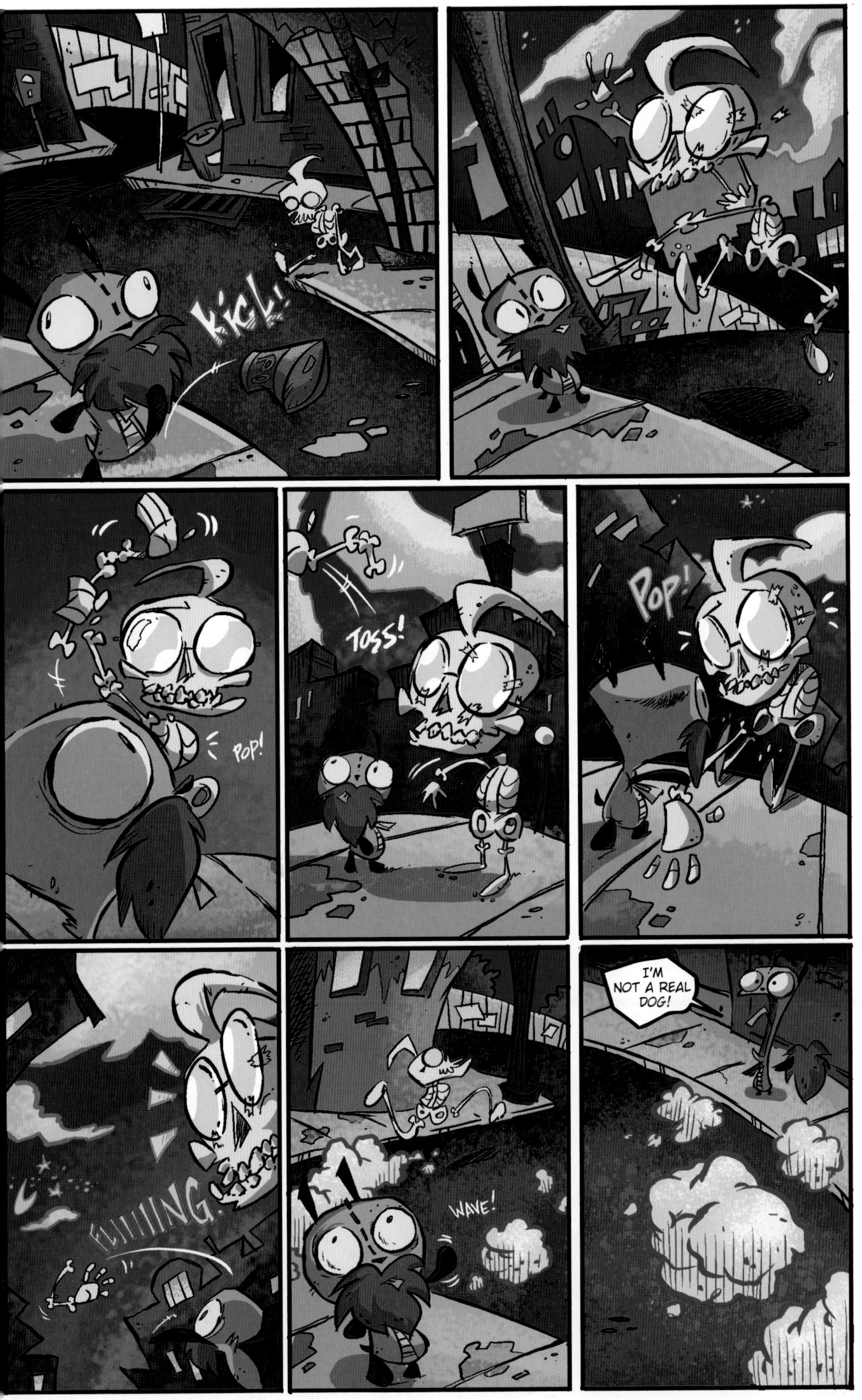
KICK!
POP!
TOSS!
POP!
FLIIIIING!
WAVE!
I'M NOT A REAL DOG!

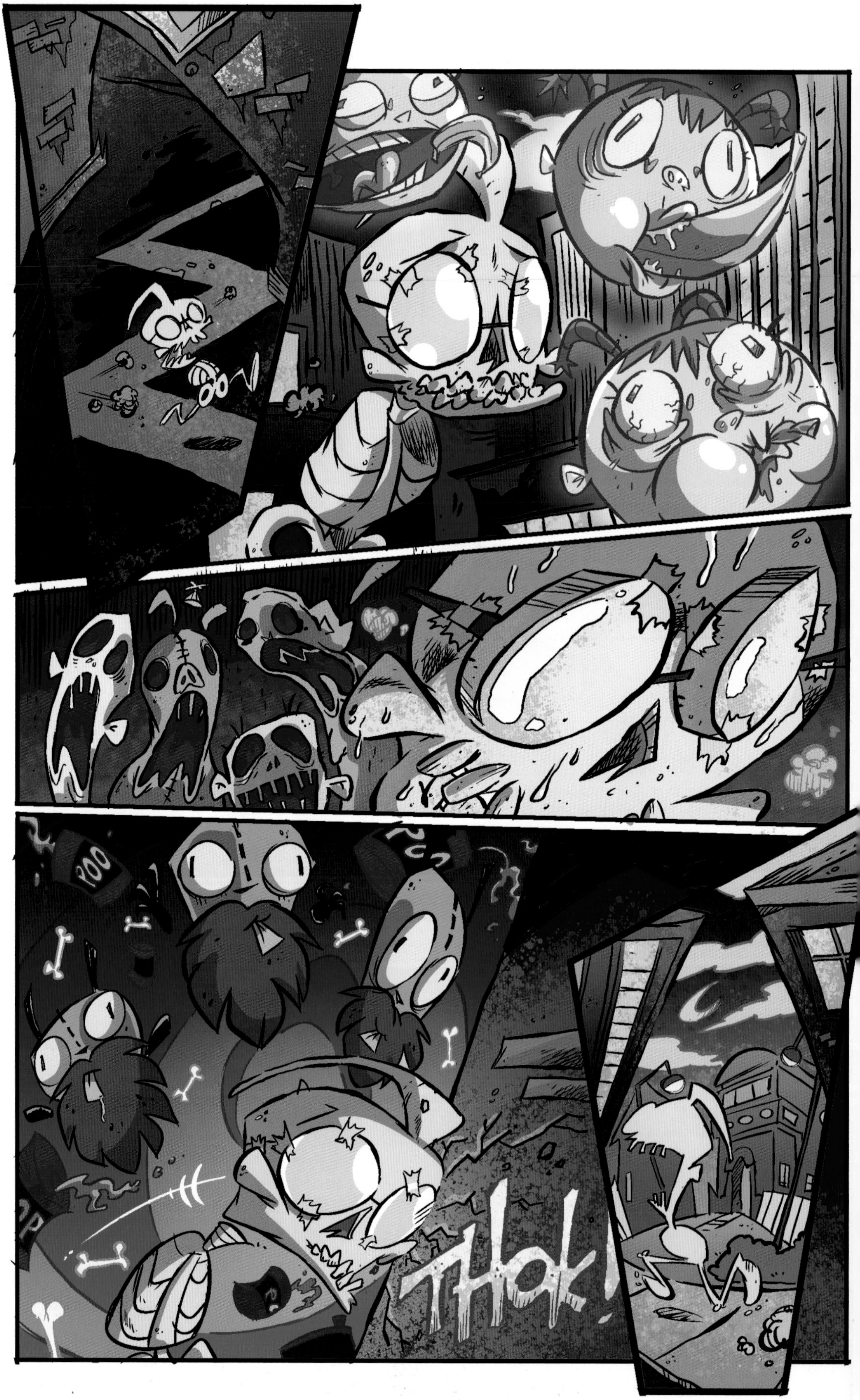
POO
THOK!

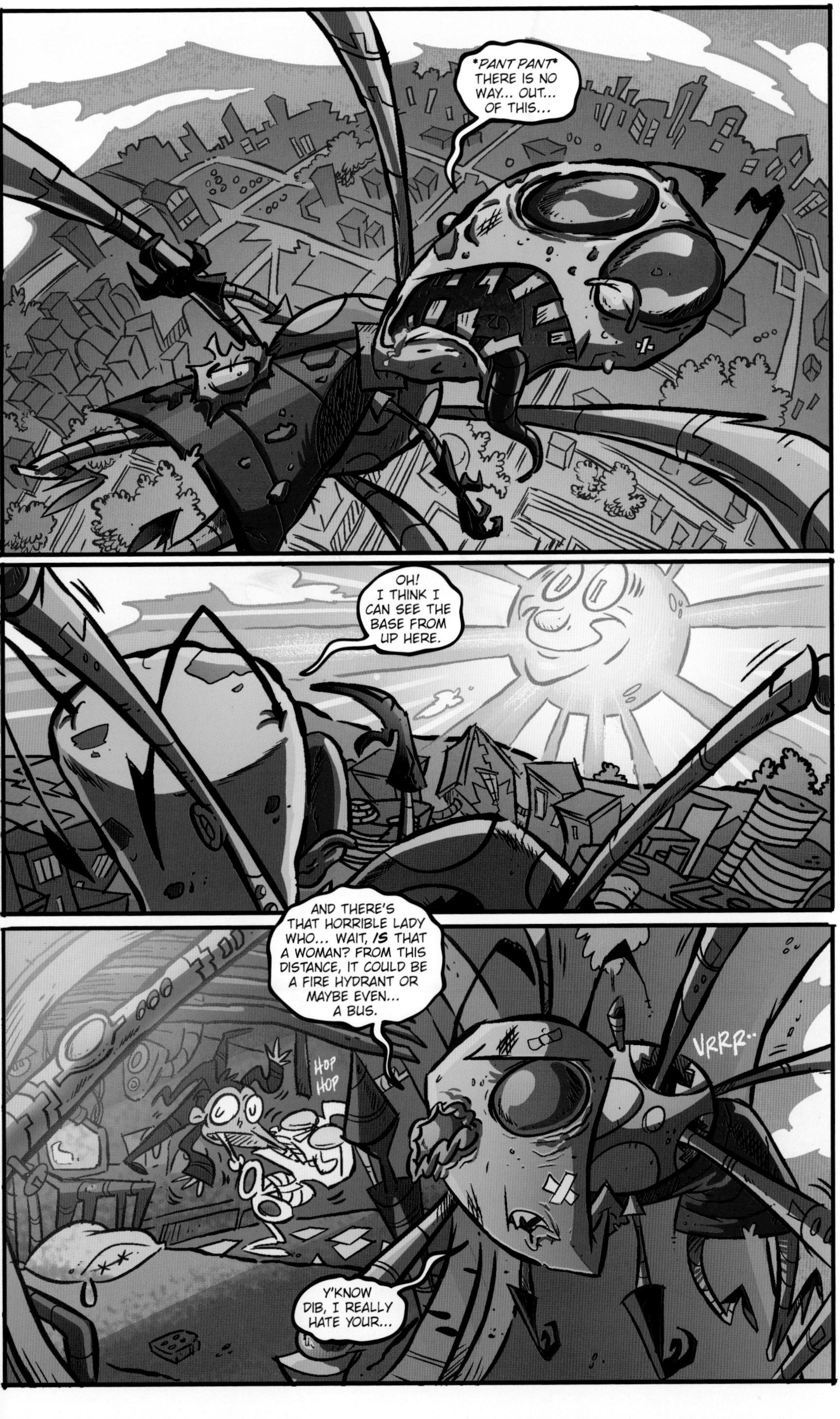
PANT PANT THERE IS NO WAY... OUT... OF THIS...
OH! I THINK I CAN SEE THE BASE FROM UP HERE.
AND THERE'S THAT HORRIBLE LADY WHO... WAIT, IS THAT A WOMAN? FROM THIS DISTANCE, IT COULD BE A FIRE HYDRANT OR MAYBE EVEN... A BUS.
HOP HOP
VRRR..
Y'KNOW DIB, I REALLY HATE YOUR...

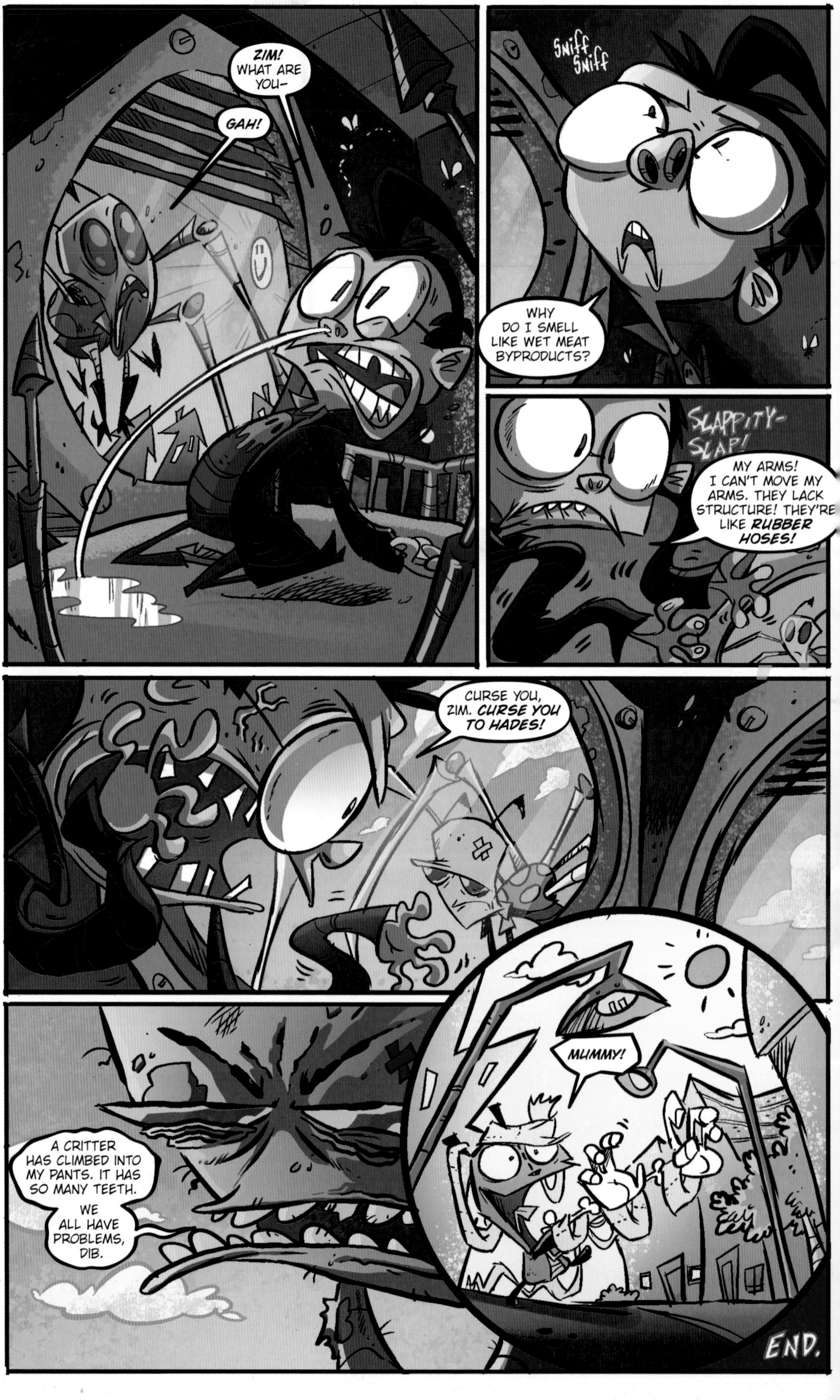

ZIM! WHAT ARE YOU-
GAH!
Sniff Sniff
WHY DO I SMELL LIKE WET MEAT BYPRODUCTS?
SLAPPITY-SLAP!
MY ARMS! I CAN'T MOVE MY ARMS. THEY LACK STRUCTURE! THEY'RE LIKE RUBBER HOSES!
CURSE YOU, ZIM. CURSE YOU TO HADES!
MUMMY!
A CRITTER HAS CLIMBED INTO MY PANTS. IT HAS SO MANY TEETH.
WE ALL HAVE PROBLEMS, DIB.
END.

INVADER ZIM™

CREATORS

JHONEN VASQUEZ

Jhonen Vasquez is a writer and artist who walks in many worlds, not unlike Blade, only without having to drink blood-serum to survive the curse that is also his greatest power (still talking about Blade here). He's worked in comics and animation and is the creator of *Invader ZIM*, a fact that haunts him to this day.

@JhonenV

SAM LOGAN

Sam Logan is best known as the creator of *Sam and Fuzzy*, a massive comedy adventure series that he has been writing and illustrating for over 15 years. He's also either partly or completely responsible for President Dog, Skull Panda, the Underground RPG, and a lot of unrelated problems. He lives in Vancouver, BC with his two dogs. (They're very good boys.)

@samandfuzzy

ERIC TRUEHEART

Eric Trueheart was one of the original writers on the *Invader ZIM* television series back when there was a thing called "television." Since then, he's made a living writing moderately-inappropriate things for people who make entertainment for children, including Dreamworks Animation, Cartoon Network, Disney TV, PBS, Hasbro, and others. Upon reading this list, he now thinks he maybe should have become a dentist, and he hates teeth.

@erictrueheart

STEVEN SHANAHAN

Steven Shanahan is a Toronto, Canada based writer, video editor, and voiceover artist. He is the co-creator of the comic *Silly Kingdom*, and has written for various animated series, such as *Super Science Friends*, *Carl's Car Wash*, and *Mr. Monkey: Monkey Mechanic*. You can find out what he's up to these days (or just see pictures of the food he cooks) on Twitter.

@shaggyshan

DREW RAUSCH

Drew Rausch is a cartoonist and the co-creator, along with Jocelyn Gajeway, of the ongoing webcomic *MY BLACKS DON'T MATCH!* He's been lucky to work on such comic book nonsense as *Edward Scissorhands*, *ELDRITCH!* (written by Aaron Alexovich), *Rick and Morty*, *Back to the Future*, and *Ghostbusters*. Proof of his artistic existence can be found at *www.drewrausch.com*.

He lives in a house that is most assuredly haunted by no less than two ghosts with his Bride in Pasadena, CA and their one black cat, Spooky.

Currently there is a tombstone in his hallway.

@Drew_Rausch

WARREN WUCINICH

Warren Wucinich is an illustrator, colorist, and part-time carny currently living in Durham, NC. When not making comics he can usually be found watching old *Twilight Zone* episodes and eating large amounts of pie.

@warrenwucinich

FRED C. STRESING

Fred C. Stresing is a colorist, artist, writer, and letterer for a variety of comics. You may recognize his work from *Invader ZIM*, the comic you are holding. He has been making comics his whole life, from the age of six. He has gotten much better since then. He currently resides in Savannah, Georgia with his wife and two cats. He doesn't know how the cats got there, they are not his.

@FredCStresing

MORE BOOKS FROM ONI PRESS...

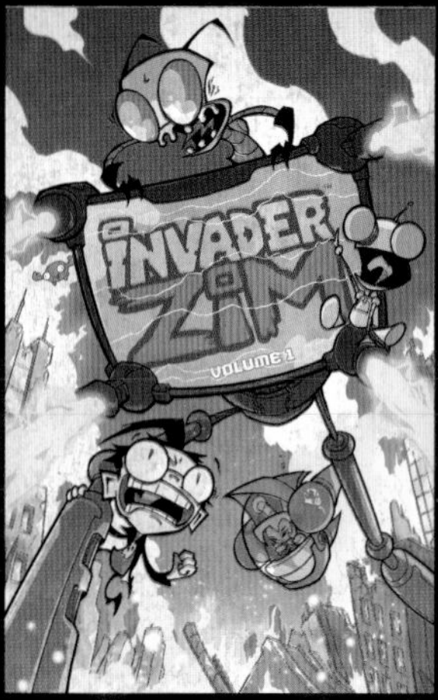
INVADER ZIM
VOLUME 1

INVADER ZIM, VOLUME 1
Collects issues 1-5!

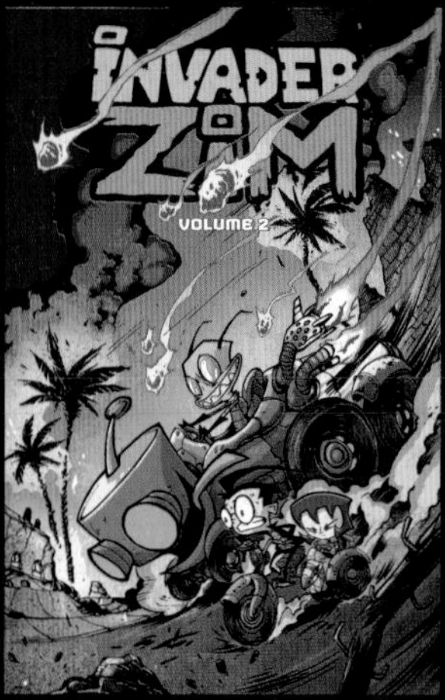
INVADER ZIM
VOLUME 2

INVADER ZIM, VOLUME 2
Collects issues 6-10!

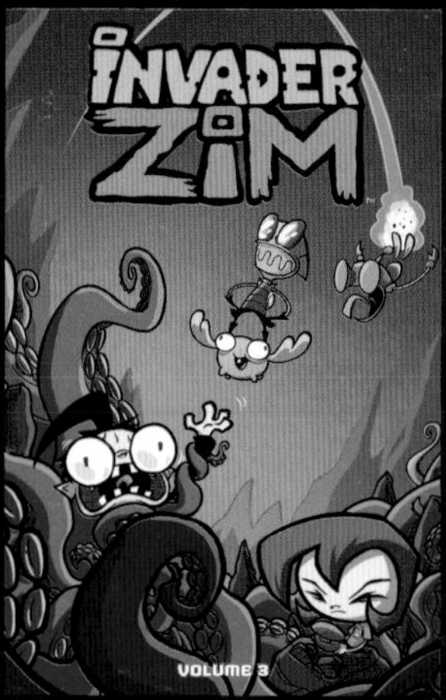
INVADER ZIM
VOLUME 3

INVADER ZIM, VOLUME 3
Collects issues 11-15!

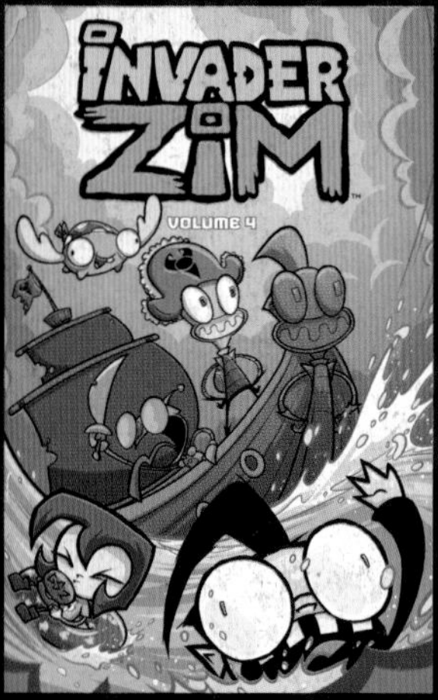
INVADER ZIM
VOLUME 4

INVADER ZIM, VOLUME 4
Collects issues 16-20!

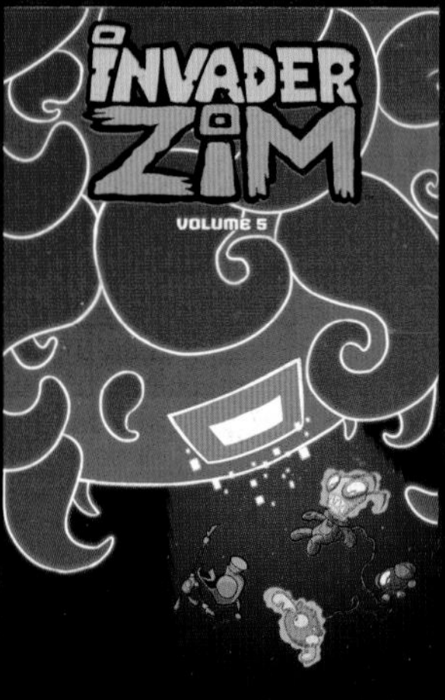
INVADER ZIM
VOLUME 5

INVADER ZIM, VOLUME 5
Collects issues 21-25!

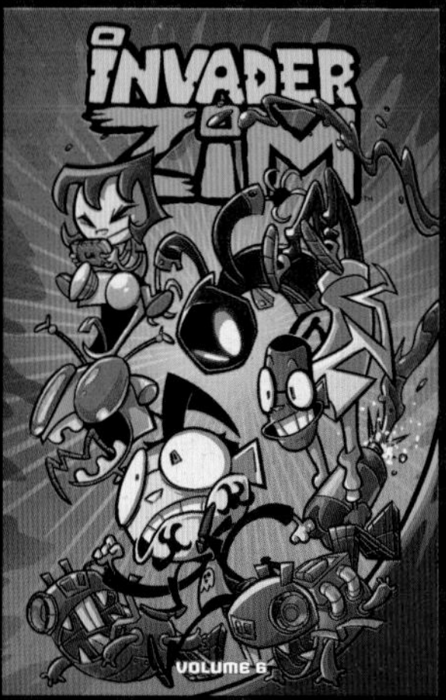
INVADER ZIM
VOLUME 6

INVADER ZIM, VOLUME 6
Collects issues 26-30!

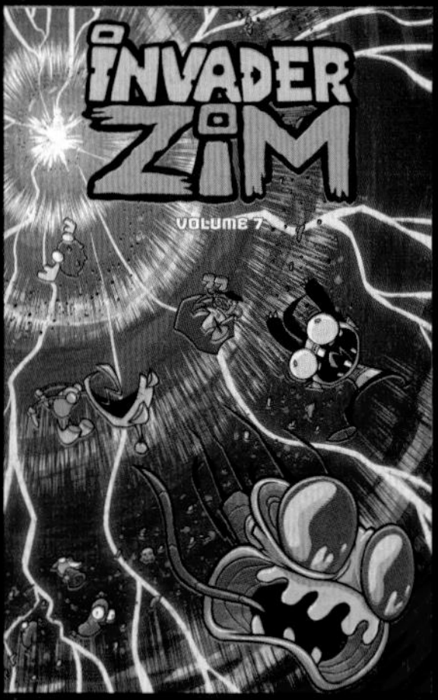
INVADER ZIM
VOLUME 7

INVADER ZIM, VOLUME 7
Collects issues 31-35!

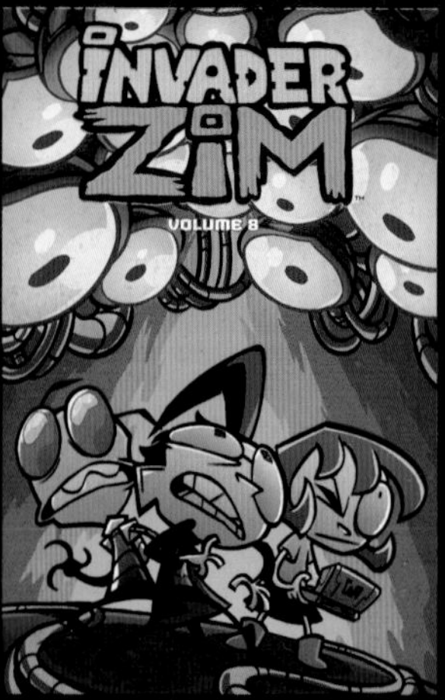
INVADER ZIM
VOLUME 8

INVADER ZIM, VOLUME 8
Collects issues 36-40!

ONI PRESS

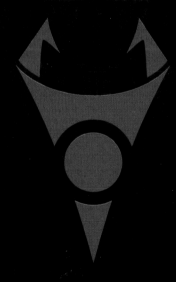

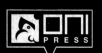

For more information on these and other fine Oni Press comic books and graphic novels visit www.onipress.com. To find a comic specialty store in your area visit www.comicshops.us.